A LOVE REUNITED

"Aurora. Oh, gods, how I have missed you!" Frayne murmured feverishly when at last his lips left hers to devour her eyes, her cheeks, her throat and finally the sweetness of her mouth again.

"Frayne, Frayne, my beloved!" she exclaimed. Aurora felt herself borne upon the swelling tide of an empyrean need and knew at last the one whose vassal she was had returned to her, searing her, body and soul, with the purifying flame of his power.

Together, she and Frayne, who had reawakened her very being, soared into the divine heights where only gods or mortals touched by the power of a god may go. And as their passion crested, their spirits were forged anew. Aurora then knew herself at last to be complete and unafraid—for she was the enchantress, and he was Frayne, the touchstone of her being. Together, they were one. . . .

Beloved Paradise

Johanna Hailey

ZEBRA BOOKS
KENSINGTON PUBLISHING CORP.

ZEBRA BOOKS

are published by

Kensington Publishing Corp.
475 Park Avenue South
New York, NY 10016

First printing: March 1987

Printed in the United States of America

To Steve

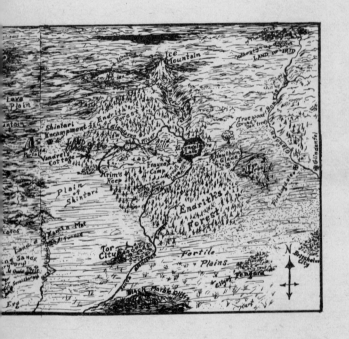

Prologue

Far to the north, indeed, at the farthermost reaches of the land of the Mages, a harpist sang the Song of Engolad, the Eilderood whose heart was stolen by Llynis of Throm and borne to the lightless depths of Somn. It is a song that is sung in the darkness before dawn when there is no moon and the stars are pale lights fading before the approaching glory of day, for it is a song of grief and despair, the lament of one cursed forever to behold the light of the One and yet to be dead to its sustaining warmth. It is not often sung, for the words come unbidden from the secret depths of the soul that has divined the true meaning of sorrow, and they are forgotten with the first light of day. Thus, as Ciaron, the god of darkness, fled before Eo, the harbinger of daylight, the bard's slender fingers stilled against the harp strings and the golden voice grew silent.

The harpist gazed out over Marmacle, the sea of crystals, to the shimmering pinnacle of Estrelland, which is the birthplace of the twin gods, and waited, his spirit heavy within him. He had not welcomed the god's summons, for though he had been born to the sword, he was weary of the battle. He had had enough of the endless conflict, the constant struggle for definition and for the answer to the riddle that, in the continuum, was forever and always only another question. Indeed, he had lived too long and would have preferred to remain for all eternity in the Flux of Timelessness where truth was merely the sum of all possibilities. For what meaning could be derived out of history that was only one endless repetition of the same question—Why?

"And does not the answer reside within the One, whom we were created to serve?" queried a voice gently out of the shadows. "And is it not Dred himself who would be best served if no one sought the answer to the Gandorf? Indeed, is that not the reason Dred must not be allowed to win the coming battle, for is it not the constant seeking for the Light of Truth that dispels the darkness of dread?"

The bard did not answer, but remained staring fixedly at the glittering tower of crystal, his eyes like twin fathomless pools in the lean, hard face. There, in Estrelland, resided Vendrenin, the Sword of Harmon, warrior-god of the Eilderood. Dragus himself had forged the god's weapon at the behest of the One for his chief lieutenant, and Harmon alone had wielded it in all the ages since the Second Uprising of the Thromgilad led by Prince Dred. With it he had banished the Prince of Throm once more to the Land of Somn, called Limbo, and had thus restored peace to the Realm of the One. Whereupon, heartsick and weary of strife, the

10

warrior-god had relinquished the thing of power to Estrelland and the safekeeping of Efluvien, his twin, that the balance might be maintained till the time of the Third Upheaval when it was foretold that Dred should walk the land again.

"Shall you never descend from your crystal tower, Efluvien, and learn what it is to love?" the bard said suddenly and turned his head at last to view the shrouded figure of the god sitting on the far side of the small campfire from him.

Efluvien shrugged.

"I am the peace-keeper. I strive only for balance and harmony. It is for warriors and poets to love and hate. You know that."

'And when the peace is shattered and Estrelland is no more? What then?" the bard demanded curiously. "Shall you return to Galesiad to await the victory of Throm?"

"Nay, not to Galesiad," murmured the god, seemingly undisturbed by the other's contempt. "My brother's sword was entrusted into my keeping till one should come to wield it whose heart is innocent. My way lies with the Vendrenin."

A fleeting shadow like pain or stunned disbelief flickered across the bard's stern countenance.

"You mean to follow the Vendrenin into darkness! Why, Efluvien? Surely that should be a task for Harmon, the warrior, and not for you."

"My brother knows the Sword of Vengeance has gone forever out of his keeping. It is a thing of pure power, neither good nor evil. Yet it feeds upon the soul of the user. It was the poet who foresaw that in the end it would make the warrior-god more terrible

11

than Dred himself, for even a god soon learns to love the power of Vendrenin for itself. You know that better than anyone. Nay. It is not for my brother anymore but for the one who fears its power and who desires it not. Dred will wrest it from the tower and seek to use it for his own evil purposes, but the Chosen One must discover its true essence if ever Vendrenin is to be restored to its rightful state. Harmon's battle shall lie elsewhere."

"Then why have you summoned me here?" demanded the bard with bitter vehemence. "Do you think I have not felt for myself the first crack in Estrelland or do not know that the forbidden spell of binding and concealment was evoked, the door between our world and Limbo opened and then shut again? I have felt the disturbance in the Flux. I have sensed the winds of change. The forces of Dred are at work in the world again. The creatures of Somn clamor at the gates and wait to be released into the Realm of the One. Soon it will be time to lay aside the harp and take up the cudgel and the sword. But that time is not yet. So why have you called me from the Flux?" He paused, one eyebrow arching in sudden enlightenment as he gazed speculatively at the peace-keeper. "Did one of the Immortals of Somn slip through the portal? Is that it? Was it Dred himself?"

"It was Sehwan, but that is not why I called you here."

"Sehwan!" exclaimed the bard in obvious disbelief. "But why should Dred choose that one to lead the vanguard? Like you, Sehwan is no warrior."

"We do not know why such a choice was made. But we cannot be mistaken. There has been no attempt to hide either the presence or the identity of the intruder. Sehwan has made clear the objective of Throm."

"You surprise me, Efluvien," returned the bard with a grim laugh. "What is Throm's purpose here?"

"Sehwan seeks the Thromholan. Messages have been left which ask the one called Frayne to meet the Seer of Throm at the Sacred Grove ere the final waning of the moon."

"And will the knight of Tor keep his assignation?" the bard queried curiously.

"We do not think it would be wise. Throm has not sent a warrior, but one who is yet both cunning and dangerous, and Dred has made more than one attempt in the past to rid himself of the heir who prophecy says will supplant him. We cannot, however, interfere with the fates of mortals. The One has forbidden it. In the end Dred's son will do as destiny dictates. As shall we all. Meantime, we can only wait and watch."

"Ah, yes. Destiny," murmured the bard and ran his fingers harshly across the harp strings. "Methinks that destiny shall have a great deal to answer for when the world comes finally to an end."

"You are bitter," the god said, as though surprised. "Did the child mean so much to you?"

The bard smiled grimly and glanced away.

"She was more mortal than most," he said, his look distant. "It pained me to watch her fleeting life pass before me. Hardly had she drawn her first breath ere she had breathed her last. Or so it seemed to me. It was much the same with her mother, whom she little resembled in any other way. At least I did not send the child to her death as I did the warrior-woman who

13

bore her. But then that was destiny, too, was it not? Or at least that is what you have told me."

"It was Almira's destiny to die that her child might live for a greater purpose," observed the god dispassionately.

"A greater purpose? That poor, sickly creature who never lived long enough to know what it was to be a woman? Take care, Efluvien. You are becoming something less than a seer and more the philosopher."

"Nevertheless, it is the truth. Even as it is the truth that the child you took into your keeping was a changeling. Almira's daughter is alive, Alain of Naefredeyan. It was she who closed the door which the shape-changer opened. I have seen her triumph over Dred himself and heard her sing the song of power. She knows not her true name, but forges her own, for she is Aurora and Andruvien, and she commands the Cloak of Power."

The bard stared hard at the shadowy figure of the god. Within him disbelief warred with the sudden birth of hope like a blaze of light in darkness.

"How do you know this? If it is true, why did I not see it in the changing flux of possibilities?"

"Perhaps in your grief you did not seek the alternative explanations for Almira's strange behavior?" the god suggested gently. "Or perhaps the sorceress, aided by the Lord of Somn, did her work all too well in poisoning your thoughts against the warrior-woman. Yet know this. Almira and the young prince of Garn were friends and cousins, but they were never lovers. Neither did they betray by word or deed their oath of fealty to the One."

A look of rending agony swept the bard's hard features.

"You are mistaken, Efluvien," he said harshly. "Almira condemned herself when she fled."

"Only in your eyes. Look into your heart for the truth, harpist. Which was the false sister? Almira or Leilah?"

The bard of Naefredeyan drew in a long, shuddering breath.

"Leilah, curse her black soul," he said. "Leilah, who is Dred's concubine." For a long time he was silent, his thoughts turned inward. But at length he raised his head, and the strange, unfathomable eyes were sudden piercing flames.

"I have been away too long, Efluvien," he said. "Tell me everything which has passed since I renounced the sword. Tell me of Almira and Garn and the young enchantress who forges her own name."

Thus it was that Efluvien related the tale of Almira, the warrior-woman, who fled with her infant daughter into Endrith's Forest in the company of the prince of Garn and three of his lieutenants because Leilah, the sorceress of Tor, plotted against the child. But the sorceress's Black Guard caught up with them in Hawthorne Glade, and after a great battle slew the warrior-woman and her companions.

"During the battle the elves of the Glade stole the infant away. They named her Anduan, Elf-Foundling, but the dryads, who fostered her, called her Tree-Child. She speaks the language of the Old Ones and has the power to converse with the beasts of the forest. But one day the knight of Tor came into

Endrith's Forest on a quest for his mistress, the sorceress. Beside the still waters of Grendylmere, the destiny of Almira's child was forever joined to that of the Thromholan. It was Frayne who named her Aurora and who awakened her to her power, the power of the enchantress, which was her birthright, and the power of the god whose vassal she is. Together they made their way to Shalandorwas and the Black Mountain, but it was Aurora who mastered Andruvien, the sliver of Vendrenin, and Aurora who on the quest for her true name freed Myrialoc from the Crystal Kingdom. And now begins the true quest, the final quest. Alain of Naefredeyan, she comes in search of you."

Chapter 1

In the Beginnings it is recorded that the Creator peopled the land with the magic folk to serve as guardians over all creation. To the children of Boreas, creatures of wind and storm, he gave dominion over the north that they might carouse freely amidst the shimmering splendor of the Mountains of Yss and the vast frozen Plains of Nyf. To the faeries, creatures of field and flower, he granted the rich, rolling grasslands, the Grenesweard, which men now call the Fertile Plains, and to the elves, he bequeathed Gwyddllan, the verdant, wooded hills and valleys of the east, which comprise Endrith's Forest. But the halcyon lands of the west, the blessed country of peace and plenitude, the domain of Blidseafeld—the happy land of eternal spring—he gave to Thromgilad, the first generation of Immortals.

Here, amidst the bounty of flora and fauna, the fairest of all the races sported, creating at whim marvelous creatures that no man has ever seen. And in honor of the One, who had brought them forth, the lords of Throm caused to be raised on the sloping sides of Mount Pelesias the mythical City of Shalandorwas, and at the center of the city, the Vardos, a marvel of perfect symmetry in reflection of the symmetry of a universe in perfect harmony.

Thus did the lords of Throm live in gladsome unanimity with the Nous, which is the Universal Mind of the One, and all the world was in accord, save for one—the fairest of all that fair race of Immortals—Dred, the prince of Throm.

'Twas Dred who caused the gnomes to excavate the great mines within the lightless bowels of Pelesias and to delve the magnificent halls—the Chamber of the Lords, the Hall of the King (for such was Dred's ambition), and—the most splendid of them all—Helynderne, Dred's private sanctum, which later was to be the Treasure Trove of the gnomes and finally the Crystal Room. Such was the beginning of the end of Blidseafeld, for it was in Helynderne that Dred communed with the dark things, the dread things, the creatures of an ancient time and place who have never known the blessed light nor ever shall. Then did Dred, in his overweaning pride, spread discord among the Thromgilad, and, inciting them at last to rebellion against the One, call forth from the bowels of the world the fire and molten lava that decimated Shalandorwas and the Happy Land of Throm.

Thus it was that Dred incurred the wrath of the One against all that unhappy race. To the Land of Somn on the plane of Limbo they were banished, and in their place the Second Generation of Immortals, the Eilderood, was brought forth, thenceforward to serve him who was Creator. Yet so aggrieved was the One at the treachery of Thromgilad, heretofore the most favored of his creations, that he forbade dominion of any earthly region to any gods, but gave the new Immortals Galesiad instead, the Eternal City in the Land of the Silver Clouds. Nor from that time forth, the One decreed, should any eye behold again Pelesias rising in splendor above the bountiful country of Blidseafeld, but only the Black Mountain brooding amidst the charred and blasted wastes of the dread Confounded Lands.

So ended the Beginnings, which was the Age of Throm, and thus commenced a new day, the Age of Men.

At the end of the First Age of Men, Dred rose up again to spread rebellion through the Realm of the One. In the Second Great Uprising, Eilderood, elves, and men joined forces to do battle against the combined armies led by the lords of Throm, but it was Harmon, the warrior-god with the power of Vendrenin, who in the Treasure Trove beneath the Black Mountain fought and defeated the prince of Throm, banishing him and all his race once more to the lightless depths of Somn.

Yet still was it written in the Tome of Prophecy that Dred should rise a third time, and still were there among the races who walked the earth some who would seek to do Dred's bidding for the sake of his ambition, or their own. One such was the Mage-lord Krim, who, deceived by a false dream sent from Somn, plotted to steal Vendrenin from Estrelland that he might achieve the immortality of a god. But his fate has been recorded elsewhere, and there was yet another whose appointed lot remained to be apportioned. Indeed, the final events whose culmination would usher forth a new age in recorded history had been set into motion by the sorceress, Leilah, who, in her secret aspirations for a godly power, had caused her sister's daughter to be abducted and imprisoned in Skorl, the black tower fortress perched atop the pinnacle of Tor.

Thus it was that Aurora, the raven-haired enchantress restlessly paced the confines of a cell within the sorceress's drafty tower, whilst Leilah, her mother's wicked sister, remained free to work her dreadful schemes. Despite the relative comfort and luxury of her surrounds, which she owed to the knight of Tor, whose slave she was, a frown marred the lovely purity of her brow and her marvelous eyes the color of gold coins flashed dangerously.

"Blast!" she uttered out loud, her slender hands clenched in vexation at her sides. "I shall go mad do I not soon discover what Leilah is about. Where in blazes has Frayne taken himself? How *dare* he stay so long away when 'tis obvious she is up to something and I alone am kept in ignorance!"

And, indeed, the entire castle had most indubitably to be aware that something momentous was afoot, for the sorceress had emerged after two weeks and three days of uninterrupted brooding before her dreaded Seeing Eye to issue a flurry of orders. For days now the usually silent halls had echoed with constant, harried activity, and Aurora, much to the detriment of her nerves, had been locked in her room and denied even so much as the company of the knight of Tor, who nonetheless had made sure his

lovely slave did not starve during her confinement.

Every morning at Frayne's orders a thrall whom
the sorceress had rendered mute delivered to the
enchantress a sumptuous repast, and on the heavily
laden tray was ever a perfect red rose, the symbol of
the knight's heart, which belonged only to Aurora,
and the sign that her love was yet safe and well. And
each morning Aurora, breathing a silent prayer of
gratitude to the One, pressed the fragile bloom to her
lips, then, placing it reverently with the others in a
silver vase, proceeded to drive herself to the brink of
collapse.

She was Anduan, Elf-Foundling, and Tree-Child
of the dryads. She was one with the great forest that
had nurtured her, and ever had she drawn strength
from the earth and all the living things that abounded
thereon. Thus, confined in the sorceress's cold stone
fortress, she had grown daily thinner, her golden skin
paling to a white translucence and her eyes appearing to burn with a feverish intensity. Indeed, it was as
though she were being consumed from within by the
same unquenchable spirit that had challenged the
judgment of Gesh, defied the prince of Somn, and
mastered Andruvien, the Crystal of Power. She was
the enchantress, the vassal of a god, and she chafed at
her own impotence as she mulled over and over the
probable significance of the sorceress's extremely odd
behavior and waited for the time when Frayne should
come to her at last with news.

But this day the mute slave had not appeared with
the tray bearing Aurora's breakfast, and, more
important, the anticipated rose, and thus she was

made doubly anxious for the safety of her beloved. For had he not warned her some weeks past that since the crafty Leilah now possessed all the ingredients required for her secret potion she had no further need of the knight's services? Oh, gods. Had Frayne waited too long to make his move?

"Where is the dratted man?" Aurora fumed out loud and flung herself petulantly across the fur-covered bed. "He gave his word that we should escape this dreary place ere Leilah discovers the crystal of Ariana is not Andruvien. Oh, *why* does he not come? Crane and Janine have need of me. I feel it."

Inevitably she began to fret over the tormenting uncertainties concerning the whereabouts and safety of her two young friends. The last she had seen of Crane, the Shape-Changer, he had taken the form of an eagle winging into the falling shadows of night, Aurora's golden bracelet clutched in his mighty talons as he carried Andruvien to safety. Had his wounds been serious, perhaps even mortal? she worried, not for the first time. The thought of the courageous and ever-loyal Crane lying dead some-where in the forest chilled her heart. Indeed, she could not imagine a world without the homely, freckle-faced young mage-lord with his hair flaming red and his grin absurdly sheepish and lopsided. He had been a part of the perilous quest for her true name almost from the beginning. It would not seem right if he were not at her side for the finish. And as if that were not enough to plague Aurora's every waking moment, there was the even greater uncer-tainty of Janine's fate to contemplate, for the girl, hardly more than a child, was presumably alone and lost in the forest.

A dire circumstance, indeed, Aurora agonized, when one considered that Janine was Wendaren, a daughter of the desert, and that she had consequently been born to the life of a nomad in the vast open spaces of sand dunes and sky. To her the forest had seemed dark and perilous, fraught with *ghuwalin*, demons of the woods. And who could blame her? After all, on her first foray into the forest depths she had been stalked by wolves, and on her second she had been abandoned to her own fate.

Yet no doubt Frayne had been right to make haste in leaving the camp without calling attention to the missing slave girl or to the packs, in one of which had resided the Crimson Cloak of Power, Aurora argued to herself. 'Twould have been disastrous for the cloak to fall into the wrong hands, for it bore the symbols that commanded an empyrean power greater than any god's. Nor would it have done for Janine to be discovered, for the band of ruffians had been in a dangerous mood and doubtless would have welcomed the sport offered by the beautiful and defenseless slave girl. Nor could Frayne have helped her, hampered as he was by the need to seem as calloused and depraved as the other servants of the sorceress. Indeed, the stakes in the dangerous game he played were too high, for in the balance was the life of Ariana, the Valdoran Virgin, whom the sorceress kept hostage in the Flux of Timelessness. Still, the child had deserved better treatment than to be left unprotected in a hostile land.

Oh, why had she not left the blasted crystal in Dred's secret chamber beneath the Black Mountain?

Had she done so, perhaps Crane and Janine would be safe and unharmed even now and the Andruvien no closer to falling into Dred's power than it had been in all the centuries it had lain hidden in the Crystal Room. She had been a fool to suppose she was meant to keep it safe. Indeed, it seemed to her that she had brought nothing but grief upon herself and her faithful companions in all that she had done since leaving Hawthorn Glade. After all, she had lost the Andruvien, and the Crimson Cloak of Power as well, and, thus rendered powerless, had been made to suffer the humiliation of being made a prisoner and a slave. But that was not all or even the worst that troubled the young enchantress. Nay. For during the days and nights of her captivity, she had been granted ample time to brood over the death of the man who weeks before had come to Vandrel's hidden valley in search of a mage to stop the spreading evil in Endrith's Forest, the man who had taken the life of Phelan, Father-Wolf, to save hers, the man whom *she* had slain—Elwindolf, Wolf-Friend of the elves.

Oh, gods! At times she thought she could not bear the torment of remembering, and still she could not stop herself. Again and again she saw him, savage and wild with blood-lust as he fell upon the pitiful, fear-crazed creature, Groul, the master lapidary who had stolen the Virgin's Tear and thus released the madness upon the land. And over and over she relived the horror of raising the stone up in her hands and bringing it down against Elwindolf's unprotected head. There had been no choice but to stop him, for without the lapidary the crystal tear should have remained lost to them and the curse of Dred's

24

madness eternally upon the land. Yet Aurora must ever ask herself if there had not been some other way. Had Elwindolf indeed to die that the miserable Groul should live?

Egad, she would go mad if she were made to linger much longer with only her thoughts to keep her company. Indeed, she must make her own escape if Frayne did not soon make his appearance, for there was much to be done and so little time left in which to do it.

Even during the first weeks of her captivity in Tor when Aurora was just learning the sweet marvel of Frayne's love for her, she had begun to feel the press of time, which did not cease to flow beyond the castle walls simply because she might wish it to. While she lay in the arms of her love, the forces of Dred might already have begun the game in earnest, for Andruvien could be anywhere, and even the Crimson Cloak of Power was beyond her reach. Nor had she felt the hand of the god upon her since she had entered the sorceress's dreary domain. Doubtless she had been judged unworthy to be his vassal, for she had failed miserably in all that she had set out to accomplish.

"Blast the knight of Tor and his cursed secrecy!" she uttered in sudden exasperation, and bounding up from the bed, began to prowl fitfully about the chamber once more, her silken gown shimmering golden in the muted light from the single window.

Frayne had said they would make their way from Tor as soon as he was certain he could free Ariana from the Flux of Timelessness. But other than affirming that Aurora herself had provided the means by which this might be accomplished, he had told her nothing of his plans. Was he even now setting his scheme into motion? Had the sorceress found him out and retaliated? Oh, *why* had he kept Aurora in the dark? Had she known what he intended doing, could she not have helped?

Yet it had ever been thus. Frayne must have his secrets, and though she now knew the most damning of them—that he was Dred's only offspring, the Thromholan of prophecy—still he had not learned to trust her. At least she knew him well enough now to realize he was motivated by a desire to protect her, but the thought gave her little comfort. She was no longer a child. She was Aurora, the enchantress of the Glade. She had no need to be protected.

Nor would she wait any longer for the knight of Tor. If he could not come to her, she must find a way to go to him, she decided impetuously and crossed the room to the door. Laying her ear against the rough wood, she strained to her any sounds of activity in the hall outside her chamber. Whatever had been going forth earlier was apparently at an end, she thought with a prickle of her nerve endings, for other than the scutter of rats scrounging for food, she could hear nothing.

The door was barred on the outside and the single window in the chamber overlooked a sheer drop of fifty feet or more, but still there must be some way to win her release, she fretted. If only she had Andruvien. No mere door could withstand the crystal's scintillating flame. Yet there was little use grieving over what could not be helped. The crystal was gone from her, and she must simply discover some other way to win her freedom.

With a sigh the enchantress leaned her head against the door and squeezed her eyes shut as she pondered the problem. Then suddenly she uttered an explosive oath and jumped as a small grey wood-mouse, stealing through the crack beneath the door, scampered across her bare foot.

Drat the sorceress and her miserable, old drafty tower! No wonder her mother's sister was ill-tempered and perverse, living as she did in such uncongenial surroundings. Never had Aurora longed more to feel the sun warm against her skin or to behold a green, living thing. Indeed, she thought she could not bear another day shut away in the sorceress's gloomy fortress, and she sank to the floor, her back against the door, and despondently watched her small uninvited guest skitter about the room.

Aurora remained thus for several moments before she became gradually aware that the nondescript little creature exhibited none of the timorousness natural to one of its kind in the presence of a human. Indeed, the rodent, having ceased its perambulations, had settled on its haunches a scant foot or so from her and was involved in what had every appearance of delivering the enchantress a tremendous scolding.

"Softly, Langtayl, Grey-Mouse," she scolded in silent thought sent outward to touch the mind of the minikin. Yet though she had couched the thought in the language of the Old Ones, which was the tongue of elves and beasts, still the creature answered not.

Her curiosity by now thoroughly aroused, Aurora leaned forward the better to examine her odd visitor. In appearance the creature was not unlike others of its kind, being mousy grey in color and possessed of the usual long tail and bristly whiskers characteristic of the common woodmouse. She fancied, however, that she distinguished an unusual sapience in the lustrous black eyes regarding her with unmouselike boldness, and all of a sudden her pulse leaped with the dawning suspicion that her guest was something quite different from what he appeared to be.

"Crane?" she whispered thrillingly. *"Can* it be you?"

Whereupon the tiny creature began to shimmer and grow, until instead of a mouse a tall, lanky youth with red hair and freckles stood blinking down at her as though a trifle bewildered at the precipitous transformation.

"Oh, it *is* you," Aurora cried and bounded to her feet to fling her arms ecstatically about the skinny neck. "I've been so worried about you. Where have you been? Is the crystal safe? What *took* you so long in getting here?"

The shape-changer wrapped Aurora in a brief, fierce hug. Then, blushing furiously, he straightened and held her at arm's length. His prominent adam's apple bobbed convulsively as he glanced fleetingly down into the lovely face turned up to his and was dazzled by the golden eyes shimmering with joyful tears.

"Aw, gee, Aurora," he grumbled, ducking his head. "You don't have to yell at me. I came as soon as I could. You have no idea the trouble I've had trying to find you in this wretched pile of stones. Egad," he grimaced, a shudder running the length of his scrawny frame, "have you any notion of the number of rats in this place? It's a wonder I made it here at all."

Aurora, dashing the back of a hand impatiently across her eyes, suppressed the sudden urge to giggle. Poor, dear Crane. There would never be another like him. Still, she could not quite resist the urge to tease him just a little.

"But then why choose to come as a mouse, you gudgeon? Surely a cat or a dog or even a wisp of smoke would have been more sensible."

The shape-changer flushed to the roots of his fiery hair.

"Drat! If you must know, I never meant to change into anything. Well, this is a big place, and you could have been anywhere. So I thought it'd be a whole lot simpler to bring *you* to *me* than for me to try to find you."

"So you tried Lil's spell of summoning," Aurora deduced, shaking her head slowly in dumb disbelief.

"Yeah, only when I got to the part about becoming one with the universal mouse in order to find the hidden portals in the cosmic flux . . ."

"Y-you became a mouse," Aurora choked, trying desperately to subdue the rising bubbles of laughter.

"I just don't understand what went wrong," grimaced the shape-changer, drawing forth a crumpled paper blotched with purple berry stains, mute evidence that he had been sampling Vandrel's elderberry jam at the time he copied down the spell. "I wrote it down just like Lil had it in her Book of Summoning."

"Oh, C-Crane, you poor chucklehead. Don't you see? It's supposed to be an 'n' instead of an 'm.' And

29

there's no 'e.' It's 'the universal *nous*—the mind of the One—and it rhymes with *goose!*"

Suddenly it was just too much for her to contain her glee. The chamber rang with the sound of her golden laughter, and instantly the shadows seemed to recede and the room to grow less dreary.

"B-But, of course, it could be w-worse," she gasped when her hilarity had subsided sufficiently to allow for speech. "You could have become a *m-moose* or a *n-oose!*"

"Oh, thanks a lot," muttered the youth grudgingly. Then he glanced into the golden eyes yet brimful with mirth, and a sheepish grin tugged irresistibly at the corners of his mouth. "Oh, well. It all worked out for the best. I'm here, and so is your blasted Andruvien," he said, and he drew forth the gold bracelet that had belonged to Almira, the warrior-woman, and that Kev, the dragon of Myrialoc, had given to the enchantress to house the sliver of Vendrenin.

Abruptly Aurora's laughter stilled.

"Andruvien," she whispered and briefly closed her eyes as suddenly she felt her stomach churn and her limbs grow weak. Oh, gods, she was not ready yet, she thought, and in that instant she realized how gloriously contented she had been simply to be Aurora, Frayne's beloved. Indeed, she wished she had never to take the thing up again, had never again to feel the icy flames sear her mind and feed upon her very soul, to be joined with it as one entity with two wills vying for mastery, one over the other—to become once again Aurora and Andruvien, a thing apart from other mortals. And yet she must, for, foolishly, she had removed the crystal from the Crystal Room and, in so doing, had taken the burden unto herself.

Drawing in a deep breath, she straightened to her full height and looked once more upon the sliver of Vendrenin. It seemed a small thing, a lovely thing, naught but a diamond with a heart of fire, yet she knew that it only slept, as did the power that was its essence and that long ago had been absorbed into herself. She alone could awaken it, for even apart, they two were one.

Slowly, with a hand that trembled slightly, she reached toward the thing of power.

"Nay!" she cried suddenly, snatching back her hand. "'Twere best to wait till we have found Frayne. *She* would feel the thing awaken. *She* would know 'twas here. 'Twould mean the end of all his plans. Nay. You keep it yet awhile longer."

A puzzled frown creased the shape-changer's brow as he watched Aurora clasp her hands tightly together at her waist and wheel away. Egad! What had Frayne and his cursed mistress done to her? he wondered, feeling a sudden, rending pain like a knife thrust through his vitals, for in that instant before she turned from him, he had caught a glimpse of something in the golden eyes he had never seen there before. The gods be merciful, he groaned inwardly. The enchantress was afraid!

Shaken by what he had seen, Crane numbly tucked the bracelet bearing the crystal in his shirt again and tried to think of something to say to fill the sudden, uneasy silence. But it was the enchantress who spoke, and suddenly the world seemed bleak indeed.

"I'm glad you're here," she said, glancing up into his face and then down again. "I've been so worried about you. Where have you been all these weeks? And Janine. Did she come with you?"

"Never mind where I've been," replied the shape-changer in quick alarm. "What do you mean, 'Did she come with me?' Isn't she here with you?"

Instantly Aurora paled, one hand going instinctively out to him.

"Oh, Crane! No. Frayne and I have not laid eyes on her since she ran into the woods that day. After you and she had that silly quarrel. I was hoping you had circled back to look for her when everyone was gone."

"But I couldn't," groaned the youth, wheeling sharply away and beginning to pace in nervous agitation. "I was lucky to get away at all. Cranith darned near did for me, but I managed to find a cave not far from the grove. I stayed there till I was fit enough to come after you. Egad! You mean the poor kid was left to fend for herself in that blasted forest?" he exclaimed harshly and turned to impale the enchantress with accusing eyes.

"I-It couldn't be helped. I swear it," Aurora affirmed miserably and looked away from the shape-changer's anguish that he might not see her own. "She was nowhere to be seen when the fighting broke out. And afterwards . . . well, afterwards I was in no position to search for her," she ended vaguely, all too aware that nothing would be served in letting the hotheaded Crane learn she had been knocked unconscious by the knight of Tor.

Crane's face worked convulsively. His fists

clenched and unclenched at his sides as he struggled with the bitter knowledge that he had failed Janine, the naive little slave girl who foolishly had believed he could do anything. She had called him *mogush*, a great magician, and she had trusted him to keep her safe. Suddenly he was swept with a terrible, grief-stricken rage.

"Curse the knight of Tor for a traitorous black-guard! This is his doing. By the gods I'll find a way to make him pay. I'll change into a grizzly and rip his heart out. Or a viper waiting to strike him in his bed. Or a vulture to pluck out his eyes. Or a worm gnawing at his . . ."

"*No*, Crane! You mustn't!" Aurora cried and reached out frantically to grasp the youth's wildly flailing arms. But she was too late. For suddenly the shape-changer shimmered and just seemed to vanish into thin air.

"Crane! How *could* you," Aurora groaned as she dropped to her knees on the floor and reached out to gather up the wriggly little earthworm attempting to burrow beneath a mohair rug. "This is no time to lose your head. Now cease such foolishness at once. I have something to say to you, and, if you don't mind, I should rather say it to a man than to a worm."

It was, however, quite useless to remonstrate with the squirming little creature trying to squiggle up her arm, as she knew full well from a great deal of experience with the shape-changer's sudden starts. Indeed, Crane would come back into himself only when he was good and ready to, or, more probably, when the spell itself took a notion simply to wear off. Such was the quixotic nature of the shape-changer's

33

peculiar gift that she had known him to remain for days as a shrub or a stone, or to alter in a seemingly endless succession of shapes—from flower to butterfly to teacup to soap bubble and so on and so forth—till at last he had got the spell to work as it should and he became himself again. With an exasperated sigh, she settled cross-legged on the floor and prepared to wait.

Unfortunately it was soon to transpire that her patience had worn quite perilously thin, which in the circumstances was not surprising. After all, she had already expended a deal of forbearance on the elusive Frayne's behalf, and she had never been one to wait when something was in need of being done.

"By the gods, Crane," she uttered in no little exasperation when several seconds had crept by and still she had naught but a brainless worm for a companion. "I swear I shall feed you to the first bird to perch on my window ledge do you not change back by the time I count to ten. *One. Two. Three . . .*" she began in ominous tones when suddenly a raucous squawk issued forth from behind her as if in summons to her ill-conceived words.

Hastily Aurora closed her fingers over what could only be a tempting little morsel to even the most finicky of birds but an absolute delight to the sorceress's familiar had the loathsome old crow the least inkling it was Crane she was ingesting. Then, thrusting her hand casually into her pocket and assuming a nonchalance she was far from feeling, the enchantress turned with an imperiously arched eyebrow to greet her unwelcome guest.

"Looking for Frayne, Kreekow?" she queried of

the large black crow eyeing her malevolently from the window ledge. "Well, as you can see he isn't here, there seemes little point in your remaining. Doubtless you have more pressing business elsewhere?"

"Why should Kreekow search for what the Seeing Eye can see? Kreekow knows what the sorceress knows. But not so the witch-child," taunted the crow as she cocked a crafty eye at the raven-haired enchantress and glanced suspiciously about the room.

Aurora gritted her teeth and with a deal of effort preserved an unruffled front. Egad, as if it was not enough that at the very moment that should have seen them free of the sorceress's power Crane should suddenly take the notion to become a worm—must she now suffer the yammerings of Leilah's feather-brained familiar as well? Still, it occurred to her that Kreekow was being deliberately evasive, for she could think of no reason that the crow should come to her chamber, except in search of the knight of Tor. Indeed, she was suddenly very nearly certain that neither the bird-wit nor its mistress had the slightest notion where Frayne was to be found, a circumstance fraught with disturbing possibilities. Had something happened to the magic looking glass, the Seeing Eye the sorceress had stolen from Sheelar, the Serpent-Lord of Somn? Was that what Frayne had been about the past few days? she wondered with an excited fluttering of her heartbeat. Egads. She must rid herself of the blasted bird, she thought in a sudden quake of impatience, and jolt Crane back into himself so that they could be about the business of finding Frayne.

"Oh, 'tis a fine-witted bird indeed," the enchantress agreed airily and wished she might throttle the wretched creature on the spot. "And now that we have fluffed your fine feathers, Kreekow, Flesh-Eater, mayhap you should begone to whatever dark and loathsome place appeals to one of your kind—the charnel pits, I shouldn't doubt—that I might continue to languish in solitary confinement. That is what my mother's dearest sister intends for me, is it not? That I should starve for want of food and company? And indeed I should prefer it to being bored to death by you."

"Silence!" shrieked the crow, hopping from one leg to the other in an instant fit of anger. "A slave speaks not so to Kreekow. 'Tis insolence. *Insolence* to speak so."

"Then doubtless I should beg your pardon," observed the enchantress, her forefinger pressed to her lips as she appeared to consider the matter with all the seriousness it deserved. "Aye, I believe that is the behavior proper to a slave in the presence of her betters. However, you will be gratified to know that heretofore I have forborne to eat crow and that, further, you have given me very little reason to suppose I should ever wish to do anything quite so revolting. Now, was there something that you wanted, or was this meant to be a friendly chat?"

"Witch-child! Serpent-tongued changeling," Kreekow croaked, nearly beside herself with venomous dislike. "The sourceress will hear of this. And 'twill be the knight who pays."

"Only if you can find him," Aurora pointed out and smiled grimly as she watched the loathsome creature vanish into the narrow aperture and take flight still shrieking virulent invectives. Thus she did not hear the faint rasp of the bar sliding free or the slight groan of the door moving on its hinges. Inhaling a deep breath to calm her nerves, then letting it slowly out again, she turned.

"Now, my writhy little angleworm," she began, drawing forth the troublesome creature from the pocket into which she had earlier deposited him, "'tis time you . . ." But she was not allowed to finish whatever she had been about to say, for all at once two strong arms closed like steel bands about her slender form to crush her mercilessly against a hard chest. As Aurora's startled cry was silenced by a warm, demanding mouth pressed hungrily to hers, the unfortunate Crane flew from her hand to vanish into the depths of a great oviform jar.

For the first stunned instant, the raven-haired enchantress stood rigid with surprise, then all of a sudden she uttered a small, strangled cry, and flinging her arms about her assailant's neck, launched herself bodily against the lean, powerful form. He staggered back, his arms clenched about her slender waist, and swung her dizzily round and round the room until at last they both collapsed, laughing, on the bed.

When she had got her breath again, Aurora struggled up and turned a mock-censorious frown upon the third of her unexpected visitors.

"Oh, Frayne! How *could* you?" she gasped, the mirth but slowly fading from her glorious eyes as they lovingly embraced the knight of Tor's almost perfect, godlike countenance. He looked weary, she thought, raising a hand to tenderly brush a stray lock of fair hair from the high, sensitive forehead. There were fine lines of fatigue about the marvelous silvery-grey eyes, which were piercing, like a falcon's, and rather sinister-appearing, with the dark rims about the irises. He had the hard, lean aspect of the warrior, the nose long and straight, the mouth stern and finely chiseled, a small scar at the corner giving his lips a slightly bitter cast. It seemed he had not found time to shave since leaving her some six or seven days past, she noted with interest, for the beard that covered the strong, stubborn jaw was soft and flaxen against the smooth skin tanned to a golden brown by the sun.

A suspicious gleam lit the silvery eyes as the knight captured Aurora's slim wrist in his strong, shapely hand.

"Hush," he murmured, drawing her irresistibly down to him. "The time is short. Let us not waste it in pointless talk."

She tried to pull away. There was so much she needed to know. But suddenly she was lying on her back beside him, her wrists pinned to the bed at either side of her head.

"How dare you!" she cried, her eyes flashing golden sparks of anger at his arrogance. She was not one to be taken lightly. She was Aurora, the enchantress, and she had been kept in ignorance of the sorceress's activities for far too long.

"I dare what is mine by right," drawled the insufferable knight, his smile lazy and maddeningly cool. "Or must I teach you again that I am the master, and you naught but my slave."

"OH!" she uttered in a terrible voice and began

furiously to twist and turn. But she was no match for his great strength, and ere she could break free, he had rendered her powerless beneath his lean, muscular weight.

Panting for breath, her breasts heaving with indignation, she collapsed at last against the bed. Blast the knight. Had she had Andruvien, she would have taught him a thing or two. Then all at once her mind reeled in sudden horror. Oh, gods—Crane! The last she could remember of the shape-changer, she had flung him from her to save him in his peculiar state of vulnerability from what she had believed to be one of the sorceress's ruffians come to bear her to the dungeons. Egad, they could not leave him crawling about on the floor to be crushed beneath a boot sole. They must find him! And at once!

Her lips parted to tell Frayne of the shape-changer's plight, but ere she could speak, he had covered her mouth with his, and for a time she was lost to everything but the knight's lips rubbing sensuously over hers and her blood leaping like liquid flame within her veins. All at once she ceased to struggle.

"Aurora. Oh, gods, how I have missed you!" Frayne murmured feverishly when at last his lips left hers to devour her eyes, her cheeks, her throat, and finally the sweetness of her mouth again. She sighed, letting her lips part to admit the probing madness of his tongue, and he kissed her deeply, passionately, drawing so fiercely upon her very soul with his need that she uttered a small cry when at last he pulled away. Whereupon she felt his hands warm against her bare skin and she arched urgently upward as he worked the fabric of her gown up and over her hips

39

and waist, the upthrust promise of her breasts, the nipples rigid with desire, till finally she was gloriously free of the confining fabric. She saw the knight's silver eyes embrace her silken loveliness, and then he left her, quickly to disrobe.

She thought she must die with yearning before at last he lay beside her, his hands probing the sweet tenderness of her flesh, till she was aflame with desire, the blood pulsing in her veins with the strange, mystical passion that was the gift of the gods. She arched against his lean strength cradled between her thighs, her breath coming in deep ragged gasps as she willed him to come into her. She felt him draw up and back and bit her lip to keep from crying out in her unbearable torment. Then at last he thrust deep within her.

"Frayne!" she exhaled on a shuddering sigh. "Frayne, beloved!"

Aurora felt herself borne upon the swelling tide of an empyrean need and knew at last that the one whose vassal she was had returned to her, searing her, body and soul, with the purifying flame of his godly power.

Together she and Frayne, who had reawakened the puissance of the god within her, soared into the divine heights where only gods or mortals touched by the power of a god may go. And as their passion crested, their spirits were forged anew and melded into a single entity—hers and her beloved's. Whereupon she knew herself at last to be complete and unafraid. For she was the enchantress, and he was Frayne, the touchstone of her being. Together they were one.

Chapter 2

Stahn was the first to scent the spoor of the man-cub, but it was Arthane the Black who growled the warning.

"They are come back again," he snarled, hackles raised, his eyes yellow in the faint light of the new moon. "It is the cub of the Long-Knife. And one other who carries the stench of death."

"Aye, it is the cub," agreed Stahn, Hlafard of the Bredan, as he sniffed the air. "But it is alone and afraid. The other stalks the trail of the cub. He is the hunter. Without the aid of the Bredan, the man-cub will die."

"How can we be sure?" grumbled Engar of the Broken Tooth. "Once Phelan tracked the man-cub, and now Phelan is dead, for the one who speaks the tongue of beasts appeared out of the air and summoned the shape-changer and the Long-Knife to defend the cub. Let us leave it to find its own trail. It is taboo."

The others of the Bredan romped or lazed about the

small glade. Mostly they were young cubs on their first hunt, for many of the Bredan had fallen to the Long-Knife at the Battle of Sedgewick some three weeks before, and now those left who were wise in the ways of the hunt numbered few.

Stahn sat quietly on a raised knoll and waited. After the old Hlafard's death, he had fought for and held the Fehald, the stone pinnacle atop the Crag that was the place of the Hlafard at Hilgemot where gathered the wolf-clans. Already he had the look of Phelan, his father, who had been Hlafard before him. He was long and rangy, with a deep, muscular chest that bespoke strength and endurance. His pelt was thick and grey, mingled with black about the pointed snout and the watchful eyes. There was about him a certain restraint that set him apart from the others, a keen intelligence coupled with a heedful patience, which had marked his father before him ere Phelan had been taken by Dred's madness and transformed into a creature of mindless hate.

Stahn had held the Fehald for less than a single passing of the cycles of Shin, the Moon Goddess. Even so, the new Hlafard had led the pack well. Earlier they had made a kill, and their bellies were full. Had it not been for the strange scent, they would have been stretched out in sleep till the first stirrings of hunger awakened them once more to the hunt. But Arthane had sounded the warning, and now would come the first real test of his leadership, Stahn knew as he studied each of the elders in turn and waited for them to convey their thoughts.

Saureth, the Grey, was old in the ways of the Bredan. He could be depended on to reserve judgment till the others had spoken their piece. Only then would he voice his sentiments, which would cut straight to the heart of the matter. His opinion always carried weight with the others, but Stahn knew it would be fruitless to attempt to woo him to his cause. Saureth would ever do and say as Saureth saw fit.

The trouble would begin with Engar of the Broken Tooth, as was usually the case. For he saw only the dark side of everything. If the pack had eaten well, he would say it was a sign their luck was sure to change for the worse, for fat wolves were poor hunters. He was the grumbler, the whiner who bred discontent among the others. But he was only an irritant. The real danger lay with Phelan's half-brother, Arthane the Black, who coveted the right of Hlafard.

Briefly Stahn regretted the absense of Alwyf, Fealu, Zerla, and the others. It was the time of the whelping, and the she-wolves of the Bredan had sought the solitude of the den weeks past. There was always less grumbling when the Circle of the Bredan was complete. Then, too, there was still the need to provide the wolf-mates with game. Already they should be on the move back to the *hoom-dennen* where the nursing females waited. But, still, he was Hlafard, and he was troubled by these strangers in the woods. For he yet owed the debt to the Long-Knife and the she-man who had freed the Bredan of the madness. But perhaps it was even more important to Stahn to save the man-cub because it and the Long-Knife had been friends to his brother Elwindolf.

"The man-cub has need of those who know the forest," he said at last. "It would not take us far from

43

our trail to follow the man-beasts. It was the Long-Knife and the tree-child of the dryads who banished the evil from the forest," Stahn reminded him. "They be neither taboo nor our enemies. And it was Phelan who invited death unto himself. Or hadst thee forgotten the madness brought upon us by Ommat?"

"We have forgotten nothing," growled Engar, his gaze falling uneasily away from that of the Hlafard. "And still I say it is best to give the man-beasts a wide berth. For wherever they go, they bring nothing but trouble."

For a moment the Hlafard was silent as he watched the cubs cavorting about the glade. What Engar had said was true. Whenever the man-beast appeared, death was seldom far behind. And yet it had not always been so. For in the old days before the madness had changed everything, Elwindolf, Wolf-Friend of the elves, had been one with the pack and the times had been good. Phelan's foster-man-cub had led the young wolves with the cunning of the man-beast and the courage of the wolf, and their bellies had ever been full. Then Stahn had called the man-cub brother and had looked with pride to the day when Elwindolf should be named Hlafard of the Bredan. But things do not always come to pass as one expects, and now Stahn was Hlafard and Elwindolf was no longer.

He wondered what had become of the she-man who had walked away in grief from the slain Elwindolf. If the man-cub of the Long-Knife had returned, would the she-man with the golden eyes return also? It would be well if she did, thought the Hlafard, for weeks earlier he had sensed a dangerous presence in the forest, the presence of one who was neither man nor beast but *aljis*—other—indeed, a creature from outside the Realm of the One, and one, moreover, possessed of a dark aura of power that made the wolf uneasy. In his heart he knew that the coming of this outworlder to the forest meant trouble against which only one such as the she-man with the Sword of Power could hope to do battle.

Still, even if there had not been the threat of the stranger of power, old loyalties die hard to one trained in the ways of the Bredan, and Stahn knew he would do this one last thing for Elwindolf, his brother.

"The Hlafard runs not from danger lest it be the greater wisdom, but I would not have the pack imperiled needlessly. Arthane, thou shalt lead the Bredan to the *hoom-dennen* and wait for me there," he commanded. "He who calls himself Ealan, the Loner, must be told that these two are come to the forest. Engar shall carry the word to him."

Engar bristled and began to pace, his head lowered to hide the hard gleam of fear in his eyes. The one who had chosen to follow the ways of the rogue-wolf was not like the others of his kind. He was *faege*—one doomed to walk in death.

"That one is renegade and outcast," he whined. "To break silence with such a one is to deny the Law of the Pack."

Knowing the moment he had been waiting for had come, Stahn leaped from his place on the knoll above the others and faced the troublemaker squarely, his lip curled back over bared, gleaming fangs.

"Beware, Engar," he growled in warning. "Thou

45

speakest of one who was cleansed by the Rite of Blood. Though he was cast out, yet did he earn the right to be called brother. I, Stahn, say it is so. Be there any among you who would challenge the word of the Hlafard?"

Suddenly sensing the peril into which his brash tongue had led him, Engar of the Broken Tooth sank into a low crouch, his ears laid back against his head and his tail curled between his legs in the sign of appeasement.

"Nay, nay, son of Phelan," he whined. Yet, though his manner was obsequious, his discourse was full of cunning. "It be not for Engar to question the word of the mighty Hlafard. I meant only to suggest the need for caution. The Circle of Bredan hath suffered grave losses. The young and inexperienced make up our ranks. Is it wise to risk the life of the Hlafard for one who hath chosen the way of the rogue? Indeed, is it wise for the Hlafard, who serves as an example to us all, to set aside the Law of the Pack even for one who was once a son to Phelan?"

"The Hlafard lives or dies for the good of the pack," Stahn countered dangerously. "I am Hlafard. It is for me to decide what is for the good, and it is for you to obey. Anything else is to challenge the right of Fehald in open battle. *That* is the Law of the Pack. Dost thee choose the right of challenge, Engar of the Broken Tooth?"

Aye. Engar would like nothing better than to challenge the high and mighty Stahn, for envy was like a worm forever gnawing at him. Yet Engar was no fool. It would mean his death to battle Stahn. Sullenly Engar retreated before Stahn's bold front.

Whereupon Arthane bounded forward to stand stiff-legged and defiant before the Hlafard of the Bredan.

"Engar of the Broken Tooth hath spoken truly," he snarled through bared teeth. "Thou hast taken and held the Fehald in fair combat. Yet even Hlafard be not outside the Law. I, Arthane the Black, say the one called Ealan be neither wolf nor of the Bredan, but taboo."

Thus did Arthane claim the right of challenge. Yet Stahn was a true son of Phelan the Bold. The time for talk was past. Swift was his attack. As Arthane hurtled toward him, Stahn leaped for the throat.

The two wolves closed in deadly combat, one black as the eternal night of Somn and the other grey, but both of an equal size and weight and both of the same blood as Phelan. Yet only one could be Hlafard.

Thus the battle raged, and the woods resounded with the fearsome growls of the great beasts as they ripped at each other with savage teeth and the others of the Bredan circled nervously, their ears flattened and tails down to show that the fight was Stahn's and Arthane's and none of theirs.

Then Arthane went down beneath Stahn's greater fury, and Stahn's jaw closed about the black wolf's throat. Arthane went still. On his back in submissiveness he lay lest the ruthless fangs tear the life from him.

"Spare the life of your father's brother, Mighty Hlafard," whined Arthane, who had thought to win the Fehald.

Stahn tightened the death grip.

"Silence, *kur-dogge!*" he growled, his eyes glazed and his veins afire with blood-lust.

47

In dread fear for his life, the downed wolf subsided. "Hath the Hlafard of the Bredan no mercy in his heart for the vanquished?" queried a voice gently from the outer fringes of the Circle. "It was not the way of Phelan, Father-Wolf, to kill needlessly."

The newcomer had spoken quietly, yet his voice penetrated even the red haze that clouded Stahn's mind. With an effort the wolf triumphed over the savage desire to slay. Slowly he loosened his hold and, without moving from his menacing stance, looked up into the still, pale eyes of one who has known the embrace of death and still endures.

"Our brother speaks truly," Stahn replied in the tongue of beasts and elves, which is also the universal tongue of the Beginnings. "Yet did Arthane challenge the right of Fehald. Lest none from the Circle speak for him, his life is forfeit. Such be the Law."

"Then I shall speak for him," Saureth snapped impatiently. "Spare the fool and let the matter be ended."

For a telling moment Stahn stood over the vanquished Arthane. But at last, satisfied that the pretender had been taught his proper place in the Circle of the Bredan, he relented and moved away deliberately. He was Hlafard, and he had met the first challenge to his right to lead. For a time there would be no other.

Stahn watched the wolf-pack vanish into the deep shadows of the forest before at last he turned to the one who waited.

"Now, son of Phelan," said Ealan, the Loner, in a quiet voice. "Tell me why Hlafard battles Bredan."

*   *   *

Janine, the desert slave girl, stumbled wearily along the faint woodland trail, which led ever northward, her precious burden clutched tightly to her chest. It seemed an eternity since she had fled the Grove of Tamaracks in the wake of the knight of Tor's betrayal. Her heart ached, for she could not believe even yet that her beloved master could be so false, and yet she had watched in stunned horror as he had struck the enchantress unconscious and had then ridden off with her toward the south, toward Tor and the evil sorceress.

Lord Frayne had turned against them all; indeed, it seemed likely he had plotted their destruction from the very beginning, for had she not overheard Kreekow, Carrion-Crow, command him to deliver to the sorceress Aurora and the Andruvien, which was the sliver of Vendrenin and Aurora's Sword of Power? And had he not helped Leilah's vile minions to capture the enchantress—Baldrac, the evil one who had stolen Janine from the slave caravan, and Cranith, the Imposter, who in the form of *saqr*, the hawk, had attacked Crane? Had she not seen her beloved Crane take the shape of a great horned owl and rake the knight of Tor with punishing claws? And then, gravely wounded by the wicked Cranith, had he not changed into the eagle, who is *al-mar-ur-rih*, the lord of the wind, and fled with the Andruvien into the night? And, most damning of all, had not the one called Frayne confessed to being Thromholan, the mortal son of Amaur, who was Dred to the infidels and prince of Somn?

The girl cried out as her foot caught on a hidden snag and she fell heavily to the ground. For a long while she lay where she had landed, her thin body racked with bitter sobs.

She could not go another step, she told herself when at last her weeping had subsided to leave her spent and filled with an odd sort of languor. She had not eaten for two days, for she had not thought to bring food with her from the abandoned camp beneath the tamaracks. In her panic she had been able to summon only enough courage to retrieve Aurora's pack in which resided *al-mandil-baraka*, the Crimson Cloak of Power. She would starve to death if she were not slain first by the wild beasts of the forest or by *ghuwalin-ghawl*, the attack of the wood-demons. But what did it matter? *Marhakim!* She was *wazara-ur-fatwa*, judged unworthy by the gods, for had she not been forsaken by her master and abandoned by her love? Indeed, she had been made to suffer the torment of *hijrah*, the separation from all whom she had ever loved, and she was *sifr*, an empty thing. With a long, shuddering sigh, Janine, the desert slave girl, closed her eyes and succumbed to the weariness of despair.

How long she slept, Janine did not know. She was awakened by the sun streaming through the branches of the trees and by a sudden instinct of danger. With a startled cry, she bolted upright, then shrank back as she looked up into the hideously scarred face and gloating eyes of the man she feared most in this world.

"Aye, wench, I've caught up with you at last," sneered the red-bearded brute of a man as he let his heated gaze roam deliberately over the slave girl's slender form. His glance lingered on a shapely leg bared to the thigh by a long rent in the girl's soiled *dolama*, the white robe of the desert clans. He licked dry lips. "You've cost me a deal of time and trouble, my little desert jade. You'd best pray to your heathenish gods that you're worth it."

Seeing the blood leap in the brutish eyes, Janine scrambled hastily to her feet.

"You will not dare to touch me," she said, lifting her head in defiance born of desperation. "I am *mamluk* to Sayyid Frayne. He is a jealous lord who will wreak terrible vengeance on any who would seek to harm his slave."

She winced at the man's harsh laughter but forced herself to stand her ground. Lest she lose her courage, she kept her eyes from the stump of the man's right arm, which ended in a wicked hook. To retreat or to show fear now would be to invite the attack of *shaghal*, the jackal, for so she knew him to be. He was Baldrac, and he had the soul of a pig.

Once before she had been made to suffer his vile touch upon her body. He had not taken her then only because in the *saray*, the loathsome inn in the city of the sorceress, he had been distracted by a greater hunger. The hunger for *al-zahr*, the dice. The gods had smiled on her, and the knight of Tor had won her from him. And her kind *sayyid* had given her to Crane, the young *mogush*, which in Wendaren means "magician." It was he who had awakened in her the sweet yearnings of womanhood, for his was a generous heart and he had treated her as an equal. *Marhakim!* He had given her her freedom!

Though her stomach was queasy with fear and her limbs trembled with the awful realization of what the infidel intended for her, Janine straightened to her full height and defiantly tossed her head so that her tangled mane of raven hair fell away from her face. She was the daughter of Ahbin-ben-ami, Khan of the desert tribes, and though it was he who had sold her to the slavers, yet was she still *bgim* of the Wendaren—a princess of the royal blood. And her beloved *mogush*, in freeing her, had restored her to honor. Never again would she be *mamluk*, the possession of another. She would die by her own hand before she submitted to this pig-man.

"You laugh, *al-muwallad-ur-khar*," she said contemptuously, for she had called him the begotten son of a she-ass. "But if you dare to anger Frayne, the son of Amaur, whom you call Dred, you will not laugh for long, I think."

A hard gleam came to Baldrac's eyes at the slave-girl's unexpected show of spirit. The brazen little baggage had been meek enough before the cursed knight of Tor had won her off him. She'd been a proper little "harahmie-girl," trained from birth to be obedient, humble, and subservient to the lord of the house. The fifteen-year-old princess had been taken straight from her mama's arms—untouched and as virginal as a spring lamb—a rare morsel, which he'd meant to have all to himself. But Frayne—the gods rot him—had robbed him of that pleasure, and from the looks of her, he'd made a proper job of it. She was as haughty as her high-flown sire, ol' Ben-Ami, the desert Khan.

A terrible hatred for the knight of Tor seethed in Baldrac's brutish soul. Over and over again he had pictured Frayne in his mind—Frayne with the exquisite creature most men only dreamed of, Frayne savoring the sumptuous delights that ought to have been his, *Frayne* deflowering *his* virgin slave—until the torment of his own depraved fantasies had nearly driven him mad. Still, he speculated suddenly, as he took in the tantalizing vision of violet-blue eyes exotically slanted and set in the perfect oval of the delicate young face, skin soft and smooth and the color of fine ivory, and trembling lips like rosebuds parted slightly over small, even white teeth, she was a luscious piece. And doubtless breaking the little bitch to his will would afford him a certain pleasure, especially if it were true that the knight of Tor prized her even in a small way.

Without warning, Baldrac struck the girl a back-handed blow across the face. Janine's head snapped back and she staggered, then caught herself. One trembling hand rose to her cut and bleeding lip as she slowly backed away from the leering brute. He would beat her until she was senseless, she thought with the despair of one who has known the pain and terror of *al-darb*, the chastisement of the stick. And when at last her will was broken, he would thrust himself upon her like a rutting boar. She had seen the daughters of the *fellahin*, the peasants who tilled the farms around the great oases, after the horsemen, the *sipahi*, of the Bakhshidan raided their villages. Those who were left alive had yet the eyes of death, for the ravishers had robbed them of *kaif*, the joy of life, which is of the soul and which bubbles forth in laughter. It would be better to die than to be slave to this whoremaster, to be made to submit again and again to his bestial lust.

Whereupon it came to her what she must do. She

would awaken in him *al-nar-ur-ghadib*, the engulfing flames of rage, so that he would end her life quickly.

From somewhere she summoned the courage to smile in the manner of Zuleika, the newest wife to Ahbin-ben-ami, who, because she was favored by the Khan, treated the other women of the *haram* with open contempt.

"So. It is even as my master has said. The man who is a man shall know the true pleasure of a woman's love. But the man who is a beast can only take by force what he can never win." Suddenly she spat on the ground between them. "Bah! You will never know what it is to be a man like the knight of Tor. *He* is a man for a woman."

With the sure instinct of one nurtured in the ways of the *haram*, she had attacked Baldrac where he was most vulnerable. Indeed, she could have found no surer way to rouse him to a mindless fury. Bellowing like a crazed bull, he came at her, the jagged scar across his hate-filled face pulsing an angry red. Terror rose like bile in her throat, for all at once he seemed not a man, but *ghuwal*, the wood-demon, and suddenly she knew she did not want to die. A silent scream of despair welled up inside her.

Then Baldrac's hand was in her hair, and he dragged her ruthlessly to him. The blood drained from her face and she bit her lip to keep from crying out as he ran the point of his hook lightly over her cheek. In dread fascination she stared into his glittering eyes and prayed for the strength to meet her end bravely.

"So," he said, his breath hot against her face, "you

54

think I'm less a man than the bloody knight who woos an unbroken filly with soft words ere he mounts and has his ride. Oh, he has his ways, all right. As I have mine!" he uttered hoarsely. Then brutally he jerked her head back.

For a stunned moment she stood helpless and unmoving in his cruel grasp. But then he forced his mouth over hers, and suddenly she erupted into a frenzied struggle. She fought desperately, but her young strength was no match for his. She could not breathe, and the darkness of Amaur seemed to fill her mind.

Struggling to remain conscious, she managed somehow to free one hand. He cursed as she raked his scarred cheek with her nails. His grip loosened, and she brought her knee up hard into his groin. He grunted and doubled over, his face grey, and Janine lurched backwards. Retching violently, she turned and started to run, but he lunged after her. The deadly hook lashed out and down. With a strangled cry, she jerked upright, her hands clutching spasmodically at her back as the point ripped a jagged gash through the tender flesh. She staggered and pitched forward on her hands and knees, her breath coming in ragged gasps.

She must rise and flee, she told herself, but the world tilted and turned and she had no strength. She heard him coming, his breath harsh in his throat, and in mindless fear, she began to drag herself forward.

A low, savage growl sounded somewhere near. Dully she lifted her head in time to see a grey shadow hurtle past her. She heard Baldrac's terrified scream cut short and the blood-chilling snarls of a ferocious beast. A man's curt shout cut across the sounds of battle followed by the soft twang of a bowstring. Then suddenly everything was deathly still.

A shadow fell over her, and strong hands gently lifted her. I am dreaming, she thought as she looked up into the still, hard face of a man dressed in buckskins. He was the man of the woods, and she knew at last that she need no longer be afraid in the forest, for she had found *al-pava-ur-shagg*, the brave protector.

Her lips parted to say his name. But the effort was too much for her. With a shuddering sigh, she sank into a deep well of darkness.

Janine drifted in and out of a strange dream filled with pain. She groaned as gentle hands turned her over on her stomach, then cleansed and bound the wound in a snug-fitting bandage. She must have fallen into the oblivion of sleep for a time, because the next thing she knew she had surfaced from the darkness to a vague awareness that she was being carried. Her head lolled against a broad shoulder clad in buckskin, and for a time she concentrated on trying to force her eyes open. But at last even the effort became too much for her and she drifted off once more. A long time later she was roused once more to semiconsciousness by the indistinct sounds of voices—a man's quiet one and then a woman's, warm with concern.

"You say she's been wounded? The poor dear. Bring her inside at once. Quick. Lay her here on the cot."

Janine struggled against the lethargy that held her between wakefulness and slumber, but she seemed powerless to open her eyes. A sudden stab of pain as she was lowered gently to the bed brought a groan to her lips.

"Easy," scolded the woman, and Janine sighed as she felt the touch of a cool, soothing hand against her feverish brow.

"Why, she's little more than a babe!" the woman exclaimed softly. "What sort of brute would do this to a child?"

"The one called Baldrac," came the curt response.

"I see. The Renegade of Fengard." There was a telling pause before she added meaningfully, "I believe your trails have crossed before?"

"Aye. Our trails have crossed, but his ended a mile south of here."

The woman made no comment to her companion's chilling observation other than to instruct him to lift the child that she might be given a healing draught to ease the pain.

Janine frowned crossly and tried to tell them she was not a child. *Marhakim!* It had been the same with Sayyid Frayne and the young *mogush*, Crane, who had called her a silly kid of a girl, for which she had been very angry and so had run away from him into the forest. Oh, how she wished she had not done so, for that was when the evil ones had come to the camp beside the Shrine of the Holy Maiden to make the enchantress their prisoner and Crane had flown away with the wings of the eagle. The thought that her last words with her beloved should have been the words of *ghadib*—anger—saddened her, and a single tear slid from beneath her eyelid. But then a firm arm had slipped beneath her shoulders to lift her, and a sharp stab of pain drove all such thoughts from her mind. A cup was placed against her lips and someone ordered her to drink. Obediently she swallowed the sweet liquid having the fragrance of roses.

"*Shukran*," she murmured as she was allowed to sink gratefully back against the pillow. "Thank you."

Then slowly the pain began to ease as she was filled with *kaif*, the feeling of well-being, and at last she succumbed to the restorative power of sleep.

Janine slowly emerged from the healing cocoon of dreamless repose to an awareness of sunshine streaming through curtained windows on the far side of the bright and airy room in which she lay. Filled with a delicious sort of languor, she snuggled more deeply into the cozy warmth of her bed and delighted in the cheerful cacophony of birdsong and the sweet scent of dew-laden lilacs carried on a breeze through a door open to the morning. At last, her curiosity piqued, she let her gaze drift aimlessly about her pleasant if rather peculiar surroundings.

Never before had she seen the like of this little house made of wood the reddish-brown of the desert sand as the sun sets. There was a homey warmth in the colorful woven rugs strewn about the polished stone floor and a strange feeling of comfort about the wooden chairs padded with worn cushions, the walls lined with shelves filled with leather-bound tomes and yellowed parchments, and the narrow staircase rising from the center of the room to the attic above.

The far side of the rather spacious living quarters held a soot-blackened fireplace, a littered table flanked by long wooden benches, and cupboards boasting an odd assortment of chipped dishes, well-used cookingware, and a sundry of dried herbs, fruits, and teas stored in woven baskets.

What was this place? And who lived here? she wondered in mounting bewilderment, and, laying the crook of one arm across her eyes, tried to remember how she came to be there.

"I live here," observed a jovial voice, apparently in response to the girl's unvoiced thoughts.

Janine started violently and quickly lowered her arm to encounter twinkling blue eyes regarding her with kindly interest from behind rimless spectacles.

"Forgive me, my dear. I didn't mean to frighten you. You must take care not to move about too freely for a day or two. The wound is coming along nicely, but even Vandrel's healing spells require time to do their work properly."

Janine uttered a small gasp.

"You are this Vandrel?" she whispered throatily. "I-I have truly found the learned one who is friend to Sayyid Crane?"

"Heavens!" chuckled the old scholar in no little amusement. "So it's *Lord* Crane now, is it. 'Twould seem the lad's come up in the world since last he crossed old Vandrel's doorstep. But then there always was more to the young scamp than most gave him credit for. Like as not he'll have a tale or two to tell. But what's this?" she exclaimed, alarmed to behold her young patient burst suddenly into tears. She settled on the bed and gathered the weeping girl to her generous bosom. "There, there, child. Just you go ahead and cry. You'll feel all the better for it."

In the wake of all the pain and terror of the past few days, such unexpected sympathy was too much for Janine. She clung to Vandrel's comforting warmth and cried until she thought her heart would burst. But at last, spent and deeply chagrined at so childish a display of emotion, her weeping gradually subsided, and she pulled away, her head bent in shame.

"I-I beg that you will f-forgive this weakness," she sniffed convulsively and glanced shyly up through luxurious dark eyelashes at this friend of her beloved *mogush*, Crane. He had spoken often and with great fondness of the *hakim*, the wise one who possessed the power of healing, for Crane had been her pupil, as had Aurora, the beautiful golden-eyed enchantress.

"Nonsense, child," said Vandrel bracingly. "There's nothing wrong with a little weeping now and then. After all, the Creator gave us tears to cleanse the soul of grief and despair. And to be a sign of overwhelming gladness, as well." The old scholar pulled a handkerchief from her apron pocket and held it out to the girl. "Now dry your tears and tell old Vandrel how a daughter of the desert clans should find herself alone and unprotected in Endrith's Forest."

Gratefully Janine took the hanky and obediently dabbed at her wet cheeks. Then, blowing her nose and drawing a deep, shuddering breath, she turned tragic eyes upon the woman smiling in kindly encouragement.

"I am called Janine," she said, "and once I was

slave to the pig-man Baldrac. He came with others to our camp at the Shrine of the Holy Maiden. There was a terrible battle. I saw Sayyid Crane become an owl and take up the *tilsaman* of the enchantress, the thing of power. But the other one of many shapes descended from the sky in the body of *saqr*, the hawk, and felled Lord Crane to the earth. I thought he would die, and my heart wept for him. But then he was *al-mar-ur-rih*, the lord of eagles, and he escaped. Yet still I fear for him, for I know he was gravely wounded. I-I hoped to find him here with you, for he had thought to send me to the so-kind Vandrel that I should be safe. But I would not let him, for I did not wish to suffer *hijra*, the pain of separation. And now I know not where he is or even if he yet lives. And I am afraid, Hakim Vandrel. I am so afraid for him."

Janine swallowed hard and looked away lest she disgrace herself again with tears. Thus she did not see the flicker of anxiety in the old scholar's eyes or the brief tightening of her lips in a grim line. After a moment Vandrel reached over to pat the girl's hand clenched tightly on the coverlet.

"Now, now," she scolded lightly. "Don't you fret about Crane. That young skalawag can take care of himself. It sounds as if he did just as he ought. You know it wouldn't do for the sliver of Vendrenin to fall into the wrong hands, now don't you? But what about Aurora? Even without the crystal, I shouldn't have thought she would run from the likes of Baldrac and Cranith. Why isn't she with you?"

"We . . . we were betrayed!" Janine uttered in a voice hardly above a whisper. Suddenly she lifted anguished eyes to the old scholar's face. "He told her he was the mortal son of Dred and he struck her unconscious. Then he-he carried her away on his horse."

A harshly uttered curse shattered the sudden stillness as the girl's voice faltered and died away. Janine's startled glance flew to the doorway. In frightened awe she beheld the shadowy form of a tall, lean man with powerful shoulders limned against the sunlight, and at his feet a great grey wolf.

"Who betrayed ye, lass?" demanded the newcomer in a voice of tempered steel.

Janine lifted a quivering hand to shade her eyes against the blinding light.

"I-It was Sayyid Frayne, my master," she answered in a troubled voice.

She heard the man inhale sharply.

"So. The trail twists and turns and grows ever more treacherous. And the gods play out their deadly games whilst mortals search their hearts for meaning. In the end 'twill be her own heart she battles. And the Thromholan who wins. Or so it be foretold. Where, I wonder, lies the meaning in that?"

For a moment longer he stood unmoving, his shoulders bowed as if he waged some inner struggle. Beside her, Janine felt the old scholar watching him, waiting—for what?

Suddenly he straightened. Janine felt her pulse quicken. The man took a single, long stride into the room, and the girl saw him clearly at last.

He was lean and powerful, with the still, hard face of the hunter. His cheeks were smooth and tanned, the finely chiseled lips stern and the beardless chin firm. His nose was long and hooked and bespoke a quiet strength reflected in the pale eyes like grey, piercing points. His hair, dark and peppered with grey, had been shorn close to the head. He was dressed in buckskins and tall, supple boots, which reached to the knees. A long knife in a beaded sheath hung at the wide leathern belt about his lean waist. He was the man of the forest, and yet she knew him not.

"Begin at the beginning," he said, his grey eyes light and piercing on the girl. "Once ye were squire to the knight of Tor. What be ye now? And why have ye the talisman of the enchantress—the Crimson Cloak of Power?"

Janine uttered a small, strangled cry, her eyes wide and staring on the face of the man who had saved her life.

"I feel I know you," she whispered. "A-and yet you are a stranger to me. Please, I beg you. What is your name?"

The man's lips twisted in a bitter smile.

"I am called Ealan, the Loner, since I walk outside the pale. I claim neither man nor beast as brother, nor any other living thing. But this day I forsake the vow of solitude to repay a debt of blood. When ye be well enough, we three shall travel the path to Tor."

Chapter 3

"But he was here, I tell you!" Aurora insisted as she continued to work her way on hands and knees across the floor, pausing to peek under the hand woven throw-rugs, discarded articles of clothing, and various and sundry other objects strewn about the chamber.

The knight of Tor stretched lazily, a slow smile hovering about his lips.

"I never doubted it for a moment," he said, observing his love's extremely odd behavior with a deal of enjoyment. "Or that our young friend should be a worm. One expects such eccentricity from Crane. But how could *you* have been so magotty as to misplace him?"

"Oh, how like you to blame *me*," Aurora retorted, pausing in her search to fling a resentful glance over her shoulder at the knight reclining at ease against the pillows, his muscled torso bared most unfairly to the waist. Suddenly she shivered in the chill draught and eyed with longing the cozy hollow at Frayne's side, which she had abandoned only with the greatest reluctance for the cold discomfort of the floor.

Blast the vagaries of men! she reflected ill-humoredly. Why must Crane choose now of all times to make a nuisance of himself! And Frayne with his teasing smile and infuriating air of amused tolerance! As if she were some precocious child not to be taken seriously. He was even worse than Crane.

"If you must know, this is all your fault," she stated emphatically and for the third time in less than half an hour, proceeded to grope gingerly around the base of a great clay jar situated against the wall a scant yard from the window.

"But how not?" agreed the knight, his lips twitching at the corners.

"How not, indeed," she said bitterly, "when I had him in the palm of my hand at the moment you so unceremoniously thrust yourself upon me. Poor, dear Crane. He just sort of flew out of my grasp ere I knew what was happening. And to make matters worse, he has the Andruvien on him. I do wish you would make some effort to help me find him."

The knight of Tor obligingly raised himself on one elbow the better to behold his love intriguingly attired in naught but his own woollen tunic, which only just managed to cover her shapely posterior as she tried to peer beneath a carved oak coffer.

"Naturally it is my greatest desire to have your slightest wish fulfilled, my love," drawled the knight, an appreciative gleam in his eye. "Yet in this instance I think I must beg to be excused. One of your—er—dainty proportions is much better suited to the task than I. Indeed, I find the possibility of unexpectedly discovering the elusive Crane flattened beneath any part of my anatomy a damned distasteful proposition.''

Of a sudden Aurora bolted upright, nearly braining herself against the wood chest in her hurry.

"Oh, Frayne!" she blurted, looking distinctly off-color. "You don't think we could have tr-trampled him when w-we . . . that is, when y-you . . .''

"I *think*," interrupted the knight in no uncertain terms, "that Skorl is affecting your mind if you can suppose for an instant that Crane even now graces the bottom of my boot sole."

Still, a shudder shook Aurora's slender frame.

"Oh, gods," she groaned. "I never thought to look for him there."

"Nor need you, you absurd child. Indeed, I consider such a possibility remote in the extreme. Crane, in case you haven't noticed, possesses an uncanny ability to whisk himself from harm's way."

"Aye, and yet not even he is infallible," Aurora pointed out in a troubled voice. "Mayhap you did not realize how grievously Cranith wounded him in the Tamarack Grove. I fear he suffered terribly, for 'twas his wounds which kept him from us all these weeks."

A shadow flickered in the silvery falcon-eyes and then vanished as Frayne arched an arrogant eyebrow and shrugged.

"And yet he did survive and has as always managed to turn up when least expected. As he doubtless will again, when the time is ripe," he drawled with the air of one fast losing all interest in the subject, then, yawning, rolled over on his back, his hands clasped firmly behind his head. "Meantime, I suggest it is little to the point to wear oneself out needlessly when the time could be put to much better use."

"Meaning that you have no intention of helping me to find him," Aurora stated emphatically, her expression one of outraged disbelief.

"Meaning, my love, that I am exceedingly weary and fully intend to go to sleep."

"Oh!" gasped Aurora, and scrambling to her feet, crossed to the bed to stare furiously down at the knight, who did indeed display every appearance of one on the point of falling into deep repose. "How *can* you be so unfeeling?" she demanded and had the satisfaction of seeing her beloved's eyes drift partially open to fix with stoic patience on her face.

For a moment she hesitated, for he did indeed look uncommonly worn, as if he had not slept for many hours. Yet somehow she could not seem to stop herself; indeed, she felt compelled by some strange perversity to pursue what was doubtless better left alone.

"Have you forgotten," she said, plunging recklessly, "how Crane rescued us from Girmizi and the Bakhshidan desert-raiders? And then again saved us from certain death amidst the suffocating wind and dust of Simoom in the Land of Erg? He has always been there when we needed him. Surely it is little enough to ask that you display at least a semblance of concern for *him* now that he may be in trouble. And—and all because *I* betrayed his trust."

Her voice breaking on the final utterance, the enchantress wheeled abruptly away, a hand flying to her lips.

Oh gods, she had let it slip. That which she had

kept so long at bay and which had yet been slowly eating at her like some dark and loathsome thing. Desperately she wished she could snatch back the words. But it was too late. Already weakening were the tenuous bonds of the spell they two had together fashioned, the illusion, like a lovely dream wrought in hyaline fragility, on the verge of splintering into a thousand thousand pieces.

The silence stretched unbearably, as she felt his eyes on her. Then at last he spoke.

"You are mistaken surely," he murmured, ironically cool. "'Twas never *you* who betrayed him."

"But it was," cried Aurora, turning swiftly back again. Dropping to her knees beside the bed, she transfixed him with huge, tormented eyes. "With every waking moment spent in contented bliss, I have betrayed him, and Vandrel and all the others who trust in me. Each time I lay with such sweet abandonment in your arms, loving you, rejoicing in your love for me, I betrayed them, because I did not seek to make my escape from this prison, which has been like a lovely, fantastical dream to me. Because I abandoned everything—the Cloak of Power, Andruvien, the quest for my identity. Oh, do you not see? My happiness has been purchased at their expense! Crane is bereft and mayhap fled from me forever, for Janine is lost and likely dead because of me."

Frayne's heart suffered a wrench as he looked into Aurora's lovely, upturned face, her great, tragic eyes shimmering golden with unshed tears and her lips trembling like luscious rose petals begging to be kissed. Egad, he groaned to himself, she had ever the power to bewitch him; indeed, to rob him of his very manhood. For even now, when the object of all his years of labor was finally within his reach, he would have—had it not been for the noble Ariana—gladly forsaken everything for this slender child-woman and fled with her to the farthest corners of the earth rather than lose her. And lose her he must, for they two were pawns in the inescapable tides of kismet. She, the enchantress of prophecy who was come into the world to be the savior of her people, and he, Ariana's son and Dred's—the Thromholan, born to lead the Thromgilad to victory.

He had known always that it must end, had tried with all the strength of an iron will not to love her. Even so, he had been powerless against her spell. He, the knight of Tor, whose heart he foolishly had believed invulnerable to love, had pledged that selfsame heart to her. And she, in turn, had for a few precious weeks created a paradiasical haven for him amidst the ugliness of Skorl. Never had he dreamed to know such sweet madness, such transcendent bliss! And now that the time was come when they must flee enchanted paradise and return again into the world, Aurora's sweet and lovely innocence pierced him to the core.

Still, though he cursed himself for a base-born coward and a fool, he would not have her know just yet how very little of their precious time together was left them, or that, once free of the sorceress and Tor, he would be riding on alone. Nay. He would play out the charade to the bittersweet end. Indeed, 'twere better thus, he told himself with a cynical twist of the lips. For how much greater must be her loathing of him at the final moment of total disillusionment, his

70

last and greatest act of betrayal.

Thus, sternly hardening his heart against Aurora's beguiling innocence, Frayne slipped once more into the role he played with such consummate skill. Assuming the cynical mask of the courtier, he became the impenetable knight of Tor.

"You, my love, are being absurd," he said, grasping her by the wrist and pulling her, resisting, toward him. "We don't know that Janine has come to any harm," he murmured deliciously against her ear so that she breathed in a quick, short breath and closed her eyes against the sudden whirling of her senses. "And Crane, I vow, shall materialize at any moment."

Whereupon an explosive crack blasted through the chamber, followed instantly by the telltale clatter of splintering ceramics and a string of vociferously uttered expletives.

"Ye gods. Crane!" Aurora exclaimed, having lurched to her feet in swift alarm to behold the shape-changer, red-faced and seething, sprawled ignominiously amidst the shattered remains of the great, painted oviform ceramic jar that had stood across the room near the window.

"Blast and double blast!" fulminated the youth in tones of self-loathing. "May I be swallowed by a fish and carried out to sea if I ever again become anything so futile as a worm."

"Oh, no, Crane," Aurora giggled helplessly, nearly overcome with relief. "Just think of the poor fish when suddenly you became yourself again."

The enchantress, still choking with mirth, helped the youth climb awkwardly to his feet.

71

"Oh, you may well laugh," Crane said in no little disgust, as with a great show of dignity he straightened the sleeves of his tunic and brushed ineffectually at the dust and debris clinging to his mop of hair. "Criminy, Aurora. I'd never have believed you could toss me into the nearest handy receptacle like so much unwelcome rubbish and then forget about me. Did you even once consider that I might be cold and hungry? You might at least have deposited me in a flower pot. You can have no idea what it's like to knock your head repeatedly against baked clay when you're nearly mad for a little dirt to burrow into."

"I-Indeed. I'm afraid I cannot," Aurora granted a trifle unsteadily, but then, suddenly reminded of the anguish she had been made to suffer on his account, she radically altered her demeanor. "But then you did bring it all upon yourself," she observed pointedly and folded her arms firmly across her chest. "Indeed, I shan't soon forgive you for all the trouble that you have caused. Do you know," she demanded, moved to emphasize each word with the admonitory shake of an index finger, "that I have been groveling about on the floor for the better part of an hour trying to find you! How could you be such a puddinghead?"

Crane's habitual attitude of doleful acceptance went suddenly into eclipse.

"Oh, so now I'm a puddinghead," he retorted with such righteous indignation that Aurora blinked. "I've been a bird, a mule, a rock, and a camel for you, and any number of other things besides. But what do you care? One tiny mistake and I'm nothing more to you than a—a *puddinghead!* But you, Aurora, are an ungrateful female. And that's about the worst thing I

72

can think of to be. In future I'll thank you not to call me names."

"Why you—you *worm!*" Aurora stammered, nearly speechless with startled resentment. "And to think I almost went mad with worry over you. Why, I should be glad if you took yourself away and never came back again."

"*That* does it. If you'll be kind enough to take back your dratted crystal, I'll do my best to oblige you. And good riddance," adamantly declared the shape-changer, and, drawing out the gold bracelet bearing the Andruvien, he unceremoniously thrust it at the seething ingrate.

Aurora drew involuntarily back, her lips parting in unspoken protest. Her gaze flew to Crane, but the shape-changer, apparently impatient to be quit of his obligation and quit of her, was waiting expectantly for her to accept Andruvien once more unto herself. She struggled against a queasiness in her stomach. Never had she thought Crane could turn so easily against her. But then he was goading her to take the crystal, saying he didn't have all day, and suddenly her eyes flashed golden sparks of anger. If he was in such a blasted hurry to leave her, then she certainly had no wish to detain him! Snatching up the thing of power, she slipped it defiantly on her wrist.

For a moment neither spoke as the crystal throbbed, its heart of cold fire quickening to Aurora's pulsebeat. The enchantress gasped and closed her eyes, her brow furrowed as if in pain, and at last the Andruvien stilled again.

Weaving slightly on her feet, Aurora opened eyes

glimmering with the subdued power of Andruvien.

"There," she breathed, " 'tis done."

Still reeling from the searing leap of the crystal's icy flame within her, Aurora stared vaguely up at Crane, who in turn was regarding her—rather oddly, she thought. Indeed, if anything, the shape-changer displayed every manifestation of one inordinately pleased with himself. Whereupon it struck her with dazzling certainty that she had been masterfully and most thoroughly duped.

"Uh—yes, so it is." Crane coughed and shifted his weight nervously from one foot to the other, feeling inexplicably as if someone somewhere had just pronounced his doom. Swallowing hard, he began to edge back, away from the glittery-eyed enchantress. "Well, I suppose I should be going now," he mumbled half-apologetically.

"Aye, I suppose you should," Aurora said shortly and abruptly crossed to the window to stare blindly out at the small patch of sky visible through the narrow recess.

Oh, gods, Crane was really leaving, she thought with a dull sense of disbelief. Blast, but she would be hard-pressed not to keep him with her, nor did it help knowing that it was perfectly within her power to do so. 'Twould be wrong, she told herself, for she could feel how desperately he himself was torn between his sense of loyalty to her and his fear and longing for Janine. In time he would come to hate Aurora, if he were not first utterly destroyed by his torment. Nay, she must set him free to go after his Janine. It was, after all, little enough payment for all that he had done.

And so she would, she vowed, quite suddenly straightening her slender shoulders, but not before she had paid him back in some small measure for his deceit. For she saw clearly now that, having somehow guessed her debilitating dread of Andruvien, he had baited her deliberately, had deliberately forced her to take up the burden. Dearest Crane! How well he knew her.

Thus it was that the enchantress, sternly suppressing the telltale gleam in her eyes, turned to face the shape-changer with a disarming air of meek acquiescence.

"Aye, doubtless 'tis time we pursued our separate paths," she sighed. "I have kept you with me longer than I should; indeed, have demanded far too much of you. But what would you? I perceived it as my duty to call out the very best in you. If I was wrong, I do most humbly beg your forgiveness."

Crane's eyebrows snapped instantly together.

"Naturally, I shall not harbor any grudge for the manner of our parting," she assured him on a note of long-suffering that left little doubt in his mind that she held him entirely accountable. "Further, I shall entreat the gods to grant that your journey be made without mishap. And why should it not?" She paused, frowning, as if suddenly struck by some previously unconsidered potentiality for disaster. "If, that is," she added, perceptibly brightening, "you take every care not to materialize in some place wholly unsuitable, like—oh, the River Glendaron, for instance. For I shan't be there any longer, you know, to fish you out of trouble."

"Egads! As if I needed you to!" spluttered the

shape-changer in red-faced indignation.

"Well, Vandrel did charge me to look after you," Aurora shrugged, guilelessly arching her eyebrows and eloquently giving a shake of the head, thus indicating clearly her own position of unassailability. "And belike she shall blame me for your heedlessness when she discovers you have so foolishly drowned yourself."

"Drat it, Aurora! I do *not intend* to drown."

"Well, but you never intended to be a worm either, did you," she said, smiling sweetly. Whereupon Crane abruptly threw up his hands in utter exasperation.

"The gods have mercy! Of all the insufferable, pigheaded *conceited! . . .*"

"I hesitate to intrude on so tender a scene," interjected a cool, ironic voice. "However, it would seem your unorthodox manner of making an entrance, my young friend, has brought the guard down on us. Might I suggest that you table your grievances for a later time?"

Crane, made thus unexpectedly aware both of numerous muffled voices issuing from beyond the closed door and of Frayne's hitherto unobtrusive presence, blanched as white as he had previously been red.

"*You!*" he uttered in a strangled voice and whipped sharply around to come face to face with the man who once had been, if not precisely a friend, then most certainly a hero after whom Crane had thought wistfully to pattern himself.

Bitter resentment oddly touched with a sort of hurt bewilderment flared in the youthful countenance.

With a sweeping glance he took in the daunting aspect of the manly knight, who, unnoticed in the heat of the others' exchange, had donned his boots and breeches. The bare muscled chest and lean, hard torso enhanced by a golden mat of hair seemed painfully to emphasize the youth's gangly immaturity. The knight was like some blasted god, and he—well, he was Crane, Krim's bumbling grandson.

All at once the knight of Tor raised a warning hand as the voices abruptly faded away.

"They've sent for reinforcements," he said, glancing at the enchantress, who was watching him with bated breath. "Quick, Aurora, dress and be ready to move. And, my love," he added meaningfully, "fetch what you would not leave behind. 'Twould seem we have outstayed our welcome."

Magically Aurora's face lit up. Eagerly she started forward, then halted uncertainly as her gaze fell on Crane. A look of tenderness came into her eyes.

"Crane," she uttered brokenly, and reaching up on tiptoe to pull his head down, brushed her lips fleetingly against his forehead. "I shan't ever forget you, dearest friend," she whispered, her lovely eyes abnormally bright. "Thank you—for everything."

Aurora quickly turned and fled without another word. Sternly blotting from her mind everything but the need for haste, she pulled a small bundle from behind the oak coffer and exchanged Frayne's shirt for her own elfin tunic and breeches, tall, supple boots, and a hooded cloak. A glimmer of a smile touched her lips as her hand closed familiarly about the haft of a silvery blade inscribed with elfin runes of protection—Glaiveling, it was, or "Little-Sword" in the tongue of men, and it had been given to her by Garwin and Gleb, her father-elves of Hawthorn Glade.

A splintering crash jarred the door. Aurora wheeled sharply, her eyes flashing, as dust and bits of debris trickled down from the ceiling.

"Frayne!" she shouted and ran to the battered oaken barrier sagging ominously on its hinges.

Frayne's grip tightened on the sword in his hand, but he made no move to follow her as his glance rested speculatively on the shape-changer, who stared rigidly before him, his freckles dark splotches against the pallor of his face. For an instant the silvery eyes like daggers appeared to soften.

"You may stay or go," he said quietly. "Either way, no blame attaches itself to you. Least of all from her."

Crane blinked once and stiffened, his hands clenching at his sides, but doggedly refused to look upon the knight of Tor. He said nothing.

A muscle leaped along the man's lean jaw. Then, smiling mirthlessly, he stepped close to the boy.

"Whatever else you might think of me," he murmured, a cold gleam in the falcon-eyes, "you may believe I shall let no harm come to her. So far as it is in my power."

Without waiting to see what effect his words had wrought, the knight strode quickly away, leaving Crane to his own torment of indecision.

"I sealed it earlier with a spell of binding," Aurora informed the knight as he pulled the returned tunic over his head, "else they'd have broken through already. Still," she frowned, "I should have thought Leilah could revoke the charm with a word or two."

"Leilah is otherwise employed just now," murmured Frayne, an odd little twist to his lips. "And it were best that she remain undisturbed yet a while longer."

"Aye. And just what has my mother's sister been about?" Aurora demanded with a darkling look. "And where have *you* been this se'ennight past while I have been made nearly to go mad bottled up in my prison chamber?"

"It shall all be made clear to you directly, I promise," grinned the knight, maddeningly cool, as he finished belting his sword about his waist. Then, blade in hand, he drew Aurora safely to one side of the door and kissed her lightly on the lips.

"For now, my love, you may open the door, and be prepared to follow my lead. And whatever happens, mark this well: Leilah must not be made to suspect the crystal in her possession is not Andruvien. No foolishness, understand?"

The enchantress, favoring the gimlet-eyed knight with a moué of disgust, tossed her raven curls defiantly. Had she not suckled at the breast of the warrior-woman? Had she not mastered Andruvien's lust to slay, not once, but twice before? Was she not Aurora, the enchantress of the Glade? She had no need to be enjoined to caution. She knew the seductive power of the crystal better than anyone. Glaiveling clutched firmly in her hand, she spoke the words to remove the spell:

"Weft from warp, warp from weft.
Unseal the heal, unheal the seal.

Unweave the web, unweb the weave.
Unbind the twine, untwine the bind.
The spell bespoken is now revoken."

No sooner had she uttered the final word than the door came crashing down, bowled over beneath the hurtled weight of two armored knights who landed all asprawl amidst the wreckage.

A triumphant outcry went up, and the clamor of shouts and clashing weapons spilled into the room, along with two more unhandily encumbered knights, who, aided by Frayne's ungentle nudge, stumbled over their floundering fellows to topple ignominiously athwart them.

"Now!" Frayne said, and hauling Aurora after him, bounded past the fallen wretches wallowing in a tangle of steel-clad arms and legs, only to be met by the daunting sight of the staircase turret bristling with men struggling to press upward through the newel stair's winding gullet.

"Careful, lads! He's coming out!" rasped a harsh voice.

"That way!" Frayne yelled and thrust Aurora roughly toward the stairs spiraling upward to the right.

Aurora screamed as she saw a burly rogue come at Frayne with a barbed pike. The knight dodged. His teeth flashing in a grin, he caught the shaft in a steely grip and rammed the butt hard into the rogue's belly. With a sickening whoosh, the villain jackknifed. Moving with a catlike quickness, Frayne brought a booted foot up hard against the rogue's shoulder and shoved, driving the pikeman backward into the jostling ranks. A concerted wail went up as with a clatter and clash the rogues toppled hind over head down the stairs.

In a single bound the knight reached the enchantress, a devil of laughter in his eyes. Never had he seemed more human, she thought, her heart lurching at the sight of his boyish grin. Then he grasped her hand and pulled her round the newel out of sight of the scene of pandemonium.

Narrow crossed slits, which had been hewn for archers to defend the fortress, admitted only a feeble light, and the stairway was dark and damp with cold. Thus Aurora was not sorry at first that Frayne soon led her from the turret stair into a great, pillared hall enshrouded in cobwebs and shadows. Dust motes swimming in the muted light seeping through an alabaster mullioned window created an aura of long disuse. Aurora shivered, feeling the chill draught, which breathed through the cobwebs like the touch of an icy hand against her cheek.

'Twas a lifeless, brooding place, she thought, a place haunted by memories of the ancient dead. Nor were they like to have been memories of fair and happy times, she reflected wryly, eyeing with distaste the darksome splendor of pillars wrought from purest black marble. Belike the Eidola, the shadow phantoms of Somn, issued forth in the darkness of deepest night to weave amidst the shrieking silence of the hall the false dreams that plague men's sleep. Shuddering, she tried to summon an image of Truewood, Father-Oak, with the sunlight slanting through the thick, leafy branches and Minta and Valesia, her dryad mother-pair, reclining at ease

81

among the sturdy boughs, their limbs entwined in a loving embrace. But somehow the vision was distant and blurred, like a memory of a time forever gone that can be only imperfectly recalled.

Frayne's voice echoing hollowly in the vast, empty hall startled her from the somber spell into which she had fallen. Her head came up with a little jerk, and she turned to see the knight beckoning to her from behind a black marble throne of princely proportions set upon a stone dais at the far end of the room. Chiding herself for letting a few cobwebs and shadows disturb her, the enchantress made her way quickly down the pillared arcade and sprang lightly to the dais.

"What is this place?" she demanded petulantly, then winced as "PLACE, PLAce, PLace, place," richocheted mockingly from wall to wall. Grimacing in disgust, she fell into a whisper.

"If you mean for us to hide in here till Leilah calls off the search, I should rather take my chances out there against her guard. This is no place for the likes of living flesh and blood."

"No," murmured Frayne, the gleam of amusement in his eyes hardening to a strange glitter. "This is the throne room of the Black Kings, the Kerrin, whom Dred seduced to his cause in the First Rebellion. He promised them a fair kingdom on the shores of the Sea of Hythe and caused a monument to be erected as a token of his pledge to them. Unfortunately for the Black Kings," he grimly laughed, "Dred's promises most oft are turned to vapor, as was the Sea of Hythe before it was all over. Naught of either remains but the black monument."

"And the Black Kings?" queried Aurora, watching in a sort of dread fascination as the knight of Tor reached casually toward two intricately wrought figures atop the throne back: one, a crown in which was set a magnificent black diamond; and the other, a black cobra poised to strike. "Is this all that's left of them? An empty hall of pillars in a miserable black fortress?"

"This,—" replied the knight, touching a finger to the glittering gem. Aurora uttered a strangled scream as the cobra appeared to come suddenly to life, darting at Frayne's hand with venomous quickness. "—and the kings' treasure, which lies beneath," ended Frayne, who had moved with an even greater speed.

Instantly the throne began to swivel to one side, and in the place it had stood before was now revealed a secret stairway spiraling into darkness.

"Oh! I could *kill* you for that!" cried the enchantress, still shaking from the swift stab of terror she had felt for the insufferably grinning knight. "Why did you not see fit to warn me?"

"To what purpose, my love?" Frayne said, laughing easily as he pulled her irresistibly into his arms. "You would only have been made needlessly anxious and very likely moved to argue endlessly about which of us should try the kings' deadly serpent."

Aurora, perceiving the futility of arguing a moot point, awarded him a darkling look.

"Nevertheless," she said with a lift of her chin, "I would not have used you in such a way. Nor will I soon forgive you for the fright you caused me. Now, tell me about this treasure. How can you be sure it is there, and how did you know where to look for the stair?"

"I am sure because I have seen it in the sorceress's Seeing Eye," he answered, kissing her delightfully on the tip of her nose. "And I knew where to look because that, my love, is what I have been doing this past se'ennight—day and night—since the sorceress first emerged from her meditation and began preparations for her final and most devastating spell."

"Day and night for seven . . . but why? What can be so important to warrant such an effort?"

"He was looking for the amulet," said a cold voice from the shadows. "The Circlet of Throm, which Dred gave to Hedron, the last of the Black Kings of Kerr."

Startled, Aurora whipped around to sweep the hall with a searching glance.

"Crane?" she called out uncertainly, trying to make out a tall form standing in the shadow of a black pillar near the dais. Then, as the mage-lord stepped out into the open: "Crane! Why are you still here? You should have been on your way long ago to find Janine."

"I stayed to see that *he* kept his word," replied the youth, pointing an accusing finger at the knight of Tor, "that *this* time he would keep you safe."

"How noble of you, to be sure," drawled the knight, infuriatingly.

"Frayne! That's enough. It was indeed noble," Aurora interjected sharply as the shape-changer scrambled belligerently onto the dais. "But hardly necessary," she added, shooting Crane a disapproving glance, "as I am well able to take care of myself.

84

But since you have seen fit to act so foolishly, you might as well tell what you know about this amulet."

"It's the reason he had Krim send him into the Land of Somn to see Dred. Ask him. My grandsire told me all about Dred's magic circlet. It was a—a sort of key that unlocked portals in the Flux so that Hedron could come and go from here to his promised kingdom on the Sea of Hythe in a matter of seconds."

"Is that true?" demanded the enchantress, turning to glance at Frayne. He wore the hooded look of a falcon, the silvery eyes opaque and unreadable. "Were you after this key of Dred's?"

"Actually, there were two of them," Frayne said matter-of-factly. "One to open the portal and the other to lock it. It's the latter that interests me. In a matter of hours the sorceress will add the final ingredient to the potion she believes will grant her control over the Vendrenin. Only, when she drops the tear of Ariana into the broth instead of Andruvien, she will create a rift in the Flux of Timelessness as shall be felt from here to the farthest reaches of the Realm. I must be ready to enter that rift at the moment of its creation. And when I have Ariana safely out, the fissure must be sealed. It is for that purpose that I must have the circlet. Without it, the Realm of the One will be overrun in a matter of days by every vile creature imaginable."

"But then we must stop her before she completes the potion!" exclaimed the enchantress, white-lipped with horror.

"On the contrary, we shall do nothing."

The knight had spoken calmly, even quietly, but

his words were all the more terrible for that.

"Would you indeed risk so much for a single being, even if it is Ariana?" Aurora marveled, feeling suddenly as if she had never come even close to understanding this strange, iron-willed man.

"You have it all wrong, enchantress," Crane said bitterly. "He doesn't risk anything. He's the Thromholan. It would suit him just fine to have Dred's creatures loose and running wild. That's probably what he's been planning all along."

"Nay, never, Crane!" Aurora swiftly countered. "You do not believe that anymore than I. You once loved him, too."

A look of agony twisted across the boyish face.

"Maybe, once. But I know what he is now. Wake up, Aurora. Don't let him use you like some stupid female who can't see beyond the bedsheets."

Aurora's golden eyes flashed dangerously.

"Mayhap you should speak plainer," she said, coming to stand squarely before him, her fists planted firmly on her hips.

Crane gulped and shifted nervously. This was not the hurt and angry girl he had faced earlier in her prison chamber, but the enchantress whom it was better not to rouse to too great a fury. Still, he was Crane, and he could not hold his tongue.

"Egads, Aurora," he blurted poignantly, flaying her with a look, "how could you sink so low? He's not just a liar and a traitor, he's the Thromholan!"

"Enough! I will not listen to you play the fool. Do you honestly believe I could love him if he were really evil? Frayne never betrayed us. Oh, he deceived me at first, too, but it was just an act to keep Baldrac and the

86

others from killing us all right then. Think, Crane. What chance had we otherwise? They were on us before we knew."

"But he took you by force and brought you here," Crane insisted, beginning to pace agitatedly back and forth. Then suddenly he stopped, and Aurora knew what he would say before he spoke. "He left Janine behind, Aurora. Maybe you can forgive him, but I can't."

"Then go, Crane," she answered steadily, "and find her. And may the gods grant you both happiness."

She made as if to leave him then, but he caught her wrist.

"Come with me, Aurora," he pleaded, his homely face working. "We'll find Janine, and then, when she's safe with Vandrel, we'll go on with the quest. We'll find your true name just like we started out to do. Drat it, Aurora, I *can't* leave you here!"

Torn between hurt and anger, the enchantress twisted free, her lips parting to deliver a chilling retort, when Frayne stopped her.

"Aye, go with him, Enchantress," the knight drawled cynically. "The boy is right. Dred's misbegotten son should be shunned. In the end I can only hurt you."

"Nay, I know what you are trying to do. I will not let you leave me again," she cried, flinging herself in his way as he moved to enter the secret stairway. "I am not powerless to help you. And if you believe so strongly that this must be done, I *want* to be with you."

Briefly the stern features softened as the knight

gazed upon the slender girl, her eyes shimmering with the reawakened power of Andruvien.

"No, never powerless," he murmured with a wry smile, and cradling her face between strong hands, held her with his eyes.

"Can you not tell me why it must be done like this?" she whispered. "Indeed, is there not some other way to gain her freedom?"

"No. The sorceress bound the Valdoran in the Flux with a spell that only she or a crystallized essence of Ariana's noble heart can break. Leilah must fling the Virgin's Tear into the miasma of the Seeing Eye. There is no other way. Nor will there ever be another time. But even so," he added, too low for the shape-changer to hear, "Crane *is* right about one thing: I could be helping Dred, for if I fail . . ."

"We will not fail," she said steadily, her eyes golden with love. "We will free Ariana and reseal the rift. I know it."

"Then so be it," he said huskily and kissed her with such sweet and passionate tenderness that he sent her senses reeling.

Aurora took a deep, steadying breath when at last Frayne released her, and turned to face the shape-changer with her slim shoulders back. But at sight of the youth's stormy countenance, the brown eyes downcast and miserable, she suffered a sharp pang of remorse. It should never have happened like this, their parting, not with anger and misunderstanding between them, she grieved. How she longed to be able to make Crane understand what was in her heart.

"We must go now," she said instead, though it hurt her.

He nodded, refusing to look at her.

"Crane, I . . ."

"I know," he interrupted gruffly. "I didn't mean it either—what I said about you. Just you be sure you know what you're doing. And, well, don't walk around with your eyes closed, if you know what I mean."

"Aurora." The enchantress glanced fleetingly at the knight waiting impatiently at the mouth of the stairway.

"The One be with you, Crane, as is my love," she murmured hastily, and wheeling away from the tall, lanky youth, hurried to join Frayne. Seconds later the two had gone, leaving Crane staring desolately into the deep well of darkness.

"Blast!" swore the shape-changer, slamming the side of his fist down hard against the marble throne, then he jumped as the thing of marble began to move back into place. A look of terrible desperation distorted his face.

"Oh, gods, Aurora!" he cried. "I can't let him do it."

Suddenly what once had been a boy was a mouse, slipping quietly through the narrowing crack beneath the Kings' Throne.

Aurora followed the knight blindly, clinging with silent desperation to his hand, her sole anchor to reality within the black nightmare of the winding stair. Egads, her destiny seemed cursed with an absurd propensity for sending her into the darkest depths. Her precipitous descent into the bowels of the Black Mountain had been bad enough, but then there had been Rab's Kingdom of Crystal beneath the shifting sands of Erg as well. No doubt it was ironic that they could thank Dred for Frayne's peculiar gift of being able to see in the dark, she mused wryly. It was proving to be most darned useful!

It was perhaps inevitable that the thought of Frayne's nefarious parent should remind her of an even more terrifying excursion into darkness, and, indeed, the enchantress, groping her way down the spiraling stairs, felt rather as if she had been returned to that lightless Land of Somn. Almost she expected Krim or Dred himself to materialize at any moment. In which case, she would have vastly preferred the former to the latter, she reflected a trifle giddily, for at least Krim, consumed by the immortal flames of Vendrenin, might have illuminated their passage.

No sooner did the absurd notion take form, than suddenly a glimmering light leaped out at them from the darkness to crawl along the wall before them. Cursing beneath his breath, Frayne backed against the newel and waited, Thrimheld drawn and ready.

Aurora willed her heart to cease its sudden hammering as the steady scrape of footsteps and the low rasp of voices echoed eerily up the stair.

"Drat! What a dreadful hole. Hold the lamp up high, lad. I've little wish to crack me bones on these wretched stairs. I cannot think how I let you two talk me into this. I'm far too old, I tell you, for such goings on. 'Tis bad enough to be traipsing about in the dark without it must be up an infinitude of drafty stairs as well."

Aurora caught her breath as a delightful giggle

bubbled forth from around the corner.

"But, Hakim, was it not at your insistence that you have come?"

"Oh, dear, perchance it was," admitted the unseen sufferer of decrepitude, and suddenly Aurora's heart leaped within her breast. "I've heard it said there's no fool like an old fool. Hurry up now, lad. The sooner we are done with this, the sooner I can take me old bones home where they belong."

And with that the peculiar threesome rounded the newel in a blaze of light.

"Vandrel!" cried Aurora in stunned amazement. "And Janine! Oh, gods, it *is* you. But—but who—?" she faltered, one arm raised against the blinding glare as she tried to make out the tall, lithe form of the man holding the lantern.

Then Frayne sheathed his sword and stepped out of the shadows.

"Elwindolf," he said in a quiet voice tinged with wonder. "You appear remarkably hale for one presumably dead."

Whereupon utter confusion reigned as everyone seemed intent on speaking at one and the same time, till all of a sudden Janine's shriek of utter horror sent them grabbing for their weapons.

"Good gods, Janine, what is it?" demanded Aurora when it was soon made evident that they had not been set upon by a band of cutthroats.

"I-I beg you to f-forgive me," the girl whispered, her head bowed in shamed embarrassment. "I-It was *al mush*, I think. I-It was trying to climb my dress."

"A mouse? Egad, not again!" exclaimed the enchantress in a mixture of mirth and vexation.

"Crane! You will manifest yourself at this very instant, or we shall leave you to the other mice and varmints. Come now, what do you choose to be? A man or a mouse?"

Crane, apparently caring little for the alternative, erupted suddenly into their midst, a slightly shame-faced but unmistakably human male.

"Janine," he groaned, "can you ever forgive me? I should have died defending you with my last ounce of strength instead of leaving you to make it alone in the forest. I *have* died, a thousand deaths, since Aurora told me you were lost."

He would have gone on, but suddenly Janine was in his arms, and he found he could not think at all succinctly.

"Oh, but you are the *maskharat*—the big fool," she cried, laughing and weeping at the same time. "Of what good would you be to me dead? No, I would have you alive and with me always. Now you will cease to be so stupid, or I will run away as I did before, and you will be of the most sorry."

Since there seemed no other way to stop the slave girl's nearly hysterical tirade, Crane settled the matter most satisfactorily. Awkwardly bending his head, he kissed her full on the lips.

The shape-changer wore a decided look of be-dazzlement when finally he lifted his face to gaze upon the shyly blushing girl, rather with the air of a man who has just been bludgeoned. Egads, he had never dreamed a kiss could be like that, he marveled, seeing the daughter of the desert Khan with new eyes. Indeed, perhaps he had been mistaken in thinking she was just a helpless kid of a girl, for despite the untutored innocence of her lips pressed against his, she had roused in him a riot of bewildering sensations he had never felt before. In truth he did not know whether he should bolt and run or clasp the delectable and mysterious creature desperately to his lonely heart. Good gods, was this what it was to be in love? he wondered, not at all sure the turmoil of conflicting emotions churning just then in his stomach was all that greatly to be desired. But before he could make up his mind to do one or the other, he was further distracted by the enchantress, who, laughing and weeping just a trifle, had come near to hug the precipitator of his latest state of total discombobulation.

"Thanks be to the One you are safe. I would never have forgiven myself had it been otherwise. But where *were* you when we were attacked at the grove? And how do you come to be with Vandrel and Elwindolf? Indeed," Aurora added, turning to regard the hunter with a great deal of joyous perplexity, "how is it that *you* are not dead, my dear friend?"

Thus it was that Aurora and those not already acquainted with the tale of Janine's escape from Baldrac were quickly apprised of the events following their separation at the Grove of Tamaracks nearly a month earlier.

"I could not believe what my eyes had seen," murmured Janine her head bowed to hide the terror she had felt in those dark days alone in the forest. But suddenly she lifted her eyes to Frayne's. "My heart was heavy with sorrow. Foolishly, I thought *alghuwal,* the demon of the woods, had taken your body, for I knew my kind protector could not have the heart of *shaghal,* the jackal." Ashamed that she had been so lacking in faith not to have penetrated her former master's charade, Janine glanced guiltily away. Thus she did not see the almost imperceptible softening of the knight's stern features or the sudden clenching of his hand into a hard fist.

"I was bereft and filled with fear. I knew only that I must find the *hakim,* the wise healer, about whom Sayyid Crane had spoken, that she could tell me what to do with this."

Removing the bundle she had worn strapped to her back, Janine smiled shyly at Aurora.

"I took it from the camp that the evil ones should not have it," she said, offering the pack to the mystified enchantress, "for it is meant only that the daughter of Al-Murabit should ever wear Al-mandil-baraka."

Aurora drew in a sharp breath. How mysterious were the ways of the gods! She had thought never again to see Janine or Elwindolf, and yet here they were, alive and well, and all because Vandrel had brought Elwindolf back from the Land of Death that he might come upon Janine in time to save her from the villainous Baldrac. And as if that were not marvelous enough, they had brought with them the Crimson Cloak of Power!

"I believed the god had left me," she said, her voice husky, "but I was wrong to doubt. For with such friends, one must be truly blessed. I am humbled by what you have risked for my sake, and by what you yet would risk. Indeed, you give too much."

"'Tis little enough for what thou hast given us, Brenna of the Golden Eyes," surprisingly observed

Elwindolf, the habitually taciturn hunter. "And naught but a pittance for what ye shall be asked to give ere all be said and done."

For a moment his words seemed to hang over the company like a voice of doom. Then Vandrel chuckled.

"Well, now that that's settled," she commented, the decided dryness of her tone belied by a twinkle lurking in the depths of blue, bespectacled eyes, "mayhap we can get on with the business at hand. My Lord Frayne, were you and my two pestiferous former charges fleeing this loathsome fortress or had you some other purpose in mind? One way or the other, I must confess I should be grateful to find myself anon in rather more congenial surroundings. If it can be arranged."

The knight of Tor, who had been an unobtrusive witness to the tender reconciliation of the enchantress with her band of faithful friends and comrades, met the old scholar's keen-eyed glance appraisingly. It seemed to Aurora, observing the byplay, that some silent communication passed between them. Then the knight inclined his head in courteous acquiescence.

"If you would be so good as to follow me, ma'am?" he drawled ironically, waving a graceful hand in the direction from which the scholar and her two companions had just emerged. "'Tis only a step or two to our chosen destination."

Taking the elderly woman's elbow, he led her past the impenetrable Elwindolf and round a single half-turn of the newel before coming to a halt. Deliberately he ran his hands over the curved outer wall. The gleam of a smile touched his lips as his fingers found the nearly indistinct outline of a small crown etched into the stone. At last he straightened and turned.

"I fear I must beg your indulgence," he drawled, maddeningly cool, and drew his sword. "Indeed, I should be best pleased if everyone would stand back."

Aurora's pulse surged to the sudden throb of Andruvien against her wrist. In swift alarm she beheld the heart of the crystal leap with a silvery fire. It was power quickening to the impulse of power, and she staggered with the first searing thrust of the crystal's flame, the slumbering will of Andruvien stirring and stretching within her. Invoking the potency of her name, the enchantress quelled the awakening strength of the crystal and bound it within a spell of silence. Whereupon a vision of darkness flooded her mind, an inky nimbus exuding from a hard core of concentrated, cunning malice. A terrible, silent scream welled up within her, burst outward like a lightless flame and for a fleeting instant pierced the darkness to reveal an image of a black, multifaceted crystal. And suddenly she knew its name. Hedron, the Black King, dead for seven centuries.

"Frayne—!" she rasped, struggling against the groping tentacles of the mind seeking to bind itself to hers. But already it was too late. As stone grated against stone, a yawning maw of darkness opened up before them, and within it, poised and deadly, her sword scintillating black crystal flame, stood a facsimile of Aurora, who was Andruvien, the raven-haired enchantress.

Chapter 4

Aurora felt detached from her body, suspended in a dark morass through which the others moved like phantoms in some horrid dream. She heard Janine's piercing scream, oddly muffled, like a distant wail resounding through a thick, black fog, and felt Crane's hands close hard about her arms and roughly shake her. Yet she could do nothing, neither speak nor move, as she stared, entranced, at the dark, mirror image of herself and saw it raise the crystal blade of power to strike down the knight of Tor.

In helpless terror she saw Frayne twist agilely to the side and the sword's black flame slash the empty air. Then, yelling at the others to stay back, the knight vaulted, somersaulting, beneath the leaping tongue of crystal fire to spring catlike to his feet within the chamber now suffused with a pale, amethystine light.

The false enchantress spun lightly, bringing the sword around in a sweeping, two-handed pass. Frayne ducked low to the floor, then threw himself to

97

one shoulder and rolled as Aurora's spurious counterpart swung the blade up and about her head to bring it crashing down in a deadly, straight-armed blow. A jagged gash rent the stone scant inches from the knight. Frayne shoved himself to his knees, clutched at eyes blinded by a shower of splintering blue sparks. A glittery smile touched the marble purity of the apparition's face. The sword came up. Crane uttered a hoarse shout, shimmered briefly, and vanished, even as Dolfang, Long-Knife, flashed in Elwindolf's hand, the hunter's arm drawing back to send the blade winging at the false enchantress.

"No!" Vandrel cried, grasping urgently at Elwindolf. "Kill it and you slay Aurora, too."

The hunter abruptly stilled. Frayne wrenched his head up to reveal the falcon eyes glazed and streaming tears, his lips twisted in bitter self-mockery. Inexorably the sword descended, while, deep inside, Aurora uttered a soundless, despairing scream.

Frayne appeared suddenly to blur behind a glimmering galaxy of minuscule stars sparking out of thin air. Then the crystal flame struck, and rebounded from the polished surface of a great shield, flashing into silvery solidity before the knight.

A cry of rage resounded in Aurora's brain, the fury of Hedron thwarted by the valiant Crane. Again and again her darksome counterpart blasted the shape-changer with the unleashed power of the black crystal, till at last the young mage's borrowed form began to blur and waver from stalwart shield to the indistinct image of a boy, his face and body twisted and strained with his fierce struggle to hold the shape. Vainly Aurora fought to break the binding between her and the thing of ancient evil before, exhausted, the shape-changer should come into himself again.

"Crane!" wailed Janine, writhing in bitter agony within the circle of Vandrel's restraining arms. "Merciful gods, someone help him!"

Ealan, who was Elwindolf, attacked with the terrible swift silence of the wolf. In mindless dread, Aurora saw him close with the thing of evil, saw the false image of herself break the hunter's hold and with a wave of the hand send him flying across the floor. Still, Elwindolf bounded to his feet and came about, his eyes glinting coldly as he crouched, ready to hurtle himself into the arms of death. A fierce shout welled up within her as she saw the fiend bring the crystal sword to bear on the reckless hunter. *Nay!* she cried, sending her rising swell of anger outward at the apparition.

The mock Aurora seemed to stagger, as if struck a physical blow. Then, as Elwindolf came in low, his fingers clutching at the imposter's sword hand, the blade of crystal power flew from the creature's grasp to shatter as it struck the floor. And suddenly Aurora was free.

Reeling, she beheld Elwindolf grappling with a black-robed fiend and knew at once her old enemy—Cranith, the Imposter, whom long ago she had driven from Endrith's Forest. And all along he had been the wraith of Hedron, the Black King of Kerr, she thought incredulously, then blanched as she beheld Elwindolf clawing at long, skeletal fingers clamped about his throat. The woodsman staggered and sank slowly to his knees, his eyes transfixed and staring into the grinning death mask beneath the concealing hood.

Aurora's voice rang out, the cold, commanding voice of the enchantress roused to icy wrath.

"Release him, Cranith. *At once!*"

Stiffening, the fiend uttered a low hiss. Then, flinging Elwindolf's limp form from him, he straightened and turned, his eyes, like black holes of venomous despite, on the enchantress.

"Fool, have you learned nothing?" he rasped. "We two were bound, your mind to mine. Do you think I do not know you dare not use the Sword of Power? *She* would sense it—Dred's ambitious little harlot. And that would spoil everything, would it not?"

The enchantress's smile was frosty.

"If I am a fool," she said evenly, "then no less are you. I have seen you as you really are, Cranith. I know your name. Shall I tell you what it is?"

Never before had she beheld such hatred as writhed then across his face. The imposter cursed, and flinging up a fleshless hand, seemed to snatch from the very air a rune-covered staff.

"My name shall avail you nothing, witch changeling, for it shall never pass your lips!" he gloated as he bore down upon the enchantress, the black robe billowing out behind him.

Aurora's hand went to the elfin dagger at her belt. Warily she backed, her eyes never once leaving the distorted features of the wraith. She had no fear of the fiend, whom she had faced before. Yet this time she sensed something different, some hidden danger in his menacing front to which she could not give a name. Then suddenly the blood ran cold within her veins as Vandrel's shouted warning made everything crystal clear.

"Beware, child," the scholar cried, "that's the Staff of Mum he holds!"

Egad, she thought, Dred's staff, which the Master Magician Rab had stolen from Somn long ages past, and which could strike dumb a wagging tongue or give speech where before there had been none. She knew instantly the fiend meant to do worse than take her life. He meant to strip her of her power, for of what use was a spell-singer who could not speak the words to command the mystic forces of the elements?

All at once her back came up hard against a wall. Crouching, she darted a single swift glance from side to side. Blast! she cursed softly to herself. How could she have been such a dolt as to let him drive her into a corner! The enchantress pressed against the cold stone at her back, her mouth dry, as the Black King of Kerr towered over her, the Staff of Mum held high in a hideous, fleshless hand.

"You might still call forth the sword and save yourself, Enchantress," he taunted, savoring his moment of vengeance against the slender girl who once had taught him the humiliation of fear. "But, no. You wouldn't. Not you, who, even knowng who he was, gave yourself willingly as slave to Dred's bastard. He will bring you all to ruin in the end, you know, and still you would die for him. What fools women are!"

In dread fascination Aurora watched the staff begin to lower with excruciating deliberation toward her. Then suddenly she threw her shoulders back and straightened. If her tongue were indeed to be stilled for all eternity, then by the gods her final utterance should be made to count for something.

"But I shall not be dead, Hedron, King of Kerr," she declared in a ringing voice. "Only silent!"

The wraith's curse hissed above her head, and the staff plunged like an executioner's axe. Even as she tensed reflexively, one arm coming up to ward off the blow, a lean, powerful hand shot out of nowhere to catch the Black King's wrist in a grip of steel.

"Frayne!" Aurora gasped as the knight forced Hedron inexorably back.

She saw the deathmask leap in fear and the wraith erupt into a frenzied rage. Grimly the knight held to the staff-filled hand, the muscles straining against the fabric of his shirt as he slowly twisted the imposter's arm. Aurora heard the sickening crunch of bones and the wraith's shriek of agony. Then, as the Staff of Mum fell harmlessly to the floor, the Black King vanished in a swirling cloud of smoke.

Aurora flew to the knight's side, her heart yet pounding with the terror she had felt for him.

"Frayne!" she breathed convulsively, her hands clinging to his lean strength, and suddenly she was pouring out all her torment in a tumultuous rush of words. "I-I sensed the thing beyond the door, felt it crawl into my mind and try to take from me the power of the crystal. I-I bound Andruvien with my name, its potency with mine so that even linked with me, he could not call it forth against you. B-But then he knew I was powerless to help you, lest in freeing one, I should free the other. Oh, gods, he is evil! I thought I must die ere Elwindolf released me from his vile bond."

The knight of Tor clasped Aurora to him, and closing his eyes, buried his face in her raven hair.

"Thanks be to the One, you are safe!" he murmured so softly she barely heard. Then just as suddenly he straightened and put her firmly from him.

"Aurora," he said, his eyes twin blades boring into her own, "the black crystal. We must destroy it!"

Aurora's cheeks paled to a pearly white.

"B-But how did you know—?" she gasped and frowned as she saw a smile flicker in the falcon eyes. His hands lifted to frame her face.

"But how not?" he queried softly, then laughed as he beheld the immediate darkening of her brow. Suddenly the golden eyes flashed dangerously.

"You saw it, too! How *dared* you take such liberties. You invaded the privacy of my thoughts. *You,* who so adamantly have forbidden me to link with yours! And yet how could you have done it without my knowing? I felt only the imposter's loathsome presence, never yours."

"There's no time to explain. The wraith has withdrawn to the crystal to renew his strength. It is imperative to strike now, before he returns." The knight gripped her firmly by the arms. "You must summon the crystal, enchantress, and destroy it."

Aurora drew a sharp breath, her eyes wide and searching on the hard planes of his face.

"I?" she queried incredulously, then wondered if his encounter with the Black King had jarred his brain as she saw that he had meant every word. "But I cannot," she whispered, stunned at the enormity of what he proposed. To destroy a Crystal of Power, even one that had been corrupted, was to tamper with the precarious balance of things. For nothing was ever really destroyed, not in the true sense, but only transmuted into something else. The essence of the crystal was cold fire, the mystic flames of Effluvium, bound and frozen in a solid state. A crystal-master learned to command the heart of frozen flame and to wield its bridled power to his own purposes, but to break the bond and thus destroy the crystal was to unleash the awesome energy of the concentrated heart of pure fire.

"Nay," she said, "I know not how."

"You command Andruvien," he reminded her. "You found the crystal rose in which resided the essence of Rab's power, and it was you who released Myrialoc from the frozen bonds of the Crystal Kingdom. Aurora, don't you understand? You are Rab's heir. When you severed the crystal rose from its stem, his powers passed to you. *You* are the crystal-master now. To you it is given to command the heart of flame, to summon it whither you will, even to create living crystal at a whim—or destroy it."

"Nay," she said, shaking her head, "you are wrong, for I know nothing of such things."

"Look into your heart, Aurora. *Think!* You saw Cranith for what he was, the essence of the Black Crystal of Kerr. And when at last you lost yourself in anger, you banished his sword of power with a single word."

Suddenly the stern features softened, a strange light igniting in the silvery depths of his eyes as he beheld her terrible uncertainty, the innocence that was both her strength and her greatest vulnerability. He knew she would not let herself believe, because she did not desire the greatness that destiny had thrust upon her. She stood before him, a child and yet a woman, too, with an enchantress's awesome power scintillating all about her.

"Elwindolf did not free you from Hedron's mind-link," he said with unexpected gentleness. "You freed yourself. Trust in me, Aurora. Or if you cannot, then at least trust in yourself."

"You ask a lot of her, knight of Tor," observed the shape-changer coldly as he came near, Janine clinging to his side.

Aurora uttered a small gasp and turned to embrace Crane with stricken eyes.

"Oh, gods, I had forgot . . . !" she blurted, and then, seeing the shape-changer battered and weary but apparently unharmed, she sent her glance winging in search of Elwindolf.

A raw lump came to her throat as she beheld the hunter climbing slowly to his feet, aided by Vandrel. The old scholar's wry "tsk, tsk" carried clearly to the others.

"It's a hard road you've picked to travel, my lad," she scolded, fixing the taciturn woodsman with a knowing eye. "Belike you'll not be happy till you've killed yourself. Land o' the livin', Ealan, you blasted rogue. You're not some raw cub anymore that doesn't know any better. Have a little mercy on yourself!"

Elwindolf's rare, fleeting smile gleamed whitely in the tanned face.

"I have stalked death many times, Hertha Vandrel," he said, grunting a little as he bent to retrieve Dolfang from the floor, "and have lived to hunt again. An old wolf does not easily change his ways."

"Harumph! You're a man in your prime who should know enough to take a wife and settle down someplace ere life has passed you by," snorted the old woman, and she walked abruptly off, leaving the lean hunter staring quizzically after her.

"And you," she added, shaking her finger at the knight of Tor, who was observing her approach with a faint, sardonic twitch of the lips, "you needn't grin at me. You're worse than he is. Aurora and Crane might be excused for stumbling heedlessly into the serpent's lair, but you at least should have used your head. Would you have me believe you'd no notion something like this might happen when you sprang the secret door?"

"I knew," shrugged the knight, to Aurora's dumbfounded amazement. "I had not, however, planned for the eventuality of encountering you and the others before the threshold of the kings' treasure. I should have preferred to spare you the distress of Hedron's inhospital reception, but regrettably I was and am pressed for time."

"Well, you don't mince words. Indeed, I take your meaning plain enough. And since you're in such an all-fired hurry, I must suppose Leilah is up to her old tricks again. I won't detain you needlessly. Just tell me what you could possibly want among these dusty old relics of Rab's. Goodness me," she exclaimed softly, lifting up a disreputable specimen of a wizard's raiment, the fabric so worn that the symbols wrought in silver and gold appeared hardly more than frayed memories of a former glory, "here's his old robe, and the wizard's cap he used to wear to satisfy the fanciful expectations of new students coming before the Master Magician of Sib for the first time. How in the name of the One did Leilah come by these, I wonder, let alone the Staff of Mum. But then, she always was a sly puss with light fingers and a propensity for collecting whatever caught her fancy."

Realizing that at least three pairs of eyes were regarding her with a great deal of astonished curiosity, the old scholar coughed and broke off her reminiscences, which she had uttered abstractedly; indeed, more in the nature of a soliloquy.

"Ahem. Well, be that as it may, you still have not told me what we're doing in the kings' treasure, which, I must say, smacks little of those greedy old buzzards. Of course, there was a treasure at one time, but it was mostly squandered by the last of that misbegotten line in the Great Wars. These," she said, seeming to embrace with a wave of the hand the jumble of harps, cauldrons, various and sundry staffs, carved representations of animals, both real and fanciful, gilded and ungilded horns, flutes, looking glasses and crystal balls, an occasional jewel-studded sword or rune-covered shield, a curious array of green bottles containing seeds and dried essences of indescribable things—indeed everything stacked, piled, or flung in indiscriminate abandonment about the chamber, "appear to be mostly odds and ends, magical oddities, as it were, which the Master Magician of Sib collected in his various travels, then misplaced or discarded long ago. Other than the Staff of Mum and a few other items, they are of little value except, perhaps, to a student of antiquity."

"'Twould seem that you are remarkably well acquainted with the intimate history of the Master Magician," observed Aurora, feeling more strongly than ever that there was a great deal about the old scholar that she would like to have explained.

"And how not, child," Vandrel countered easily, her eyes all a-twinkle. "I've spent my life dabbling in history."

"Is that all there is to it?" demanded the enchantress. "I must ask, for I find it most peculiar that you of all of us should recognize the Staff of Mum, which vanished along with Rab and Myrialoc when he fled Dred's armies. And how can you possibly know these are his cloak and hat unless you had seen him wear them? Ye gods, Vandrel, you speak of my mother's sister as if you had known her all her life. Can you truthfully say you never once met my grandfather, or Leilah and Almira, his daughters?"

For the first time since Aurora had known her, the old scholar appeared momentarily to suffer something less than her usual equanimity.

"Oh, well, perhaps a time or two," she admitted, making light of it with a brief shrug of one plump shoulder. "I was not always a recluse, you know." The blue eyes dimmed behind the spectacles with a faraway, whimsical look. "In my youth I resolved the conundrum of Hylmut's insubstantial substance within the context of formless form and charted a course through the fluctuating loci of Myrialoc to the gates of Figenigm."

"*You* were a student at the college of magicians?"

108

marveled Crane, awestricken, his jaw comically agape.

"Farfetched as it may seem, I did study for awhile at Sib," she affirmd, very dryly, then, chuckling, thwacked the youth affectionately on his scrawny chest. "Close your mouth, boy. It was all very long ago and nearly forgotten by everyone. And unless I miss my guess, the knight of Tor has more pressing business for us." The twinkle gave way to a thoughtful gravity as the discerning eyes came to rest on the enchantress's troubled young face.

"Rab was the greatest of the crystal-masters," she said after a moment, her smile a trifle misty. "I've seen him at work, crystal fire pouring from his hands like molten rock as he shaped it to his fancy. That is the real gift of the master—that, perceiving the inner virtue of the heart of fire, he shapes the crystal only to an outward manifestation that remains true to its inner symmetrical perfectness. Rab mastered the law of crystal binding, not for power, which corrupts and distorts, but out of love for its terrible beauty."

The elderly woman blinked and appeared mentally to shake herself. Then, sighing shortly, she looked the enchantress straight in the eye.

"You are the crystal-master now, Aurora, and no one can make up your mind for you. But Frayne is right about one thing. Hedron is a dangerous enemy, and you will have to do something about him sooner or later."

The enchantress made no immediate reply, but turned away to stare blindly into the amethystine shadows as she grappled with the answer to the riddle

Vandrel had given her.

The ever-evasive scholar had been definite about one thing only: it was up to Aurora to render Hedron harmless. The question was, how to go about it? Obviously the simplest and most direct method would be to destroy the crystal that preserved his essence and was the source of his strength. Yet the most obvious way was not always the best, she reasoned uneasily. And besides, in the months of her apprenticeship to Vandrel, she had never once known her to babble haphazardly on about anything. Indeed, she had ever held firmly to the first tenent of riddlery—that answers come only from the formulation of questions. Nay. The true solution to the conundrum of the Black King must lie within the context of Vandrel's reminiscences about Rab. The question was, what had the one to do with the other?

Certainly Rab, who had bound crystals only for love of their intrinsic beauty, would never have chosen to destroy what might still have been remolded to its original perfection. Yet in order to do that, he would have had to envision its fiery heart as it had been before Hedron corrupted it to his own image, something that the greatest of all crystal-masters might have been able to do, but that seemed rather less certain to Aurora, who did not know the first thing about the law of binding. And even if she could manage by some hook or crook to restore the crystal to a manifestation of its true form, she did not see how such an achievement would neutralize the Black King. If he commanded the crystal, what difference did it make what shape it had? Would he not still possess its name and thus retain control over it?

But then that was the answer! she thought suddenly, her pulse leaping with excitement. If she indeed possessed somewhere within her Rab's mastery of crystal binding, then she need not shape the crystal to its original symmetry at all. In fact that would be the last thing she should do. Nay, she would create for it a new heart, a new name, and a form to suit the virtue of that name. Then would it truly be closed to Hedron and Hedron to it.

Aye, she had resolved Vandrel's riddle, she thought wryly, but what if she called forth Hedron only to discover she had within her neither the knowledge nor Rab's gift of crystal-mastery? She would find herself in a pretty coil then; and yet it seemed she had little choice, except to try. And besides, it would be worth the risk if in the end she had finally rid the realm of Cranith's troublesome interference. Her decision made, Aurora tossed her raven head in a gesture of proud defiance and turned firmly to face the others.

"Very well, I will make the attempt, but may the One help us if I fail." The golden eyes flickered to Frayne's and held for a long moment, a question lurking in their depths. He did not have to speak to answer. She felt him with her, his strength melded to hers as it had been long ago beneath Dred's Black Mountain when together they had mastered Andruvien and forged the Blade of Power. Slowly she nodded. She need have no fear. Their love would be her armor in the coming battle; his faith was an

111

impregnable shield.

The Enchantress of the Glade called forth the Black King of Kerr with a whisper of his name.

"Hedron, King of Kerr, Master of the Black Crystal, by the power of your name, I summon you."

He came to her like the wind scuttering through dry grass in the thick of night, a king in black, billowing robes and upon his brow a finely wrought circlet of tarnished silver. He wore not the death mask—that had been Cranith's, and Aurora had named his true name and thus had bound him to his true aspect and form. His was the haughty countenance of a king who, even when embraced by death, would not die. Aurora felt his soulless eyes, like twin blades of ice, pierce her, and she shuddered.

"I am come, witch, even as you have commanded. And now *you* shall answer to *me!*"

His speech was a silent whisper through her mind, a slithering tentacle of thought that sought to entwine itself about her. She tried to draw back, her breath quickening to a shallow, rasping cadence as she fought against the paralyzing terror of his psyche seeking to enthrall her. Yet the harder she struggled the deeper she sank into the quagmire of her own deepest fears—darkness without light, lungs without air to breathe, limbs that could neither move nor feel, a mind without memories. She was alone, her name but a dying echo of unreality, her existence but a dream.

"Anduan, Elf-Foundling, Tree-Child of the dry-ads," sounded faintly in the terrible silence of despair, and with it, the muted chords of a distant memory like the murmur of a song reawakening within her. "See him as he is, Aurora. A dream of reality, a shade of truth. Seek the essence of the lightless flame, the heart within the heart of night's illusion. Unname the crystal and unbind the crystal flame."

It was Frayne's voice, his thoughts melded to hers, and suddenly she knew she had never truly been alone. Hedron was the fallacy, a name without essence, an essence without being beyond the reality of the black, corrputed Crystal of Kerr. As a beam of sunlight bursts through a sudden rift in clouds, so did the enchantress pierce the illusion of sightlessness to behold the king, his face contorted in rage.

The black Sword of Power leaped to his hand and spouted crystal flame. From somewhere she heard Crane shout her name, then the cold fire of Effluvium enveloped her. Like the great fist of Boreas, the god of wind, it flung her back. She landed hard, lights spinning crazily before her eyes. Gasping for breath, she struggled to her feet, dazed and a little bruised but miraculously unharmed, and once more the flame leaped out at her and once more dashed her to the floor.

Bewildered to find she was yet alive after having twice sustained the force of the crystal's fire, the enchantress dragged herself upright yet again to face Hedron's wrath. Flinging her raven hair from her face, she stared defiantly at the blustering king, and suddenly her pulse quickened as she read the uncertainty in his eyes. The realization came fleetingly to her that he was afraid. Then the crystal's fiery tongue was sizzling all about her, and without conscious thought she gave herself unto it, her thoughts melding freely with the scintillating flow.

For a time she knew nothing but the terrible awareness of raw power, the living essence of unstructured possibilities, a vision of awesome unbridled beauty. Without knowing from whence the knowledge came, she began to mold the molten flame into fantastical geometric shapes, binding one to the other in crystalline, perfect symmetry, till at last she summoned the cold heart of fire, taking from it the knowledge of its name and reshaping it to a concentrated brilliance of blue flame. Finally she gave it a new name, the crystallized essence of its new being, and thus sealed it by the virtue of its own power. Then, with the last of her fading strength, she willed it to a far place where none should ever find it, a place where one greater than she had created a crystal kingdom once long ago.

Vaguely Aurora wondered how long she had lain on the edge of consciousness, her name beating against the closed doors of awareness, before at last she summoned the will to open her eyes. A crowd of anxious faces hovered over her—Crane, Janine, Vandrel. And Elwindolf, the pale eyes oddly reserved as they rested on her.

"She's coming around," observed the scholar with an air of satisfaction, as if she had in her own brusque way been assuring them all along that that would be the case. "There's nothing wrong with the lass that a good meal and a few hours of rest wouldn't set to rights again."

Aurora licked dry lips and tried to sit up. Then with a groan she sank back again, her head spinning with the unwise suddenness of her move.

"Softly, Enchantress. You'll be yourself again directly," murmured a low, thrilling voice, and she relaxed with a sigh as she realized her head rested in the protective cradle of Frayne's shoulder.

"What happened?" she whispered hoarsely, sublimely content to remain where she was. "I-I think I must have been dreaming."

"Not likely, unless we were all dreaming the same thing," Crane muttered strangely and glanced nervously away from her sudden probing look.

Feeling the cold clamp of fear about her heart, she stared from one to the other of her friends. Janine, blushing, her eyes dropping self-consciously as she caught her bottom lip between small, white teeth. Crane, his freckled face carefully averted, the toe of one boot kicking at a bauble lying on the floor. And Elwindolf, impassive and withdrawn, watching her as if she were someone he had never known before. Vandrel alone seemed unchanged, her bluff, kindly face exuding its usual imperturbable warmth, as she clucked her tongue over Aurora and berated the knight of Tor for allowing the girl in the weeks since she had left the cottage in the hidden vale to waste away nearly to nothing.

The old woman's scolding was cut abruptly short as the enchantress inhaled sharply and reached out to grasp the scholar's wrist.

"I remember," she said, her eyes huge and staring. "Hedron, the crystal—everything." She twisted her

115

head around to look searchingly at Frayne. "He thought to bind me to him as he had done the crystal. To make me his slave. But you called me back and made me see again." A hand fluttered to her brow, which furrowed in a frown of perplexity. "The rest is less clear to me. I remember the cold fire and realizing at last that it could not harm me, and then . . ." her hand slowly lowered, her voice dropping to a bare whisper, "suddenly I was not afraid anymore. Something happened. I-I have not the words to tell it. Beauty so wondrous I wanted to weep for joy. Power so terrible I wished to flee from it. And then I understood what Rab had felt when he mastered the law of crystal binding—reverence for something that only the gods can comprehend, and humility."

She realized suddenly that she was weeping, great, silent tears that seemed to come from her very soul.

"I cannot understand what happened to me. I know only that I was filled with a terrible hunger to work wondrous things such as I had never even imagined before. If you cannot forgive me for having failed you, I am sorry," she said, her chin rising in unconscious defiance, "but I am not sorry that I did not destroy what was never meant for mortals. I shall find another way to vanquish the Black King, I swear it, even if I must die trying."

A stunned silence greeted her final utterance, and suddenly her heart felt like lead. How could she make them understand, when she did not understand it herself? In hurt and slowly mounting anger, she stared at their blank faces. Why in the name of the One did they not say something? she fumed, biting her tongue to keep from flaying the ones she had believed her friends.

Her face flamed as Frayne's ironic bark of laughter rumbled over her. Twisting free of his slackened hold, she sprang to her feet and turned to face him, her glorious eyes sparkling dangerously. How dared he laugh at her! Had she so easily earned his contempt? Then Crane was laughing, too, but ruefully.

"Aurora, you silly gudgeon," he uttered in incredulous amazement, "you didn't fail anyone. There's nothing left of Cranith, or whatever his name was. Not so much as a single puff of smoke." He fell silent, his adam's apple bobbing up and down as he swallowed hard.

"Gone? Hedron is gone indeed?" she breathed, looking from one to the other. "But I don't understand. You were all behaving so strangely toward me, as if you could not bear to look at me lest I might see my shame reflected in your eyes. I thought you blamed me for having betrayed your trust."

"Aurora, what nonsense is this?" exclaimed Vandrel, but the enchantress was staring at the young mage-lord.

"Crane?" she demanded.

The youth seemed to vibrate through his whole lanky frame at the uncertainty in her voice. His head came up with a wrench.

"Ye gods, Aurora, you were wonderful! I hope never again to see anything so unnerving as you, like some incredible, detached god, calmly at work molding miracles out of flame. Egads, I didn't know you anymore!" he blurted, miserable and ashamed because he knew that he had been afraid of her and,

117

worse, feared her still. Once before he had hurt her with his stupid tongue, and she had sent him from her and then vanished for endless months in the dead of winter. He had thought then never to see her again, but she had returned, more forgiving, more enchantingly beautiful in her sublime innocence, and more powerful than he had ever dreamed possible. Oh, gods, he prayed that she should not see what was in his heart.

"But I am no different from before," she said, turning away that none should see the hurt in her eyes. "Blast! It is only this horrid place. It is as dark and twisted as its mistress, and it twists us as well. Where is this cursed circlet we have come to fetch? I would be quit of the business of the sorceress *and* her misconceived magic potion once and for all!"

"But you are quit, Enchantress. You and the others," Frayne murmured softly. "The rest is up to me."

Aurora flinched as if stung by a whiplash. Warily the knight of Tor watched the slender hands clench into fists and then relax. Now that he had flung the gauntlet down she would be at her most dangerous, he knew with wry certainty, and he steeled himself for the coming battle more fraught with peril for himself than any he had fought before.

Even so, she took him by surprise.

"I see. Then you have found the amulet of Kerr," she said, turning slowly, and suddenly it seemed he knew her not at all.

Since first he had seen her emerge from the water-willows hugging the shores of Grendylmere, like some ethereally lovely sprite, half-naked and with elfin magic shimmering in her eyes, he had beheld her in many guises, but none to equal this. In vain did he search her eyes for the spark of anger that he knew so well how to arouse, or the imps of laughter that charmed and beguiled him when the black mood lay upon him. Or at least for some sign of the childish innocence that had captivated him from the first. But none of these, not even the breathtaking marvel of her woman's passion that could drive him mad with a single look did he find.

Then it came to him that he could read her not at all. Her thoughts, which had ever been open, playing freely across her lovely features, a kaleidoscope of unabashed innocence for all to see, were closed to him, and he suffered a sudden, swift pang of regret, as if something precious and rare had just been slain.

"Even as you see," he answered, holding forth the circlet of tarnished silver that had graced the Black King's brow.

Her lips parted in surprise, and she took an involuntary step toward him. Then she was mistress of herself once more.

"So Crane was right. You were only using me. And now that I have banished the wraith of Kerr and freed the circlet for you, you plan to leave me as you have countless times before," she said offhandedly, as if they were discussing the weather or some equally inconsequential matter, and Frayne marveled at this new tack. When had she learned to dissemble? he wondered fleetingly, this surprising child-woman who had stolen his heart before he even knew it.

"Not this time, Enchantress," he drawled cynically. "This time you shall leave me, with Crane's help.

You will oblige me in this one last office, will you not, Mage-Lord?" he queried with arresting gravity, his silvery eyes peculiarly intent upon the youth.

Crane's head came up with a jerk. The knight of Tor had called him many things in the past, but nothing even remotely resembling "Mage-Lord." For a long time he was silent as he stared searchingly into the manly countenance. Then after a moment he swallowed hard. His glance flickered to Aurora and he nodded shortly.

"I'll take her wherever she chooses, so long as it's a long way from Tor," he said gruffly.

"Then do so at once," enjoined the knight, "and I shall count myself doubly in your debt."

"Aye, we must not keep Frayne from his appointment with his mistress," Aurora agreed coolly. Too coolly, thought the knight, the silvery eyes alert beneath drooping eyelids. Warily he watched her walk toward him, felt his loins stir as she leaned against him, her hands trailing with provocative deliberation up over his chest to encircle his neck. Tilting her head back, she gazed steadily up at him, her eyes weaving their golden spell.

"And so you would take back your heart again, Knight of Tor?" she queried softly, and it was all he could do to keep from crushing her to him as her sweet scent teased and tantalized his senses.

"Even so, Enchantress," he lied, his lips curling in bitter self-derision. "But then, it was never worth the having."

"And is your slave worth nothing to you, my lord? Have I so little pleased you?"

120

The knight whose bold deeds had become the stuff of legend stared with a growing sense of helplessness into the sweet face turned so innocently up to his. Drawing a husky breath, he reached up to unclasp her hands from about his neck.

"You are many things, my love," he said, putting her from him, "but never a slave. And least of all a slave to me."

"You are wrong, Knight of Tor," she murmured, a strange smile hovering about her lips. "And, worse, you are a liar."

The knight's eyebrows snapped together in a startled frown, but before he could make heads or tail of her cryptic utterance, she had changed yet again.

"May I see this amulet that I have been made to purchase for you?" she queried coolly. "That which you value more highly than myself? Surely I have a right."

"Indeed, none better," he managed without hesitation, though he little trusted this stranger who wore the aspect of his beloved. What was she about, this intriguing innocent who grew more bewilderingly complex by the minute—more the woman? Lazily he gave over the circlet into her extended hand and watched her turn it in her fingers as she read aloud the charm inscribed upon its inner surface:

> "An end to a beginning—
> 'Tis a doorless portal opened.
> A hole within a whole—
> 'Tis the all of nothing.
> A beginning without end—

121

'Tis the pathway of the soul.
To close the same,
Name the name.''

"What does it mean?" she said, glancing curiously up at him.

"That need not concern you, since you are even now leaving," drawled the knight infuriatingly, and retrieving the amulet, slipped it beneath his shirt. "Indeed, 'tis time I bid you godspeed. There are matters requiring my attention that cannot wait, I fear."

For an instant golden flame leaped in the enchantress's eyes, but immediately she had herself in hand again. Turning to signal the others with a peremptory wave of the hand, she walked away from the knight of Tor, her raven head held high.

"Very well. Take me where you will, Shape-Changer," she said imperiously, "and dally not. I mislike this dungeon and would walk beneath green trees again."

Crane, looking more than a little bewildered at her ready acquiescence, darted an uneasy glance at the tall knight, who stood unmoving, his falcon eyes watchful on the raven-haired enchantress as she waited impatiently to be borne away from Skorl and the man to whom she had sworn her undying love. Sensing something amiss but unable to puzzle it out, he shrugged fatalistically. Doubtless she thought to cajole him into sending her back again once she had him to herself. But for once she would not have her way with him, he vowed darkly. Pigs could sprout wings and fly before he fell for any more of her hen-witted schemes, which were always certain to land one or both of them in a bumblebroth. Then the others, except for Elwindolf, were crowding round, and he was trying to gather his thoughts to get right the spell that would bear them far from the sorceress and Tor.

Frayne, sensing that someone had drawn near, started from his somber thoughts to find the still-faced hunter standing before him.

"You would send Brenna of the Golden Eyes from danger," said Elwindolf in a quiet voice. "Yet danger shall ever follow such a one."

"Perhaps," replied the knight noncommittally. "There are troubled times before us all. Yet it seems certain that she will do better among her friends than at my side, where even prophecy foredooms her."

Slowly Elwindolf nodded, but whether in agreement with the knight or in confirmation of his own private thoughts, Frayne could not tell. Patiently he waited for the taciturn hunter to reveal what was really troubling him. Yet when at last Elwindolf spoke, it was of matters far more perplexing than the knight could ever have imagined.

"Once I wandered at the borders of the land of death, and Hertha Vandrel called me back again," he said, the pale eyes remote. "Since that time I have trod a solitary path. Yet I was not always alone. One night as I lay sleeping, I awakened to a stranger at my camp—one who be *aljis*, other. We talked long into the night, and just ere the breaking of day I was instructed to give you this message if ever our paths should cross again:

"'Tell the one who calls himself Frayne, knight of Tor, that Sehwan of Blidseafeld would meet with

123

him at the Grove of Tamaracks ere the final waning of the moon. Tell him I mean him no harm. Tell him it is of the greatest urgency that we meet.'"

"What matter of hoax is this?" queried the knight sharply, his eyes like daggers.

"If a hoax, it be not of my making. Walk carefully, my lord. This be no mortal who would speak with thee."

The hunter said no more, but left Frayne staring grim-faced after him. No, darkly mused the knight, 'twas no mortal, for Blidseafeld was once the Blessed Land of Throm, and its prince, Dred, the Lord of Somn!

Thus, with Frayne preoccupied with Elwindolf's startling news and Crane distracted by the fear that he would bungle the spell and land them all in Vandrel's chimney or some other equally inconvenient place, perhaps it was no wonder that only the keen-eyed scholar noticed Aurora slip Andruvien from her wrist and lay it inconspicuously on an ancient, dust-covered coffer. Smiling wisely, Vandrel held her tongue. Hadn't the lass come into her own? Indeed, she was more than a match for the hard-headed knight and anything or anyone else, short of Dred himself, that might come along.

No, she needn't worry overmuch about Almira's daughter. And as for Leilah, she'd done her best for the girl, till the wench hoodwinked the young desert chieftain—what was his name? Xavier or Xerxes or something or other—into carrying her off. Well, Leilah had always been a hot-blooded little hussy, and it was hardly strange that she had hated living out in the middle of nowhere with miles of desert between her and the things she had always yearned for. But as much as it still hurt to admit it, the chit was rotten to the core. Now Leilah was about to pay in full for all her black-hearted deeds, and that was the way it should be. Vandrel had washed her hands of the wicked sorceress of Tor ages past.

For a long moment Frayne stared into the empty space that Aurora and her four companions had occupied before the shape-changer conveyed them from the sorceress's fortress on the wings of a thought. It was done. He had sent the enchantress from her greatest peril—himself. Yet he experienced little joy in his accomplishment, which had cost him dearly, for he had paid the price of his heart's bliss.

Briefly the knight's head bowed before the lingering vision of the incomparable Aurora, her chin up and eyes aglitter with stubborn pride, refusing even at the very last to bid her love godspeed. The image would haunt him to the end of his days, he thought, his destiny weighing more heavily upon his shoulders than at any time before.

Then suddenly the fair head lifted. The muscle leaped along the strong line of his jaw. A cold gleam came to the falcon eyes, as resolutely he dispelled all thoughts of his lost love. There was one last task for the knight of Tor, which would demand every ounce of his iron will. And when it was done, the binding oath he had sworn as a knight before the Menhir would be fulfilled, the knight of Tor naught but a memory. For it would not be Frayne who rode away from Skorl, but the mortal prince of Throm, Sulwyn

Idris, the Thromholan!

Turning on his heel, he strode firmly from the kings' treasure, never once glancing back. Thus he did not witness the shimmer of lights like a small galaxy of minuscule stars leap suddenly into the air behind him. Nor did he see three familiar forms coalesce from the glitter and, after a brief, low-voiced exchange of words, gather a small object from atop a dusty chest and swiftly follow after him.

Chapter 5

Aurora, materializing once more within the chamber of the kings' treasure along with Elwindolf and Crane, breathed a sigh of relief upon discovering they were alone. To have found Frayne awaiting their arrival would not have suited her plans at all, for she little relished having to go through the whole thing again, perhaps only to lose the battle either with the hard-headed shape-changer or the flint-willed knight. As for Elwindolf, he was a rule unto himself and would ever do as he saw fit. The hunter had come at his own insistence to insure for himself that no ill befell either of the two impulsive young mages.

"Where is it, then?" demanded Crane irritably as he cast a look of repugnance about the cluttered environs of the wraith's former haunt.

"Well, it must be here somewhere. I am sure we shall discover it if we only look," Aurora replied with an air of profound innocence. Dutifully she began to rummage through the sorceress's collection of magician's bric-a-brac while the disgruntled shape-changer stood with arms folded uncompromisingly across his chest, his brown eyes narrowed in suspicion as he watched the enchantress go through the motions.

"Y'know, not that I mean to criticize or anything," he said meaningfully, "but it seems to me you have a deuced hard time hanging on to the blasted crystal. Did you ever consider that maybe the bracelet wasn't such a good idea after all?"

The enchantress paid the youth's acerbic observation little mind. Suddenly she snatched up a shiny gold object from the trunk upon which she had so conveniently placed it before Crane had transmitted them through the plasmic flux to Vandrel's cottage, surprisingly relocated, elderberry forest and all, within a cozy glen not far from the Grove of Tamaracks in which stood the Shrine of the Holy Maiden.

"Here it is!" she cried with relief that was only partially feigned. After all, she had been taking something of a risk leaving the crystal even for the ten minutes or so required to persuade Crane to bring her back again to retrieve it. She shuddered to think what might have happened if Leilah had somehow got her hands on it in the interim. But the gamble had paid off, for though Crane had been surprisingly recalcitrant, the missing Andruvien had proven, even as she had known it would, the one sure means of overcoming his mulish opposition. Thus she had contrived with a single, small deception to have her friends removed from Skorl and herself returned without a great deal of time wasted in useless argument. Or at least she would have done so had it not been for Elwindolf. He was a stumbling block she had not counted on, she mused with a wrinkled brow, and doubtless it would be nigh unto impossible to hoodwink him into going back without her. Still, the important thing was that *she* was exactly where she had determined to be, for she had never had any intention of allowing Frayne to do anything so odiously noble as sacrifice their love out of some absurd notion of duty. For that was what he had done. She was sure of it.

He had thought to send her from him to keep her safe, little considering that while his motives might be selfless, his decision had been arbitrary and arrogant. Indeed, she had been both hurt and furious with him that *still* he could be so undiscerning. And suddenly it had come to her that it was of little use to argue with someone so thick-skulled. Nor would she ever again beg to stay with him. She had *earned* her place at his side by right of countless shared perils and by virtue, as well, of the destiny that bound them irrevocably, one to the other. And if he could not see that, then henceforth she would determine her own course, the knight's pigheadedness be damned.

Besides, she vowed with a toss of her raven head, no one, not even Frayne, was going to keep her from being present when Leilah met her just recompense. For she was Aurora, the enchantress, on a quest to find her true name, and who better to tell her what she needed to know than her mother's sister?

Thus it was that Aurora, displaying a maturity of wisdom and insight far beyond that of the child Frayne still thought her to be, slipped the bracelet bearing Andruvien on her wrist, then turned to confront her two companions with hands planted firmly on hips and her raven head held high in unconscious, proud defiance.

"I am grateful to you both for your forbearance. It *was* careless of me to misplace the crystal," she said, acknowledging Crane's quite audible snort with only the tiniest flicker of an eyelid. "But now I bid you farewell and godspeed with the hope that one day we shall meet again under more auspicious circumstances."

She had expected the shape-changer to oppose her, but she had not at all anticipated the nature of his argument when at last it came.

"You can talk till you're blue in the face if you want to, Aurora," he began with the air of one laying all his cards on the table. "I know I'm only Krim's bumbling grandson. But I'm still coming with you. I have in the past managed now and then, after all, to be of some small use to you and that sorry excuse for a son of a Thromgilad."

The enchantress, feeling the prickle of tears behind her eyes, swallowed and looked hastily away. She had thought to hear him demand she return to Vandrel's cottage in the hidden glen, but instead he had determined to come with her. How could she have been so misled! For Crane could not have expressed more clearly his stubborn loyalty to her and Frayne. The youth's heart had ever been true, his generosity without bounds. Indeed, he shamed her, for she had failed in her trust, believing him Frayne's enemy and therefore hers. Silently she berated herself for a fool. She should have realized when he'd thrust himself before the wrath of Hedron's crystal sword to save the knight that he had done so out of love for Frayne, a love that might suffer times of doubt but that deep down survived intact. For it was Frayne who had believed in Crane, and Frayne who time and again in the past had with sensitivity and insight sought to countervail the boy's debilitating lack of self-esteem, the legacy left him by the powerful Mage-Lord Tarn, the father who had despised him, and by Krim, who had felt nothing but contempt for his only grandson.

So be it. She would put no obstacles in his way. He, too, had earned the right to see the quest to its end.

"Very well, if that's the way you want it, I certainly do not intend to waste time trying to change your mind," she said as forbiddingly as she could manage, when actually she was experiencing an overwhelming compulsion to fling her arms about his scrawny neck and hug him dearly, an act that she well knew would only have caused him a great deal of embarrassment. Suddenly she grinned, a devil dancing in her eye. "Besides, I would not miss for the world the look on Frayne's face when he realizes that not only has he failed to rid himself of my troublesome presence, but that he's stuck with you, as well. I only hope that *you* do not come to regret it. He can be fiendishly sharp-tongued when he's vexed. You must simply promise not to go off in one of your huffs and become some troublesome, deplorable thing. You have never been at your best, you know, either as a red-spotted toad in a mass of warts or as an extremely insignificant and disgustingly squirmy worm."

"Blast it, Aurora. You've a fiendish tongue yourself when you're of a certain mind," complained the shape-changer, blushing at the memory of the havoc he had created in Vandrel's kitchen the time he had turned into a toad because Aurora had provoked him. Then all at once they were both laughing in remembered mirth, for it had been funny when in all the confusion of trying to capture the obstreperous toad, the unfinished potion for the prevention of warts had spilled, causing the floor to sprout a proliferating host of the things it had been meant to avert.

"I should have missed you had you chosen not to come," Aurora said after awhile, sobering to a fond smile before at last she turned her gaze speculatively upon the taciturn hunter.

"And you, my friend?" she queried softly. "Can I at least persuade you to be sensible?" But Elwindolf, like Crane, would not be swayed from accompanying the enchantress into danger.

"Once I was the foster-son of Phelan, Father-Wolf. Till the madness came," he said, his eyes like still ponds reflecting a pale sky. "He who was Drude, called Elwindolf, Wolf-Friend of the elves, journeyed to the place of the Earth Mother in search of help to rid the forest of the sickness, but Hertha Vandrel would not come, saying the two young mage-lords could do as well as she. Though he who was Elwindolf did not believe, Brenna of the Golden Eyes and Crane of the many forms did come with him. You righted the wrongness, and it was Elwindolf who failed in strength and courage of the heart. In madness and grief he sought the Blood-Cleansing of the Bredan, seeking to slay him who had brought the evil into the forest, though Ommat was naught but a

132

little man afflicted with the madness. In choosing the way of the wolf, I dishonored that in me which is man. For to kill one of his own breed, one who is sick and weak, out of blood-lust, is to be a beast and not a man. You saved me from that final shame, Brenna of the Golden Eyes. And to you I owe the debt of Elwindolf's name."

"And yet you would call yourself Ealan, the Loner," murmured Aurora, wondering at the mystery surrounding this strange man of the forest.

"Aye, for Drude, who was Elwindolf, fled into the land of death, but Hertha Vandrel called him back again. Still, he who awakened from the sleep of death was neither Drude, who had died less than a man, nor Elwindolf, who was cast off from the Bredan and who was *aljis*, other. For Elwindolf slew Phelan, Father-Wolf, who twice gave him back his life, and only through the Rite of Blood can Elwindolf be cleansed of that which the Bredan call *faege*—one who walks with death. So long as Phelan's death be unatoned, even so long shall the wronged spirit of Phelan walk with his foster-son. Ealan may call no man or beast brother till all debts be paid.

"I would come with you, Brenna of the Golden Eyes, till Drude's debt is no more."

The enchantress gazed for a long moment into the hunter's stern face, her heart filled with pity. If only she had had the words to tell him that whatever debts there might have been between them lay all on her side. For in slaying Phelan, Elwindolf had spared her life. Yet had she repaid him by taking his. Still, she saw no way to right the injustice. Despite everything that he had said, Elwindolf was yet the man-cub,

133

reared in the strict ways of the Law of Bredan, and Drude as well, a man who believed in honor. Wisely she forbore from pursuing the matter further.

"So be it," she said instead. "You, too, shall share the moment for which I have waited. Leilah knows why my mother was slain in the Hawthorn Glade. I know it in my heart. She can tell me about my father and why I have been singled out for such a strange destiny—to be raised by elves and dryads in Endrith's Forest, then finally to discover within myself strange and terrifying powers. The end of the quest to find my true name lies here, with the sorceress of Tor, if only she can be made to reveal it."

"Well, there's only one way to find out for sure, and it isn't standing around here talking about it," observed Crane fatalistically. Somehow she had made it sound much too easy, and if there was one thing he had learned since he'd first set out on this fantastical adventure with the enchantress, it was that things were seldom so simple as they seemed.

It was Aurora who led the way from the secret chamber to the threshold of the dark, winding stairway. There she halted and signaled briefly for her two companions to stay back.

"I must know where Frayne has gone," she said, and assuming a distant look, began to sniff the air the way the wolves had taught her long ago, when she was a child in Endrith's Forest.

Crane watched curiously, for though he had never actually seen Aurora go through her own unique process of scenting a quarry, he yet knew that the enchantress was forming a mind-link of sorts with the knight of Tor, a link that was undetectable to the one she wished to track. She had told him all about it when she and Frayne, upon the quest for the unicorn horn, had been taken prisoner in Krim's Keep, the magician's castle of illusions. She had been joined that time to the dying unicorn, till she had lost the spoor at the foot of Krim's mountain because Crane, in order to save the magical creature from the Asgeroth, the monstrous half-boar, half-jackal that wandered the castle halls, had caused the unicorn to be transported a day's journey ahead in both time and space.

That had been the beginning of their sometimes turbulent but always steadfast friendship, which had led eventually to Aurora's apprenticeship to Vandrel and any number of harrowing adventures together. He had loved her and always would as something exquisite and totally unattainable, and she would ever think of him as the brother she had never had. In time he had learned to accept that, though it had caused him much suffering. Yet destiny had been kind, for it had given him another to fill the empty place in his heart—Janine, who was like a rare and lovely desert flower only just beginning to blossom forth before his very eyes.

The enchantress's hand clutching his arm startled the youth from his reverie.

"He is making his way to the sorceress's own tower wherein resides the Seeing Eye," she said, her eyes still glimmering with her inner vision. "Come. We must hurry if we are to reach him before it is too late."

Guided in the darkness by the lingering memory of Frayne's footsteps, Aurora bounded heedlessly up the twisting stairway, Elwindolf swift and silent at her heels. It was not until they came once more to the Hall of Kings and the passage sealed by the marble throne that she missed the shape-changer's gangling presence.

"Crane!" she called impatiently over her shoulder. "Where in blazes are you?"

Instantly she was assailed by a sudden, high-pitched screech and the rush of wings about her head. Aurora uttered a startled oath and ducked.

"Blast, Crane, you know how I feel about bats!" She shuddered, swatting furiously at the air, and at last the shape-changer, belatedly recalling her aversion to anything remotely resembling the Valkar, the man-bats who had sought to drink her blood as she lay asleep beside the steaming baths of the Vardos, relented.

"Criminy, Aurora," he muttered plaintively as he materialized beside her in his own familiar shape, "you might have knocked me silly slinging your arms around like that."

"Indeed I shall do worse than that if ever again you assault me in the form of a bat," she promised feelingly before turning at last to search for the hidden spring to move the throne from the opening. But Elwindolf, who knew from past experience to ignore the never-ending bickering between the obstreperous young mages, was before her. With a rumble the throne rolled ponderously aside, revealing the dim light of the great hall above.

Caring as little for the brooding Hall of Kings as they had for the dungeon below, the three stole swiftly past the marble pillars to the door leading to the turret stairway. A brilliant flash of lightning leaped and crackled about the tower as they entered the winding stair, the light coruscating eerily through the crossed slits hewn through the stone.

"Oh, gods, the time approaches," Aurora groaned, her eyes distant and fey. "The sorceress speaks the words of incantation even now. Frayne is within the chamber, unseen. The potion is nearly complete. We shall never be there in time!"

"Maybe not this way," declared the shape-changer, eyeing the forbidding turret with distaste. "But if you can form a clear enough mental picture of the sorceress's cursed chamber, we can be there in a heartbeat."

"Aye, we could," she breathed and glanced with a suddenly arrested look at Crane's shadowed face. Crane could take them anyplace either he or she had been before, for he needed only to have an image of it in his mind, and she could supply him with what only she had seen in the same way she conveyed her thoughts to animals when she communicated with them. Indeed, she had only to visualize the interior of the sorceress's private quarters—the curtained recess beyond the Chamber of Visions, for example, which contained Leilah's couch and other intimate possessions. She had certainly seen it before, the night Frayne had dragged her in front of the sorceress and ordered her to kneel before her betters.

Unconsciously she bit her lip till it nearly bled as she felt again the bitter humiliation and anguish she had been made to suffer. And yet, though Aurora had not realized it at the time, Frayne's callous behavior toward her had been necesary to save her from being confined within the Flux of Timelessness or worse,

137

for Leilah was as vindictive and merciless as she was beautiful, and it would not have done for the sorceress to have even an inkling of Frayne's true feelings for the young enchantress.

Sternly suppressing the remembered pain of that night, Aurora sought to recall the sumptuous inner chamber. The image of the sorceress reclining amidst plush cushions on a bed covered with a luxurious rug of white fur came all too vividly to her mind. Leilah, with her coal-black hair streaked at the temples with wings of silver and her eyes like black diamonds, hard and gleaming. With her full, luscious body, shimmering palely through translucent ebony silk, she had exuded seductiveness. Rather like the white-petaled sundew, whose delicate white flower drew unsuspecting insects to be trapped and devoured, mused Aurora with a wry smile. She had had an impression of silk hangings draped from the ceiling and walls that had seemed to breathe as the restless draughts played among their folds, of plush cushions, velvet and inviting, strewn seductively about the room, and of the scent of musk, heavy in the air. There had been, as well, a magnificent screen set across one corner of the room. Black- and gilt-lacquered, with eight folds, it apparently served to shield the sorceress from the draughts when she dressed or bathed. Or to hide her from the interested eyes of nocturnal visitors as she readied herself to lure them into her bed, bitterly reflected Aurora, recalling the way Leilah had clung to the knight, her arms draped about his neck and her voice husky as they discussed in what matter they should dispose of their captive.

138

"Aye," said the enchantress, her eyes golden and dangerous. "I can picture the spider's lair clearly enough to carve it in stone, if you like."

Wisely Crane refrained from commenting on the absurdity of such a notion. Indeed, after a single look at Aurora, he sent a silent prayer of gratitude to the One that he did not stand in Leilah's shoes. As a matter of fact, he doubted that anyplace within the radius of several miles would be safe when the enchantress at last came face to face with the sorceress, never mind the trivial consequences if Frayne should fail to seal the portal in time. In the wake of cataclysm, after all, he reflected gloomily, what were a few score or more of Dred's multifarious creatures of darkness loosed upon the Realm?

It was decided in the end that Elwindolf would proceed on foot up the turret stair while Crane and Aurora took the less laborious route, by way of the plasmic flux directly to the corner secluded behind the sorceress's ornate eight-fold screen.

"It be the wisdom of the wolves on the hunt to cut off the avenues of escape," Elwindolf had conceded thoughtfully after Aurora explained her strategy, and though he was reluctant to allow his young charges to venture off without him, still he had gone.

And besides, the enchantress mused ruefully as she watched the tall, broad-shouldered figure of the hunter disappear beyond the newel, asking Crane to land just the two of them in the less than roomy confines of the corner without attracting any attention was chancy enough. To have included Elwindolf as well would have been to invite disaster. The equally disturbing possibilities that either the screen had been moved or that they might materialize within the wall of solid stone were simply too dire to contemplate. Resolutely attempting instead to block all else from her mind, Aurora concentrated on relaying to Crane an exact mental image of the desired area of the sorceress's boudoir as it had looked the one and only time it had been her dubious privilege to see it. Then, for the blink of an eye, she was plunged into darkness, only to emerge again, all asprawl upon a mound of velvet cushions, Crane tumbling in a heap beside her.

Crane, bless his heart, had not missed the mark by far. Though not precisely in the corner, they did find themselves within the sorceress's bedchamber. Unable to suppress the warm rush of blood to her cheeks at sight of the shape-changer's sardonic grin, the enchantress shrugged dismissively. Could she help it if the image of the seductress's bed had obtruded on her thoughts at the very last instant? Really, the horrid thing seemed permanently etched into her brain!

After leaving the treasure of the kings, Frayne made his way up the endless stair leading to the summit of the loftiest of the seven towers of Skorl. He climbed steadily, oblivious of the rats scuttering from beneath his feet or the wind groaning about the outer turret. His mistress had ever been of an arbitrary disposition, predisposed, when he was not on one of her interminable missions, to summon him to her quarters at a moment's notice. He had, consequently, long since ceased to regard the peculiarities of the fortress, and this time in particular it was enough to know that after today he need never set eyes on Skorl or its irksome mistress again. The plaguy woman had tried his patience far too long, and he was not reluctant to see the charade come at last to an end.

Perhaps it was odd then that upon coming at last to the carved oaken door at the top of the stair he should suddenly draw back, his expression singularly bitter as he contemplated his next move. He must enter the chamber undetected and remain thus till such time as the sorceress completed the potion, a task he knew was easily within his power, and yet still he hesitated. Uttering a low curse, he wheeled sharply, slamming the side of his clenched fist hard against the stone newel.

"A curse on Dred and all his ilk," he muttered, his forehead coming to rest against his hand on the wall. How the god must laugh each time his only son and heir was forced to acknowledge his detested kinship with the Thromgilad. And how galling to the knight of Tor, for as prince of Throm and Dred's mortal son, Frayne was possessed of any number of rare and remarkable gifts, all of which he heartily deplored and none of which he willingly employed, except in the direst circumstances, such as this was.

And yet what perfect irony, he reflected, his lip curling cynically as he pushed away from the newel and turned once more to regard the door beyond which his importunate destiny awaited him. He would use that talent peculiar to his father's race, and thus to himself as well, to weave a shroud of shadows in which to conceal himself from all eyes save those which ever saw him truly as he was, but he would use

141

it to save the woman whom Dred had ruthlessly violated. Perhaps there was a measure of justice in the world after all, he told himself, but he only half believed it.

Thus the knight of Tor, clothing himself in darkness, lifted the latch and eased open the door to the turret chamber. A shadow within a shadow, he slipped unseen into the presence of the sorceress weaving her spell of magic over the great oval cauldron wrought from adamant—the Seeing Eye, more ancient than the first immortals, though Dred had claimed it as his own till Leilah stole it from its guardian, Sheelar, one of the Seventy-seven Serpent-Lords of Somn, and spirited it, unbeknownst to the prince of Throm, to Skorl.

Within the sorceress's Chamber of Visions the tapestry wall-hangings moved restlessly with the unseen drifts of wind prowling about the cold stone walls. Misshapen shadows cast by the flickering tongues of candlelight writhed like participants in a macabre dance about the room as the sorceress, her eyes black, burning coals, stared feverishly into the roiling surface of the Seeing Eye and chanted the words of an incantation long buried in antiquity. The knight smiled mirthlessly. Leilah had begun to work the spell that would mean her own destruction.

Closing the door so softly that the sorceress never heard the click of the latch above the fulminations of the storm gathering about the pinnacle of Tor, the knight steeled himself to enter the rift at the very instant of its inception. Despite the chill dampness, he could feel the sweat trickle down his sides beneath his tunic. Nothing must go wrong, for he risked

142

everything—not just the Valdoran's freedom but the precarious balance maintained by the Vendrenin between Dred's world and the Realm, as well. The smallest delay going in would mean failure, for he dared not allow the portal to remain open for longer than a minute or two. Indeed, timing was of the essence, for though time within the Flux itself was meaningless, once through the portal he had in reality only seconds in which to find and bring Ariana out and then reseal the rift before the creatures of an ancient malevolence should win release, as well.

Unconsciously his hand rose to make sure the circlet was yet snug beneath his shirt, and inescapably his thoughts went to Aurora. In a sense she had been right to accuse him of using her, for he had known from the beginning that only a crystal-master could free the amulet from the crystal-bound wraith of Kerr. Aware, as well, that she was never in any real danger from the searing flames of Effluvium, he had suffered only minor qualms in maneuvering her into a confrontation with the Wraith of Kerr. It was imperative that he possess the amulet, for the circlet itself would be the sole landmark to guide him out of the dimensionless planes of the Flux within the same time frame from which he had entered.

Nor had he been mistaken to believe Rab's heir equal to the task, he reflected. A silvery light ignited in his falcon eyes at the memory of the raven-haired enchantress enveloped in blue flame, crystal fire leaping from her fingertips as she forged the heart anew. No, he had not been wrong to trust in her, and neither had he had any other choice but to force her to

143

claim the heritage of her ancestry, she who was the granddaughter of the Master Magician of Sib and the daughter of one even greater than Rab, if she only knew it.

An oddly whimsical smile touched the knight's stern lips at the success of his small deceit. If the enchantress ever once guessed that he had purposely led her to believe his life was in dire peril solely in the hopes that she would discover within herself the power of crystal-mastery needed to save him, she would be furious indeed. The keen-witted Vandrel must have realized it almost immediately, he thought, recalling how the scholar had upbraided him for his apparent carelessness in allowing her two former apprentices to walk into what could only have been a trap. Crane, however, had nearly spoiled everything with his daring, yet foolhardy, intervention.

The knight's lips thinned to a grim line at thought of what the lad had risked. And Elwindolf, too, the steely-nerved rogue. Frayne had never once taken into account the possibility that *they* would put their lives on the line to save his, and it had very nearly been an extemely costly miscalculation, one that both baffled and humbled him. For while he could well understand Aurora's reasons for doing what she had done, theirs were less readily explained. Indeed, they, and in particular the shape-changer, had little cause to hold him either in affection or esteem.

Silently he cursed himself for a fool. He was not some green boy. He was the knight of Tor, the veteran of a hundred battles. He should have known men of their mold would not stand idly by while another, even Dred's unworthy bastard, was struck helplessly down. Damn! He had been too long immersed in the dark intrigues of soulless gods and grasping mortals could he no longer recognize men of true heart and noble vintage! Still, they had fought for him, he reflected cynically, and, ironically, the results had been the same as if they had not interfered. The enchantress, in her fear for them, had unwittingly called forth the power to save them. No doubt, whatever god guided his steps had not chosen yet to desert him.

Besides, he told himself as he watched the sorceress perform her rites of incantation like some unwitting fool, in the long run none of these things mattered— Crane's inexplicable motives in risking his life for a man who had betrayed him, Elwindolf and Vandrel's unquestioning acceptance of Dred's mortal bastard, not even Aurora's unshakable love or his own wretched heart. Each walked his own foreordained path even as the gods had recorded in the Tome of Prophecy long ages past. It remained only for each to see the unraveling of his own individual tale, which in itself was naught but a single thread in the greater tapestry of the history of the ages.

Egad, but he was weary of it all, weary of the solitariness of his own existence, weary of himself. And yet even as he formulated the thought, he knew it was only half the truth, for if he were to be honest with himself, it was the prospect of existence without Aurora that filled him with such a bitter sense of desolation.

Abruptly the knight snapped to attention, his look grim as he realized how far afield his thoughts had drifted; indeed, how greatly Aurora's sweet spell had softened the battle-hardened warrior legendary for his cool nerve and reckless daring. Sternly he drove all else from his mind but the sorceress and the task at hand, until at last he was himself again, the knight of Tor, cold and as inflexible in his resolve as tempered steel.

Sensing, perhaps, the knight's gimlet eyes watching her, the sorceress appeared suddenly to falter. Her glance flickered uneasily to the shadows beyond the glaucous haze exuding from the seething cauldron and lingered for a moment. Briefly a frown darkened her brow. Were her eyes playing tricks on her or was the darkness deeper there, near the door, like a shadow lurking within a shadow? Unconsciously she hugged herself, her hands crossed at the wrists chafing the chill from her thinly clad upper arms. Then she shrugged. She was being foolish. Only the Lords of Throm knew the secret of shadow wizardry.

Molding darkness like clay, a Thromgilad could shape creatures of shadow to work mischief in the night or to do the bidding of the Master Throm. Such were the shadow-phantoms of Somn, the Eidola, who carried false dreams of greed, power, or ambition to slumbering mortals. Nor was that all. A Thromgilad could gather darkness about him like a cloak and walk unseen among men and even elves and Eilderood. Indeed, had not Dred concealed himself from Harmon, the Warrior-God, in such a manner, till the Valdoran Virgin, playing the role of sacrificial lamb, lured the Dark Prince to her in the Tamarack Grove that Harmon might find him?

Bah! The virtuous Ariana sickened her. Why should *she* have been the one to bear Dred's only offspring? It should have been herself, Leilah, Dred's willing concubine. The gods knew, he had never to force her to get what he wanted. But she, Leilah, had made the Valdoran pay in full for having robbed her of the right to be the consort of an Immortal, just as she had made her own sister, Almira, pay before her. Almira's punishment had been death, but Ariana she had imprisoned in the Flux of Timelessness, never again to set eyes on her fine, princely son. It had been revenge worthy of Dred's concubine, for she had not been satisfied merely with humbling the high and mighty Ariana. No, she had added a touch of spice to the pie, for it had suited her to make Dred's proud offspring her slave, degrading him as Dred had degraded her when at last he had cast her off as though she were nothing.

Yes, nothing! But she would show the arrogant prince of Throm. She would show them all, she exulted, her eyes black and feverish in her bloodless face. In moments she would have everything she had ever dreamed of having—power greater than any god's, the fear and adulation of lesser beings, and revenge. Revenge against Rab, her father, who had denied her the Crimson Cloak of Power that was her birthright; against Chandra, her mother, who had ever preferred the golden-eyed Almira; and against Dred, the god who had used and then humiliated her. But, greatest of all, she should have revenge at long last against the one she loathed most in all the world. He who had fathered a child on her hated younger sister. He whom she, Leilah, had loved; indeed, her one and only love. *He* had rejected her!

No! By the One, he had never seen her once he set

eyes on her accursed sister. But he would see her now, she vowed with all the bitter hatred of her twisted heart. She would brand his soul with the image of Leilah, lord of a godly power, master of Vendrenin!

Turning with a whirl of her silken robe, the sorceress gazed into the heart of the Seeing Eye, her arms outspread before her.

"Eye of the Dark Void, Motivating Spirit of the Plasmic Somn, hear me, hearken to my words. For I, Leilah, Sorceress of the Black Robe, Guardian of the All-Seeing Eye, have brought you all that you have commanded:

"A forgotten dream of a child forgot," she said, holding forth a locket in which, Frayne knew all too well, were the miniatures of the parents of a young orphaned girl trapped in Shandel, the City of Forgotten Children, on the Isle of Kylandros. That had been the object of his first quest for the sorceress, but there had been many others after it. Indeed, each successive object that the sorceress fed into the seething cauldron represented another of those endless, harrowing voyages.

"A schemeless scheme of a world besought," Leilah chanted, dropping in an unchartered map of the Unknown Lands. "Something dearly bought but never sold"—the scroll containing the words of wisdom recorded by Eldred, the Sage, who had suffered torture and imprisonment rather than compromise his ideals of honor, truth, and the dignity of all men, joined the other things. "A newly minted coin of old" had taken Frayne back to the floating Isles of Kylandros, which drifted forward and backward in time through the Flux of Timelessness, in order to find a coin of an ancient civilization long vanished from the earth. "The scale of a dragon not of dragon spawned" had come from Rab's glass dragon, Kev, whom Aurora had rendered a real, live dragon when she freed Myrialoc from the Crystal Kingdom on their quest for the perfect crystal rose.

Briefly the knight smiled, remembering his previous attempts to decipher the riddle of a dragon not of dragon-spawn, which, till the surprising discovery of the peculiar hyaline creature in Rab's hidden kingdom beneath the Palace of the Rising Sun, had been his single failure. "Day's reflection in a moonlit pond" had posed similar problems, till he had looked one evening into a still pond silvery with the light of the newly rising moon and beheld upon its surface the reflection of a day lily only just beginning to close.

The knight's aspect hardened as the sorceress came to the seventh of the riddles: "The unkept promise of an oath not spoken," for in her hands the sorceress held the never-used swaddling clothes of a stillborn infant, the unwanted bastard of a wealthy merchant of Tor. Nor did Frayne's expression ease with the eighth ingredient, "the token of a circle broken," for it was the horn of the dying unicorn that had never completed the circle of rebirth promised to those of its kind. Its trek to the Unicorns' Burial Ground had ended with the giants beneath the Black Mountain in the Confounded Lands. And yet, it had been the beginning of Aurora's quest, for there she had mastered Andruvien and forged the Sword of Light.

"Shadow of a soul in darkness bound," quoted the sorceress then, and the knight of Tor grew rigid as he

149

beheld the small cameo worked in onyx, which he himself had wrought.

"Rot her black heart!" he muttered beneath his breath, his eyes glinting silvery sparks. It was his father's likeness, which he had rendered in all innocence from a description given him by his mother. But he had not known then that he was Dred's bastard or that the Immortal had raped his gentle mother to beget him. He had been a child wondering about the father he had never known, a father whom he had believed honorably slain in the battles of the Second Uprising. He had neither seen nor thought of the cameo for so long that, presuming it to be lost, he had nearly forgotten its existence. Doubtless when he had come home to the Mountains of Thunder after the ill-fated pilgrimage to the Menhir of Tor to find Haven-House burned to the ground and Ariana vanished from the Valley of Mists, it, too, had been spirited away, he thought with a resurgence of all the old anger and grief he had felt that desolate day so long ago.

It was only with an iron will that Frayne subdued his wrath. Soon, he reminded himself, the sorceress would be made to pay the price of all her transgressions. Cool again, and all the more dangerous for it, the knight of Tor steeled himself to wait the few remaining moments.

"A thing not lost and yet not found," recited the sorceress in growing excitement and held forth an unadorned ring of purest gold.

A cold gleam of a smile curved the knight's lips as he watched Leilah feed into the still-frothing cauldron the Cirlce of Aon, emblem of the All of creation and of the Nothing from which all creation emanates, the symbol of the One. She was not lacking in gall, he mused cynically, this sorceress who dreamed of wielding a godly power.

Then he saw in her hand a crystal of shimmering fire and knew Leilah had come at last to the culmination of all the endless years of scheming. It was the tear Ariana had wept in the Tamarack Grove; the second tear, which, having fallen unheeded to the ground, had remained untouched through all the years. Untouched, that is, till Crane had unknowingly stuck it in his pocket, and then later, discovering it, given it to Aurora. Frayne himself had taken it from the enchantress and presented it to his mistress, saying it was Andruvien, the sliver of the Vendrenin needed for her potion.

Yet he had known the moment he retrieved it from the pouch around Aurora's neck and beheld it for the first time, a perfect crystal of scintillating iridescence, that it was not Andruvien. Indeed, the blood had leaped in his veins as he realized he held at long last the key to unlock his mother's prison. For it was Sorh, the Virgin's Tear, the crystallized essence of Ariana's sorrow for the loss of that which she had ever held sacred and which she yet would willingly sacrifice out of love for the One. Frayne's fingers tightened on the Circlet of Kerr as Leilah uttered the final words of the charm that would open the way for Ariana's release.

> "Elements of Fire and Flame,
>   By the power of your name,
>   Shatter stone. Unloose the wind.

The laws of twixt and 'tween rescind.
Let pass the heart whose crystal essence
Here commands its living presence."

The tower shook with the crash of thunder as the sorceress flung the crystal into the cauldron's spumous center. Whereupon the knight of Tor, seeming almost to leap from the shadows, strode inexorably toward her.

"You!" Leilah uttered like a curse and thrust herself furiously in his path, her back to the blistering eye of plasmic Somn. "Do not try to interfere. I warn you, the potion is complete. Nothing can stop it now."

"Even so, Sorceress," Frayne drawled ironically. "Now be pleased to get you hence. Your part is done."

Leilah's lips parted on a gasp of outrage. "How dare you speak to me like that!" she exclaimed furiously. He would pay dearly for such insolence on the morrow. Indeed, it was time she was rid of him entirely. In moments the potion would have done its work and she would have no further need of Dred's scurrilous offspring, or of anyone. She would have Vendrenin, and even the gods would fear her then. The sorceress drew up in proud disdain to order her impudent slave from her presence. Then something in the hard glitter of his eyes penetrated even Leilah's overweening vanity.

"What do you mean? What are you doing here?" she demanded, her tone, though imperious as ever, yet edged with a hint of uncertainty. No fool, she well knew the knight of Tor was never to be taken lightly. Indeed, she had ever savored her power over the fearless warrior, knowing that so long as she had his precious mother in her control, he dared not raise his hand against her. Nor had she lightly wielded the reins of her total command, but had flaunted his impotence, humbled his manly pride, humiliated and used him at her whim, and, detecting behind his careful mask the powerful will of the Thromholan kept rigidly in check, had gloried in it. And always he had remained her dutiful slave, submissive because he had no choice. Thus, having grown used to commanding his total obedience, she had come inevitably to expect it, so much so that she had long since ceased to regard the danger inherent in the half-god, half-mortal Frayne. Still, there was something different about him, something she could not name.

His smile chilled her soul.

"Haven't you guessed?" he queried easily, his single, imperiously arched eyebrow mocking. "I've come for Ariana."

For an instant the sorceress stared blankly at the knight. Then suddenly she laughed, a short gasp of incredulity.

"You must be mad. I've no intention of releasing the cursed Valdoran, now or ever."

Frayne, already sensing the shock waves shuddering through the fabric of existence, had little time for useless talk.

"But you *have* released her," he said, brushing the sorceress contemptuously aside. As if she were nothing, came Leilah's stunned realization, and hard upon it, the certainty that somehow he had tricked her. The Vendrenin and all she had dreamed and

153

worked to achieve was to be denied her, she knew it as surely as she knew to whom she owed the blame for the dissolution of her heart's ambition. Frayne, her slave, the treacherous knight of Tor! Abruptly something snapped inside. In sudden, mindless rage she threw herself against him, her nails like cat's claws raking at his face.

"What have you done?" she cried harshly, struggling with the fury of a crazed animal as his fingers clamped like a vice about her wrists, dragged her hands down and pinned them together in a grip of steel, till at last the pain subdued her frenzy and cleared her mind so that she went deathly still with appalling comprehension. "The crystal. *Damn* you! It was hers, wasn't it. *Wasn't* it!"

She read the answer in his eyes, those damnable orbs of tempered steel, dark-rimmed and soulless as his immortal sire's. Her mouth twisting in an ugly grimace of loathing dreadful to behold, she spat full in his face.

"Bastard of Throm!" she hissed. "I hope you rot in Somn with your accursed sire."

Flinching, Frayne went deathly pale. For the space of two heartbeats he stood unmoving, his eyes shut, before at last, raising the back of his free hand, he contemptuously wiped the spittle from his face. Then deliberately he looked at Leilah, his eyes unveiled, and suddenly the sorceress shrank before his terrible, icy stare. For it was the Thromholan she beheld, undisguised—the mortal prince of a race of gods—and his wrath was fully roused.

Never had Leilah known such paralyzing fear. For what seemed an eternity he held her transfixed and powerless, till finally the sorceress, mouthing voice-less words of entreaty, sank inexorably to her knees before him, her wrists, still imprisoned in his pitiless grip, all that kept her upright. She read her death in his falcon's eyes and knew she could do naught to save herself. Nor could she bear it longer. Why did he not slay her and be done with it?

Then she saw the beaded sweat upon his brow and the muscle leap along the lean jaw, and suddenly laughter, hideous and exulting, bubbled up within her. Gods! How well he had played the part of the impregnable, world-weary cynic. She had been a fool not to have seen it for what it was. A mask to hide his single vulnerability, his one and only flaw. The dread Thromholan fought a battle within himself. For was he not Ariana's son, the knight of Tor pledged to the One? What torment must he suffer to be the acknowledged issue of Dred's despite as well! Openly she dared to mock him, taunting him with the truth of his own despised heritage, a legacy of rapine, degeneracy, corruption, and evil.

"What is it, my lord Thromholan? Surely con-science does not stay your hand. You, the exalted prince of Dred's noble race, possessed of the power to slay with but a thought."

The sorceress gasped as the fingers like steel bands tightened ruthlessly about her wrists. Still, she forced herself to go on, goading him to a realization of his own ambivalence.

"Perhaps you seek a punishment more worthy of your illustrious sire. But of course. Death would be too quick, too painless for one who has dared to enslave and coerce the mightly Thromholan with the

155

threat of his dearest mother's own mortality. Why, you might return kind with kind: weave shadow phantoms in my mind, ghastly specters of wretchedness and despair—skin lesions and suppurating sores, broken bones, tortured limbs, visions of mutilation, disfigurement, and tormented madness. The possibilities are endless."

Deliberately she arched, her head rolling back, baring to him the throbbing vulnerability of her throat, her breasts bulging above the low-cut neck of her gown, the skin translucent, white and flawless.

"What are you waiting for?" she breathed, tantalizing him with a vision of her total helplessness. "It is only what Dred's son would do, after all. What *he* would do if he were in your place. Surely you are no less than Dred."

"Enough!"

His voice, unnaturally quiet, lashed her into quivering silence. Indeed, she quailed before his awesome, white-lipped fury. Merciful gods, she had gone too far, and now she would pay for her recklessness.

"If you are wise, Sorceress, you will hold your tongue," he said, dangerously calm. "Doubt not that you have never been closer to death than you are at this instant."

Then, unbelievably, he had released her.

Stepping deliberately past her crumpled form, the knight of Tor left the sorceress staring after him in stricken fear and loathing.

*   *   *

Dismissing Leilah from his mind, Frayne gazed at last upon the turbid surface of the Seeing Eye and knew a fierce sense of triumph. For even as he looked, the glaucous stuff of Somn began to whirl and eddy, creating a swirling vortex at its center. It was the rift forming. He could feel the membrane weakening, the web of cause and effect that separated the continuum of the finite from dimensionless time and space. It would be soon now, he thought, oblivious to the storm outside the tower, blustering, angry, and belching jagged bolts of lightning. His whole being was concentrated on entering the portal at the very instant of its creation.

Thus he was not aware either of the sorceress rising furtively to her feet or of her eyes, black and cunning and filled with hate. Like a vengeful shadow, she stole toward the knight's unprotected back, a blade gleaming silvery in her upraised hand.

A fist of wind smashed through the shuttered windows, dousing the candles and ripping tapestries from the walls. Instantly the turret was plunged into darkness fulgurating with lightning flashes from the storm. Frayne staggered with the blast, then braced himself, and suddenly the portal opened up before him, a spiraling tunnel of luminescent cloud leading into darkness. Drawing the circlet from beneath his shirt, he stepped forward into the mist. Then he heard someone shout and half turned back again, his arm coming up in an instinctive gesture of defense.

"Frayne! Behind you!"

The Chamber of Visions seemed to leap at him as a dazzling flare of lightning skirred across the sky. He caught only a glimpse of the body hurtling at him and the silver flash of a blade before his assailant was upon him, the knife slashing his forearm to the bone. A savage curse was torn from him as he felt the circlet fly from his nerveless grasp. Then, borne backwards with the force of the attack, he plunged into the rift, his assailant carried with him.

Chapter 6

"Oh, gods, *Frayne!*"

Aurora's despairing cry carried above the wail of the wind whipping about her slight form as she darted from the curtained recess toward the rift through which the knight had vanished, Leilah clinging to him in mindless hate. Her face white with grief, she flung herself forward across the portal's threshold, only to have Crane catch her wrist and snatch her back again.

"Aurora, no!" he shouted, dragging the enchantress from the maw of swirling mist.

"Let me go. Curse you, let me go!" cried the enchantress, erupting into a frenzied struggle.

Blast! thought the harried youth as he wrapped Aurora in a bear-hug and hung grimly on. Where was Elwindolf when you needed him? Then, agile and strong despite her appearance of fragility, Aurora dealt him a punishing blow to the shin with her boot heel. Yelping, Crane jerked spasmodically upright, dragging the enchantress bodily off her feet.

It was a strategic error, for, rendered precariously off balance by the frenetic welter of feminine fury clasped in his arms, the sorely beset young mage found himself weaving and stumbling helplessly backwards, till at last, blundering into a pile of cushions heaped on the floor, he toppled full length, Aurora coming down hard on top of him.

For an instant he lay too stunned to move. Then he felt Aurora struggling to her feet and dragged in a painful breath.

"*Damn* it, Aurora," he gasped, "*listen* to me!" He watched her pause uncertainly, her back to him, and searched for the words to hold her.

"Don't you understand?" he croaked, trying to make himself heard above the tumult of wind and thunder. "Frayne's lost to us in there. If we went in now, we'd just find ourselves in a different plane of time from the one he entered. They're always changing. It's hopeless. We'd never find him, and we'd never find our way back to this time either."

"Then how will *he* return to *us?*" Aurora demanded, her shoulders heaving with each labored breath. She was sick and trembling, near to choking on the bile rising to her throat. Why had they not been here sooner? Even a few seconds might have been enough to stop Leilah.

Alarmed at the appalling pallor of her face revealed in the repeated flare of lightning bolts, Crane lumbered to his feet. Awkwardly he grasped her by the shoulders and shook her a little, bracingly.

"Hey, there's no use working yourself into a stew. Frayne has the circlet. It's kind of like a lodestone, always pointing toward the beginning. It'll show

160

him the way back, just you wait and see."

The enchantress groaned, seemed suddenly to sag then catch herself. Slowly she knelt, her hand reaching for something pale and shiny on the floor. Crane, hearing her strangled gasp, bent quickly over her and pulled her to her feet.

"Aurora, what is it?"

She did not answer, but simply handed him the circlet with a shaking hand and turned to stare into the swirling vortex of the portal.

"I would rather be in there with only the faintest hope that one day our separate planes might somehow overlap than to remain here where there is no hope at all," she said after a moment, her shoulders back and ominously rigid.

Crane's heart sank.

"Stop it!" he blurted, trying desperately to buy some time. "You're talking nonsense now. There's got to be some better way. We'll go to Vandrel, ask *her*. She'll know what to do, and . . ."

Aurora's head jerked partway round and froze. "Crane—"

Instantly he bit off what he had been about to say and in exasperation ran his fingers hard through his hair. Drat! She was on her high-horse now, he thought, all too familiar with that ominous quality of her voice. He might as well whistle in the wind as try to reason with her when she spoke like the blasted enchantress she was, sure of her own power and resolute on flying headlong into certain disaster.

"As soon as I am gone," she continued in that same, chillingly flat, unyielding tone, "you will use the circlet to seal the portal. Do you understand? Do not wait. Then, when it is done, you and Elwindolf return to Janine and Vandrel. Tell Vandrel everything. Mayhap she will be able to think of something. I simply cannot risk the alternative—that there is no other way into the Flux. You must try to understand that. And, Crane . . . *Crane*, are you listening to me?"

"Yeah, yeah," muttered the youth grudgingly, unable to look at her. "I'm listening, though the gods know why I should be."

"When you are with Janine again," she said with just a hint of a tremor, "promise me you will be happy. Don't let anything come between you, ever."

"Criminy, Aurora!" exploded the shape-changer, nettled and sore beset. "What kind of thing is that to say?"

"Promise me! Swear it on your name," she said, twisting round at last to look at him.

Crane gulped. Why must she be so beautiful? he thought, staring at the slender form scintillating power. Standing silhouetted against the portal's soft glow, she seemed some illusive, ethereal creature. Indeed, her long, glorious hair feathered by the wind flowing through the gaping windows shimmered with a silvery aura, and her delicately wrought features, illuminated in the fulminations of the storm, were touched with a loveliness that seemed not of this world. With her eyes, huge and dark in the pale oval of her face, her lips, faintly curved and wistful, and her small, pointed chin, stubborn and yet proud in spite of her grief, she bewitched and mesmerized him.

"Please, Crane," Aurora murmured more gently.

"It will be something to which to—to cling, the knowledge that at least somewhere two people I love and who love each other are together and happy."

Feeling helpless and dazed, Crane nodded jerkily.

"Yeah, sure, I promise," he grumbled, hating himself but not knowing what else to do. In all the time he'd known Aurora, he'd never found a way to stop her when she'd made up her mind to a thing. He didn't know anyone who could, except maybe for Frayne, who was just as stubborn as she was, and for Elwindolf, who had seemed at times to exert a strange sort of influence over the exasperatingly headstrong enchantress.

But then she had turned and squared her shoulders, and he cursed bitterly. Where was the benign influence of the One now? he blasphemed. Surely the Creator could spare a moment or two for *some* sort of divine intervention before Aurora, like Frayne, another of his apparently ill-fated but devoted servants, was plunged into irretrievable disaster! He wasn't asking much—just a small demonstration of the omnipotence with which the One was credited but which hitherto had seemed singularly lacking as they were thrust deeper and deeper into the sinister intrigues of the Immortals.

The enchantress took a step closer to the abyss from which not even Andruvien could save her, and suddenly the young mage-lord knew that no matter what he had promised her, he could not stand idly by and do nothing. Drat! He had to stop her, even if it meant knocking her senseless and sealing the rift before she came to and pulverized him for his interference. Flinging caution to the winds, the shape-changer launched his ungainly length straight for the enchantress, who without a backward glance was even then making ready to step into the swirling vortex.

Never in a million years could Crane, who tended by nature to a fatalistic world view, have imagined that the One should choose suddenly to answer his prayer not only with stunning dispatch but in a manner most certainly calculated to make a lasting impression. Yet such is the way of omnipotents to be ever incalculable, and, indeed, before ever Crane had reached Aurora, he saw her start violently, her hand clutching at her knife, and, staring fixedly before her, begin to back up slowly. With a distinct premonition of impending doom, the shape-changer ground to a precipitous halt.

"Good lord," he gasped, having glimpsed emerging from the luminescent swirl the daunting aspect of a towering knight clad all in black, a great sword glinting in one powerful hand—his left, for the right arm had been severed below the elbow.

"Who are you?" demanded the enchantress imperiously, taking a fighting stance, her weight balanced easily on the balls of her feet and the elfin blade, Glaiveling, held menacingly before her. Crane groaned and rolled his eyes ceilingward. Egads, this was not the time to go off half-cocked. Their visitor had not the look of one prepared to do the niceties; indeed, if anything, he appeared to have taken an immediate dislike to his unwitting welcoming committee.

"What trick of sorcery is this," bellowed the knight, "that I, Xerxes, am met by the warrior-woman whom I slew at the command of Hawra?"

Aurora vibrated down her entire length at the knight's startling revelation. Xerxes, who had slain Almira! The gods had delivered him to her. Still, though the blood seemed suddenly to leap within her veins, some instinct prompted her to a cool cunning before the man who had murdered her mother so long ago in Hawthorn Glade. She was the enchantress who had braved many perils in the quest for her identity. It would not do to act in haste. Not now, when she was upon the threshold of discovery. He had wielded the sword, but some other had set him to the task, and only the knight could tell her the name of the traitor. Indeed, there was much she would know ere she exacted the vengeance that was hers by right and then entered the vortex of the Flux for all eternity.

"'Tis no trick, Xerxes," she said, casually sheathing her knife, "but fate. I have traveled many leagues to meet Almira's slayer, for I would know my enemies. Tell me, who is this Hawra?"

His sudden booming laughter tested her nerves.

"Does the warrior-woman know not her own sister?" he rumbled with sardonic amusement. "Yet even so was Xerxes deceived in her." A chill crept into his voice. "In Hawra of the black eyes, who promised Amir-al-sharq, prince over all the tribes of the east, a potentate's power and a king's treasure."

"Leilah!" uttered the enchantress in accents of bitter loathing.

"So. You begin to see, eh?" he commented in hearty approval. "Leilah, who coveting both her sister's magic cloak and her lord, commanded her

165

sister's death. And the child's as well," he added, rather as an aside, shrugging. "And Xerxes, a proud prince of a proud people, become *al-hashash*, the assassin. It was a lordly jest worthy of the gods. My reward was imprisonment in the Land of Fesh-fesh, the shifting sands of time without time. Such are the promises of *kafir*, the infidel, and Amaur, the Prince of Darkness, who purchases fools for slaves. Still, if one is patient, all things in the end come about. For as you see, Xerxes is returned to his own world, and it is the lovely Leilah who rots in the Flux."

"You saw the sorceress in the rift?" demanded the enchantress, hard put to keep the excitement from her voice.

"Saw her? The bitch flew past me with the swiftness of the wind, but I saw her," he laughed.

"And was there no other with her? A knight, perhaps?"

Immediately she could have bitten her tongue, for she could feel Xerxes come to swift attention. Drat! She had been too hasty, too straightforward in her questioning, and thus had roused his curiosity and suspicion.

"Perhaps," he answered cagily, his fingers absently stroking his pointed beard. "And perhaps not." He shrugged massive shoulders. "A thousand pardons: my memory. Sometimes it is not so very good."

He was lying. They both knew it and that it would avail her nothing to accuse him of it. She must find some other way to retrieve her error, but how? It seemed so hopeless. But wait. Did he not say Leilah had won his dubious loyalty with the promise of wealth and power? she mused, her lips curving ever so slightly in a smile.

"Ah, well," she said coolly. "'Twas a matter of no great importance. I wished only to assure myself that she had not her lover—er—her champion to give her comfort where she has gone. Is it a dreadful place which shall be her prison? I would like to think she will suffer terrible torment for her infamies."

"She will suffer," he said in a hard voice. "As will this lover. Who is the fool?"

"Oh, but I must beg a thousand pardons," demurred the enchantress. "It seems that my memory is as faulty as yours."

"Oh, ho. You are possessed of a wit worthy of a Wendaren, my little golden-eyed gazelle," he chortled. "And what should it profit me to tell you what I did or did not see?"

"Perhaps nothing, or perhaps you have forgotten along with everything else that I am the heir of Almurabit," she suggested, her raven head coming up with a regal air. "I possess the secret of Seraisharaqa, the Palace of the Rising Sun. It is something which I might be willing to share for certain information."

"You would betray the House of Doane?" queried the knight incredulously. Yet clearly she had piqued his interest.

"Nay," Aurora denied without hesitation, "for Almurabit is no longer, and Leilah . . . well, she can hardly matter now. So you see, *I* am the House of Doane."

Plainly he did not trust her, and yet he must know that the golden-eyed Almira had ever been her father's favorite. To her he had given Al-mandil-baraka, the Crimson Cloak of Power, thus establishing her as his rightful successor to the Crystal Kingdom, which legend said lay beneath the palace. It would be strange indeed did she not possess as well the secrets of Doane, which alone could release the fabulous kingdom from the magic that protected it from intruders.

"Very well, I am willing to strike a bargain, if you can offer proof you have what you claim."

Wordlessly Aurora removed the light bundle strapped to her back.

"Is not Al-mandil-baraka-ur-murabit proof enough?" she demanded, flinging about her shoulders the Crimson Cloak of Power that had belonged to Almira, the warrior-woman.

"Aye," he said on a harshly expelled breath. "It is a telling argument in your favor."

She could feel him watching her with greedy eyes and had to grit her teeth to contain her loathing of him. Not yet, she told herself. Not till he told her what he knew about Frayne and the place in which the knight now found himself.

"When you come to the outer walls of the palace," she said, the more firmly to ensnare him, "you need only invoke the power of the fire god Gawr with the prayer of Shest. The gates will open to you. It is in the Throne Room of the God that you shall find the secret stairway to the Crystal Kingdom. When you have told me all that I would know of Leilah's place of imprisonment and of the knight who was with her, I will reveal to you the secret words to open the way to the undergroud stair."

"And if I tell you there was no one with the sorceress?"

"I shall not believe you," she answered coldly, "for I saw him enter the portal with Leilah."

"Then I say they were parted somewhere in the drift, the sorceress to enter the Flux in one plane and the knight in another, for indeed I saw no one with Leilah. You need not fear your sister will enjoy the company of her lover, for they will be forever separated by timeless time."

Xerxes spoke with the ring of truth in his words, and though he might only be a consummate liar, Aurora believed him. The tiny flicker of hope and the germ of a plan to force the Wendaren prince to lead her back through the rift to the place from which he had come thus died a sudden death. What now? she thought, nearly paralyzed by the emptiness of despair stealing over her. But then her mother's murderer was demanding she fulfill her part of the meaningless bargain, and suddenly she felt insanely like laughing.

"Fool, do you think you shall profit from this day's work?" she said contemptuously. "If ever you were to find your way to the Palace of Doane, you would discover the gates torn asunder and in the Throne Room of the God naught but a gaping hole leading into an empty tomb. The Kingdom of Crystal, like its creator, is no more. Both have entered a new plane of existence far beyond the limits of your brutish comprehension."

The time for pretense was past. With a thought she summoned to her hand the Blade of Power, Andruvien, scintillating crystal fire.

"Return from whence you came, Amir-al-sharq. You shall not pass by here, for 'tis meet that my mother's slayer should suffer the punishment of eternal damnation in the Timeless Flux. I, Aurora, Almira's daughter, so say it."

The darkness retreating before the brilliance of the crystal sword, the Black Knight stood revealed in the light. Beetle-browed and dark-eyed, with fleshy, bearded cheeks and a bold beak of a nose, he had rather the look of a great black bear, thought Aurora, vaguely surprised. Yet though he might appear bluff and hearty with his wide mouth and the laugh-wrinkles etched about his eyes, she was not fooled. Nay. There was more than a little of the wolf in his grin, which bared strong, white teeth, and a crafti-ness behind the gleam of laughter in his eyes. That he had the cunning of Xantu, the Fox, and the soullessness of Snog, the striking snake, she did not doubt for an instant.

"Oh, ho! Almira's child, is it," he bellowed, sweeping her from head to toe with an appraising glance. "So you were not carried off by wolves while my men and I slaughtered your mother and the Prince of Garn, her luckless cousin. Somehow I thought it was not so."

"Nay, the elves of the glade, who witnessed your crime, rescued me. Whereupon I was reared by dryads and am become a woman grown in the likeness of my mother, Almira, the Warrior-Woman. Now get you hence ere I teach you what more I am," she ended ringingly, the blood throbbing in her veins.

The One give her strength, she prayed, for this

prince of the desert tribes was bitter gall to her. He was the hyena who dared to boast of his foul deed, and gladly would she slay him as he had slain her mother. Still, she was Anduan and Aurora, custodian of an awesome power, and ever must she guard against the Andruvien's seductive will, which fed upon the lust to kill. She dared not use it for her own selfish purposes, lest it consume her as Krim had been consumed before her by the Vendrenin's icy flames.

Thus crouched and waiting, the sword in her hand pulsating blue flame, the enchantress wished the Black Knight gone from her lest she pay the price of her soul to avenge her mother. But suddenly he was laughing, the rumble of his mirth rolling over and through her, swelling her wrath, warping her will.

"You are arrogant like your mother," he jeered, "yet she, too, was only a woman with naught but two legs and a man's borrowed blade. Come, my cocky little hen. Test your mettle against Guthsweord—Almira's sword forged by a god!"

Rage, swift and terrible, swept over Aurora as she beheld the weapon, gem-studded and shimmering silvery in the light of Andruvien's fire. It was as she had envisioned it when she had forged its likeness from the plasmic stuff of Somn to fight the Asgeroth. Pulsing in her hand with a living essence of its own, it had seemed to will her to stand and fight, to demand that she be fearless, and she had known then it was a true vision and that the sword awaited her in reality. Guthsweord, The God's Sword. By the One, the sorceress's assassin defiled it with his unclean hand!

"Then you will die, Xerxes!" she cried piercingly and raised high the Blade of Power. "For indeed I am my mother's daughter and I would take what is rightfully mine—vengeance *and* Almira's dishonored sword!"

Andruvien flashed crystal fire as the enchantress struck a two-handed blow. Yet the knight parried, catching the full force of the flame with Guthsweord and turning it aside. Aurora faltered, momentarily stunned at the marvel of a blade that could withstand Andruvien's might, and instantly the knight took the advantage, rushing her before she had recovered her wits. She heard Crane's warning shout as from a distance, then instinctively she had vaulted in a low, somersaulting arc from beneath the knight's slashing blade. With the agility of Anduan, Tree-Child, she rolled lightly to her feet and pivoted, bringing Andruvien round to deliver the knight a backhanded swipe. Again the desert prince parried the thrust, but this time Aurora was ready for him. She felt the hand of the god upon her, searing her with his awful power, imbuing her with his strength. In truth she was the enchantress, the vassal of a mighty lord. Catching Guthsweord on Andruvien's hilt, she gave a sharp twist. The knight's eyes bulged as the sword flew from his grasp, and landing with a resonant clang, skittered across the stone floor.

Xerxes, Amir-al-sarq, paled before the cold fury of the enchantress, for she looked upon him with the eyes of *al-nar-baraka*, the flames of power, and suddenly he was afraid.

"*Sajada, Banat-ur-zarcun-nar:* I bow before the Daughter of the Golden Fire," he said, sinking to one

172

knee, "for thou art *al-marmann,* the god-favored."

Aurora, her blood yet feverish with the puissance of the god and with Andruvien's insatiate lust to slay, raised the Blade of Power above the knight's bowed head.

"And you are Ga-tairan-bridd, the vulture that follows the path of death and destruction," she retorted scathingly, "for you have chosen death as your livelihood. And thus have you brought on your own untimely end."

The crystal blade quivered with desire in her hand, the throbbing will of Andruvien pulsating to the hammering of Aurora's heart and growing stronger with every pulsebeat. And suddenly it no longer mattered that in using the thing of power to satisfy her own lust for vengeance she would forever lose herself. They were one, Aurora and Andruvien—of one mind and a single will to kill the sorceress's assassin. Thus in the grips of her obsession to slay her mother's murderer, she did not see the sudden gleam ignite in Xerxes' hooded eyes or his lips curve faintly in a cold, calculating smile as he gazed with unexpected eagerness beyond her toward the portal at her back. The enchantress's hands steadied on the hilt, and Andruvien, the sliver of Vendrenin forged for a god's weapon of vengeance against a god, began its fatal descent.

"Aurora, behind you. Look out!"

Crane, coming at the enchantress from nowhere, knocked her hard to one side. She fell heavily, the shape-changer flinging himself protectively over her so that she sensed rather than saw her intended victim scramble to his feet and lumber past them toward the

173

turret door, pausing only long enough to snatch up her mother's sword from the floor. She heard a hoarse shout and the sounds of a scuffle, then mass confusion reigned as some horrid, reeking thing shambled across the floor nearby hissing obscenities and the chamber was filled suddenly with the beat of wings, the clatter of hooves, the scrape of claws, and the clamor of horrifying howls, squalls, screeches, and bellowing roars.

Aurora, blinded by her hair and nearly suffocated with her cheek pressed hard against the floor, twisted frantically beneath the shape-changer. Good gods! The creatures from an ancient time, the manticores and basilisks, the dread tadiefot and spitheythirl, aingealwyrms, glumengogshuileachen, iaranny-corns, and hyppohornboras—the evil things of the dark Before—were issuing forth from the Timeless Flux even as Frayne had warned they would.

"Get off me!" she panted, managing with the strength of sheer desperation to get her head up. "The portal . . . !" But an equally frenzied Crane only shoved her down again.

"Don't look!" he shouted into her ear. "It's death to look upon the face of a cockatrice."

It was in her mind to tell him that they would soon be crushed to death from the sheer press of creatures rapidly filling the chamber when the blast of shattering stone followed immediately by the shuddering of the tower fortress gave ample evidence to the fact that the creatures had sought their own solution to the bulging superflux of monstrosities. Then Elwindolf, shouting above the uproar, was dragging the shape-changer from her at last.

174

Bounding to her feet, Aurora found herself staring into the triangular-shaped face and goggle-eyes of a glumengogshuileach, commonly known as the glumengog. The creature of gloom, she thought irrelevantly, looked rather like a gigantic praying mantis with its green, scaly body, four legs and two spine-covered arms ending in wicked, clawed pincers, one of which was even then reaching for her with every apparent intention of pinching off her head at the neck. Held transfixed by the protruding ruby eyes, she waited helplessly for her inglorious and most damned unpleasant end, when simultaneously a blade whizzing past her frozen countenance severed the creature's hideous appendage and a strong hand grasping her by the shoulder yanked her from between the enraged beast and a charging iarannycorn. Aurora saw the glumengog impaled upon the single ironlike horn of the monstrous winged lizard with the loins of a lion and the head of a great-horned owl, then Elwindolf was dragging her and the gaping shape-changer into the shadowed recess of the sorceress's bedchamber.

No sooner had the stalwart hunter released her than she had turned to Crane, her hands clutching at the front of his shirt as she tried to make herself understood above the pandemonium of raging beasts and the howling storm.

"Quick, the circlet!" she screamed. "We must seal the rift!"

For a moment she feared the youth had lost his wits, for he stared at her out of dazed, panic-stricken eyes, his adam's apple bobbing up and down as he swallowed and tried in vain to speak.

"Crane, give me the circlet!" she demanded again, nearly ripping his shirt as she tried to shake him into rationality.

"C-can't," he choked, his expression peculiarly abject as he gestured helplessly toward the scene of utter chaos. "I-I dropped it. Out there!"

"Merciful gods," breathed Aurora and wheeled to peer out at a slithering, two-headed aingealwyrm breathing fire out of both its serpent heads as it fled the hideous toad-footed, hirsute tadiefot, green slime oozing from its tusked caterpillar's mouth. The amber-scaled aingealwyrm, having reached the gaping hole in the turret wall, spread wide its eagle wings and vanished into the blustery night even as the tadiefot gave a final leap, missed the aingeal-wyrm's barbed tail, and plunged over the side.

Aurora, taking advantage of the momentarily unobstructed view, darted from cover. Resolutely she ignored Crane's high-pitched shout of alarm, which trailed after her, and the swirling maw still spewing forth a plethora of nightmarish monsters, as she made her way straight for the downed glumengog still writhing in its final death throes. Slipping and sliding in a spreading pool of yellow gore, she looked in vain for the missing amulet.

"By the One, it cannot have simply vanished," she fretted and straightened to send a searching glance further afield. 'Twas then that she saw the man, blood oozing from an ugly wound in his chest, drag himself to his feet, then, weaving drunkenly, stagger through the gaping door to vanish down the turret stair.

"Xerxes!" she breathed, her eyes glittering fiery

176

sparks. So he had not escaped unscathed as she had previously thought. Nay, for Elwindolf had been waiting beyond the closed door!

Then a bloodcurdling cry—the cry of the wolf—sent an icy chill coursing down her spine. Wheeling, she beheld Elwindolf standing boldly before the gaping portal. Guthsweord, her mother's sword forged by a god, flashed in his hand as the hunter fought valiantly to hold back the stream of creatures seeking still to cross over from the Timeless Flux into finite reality. And beside him was Crane, frightened yet determined.

Aurora's heart lurched. The gangly youth looked so blasted vulnerable. Egads, he had not even a weapon! Then she saw a great, spidery spitheythirl emerge from the rift. A scream rose to ther throat, for it towered over the young mage and the hunter, its barbed stinger poised to strike. In helpless terror she watched Crane dart suddenly in front of the lean hunter as though to take the poisoned dart meant for Elwindolf.

"Crane, *no*, you mad fool!" she cried. Then she saw him begin to shimmer and change. Like a pillar of ice rapidly melting, he oozed over the floor, a great, mirky, viscous puddle into which the monstrous creature lumbered and, to Aurora's amazement, instantly became fast stuck. 'Twas then Elwindolf lunged for the soft underbelly, slashing upward with the sword. Then leaping from beneath the shuddering giant, he severed one by one the four waving tentacles, each of which ended in a glaring, multifaceted eye. The creature emitted a high, keening shriek and pierced itself with its own poison-laden

177

stinger. In dread fascination Aurora beheld it give a tremendous, convulsive heave and break free of the viscid stuff that had been its bane, then, lurching blindly for several feet, it collapsed in a quivering mass to the floor.

Aurora, drawing in a long, shaky breath, felt weak with relief. Yet even as the spitheythirl fell, the winged hyppohornbora, having the body of a horse and the head and hinder parts resembling a hornet, leaped into its place. Nor was it the last of the creatures of darkness caught in the rift. There would be countless others, Aurora knew. Too many for the courageous Elwindolf and the ingenious Crane. Unless she found the circlet soon, they would pay the price of their hopeless stand with the forfeiture of their lives.

"In the name of the One, where is the cursed thing?" she fumed aloud.

"Here it is, 'tis here," came an answering squawk from overhead, followed by a raucous chortle. "Mine it is, and mine it will stay."

The enchantress jerked upright, her head flung back as she searched for the seemingly disembodied speaker. Then suddenly she stilled, a dangerous glint in her eye.

"I've no time for your bird-witted games, Kreekow," warned the enchantress in dire tones, as she located the sorceress's familiar circling above the now roofless turret on a pillar of rising air, the circlet clutched in her wicked talons. "Give me the amulet that the rift may be sealed."

"And my mistress with it? Nay, I say. 'Tis not what she would do, methinks," croaked the bird, flapping its wings to climb higher before lazily circling once more.

Realizing the futility of antagonizing the crow so long as it held the amulet, Aurora suppressed the urge to invoke one of the Eleven Hundred Droonish Curses that would transform the noisome bird-wit into a featherless fowl ready for the stewpot. After all, it would not do to have the circlet plummet into the irretrievable depths, no matter how much satisfaction might be derived from having Kreekow plummet with it. With an effort the enchantress assumed a more reasonable tack.

"Surely not even Leilah could wish for the Realm to be overrun by such loathsome creatures," she urged, trying to sound calm when she must shout at the top of her lungs to be heard by the bird. "Nor can you want such a dreadful thing. Think, Kreekow. To them you would be a toothsome delight."

But nothing, it seemed, would penetrate the crow's feathered cap, and it was not long before Aurora was wishing ardently for a winged steed to bear her to Kreekow, since it was becoming increasingly obvious that Kreekow could not be made to come to her. A steed like Kev, for example, she reflected somewhat wistfully, recalling that she had promised she would send for him if ever she should need him. And, indeed, the draconian glass frangible that had been transformed into a real, fire-breathing dragon when she freed Myrialoc from her grandfather's Crystal Kingdom would have been a marvelous sight for sore eyes at that moment, decided the enchantress, as she observed Kreekow flick her tail feathers in a gesture of unmistakable derision.

"By the One, I would fain have Kev appear on the spot," she muttered aloud. "Then would you be less high and mighty, my fine feathered friend."

No sooner had the words left her mouth than a huge, darksome shadow loomed suddenly out of the black, roiling clouds—a magnificent beast soaring on great, serrated wings.

"*Dracadern*," breathed the enchantress, "the Dragon of Darkness." She gazed spellbound at the gracile body tapering to a long, serpentine tail, the slender neck outstretched and the wedge-shaped head belching orange flame. Slowly it drifted in lazy, descending spirals toward the blasted turret, till at last it seemed to curl in upon itself, the wings furled as it hovered scant feet above her, its head cocked so that she could see plainly the rufescent glitter of an eye staring back at her. Unconsciously her grip tightened on Andruvien's hilt.

"I say," called out the fearsome beast, "would you mind moving out of the way? I promise I have been practicing my landings faithfully, but as you well know, I've a most lamentable predilection for precipitating near-disasters."

Aurora's heart gave a little leap.

"Kev?" she called incredulously. Then, with quickening joy, "Oh, *Kev*, thank the One, it is you."

"I came as quickly as ever I could. Indeed, rather more quickly than I should have thought possible," replied the dragon, blinking as though a trifle startled himself at his sudden appearance above the sorceress's tower fortress. "Actually I was having some difficulty getting off to sleep and thought to take a few turns about Myrialoc—to sort of quiet my nerves, you see—when no sooner had I taken flight, than I heard someone demand my immediate presence, and, well, here I am. An apparent example of instantaneous transposition. Very interesting but somewhat nerve-shaking, I must say."

"Never mind that," broke in the enchantress, acutely aware of the battle raging at her back. Then suddenly she groaned as she searched the uneasy sky for Kreekow and beheld nothing but the lightning-riven clouds. "Oh, *blast!* The dratted crow is gone!" she uttered in accents of despair. "Whatever are we to do now?"

The great beast settling with exaggerated care upon the blighted parapet dwarfed the drooping figure of the girl, who stood with shoulders hunched, her hands over her face in an attitude of utter desolation. Hesitantly the spiked head lowered to within inches of Aurora, the fierce, dragonish face incongruously eloquent of a tender-hearted sympathy.

"Crow?" he queried, obviously puzzled. "Was it a crow you wished?"

"Nay, not the crow, but that which it stole from me," she cried, flinging down her hands in sudden, quick impatience.

"I see," replied the dragon, though in fact he did not see at all what she was driving at. If only the others would cease to carry on so, he thought, more than a little distracted by the incessant uproar issuing from the interior of the ruined turret, perhaps one could think with greater clarity. After all, it was not so very long ago that he had been naught but an empty-headed oddity of animated glass, and, indeed, all this unaccustomed cogitation was like to give him a splitting headache. Now what *was* it that he had been about to say? Ah, yes, the crow.

"Could it have been the one I glimpsed with regrettable belatedness as I burst upon the scene?"

"Oh, *did* you see it?" exclaimed the enchantress, turning eagerly to the dragon. "Do you know where it went?"

"Oh, dear, perhaps not precisely," he hedged, leveling a massive stone merlon with a nervous flick of the tail. "Actually I never saw it till it was too late. I was letting off a little ballast, the way we dragons do, you know, and the poor creature was suddenly just there. There was nothing I could do, I'm afraid."

"You mean you blasted Kreekow with dragon fire?" Aurora clarified, horrified at the notion despite her longstanding antipathy for the sorceress's unendearing familiar.

"Actually singed is more like, since the crow caught only the tail end of the blast—er—*in* the tail end, as a matter of fact," mused Kev with a hint of a dragonish grin. But immediately he sobered at sight of the enchantress, tight-lipped and pale.

"Then all is indeed lost," she murmured, her eyes curiously blank.

"It's my fault, isn't it," Kev groaned, his head beginning to droop. "I did try to save the poor unfortunate, but I'm afraid she slipped from my grasp so that all I came up with was a few feathers and," he added, extending a great, taloned foot, "this."

In startled wonder Kev saw Aurora's eyes flash suddenly golden, and with hands that slightly shook, she carefully slipped the silvery thing from one of his fearsome curved claws.

"Oh, you magnificent, lovable oaf!" she exclaimed, giving the sheepish dragon a fierce hug about his scale-armored neck. "This is what I was looking for—the Circlet of Kerr." Then, telling him to wait for her there, she hastily left Kev staring after her, his dragon eyes aglow with a distinctly undragonish affection.

The enchantress, skirting the corpses of the glumengog, spitheythirl, and hyppohornbora, was met with a daunting scene, for Elwindolf, bloodied from numerous wounds and his left arm hanging uselessly at his side, was fast losing ground before four Cyclopacephali, the headless men of the fabled land of Cecys.

Tearing her eyes away from the grotesque creatures with their hideous single organ of sight embedded in the humanoid chests bulging with muscle, Aurora searched frantically for some sign of Crane. Knowing full well that he might have been anything from a stone block to a trailing cloud of gas, she was no less amazed to discover suspended in midair a black spider as big around as a human head busy at spinning an intricate web from the remnants of the ceiling to the floor. Already the sticky, hyaline mass of fibers resembling a huge cocoon encompassed the swirl of mist constituting the portal, and trapped within it were a host of *werfleogen*, the grotesque man-flies, no greater than six or seven inches in length, which together with half a dozen of

183

their kind could with their razor-sharp teeth devour a man to the bone in a matter of seconds. Still, though they gnawed ferociously at the silken strands, they had not yet managed to escape the spider repairing and strengthening his web with untiring devotion.

Realizing in that single, swift glance that she had located the shape-changer, the enchantress waited to see no more but, summoning Andruvien, hurried to give aid to the hunter—too late. For before ever she could reach him, she saw Elwindolf stagger and go down on one knee as one of the Cyclopacephali broke through his guard to strike him savagely in the side with a great, spiked club. With a piercing cry, the enchantress sprang in front of the hunter, blue flame spouting from her hand as she wielded the Blade of Power.

In seconds it was over, and Aurora was kneeling anxiously beside Elwindolf who was still crouched on one knee and leaning heavily on Ariana's sword forged by a god. The hunter's face was grey with pain and fatigue, yet the pale eyes were steady as ever as he met Aurora's anguished glance.

"Oh, Elwindolf, my good friend," she cried softly, her voice painful in her throat. "I fear your wounds are grievous."

"Nay, they matter not." Impatiently he tried to wave her away. "Our young lord hath greater need of thee than I. Take thy mother's sword that hath served me well and go." And indeed he had spoken truly, for even as she glanced fearfully over her shoulder, Aurora saw that the spider's efforts to contain the *werfleogen* were inexorably failing.

"Aye," she said in a hushed voice and reverently

accepted the godly weapon, "I must go to Crane's aid, but I will not be long. Rest easy now, for none can ever say the man called Drude has not redeemed himself in full."

Quickly she rose to her feet and turned to leave him, but the hunter's steely hand clamped about her wrist. She stopped and looked back at him, a question in her eyes.

"Seal the portal, Brenna of the Golden Eyes. Seal it ere all our efforts be for naught."

For a long moment she answered not, for her heart was filled with dread. Aye, the portal must be sealed, and yet how could he know—how could anyone possibly know—what was being asked of her? Oh, gods—*Frayne!* Never again to see him, never to hold him in her arms or to be held by him. And worse, to condemn him to everlasting imprisonment within the Timeless Flux. Why? Indeed, *how* had things come to such a pass? Could she have been so mistaken in believing their spirits had been forged by the god's searing passion into one, their destinies thus inextricably bound one to the other? What cruel hoax had the gods perpetrated against her? against Frayne? What merciless fate to demand so cruel a sacrifice? And yet must the thing be done. With painful clarity she saw it and that she was the one chosen for the heinous task. And she saw something else as well, something she read in Elwindolf's face that had remained unspoken in his words.

Slowly she lifted her head to match the hunter look for look.

"I will seal the rift," she answered steadily, "though it be my heart's tomb. But in turn, you must promise me, Elwindolf—nay, *swear* by Phelan's name—that you will live."

She saw a shadow flit across the stern features, saw him hesitate. Then a faint smile hovered briefly about his mouth.

"It be a hard bargain, Enchantress, for I be weary unto death. Yet I so swear. By Phelan's name and if it please the gods, Elwindolf will live." No sooner had he finished the oath than a sigh shuddered through his lips, and Elwindolf, who was sworn to live, slumped, senseless, to the floor.

With fingers that shook, the enchantress sought for the pulsebeat at the base of the man's throat, and at last she sensed it, a faint throb of lingering life. Deliberately she rose to her feet, her fingers tightening on the circlet clasped in her hand.

"So be it," she murmured with a last, lingering look at the hunter's still face. Then resolutely she crossed to the portal, and lifting high the Circlet of Kerr, pronounced the words that would forever seal her heart with the knight of Tor in the inescapable Flux of Timelessness:

> "End to a beginning—
> A doorless portal opened;
> Hole within a whole—
> The all of nothing;
> Beginning without end—
> The pathway of a soul:
> I, to close the same,
> Thee 'a circle' name."

A deep rumble shuddered through the fortress,

toppling stone from the already wrecked parapet atop the sorceress's ruined chamber. But then a stillness fell, even to the bluster of the storm, hushed with a preternatural suddenness that preyed upon the nerves. Aurora backed a step, feeling the eerie, unearthly silence like the thunder of doom.

"Crane!" she called nervously. "'Tis enough. Come away—*now*—ere it is too late."

Yet already it was too late, for the swirl of mist began to quicken till it whirled about the rift, a glaucous blur, and with it was the wind leaping into a howling fury as it was drawn into the whorl of the portal inexorably collapsing in upon itself.

"Crane!" Aurora cried, seeing the spider's silk cocoon along with its shrieking captives vanish into the vortex. "Oh, gods, no."

Oblivious of the batter and blast of the tempest, the enchantress sank to her knees, her eyes clenched against the sting of tears. They were gone—Crane and the knight of Tor. Oh, why could it not have been she instead of the shape-changer? How would she ever be able to face Vandrel with the tale of Crane's horrifying fate, Vandrel, who had loved him like a son? And Janine. Oh, gods, Janine, who was just awakening to the joys of love! How could she shatter the hopes of that child in whom the mystic wonder of womanhood had only just begun to bloom? Why must destiny be so cruel? Had she never ventured forth from Endrith's Forest on the quest for her true name, a quest invented by Minta and Valesia, her dryad mother-pair, to amuse a restless child, might not Crane even now be safe in the Land of Mages? Might not Frayne be where he belonged—

in the real world of men caught up in the sweeping tides of history? And what of herself? If she had remained in Hawthorn Glade with the elves and dryads, she would never have known the agony of a love forever lost, the desperate feeling of having part of oneself torn asunder, the ache of being always afterwards incomplete and alone. Indeed, she did not know how she would endure without Frayne, her one and only love. Yet somehow she must, for there was still Elwindolf to be gotten to safety and the Realm to rouse against the creatures that had won release from the Flux. How many had there been—a score, or more perhaps? she wondered dully, then again felt the sharp edge of grief at Crane's loss, for it was because of his supreme sacrifice, which might yet be Elwindolf's as well, that the number was not far greater.

"Oh, Crane," she uttered brokenly, "I would give my life to bring you back again."

"But I am back, you gudgeon," shouted a dear, familiar voice into her ear. "And unless I miss my guess, we've precious little time to waste. I wouldn't give a groat for Leilah's precious Seeing Eye or her blasted fortress right this minute."

Aurora's head came up with a jerk. Her hair whipping in the wind blinded her and stung her face so that she must shove it back with an impatient hand ere she could see the gangly youth bent over her, his grin ridiculously awry, as he glimpsed a joyful light leap to her eyes.

"B-But *how . . . ?*" she stammered and, letting her hair fly, grasped him hard by the arms, as if only by the reassuring touch of sinew and bone could she believe he was there in the flesh and not some cruel phantom come to haunt her. "I-I saw you drawn into the vortex."

"Oh, *that*," he shouted back, shrugging it off. "It was nothing. I just thought myself out again. Which is what I'd better do for us right now. Where's Elwindolf?"

"There!" she cried, pointing toward the ominously still form of the hunter. "Quickly! Take him to Vandrel. I'll come as soon as ever I can on Kev."

"On *Kev?*" echoed the youth, halting abruptly in his tracks.

"Never mind that now. Just *go!*" she yelled, shoving him toward Elwindolf. "Before he bleeds to death!"

Something in her voice must have convinced him that for once this was not the time to argue over particulars, for, after only the briefest hesitation, he made with all haste for the injured hunter, and kneeling, cradled the man's head and shoulders against his chest. The shape-changer cast a last, troubled glance at the slender figure leaning into the wind, the raven hair wild about her face and shoulders, and suddenly it came to him that he would never see the fiery young girl, Aurora, again. For an instant he thought he could not go through with it. Then resolutely he evoked the spell that would transport him from her, and in his heart he knew a sudden, terrible fear for the lovely, golden-eyed enchantress.

Chapter 7

With a heavy heart Aurora watched Crane and Elwindolf vanish amidst a shimmer of light.

"In the name of the One, please let them come in time to Vandrel," she prayed, and made as if to go to Kev still waiting patiently atop the parapet wall. Yet suddenly she halted and for an instant stood unmoving, her back to the cauldron as the wind dropped to a low moan and grew finally still.

The hairs at the nape of her neck prickled with the feel of a danger sensed but not fully apprehended, and all her instincts warned her to flee. But something stronger than her fear held her; indeed, compelled her to turn and cross to the sorceress's cauldron, now uncannily quiet and imbued with a brooding calm that stretched the nerves. It was the silence of waiting, the hush of a held breath before a terror-riven scream. In dread she gazed upon the now still, black surface of the Seeing Eye and could not stop herself. Slowly her hand lowered, then plunged into the murky depths and out again.

The lavender nimbus of light leaping into life she had seen before, the time she had slipped undetected into the sorceress's chamber to take back her elfin blade Glaiveling and had stolen a look into the Seeing Eye. That was when she had learned the truth about Frayne, had seen him, a youth with Ariana, his mother, and known finally how the sorceress had coerced him into doing her bidding in exchange for keeping his mother alive.

"Frayne," she murmured, and, feeling her heart like a bleeding wound within her breast, she relived the horror she had known as she peered out of the curtained recess to behold Frayne limned against the portal's glaucous haze and Leilah, the knife in her hand, stealing toward his unguarded back. She remembered shouting a warning and seeing him turn. Then Leilah was upon him, the knife slashing viciously as her hurtled weight bore them both backwards into the abyss. As if in a dream, she saw herself bolt from her hiding place and leap for the yawning maw of the rift and Crane, hard on her heels, drag her, struggling, away again.

One by one the horrifying images passed before her, not in her mind, but upon the rippling surface of the magic mirror—Xerxes, the Black Knight, falling to his knees before her, Crane thrusting her from the path of the cockatrice emerging from the portal at her back, the manticores and aingealwyrms and all the other hideous creatures escaping into the Realm of the One, Kreekow taunting her with the stolen circlet, Kev appearing out of the clouds like an ill omen that had turned out good, Elwindolf falling to the Cyclopacephali, Crane spinning his web, and

192

finally herself calling upon the power of the circlet to seal the rift. With the fading image of Crane and Elwindolf at the point of dematerializing, the surface of the Seeing Eye grew gradually still, assuming once more its inky obscurity. And then suddenly Aurora understood.

The images, this time and the time before, had all taken the form of her thoughts. She had decreed their focus and direction by what she had been thinking when she disturbed the surface and created the ripples. It had to be! And if that was the way of it, then could she not direct it to visions of present and future if she wished, or even a timeless time, simply by so directing her own thoughts? To Frayne in the Flux, for example. Was he alive? And in what time plane had he landed?

"The Flux," she murmured like some half-meaningless incantation. "Let the Flux be seen." Then, thrusting her hand again into the chill stuff of Somn, she waited, hardly daring to breathe as she stared in dread fascination at the spreading ripples incandescent with a purplish aura.

At first there seemed naught but a kaleidoscopic blur of rapidly altering patterns, like an amorphous image of clouds sculpted and resculpted by the wind at tremendous speed. In mounting frustration she sought to separate one from the other, but it was impossible, for no sooner had she focused on something vaguely recognizable than it had merged into something else and that again into some other ungraspable manifestation of irretrievable fluctuation. Until at last she cried out in helpless rage.

"Stop it at once! 'Tis Frayne I would see. The

knight of Tor within the timeless possibilities."

A sharp pain like a knife thrust in the heart brought a gasp to her lips as the knight seemed suddenly to leap into view. His fair hair glinting in sunlight falling from directly overhead, Frayne stood in apparent indecision at a crossroads, one roadway terminating at the junction of the other, which seemed to stretch for miles in a perfectly straight line in either direction from him across a vast, unvarying plain of green, waving grass. Never had Aurora beheld any land so markedly devoid of hill or tree; indeed, of discernible landmark of any kind, save for the signpost bearing three identifying arrows and set squarely at the head of the T. In no little amazement Aurora saw that the place names were of the Old Tongue, and immediately she grasped at least part of her beloved's dilemma. For Frayne was not versed in the language of the Beginnings, which was of a simpler time when all the races and the beasts communicated in a universal tongue. Still, she reflected, perusing the inscriptions with much perplexity, even if he could have deciphered the words, he could hardly have been in less of a quandary. In truth, though she could read them, they made no sense to her at all.

Almost as if he sensed her watching him, the knight glanced abruptly over his shoulder, directly into her eyes.

"Oh, gods," she moaned, extending a quivering hand toward the image of her beloved. He looked so weary. Indeed, she saw fine lines of pain and fatigue about his mouth and eyes, and, too, there was something unnatural in the way he held his left arm before him. He has been hurt, she thought, feeling his pain as if it were her own. But then he had turned away again and with a fatalistic shrug had taken the roadway to his left.

It was then Aurora saw the blood-soaked bandage crudely wrapped about his forearm.

"A curse on the sorceress!" she hissed, knowing of a certainty that 'twas Leilah's blade that had wounded him. Helplessly she watched the knight make his weary way down the seemingly endless road and ached with all her being to be with him, to succor and sustain him with her young strength.

She did not know how long she stared upon the rippling surface of the magic looking glass—a few moments or hours. Yet it seemed the knight had passed through a league or more of monotonous countryside before at last he came to yet another crossroads, appallingly similar to the previous one. Indeed, so alike were they that Aurora knew with sinking certainty that no matter which way the knight might choose to go, he would always and inevitably come in time to this very crossroads. For did not the signpost bear the same three place names as had the first? And where earlier they had only served to bewilder her, did they not now stand out with bitter clarity, the clues by which were resolved the riddles of a road without curve or bend that yet ever completed a circle, and of an unchanging land of unvarying uniformity that nevertheless lay within a dimension governed by the very law of ever-fluctuating possibility?

Never had Aurora felt so miserably powerless, as she watched the knight of Tor sink heavily to his knees at the crux of the intersecting roads, his bowed head glinting golden in the steady light of a sun that still stood unmoving at its zenith, while the signpost with the three arrows reared up before him like some obscene jest of the gods. One pointed back the way the knight had come and bore the word *Hwanonswa-afre,* or "Whencesoever" in the language of men; another looked to the left toward *Hwarafre,* or "Wherever," and the third looked to the right, which led to *Anighwar,* or "Anywhere." Therein lay the hoax, for, placeless place names of undetermined designations, they pointed only to the limitless possibilities. And until the wayfarer at the crossroads declared from whence he came and whither he would go, he was doomed to wander timelessly down a road with neither beginning nor end, which traversed a boundless realm of infinite possibility awaiting specificity.

But Frayne knew not the meaning of the words, for he was Thromholan and man, a descendant of gods who had traded innocence for knowledge and of mortals who had abandoned the simplicity of the Old Ways for the complexity of vision and undefinable truth. The Old Tongue of the Beginnings was thus denied them, for they could no longer comprehend with their hearts what they could not perceive with their senses. Only the magical peoples, the elves, the dryads, and the vanishing race of faeries, could commune with the beasts and the living essences of earth, using the language that had once been universal among all the races and all the One's creations. In despair Aurora sent her thoughts outward toward her love, sought desperately to breach the barriers of time and space and his own impregnable armor of cynicism and distrust. She saw his head come up as if he had heard something from a great distance, and for a moment hope leaped like a flame within her. But then his reflection upon the surface of the looking glass began to darken and grow dim.

"Nay, not yet!" she cried in terrible anguish, and still Frayne receded yet farther into the deepening gloom. She thrust out her hand toward the rapidly fading vision as though by this she might keep him with her, but she knew it was hopeless. She, who was Aurora, the Enchantress, Rab's heir and Almira's daughter—*she* was losing him; and not Andruvien, not the god whose vassal she was, not the Crimson Cloak or the song of power, nay, not even her love could keep it from happening. There was nothing, *nothing* she could do.

"Merciful gods, there must be *some* way to reach him. Show me, I beg you, how I may go to him!"

At once the image of the signpost seemed to leap out at her so that for a fleeting instant she glimpsed the arrow that earlier had read *Hwanonswa-afre*. Then the ripples stilled and the vision vanished into an inky well of darkness.

"Show me Frayne in the Timeless Flux," Aurora cried, thrusting her hand again into the center of the Seeing Eye. But she had known even before she beheld the brief, choppy disruption of the surface settle back into its dreadful placidity that the Eye was closed to her, had known that someone somewhere had wanted her to see her beloved one last time before he was lost to her forever. For had not Frayne told her

197

once that even Leilah had never been certain of her mastery of the looking glass, that though she might command the visions to appear, she could never be sure that those she had summoned were true glimpses of past, present, or future, but only what some other, Dred perhaps, wanted her to see? And then, too, there was Sheelar, the Serpent-Lord of Somn and Guardian of the Seeing Eye ere Leilah had stolen it from him. Had not he told her the images reflected upon the Eye were distorted by the shadows of Somn from whence the magic glass had issued long ages past? It would then seem to follow that the Seeing Eye of Somn revealed only what it—or some other—would wish it to, part-truths or distorted reflections of truth meant to mislead, and perhaps even lies. Which of these was the last brief glimpse of the signpost, that which had seemed to answer her final, anguished plea to the gods? Truth, half-truth, or lie, she had seen it: *Kylandros,* carved into the arrow looking to the unseen point of departure upon the road of possibility.

Why? Were the floating isles of Kylandros, which drifted randomly forward and backward through the Flux of Timelessness, a true portal through which she might reach Frayne? Or a trap meant to imprison her? For simply to enter the Flux was not enough. If it were, Frayne would have won Ariana's release long ago. Nay. He had had to wait for a portal that led directly to the time plane in which Leilah had imprisoned the Valdoran, or at least to one within the context of possibilities that surrounded her. Thanks to the sorceress's potion, Frayne had emerged upon the roadway that, given the correct designations, would lead him to his mother, but Aurora would not have that advantage. For to enter at random, as she would do if she journeyed to Kylandros, would mean an endless search for the single strand of reality among an infinitude of related and unrelated possibilities. Not only did she face the likelihood of never discovering Frayne, but once in, there was an equal possibility that she would either never find her way out again or, at the very least, never escape back into her own finite span of reality.

Therein lay her dilemma: For either to be trapped in the Flux or to be forever separated from her own time plane would mean never to complete the quest for her true name, indeed, for her very identity. But more important it would mean denying her own destiny, and that more than anything gave her cause for anguish, for surely the god would not have chosen her to be his vassal if she were not meant somehow to serve him in the troubled times before them. And might not that be the reason she had been given the vision of Kylandros upon the signpost—to lure her from the path of her true destiny? Might not it serve Somn very well indeed to have her gone from the Realm when Dred rose up again to challenge the One? For she would go to Kylandros no matter what the risks. She had known it even as the vision had vanished from the Seeing Eye, just as he who had sent it to her must surely have known it, too.

No sooner had she reached that disturbing conclusion than suddenly the air crackled with hideous laughter.

As if stung by a whiplash, Aurora drew back from

the cauldron.

"Who is it?" she shouted, Andruvien flashing silver fire in her hand. There was no answer—only the laughter—but she knew him. Knew him as she knew the creep of flesh when a chill wind blows in the dead of a moonless night. She had heard his soulless mirth before, the laughter of a mocking god.

"You think you have won, but you are wrong," cried the enchantress. "I will find Frayne, and together we will return. This I swear to you, Prince of Somn."

Dred's laughter swelled, drowning out the rumble of thunder. Aurora staggered, her hands clasping at her ears, as the god's malevolence battered her mind and tortured her soul. He made her see herself as she was, a foolish innocent, a child who dared to believe she posed some threat to an immortal prince of Throm. Perhaps she had amused him for a time with her absurd notions of destiny, but that had been all it was. She might venture foolishly into the Flux or remain where she was. It mattered not one whit to Dred, the mightiest of the proud race of Thromgilad. The vision of the signpost bearing the false promise of Kylandros had been naught but the god's final jest in the grand hoax he had played upon them all. For he had contrived all of it.

That much she saw clearly now—the machinations of a god who sought to rework the fabric of destiny to suit his own ends. Leilah, Frayne, Ariana, herself—he had used every one of them to achieve a single purpose; and, indeed, the potion had never been other than what in the end it had turned out to be—a trap for Dred's mortal son, Frayne, the

Thromholan, who had been destined to supplant the immortal prince of Throm.

'Twould seem that Dred had had the last laugh, and yet 'twas not he who was prophesied to lead the Thromgilad to victory, but the Thromholan, whom he had imprisoned in the Flux of Timelessness. Doubtless Aurora should have rejoiced that Dred had in his scheming woven the fabric of his own defeat, but she knew only grief and the first stirring of an icy rage. She felt Andruvien responding to her anger, feeding on it, feeding it back to her, until she scintillated power.

"You should have slain the knight of Tor, Prince!" she called out ringingly. "And the Enchantress of the Glade!"

Crystal flame spouted from Aurora's hand. Andruvien's fire smashed into the cauldron and shattered and smashed again, and yet again. A resounding crack split the air—the adamantine wall of the vessel ripped asunder, vomiting forth the fuliginous hyloplasm of the Seeing Eye. In horror Aurora beheld the fundament reek miasmic fumes. Merciful gods, the very stone of Skorl was being dissolved by the vitriolic spew!

Too late she apprehended her own peril, as suddenly the cauldron lurched and heaved. The floor was weakening, giving way beneath the vessel's weight, and when at length it went, the enchantress would go with it. What a fool she had been not to have seen it sooner. While she had stood like some empty-headed ignoramus gaping at the destruction of the sorceress's stronghold, she had let herself be cut off from the only two avenues of escape, for, while the teetering cauldron stood between her and the turret stair, its spreading offal barred her from the parapet and Kev.

Aurora uttered a strangled cry as the floor shuddered beneath her feet. Blast! This was no way for it to end, she thought, searching desperately for some way out of the coil of her own making. There was still too much to be done, and she would be damned if she would allow Dred the final victory. The cauldron shifted ever more precariously to one side as the stone beneath it sagged ominously. Then she saw it—a tangled remnant of Crane's spider web hanging from what was left of the wooden roof. The fibers had been twisted into a single mass, probably by the whirlwind as it was drawn into the collapsing portal, Aurora guessed. Perhaps an inch in diameter and some thirteen feet or so in length, it was like a silken cord, the end of which dangled no more than four or five feet above the cauldron.

It took no more than a single glance to know it was her only hope, and even if she missed the leap and plunged into the spuming cauldron, it would be better to die having made the attempt than to die cravenly, having tried nothing.

Without further reflection, the enchantress thrust Guthsweord, her mother's sword, through her belt, vaguely surprised to find her hands steady. Indeed, she felt imbued with a steely calm as one last time she gauged the distance to the slender lifeline and crouched, ready to spring. She heard the floor give a final groan, then she was in the air, her fingers clutching at the makeshift rope. Even as her grip caught and held, the stone beneath her collapsed, sending the cauldron plunging with an avalanche of debris into the lightless depths. Retching, she clung tightly to her tenuous bond till her heart should have ceased its pounding. And when at last she brought herself to look over her shoulder down into the yawning maw of death beneath her, the sweat stood out on her forehead.

"Thanks be to the One," she breathed, briefly closing her eyes against the appalling reality of her narrow deliverance. "And to dearest Crane."

An ominous rumble deep within the bowels of the fortress gave ample warning of the danger that yet abounded all around her. Skorl, the ancient seat of the Black Kings and the stronghold of the scheming sorceress of Tor, was crumbling from within, felled by its own dry rot of centuries of evil. Sternly Aurora subdued the bile rising to her throat, and drawing a determined breath, began to pull herself up the twine of sticky fibers toward the roof. Chunks of rock and other rubble already loosened in the devastation wrought by the creatures from the Flux hurtled down at her from the parapet with each convulsive shudder of the stricken fortress. Still she fought her way upward, though her tongue cleaved to the roof of her mouth and her breath came in hurried gasps, till at last she was nearly within reach of the jagged ruins of the roof. So swiftly did it come that Aurora never saw the stone block catapulted out of nowhere. One moment she was struggling upward the final foot or so and the next she reeled from a glancing blow to the shoulder, a scream wrenched from her throat as she clung desperately to the fibrous cord by one hand, her left arm dangling uselessly at her side.

"Kev!" she cried. "Kev, help me!"

Her grip was weakening, the rope beginning to slide through her hand, taking skin and flesh with it.

"Oh, gods, I am undone," she groaned and felt the rope torn from her bleeding fingers.

The sudden clasp of a scaly coil about her waist sustained her fall and bore her, in a near swoon, upward. Vaguely she knew that she was laid tenderly upon trembling stone. Then, grasped with infinite care about her upper body and her legs, she was lifted into the air. For a time she hovered between darkness and a bewildering sensation that she was somehow flying; whereupon the bite of a chill wind and the sting of rain against her face brought her at last to pain-filled awareness and the realization that, cradled in a taloned grip and borne on dragon's wings, she was in truth skimming beneath a ceiling of clouds high above the spreading plain.

Briefly the agonizing torment of the injured shoulder and of her hand, the flesh raw and bleeding, was blocked from her mind as she beheld, far below her and receding with bewildering swiftness into the distance, the craggy pinnacle of Tor belching smoke and flame. Strangely detached, as if caught up in a dream, Aurora watched the final throes of the tower fortress. Skorl, the sorceress of Tor, the lingering evil of the Black Kings, even the dread Seeing Eye—they were all gone, vanquished for all eternity, and she felt nothing save only a dragging weariness and an odd sort of emptiness.

Why did nothing ever turn out the way it was supposed to be? she wondered dully. She had often envisioned the sorceress's downfall. Through all the weeks and months of poring over books, all the seemingly endless preparation, the eternity of waiting for the time when at last Vandrel should deem her ready to venture forth in pursuit of her true name and in search of Frayne; indeed, ready to confront the sorceress who had bound the knight of Tor to do her bidding, she had scarcely thought of little else. She would meet her imagined enemy boldly: the Enchantress of the Glade, with right on her side, come face to face at last with the wicked sorceress of Tor, and she, Aurora, would prove the greater power, for she would win the one thing she desired most—Frayne's freedom.

How stupid and naive she had been! A child weaving fantasies. Far from the bold confrontation she had envisioned, her one and only encounter with the sorceress had seen her flung ignominiously at Leilah's feet, a captive and finally a slave. She had dreamed of freeing her beloved from the power of Tor and instead had stood helplessly by as he was hurtled into a prison far worse than Leilah's loathsome bondage.

Oh, gods, she had lost him, and though her heart had thus been wounded unto death, she was yet cursed with the aching emptiness of life without him—Frayne, her godlike knight, her one and only love. 'Twas then the darkness took her, and she knew no more.

Aurora lay wrapped in a snug blanket of darkness, reluctant to let go of sleep's sweet oblivion. Yet the gladsome trill of a woodthrush issuing from somewhere overhead teased her with its cheerful persistence, as did the rustle of wind-kissed leaves and the tantalizing fragrance of wild mint, sweet pepperbush, and lemon-scented horse balm. A sigh breathed through her lips, as at last she stirred, the sun's growing warmth and the tickle of grass against her cheek further wooing her to unwelcome wakefulness. Still, burdened by a heaviness of spirit, the unremembered cause for which she instinctively sought to hold at bay, the enchantress lingered yet a while longer with eyes closed and sought to return into the safe haven of dreamless slumber.

It was not to be, however, for no sooner had she burrowed more deeply into the makeshift pillow of her arm than she became aware of the protest of stiffened limbs and the inescapable torment of parched lips and throat.

"Oh, gods," she groaned, coming irretrievably awake. Then, rolling heavily onto her back, she gasped as a searing pain lanced through her shoulder, and with it, the agony of returning memory.

She thought she must perish from that first terrible, swift stab of inconsolable loss. Indeed, she lay there for a seeming eternity, her every breath coming like a knife thrust, quick and hard, as she struggled to come to grips with her grief. And when at last her brain ceased to reel and the world to tilt and whirl about her, she was trembling and weak, her brow damp with sweat as when a morbid fever has just broken. Staring blindly at white drifts of cloud in a blue expanse of sky, she yearned for the solace of oblivion.

Still, she was young and basically healthy despite her wounded heart and body, and it was not long before Aurora hearkened to the irresistible allure of birdsong and the chuckle of a brook somewhere close by.

"But what place is this? And how came I here?" she muttered fitfully to herself. Then, her hazy recollections of dragonflight springing of a sudden to her mind, she called out, "Kev? Kev! In the name of the One, Kev, where are you?"

There was no answer and no sign of Kev anywhere around. Still, since it was a peaceful place in which she found herself and since there seemed little point in worrying about her missing friend—he was a dragon, after all—she felt her racing heart begin to slow to a normal pace, whereupon she experienced the first vague stirrings of curiosity about her surroundings.

Lifting herself cautiously to one elbow, the enchantress gazed with slowly awakening wonder upon a forest of giant oak, all bedecked with white Virgin's bower and purple nightshade trailing round the ancient trunks and draping from the outstretched limbs. She lay in a clearing beside a still pool fed by a small stream rife with pussy willow, horsemint, and cattail. Imperceptibly her blood began to quicken, her senses coming alive to the breeze sweet with the promise of a morning shower, to golden shafts of sunlight filtering through tree branches thick with leaves, to the drone of honeybees and the flutter of butterfly wings. There was power in the fecund soil, rich and black and efflorescent with fairy wand and toadshade, painted trillium, yellow lady's slipper, goldenrod, and everywhere, the feathery, white foamflower. She could feel the earth's potency like an elixir working its healing spell on her, purging her of the lethargy that weighted her limbs and deadened her nerves, awakening her to the pain in her body even as it eased the aching torment of her heart.

With the quickening of life within her veins, she found herself gazing with longing at the clear waters of the pool. She felt gritty from the deep, druglike sleep into which she had fled to escape the agony of her soul and soiled with the lingering horror of Skorl and the infamy of the sorceress who had had her mother murdered and her lover bound forever in the Timeless Flux. She recoiled from all thoughts of Dred and the mockery of the false vision of hope with which he had taunted her. It was too soon for that. First she must heal the wounds of body and spirit.

Slowly, her teeth gritted against the unavoidable wrench of her injured shoulder, Aurora dragged the boots off her feet and worked her way out of the clothes that had ever chafed and confined her, till at last she lay, weak and panting from her exertions, but feeling inexplicably as if she had somehow rid herself of a heavy burden. Indeed, the sun, warm against her bare skin, was like balm, easing the soreness from her muscles and infusing her with a wondrous sense of returning gladness in being alive so that she hardly knew that she had risen to her feet, her face uplifted to the golden shafts of sun in unconscious celebration of the rebirth of Anduan, Elf-Daughter and Tree-Child, a spirit free at last from the fetters of the man-beast.

Buoyed by that which she could not explain, but

208

which she knew in her heart to be the power of the enchantress to which Frayne had awakened her but which had ever derived from the earth itself, Aurora made her way to the beckoning pool. She paused only long enough to gather some of the fragrant white blossoms from the sweet pepperbush growing in abundance along the bank, before she entered the crystalline waters. Crushing the flowery heads till they formed a soapy lather, she cleansed her hair and then her body until her skin, save only for the great, purplish bruise that marred the purity of her left shoulder, tingled and glowed from the scrubbing. Satisfied at last, she slipped beneath the still surface. Glorying in the sensuous fluidity of her hair streaming about her head and shoulders, she swam until her small store of strength was spent and she was forced to leave the invigorating ambience of the water. Then, shivering with cold, she sought the warmth of the sun, and like a healthy young animal basked upon a flat rock near the rippling waters till she was dry again and filled with a delicious languor.

How long she lay in blissful harmony with the mystic forces of earth, air, and water, she did not know, but when at last the stiffening of her shoulder and the raw stinging in her lacerated hand roused her from her semitorpid state, the sun had receded behind the thickening rain clouds. Conscious at last of the gnawing in her belly, she recalled that she had not eaten for two days. Still, she must first tend her wounds ere she satisfied the cravings of her belly, she decided, and began to gather cattails, horsemint, and strips of bark from an oak sapling. Quickly she went about the tasks of preparing the downy seeds of the cattail to be sprinkled over her several cuts before bandaging and the horsemint and strips of bark into a healing salve, when suddenly she paused in her work, surprised to discover a song had come unbidden to her lips.

In truth, she mused, Kev had brought her to a wondrous place wherein resided an ancient power, and hard upon that realization it came to her to marvel that he had known of it, for the magician's glass dragon had never ventured forth from her grandfather's Crystal Kingdom ere she and the others had discovered him beneath Seraisharaqa. Doubtless Rab himself, in his lonely vigil for the return of Almira, his golden-eyed daughter, had told Kev of the forest of healing ere the magician confined his own essence in the perfect crystal rose till his heir should come to release it and Myrialoc from the Crystal Kingdom he had wrought. Well, no matter how it had come about, Kev had brought her here, and already she felt more herself than she had since leaving Hawthorn Glade long months past. He had more than repaid her for her small part in transforming him into a real, fire-breathing, dragon-scaled example of flesh-and-blood *dracadern*. But where in blazes had he got himself off to? she puzzled, a trifle uneasy at the thought of being marooned in the sylvan paradise, despite its peaceful loveliness. She could not remain there forever no matter how much she might like to, for in spite of everything that had happened, she was still the enchantress and Andruvien, the vassal of a god. Though her heart might be wounded unto death, she yet lived, and soon she must come to a decision as to what course next to pursue.

The thought brought her no comfort. Indeed, she recoiled from any consideration of her uncertain future. There was yet time, she told herself, and firmly shrugged off her momentary pique at the dragon for his protracted absence. Kev would come when she needed him, and she was not yet ready to venture forth into a world in which she would know only peril and strife—and loneliness too terrible to contemplate.

Yet time in the sylvan glade seemed to stand still, as Aurora quickly mended in all but spirit. The days and nights she spent daydreaming beside the hyaline pool or delving into its shadowy depths soon blurred into a never-ending dream of peaceful solitude, and, in truth, she soon lost any desire that it should ever end. She had long ceased to wonder about Kev's absence or even to ponder the eventuality of his return. It was as if he and everyone and everything that she had known before awakening in the oaken wood had ceased to exist for the raven-haired enchantress. Even Frayne was naught but a painful memory kept firmly locked within the deepest recesses of her mind, to be glimpsed only in her dreams and then resolutely forgotten.

Nothing was allowed to impinge upon that tranquillity that she gathered about her like a cloak to ward off the chill reminders of all that had hurt her. Telling herself that it was better that the thing of power be secreted in a place of safety, the enchantress confined the crystal along with Guthsword and the Crimson Cloak of Power to the dark recesses of a hollow oak, then immediately forgot them. No longer need she be troubled by remembrances of a destiny she had never asked for or desired. Nor need she ever feel again the sharp stab of conscience at the sight of her mother's sword, the blade Elwindolf had wielded in her defense before returning it and giving his solemn oath that he would live. The blade was gone from sight as was the cloak that bore the undeciphered symbols of a power she need never wield again. And if it was the symbol of her unknown identity as well, the standard of her sworn quest to go forth in pursuit of her true name, it mattered not. Indeed, nothing mattered, nor ever would again so long as she need never think or dream or remember.

Thus the days passed, and Aurora regained her strength. Aided by the herbal poultices and the magic inherent in the glade, the torn flesh of her ill-used palm knit and the bruise upon her shoulder gradually faded, till naught was left to remind her of her harrowing escape from Skorl's utter devastation, or of a fleeting image of a signpost in the midst of a darkening vision, or of laughter mocking her, stripping her of all illusion and leaving her bereft of all purpose or meaning—bereft of hope.

Then indeed did the enchantress know in its fullest the false tranquillity of a mind that need no longer contemplate the dark visions, the nameless fears of a dread evil that ever hovers on the outer-fringes of paradise, always waiting, till the inevitable day of reckoning shall come. Thus she did not know nor even wonder that Elwindolf drifted ever further from the realm of the living, sensing, as the wolf senses the unseen presence in the forest, that the spirit of the enchantress had withdrawn into a darkness not unlike the darkness of death. Neither did she know how Crane fretted over her absence, fearing she had fallen to some unknown peril, blaming himself for having left her, till Vandrel fussed at him, saying that if he did not cease to carry on so, she would soon have two patients instead of one. Nor did Aurora guess at the havoc wrought upon the city that had nestled at the foot of the craggy pinnacle from whence it derived its name. Tor, the city of the Menhir before which Frayne had given oath of fealty to the One, Tor, the prosperous city of merchants, the boasted center of the world, was no more.

Those who escaped the devastation told the tale of the coming of the Bodan, the messengers of doom that swoop down upon the unsuspecting to ravage and destroy. Yet they are only the harbingers of a greater force of upheavel yet to come. And so it was with Tor. First visited by the monstrous emanations of an ancient evil, many fled into the fertile plains with naught but the clothes on their backs, while others sought to barricade themselves along with all their cherished possessions behind solid doors. But in the end not even the barriers wrought from Sedgewick lumber could save them from the molten rock spewing from the pinnacle of Tor.

Crane, the shape-changer, had himself witnessed the aftermath of destruction some three days following the flight of the enchantress from Skorl. He had come in the shape of a large falcon, Vandrel having forbidden him simply to think himself to the black fortress.

"Don't be a fool, lad," she had said, her old eyes

213

wise behind the spectacles. "You said yourself the tower was ready to tumble down about your ears before ever you left it. There's no telling what you'll find, and it would hardly do to materialize inside a solid pile of rubble, now would it."

Janine, too, had proven uncommonly stubborn in her opposition to his proposed venture, but much to his surprise his former slave was against the plan no matter what unorthodox method of travel he might choose.

"She is Banat-ur-zarcun-nar, the Daughter of the Golden Fire," she insisted, and he had been stricken to the core at sight of the violet eyes blazing up at him with a woman's fiery passion. "And the dragon of Seraisharaqa is with her. Why can you not understand that she has no need for you to take such risks with your life? I have seen her call down the fire of Gawr and with a word command Al-tabl-ur-ras, the Drum of the Heavens, to rise. I tell you she has come to no harm."

Still, though he heeded Vandrel's strictures against using the more direct method of attaining his desired destination, he could not bring himself to give over the nagging conviction that Aurora was in some sort of peril. He could not explain it even to himself. It was just something he felt. Besides, there was a more pressing reason to find the elusive enchantress than just his vague premonition of danger. There was Elwindolf to consider, as well. And even if Janine kept to her word never again to speak to Amir-al-maskharat, the Lord of Fools, he had to return to Skorl to find out what had happened to Aurora, if he could.

Thus, one morning before even the sun had risen above the treetops of Endrith's Forest, Crane went one last time to the sickroom wherein Elwindolf lay as one who had already passed beyond the borders of death. His eyes, sunken into fleshless hollows of suffering, were open as always, fixed and staring on something only they could see. The young mage shivered, wondering at the indomitable will that would not let his friend die. For not all of Vandrel's healing herbs or magic potions could lure the man-wolf's soul back from wherever it wandered. He was *faege*, had declared the scholar in the Old Tongue, her wrinkled face looking suddenly weary and aged, as Crane had never before beheld it. Elwindolf, Wolf-Friend of the elves, walked with death, his spirit yearning after the dead soul of the Father-Wolf, Phelan, whom the man-wolf had slain. Nor, not knowing of the oath he had sworn to the enchantress, could Vandrel explain what unearthly bond kept him from abandoning the poor tortured body wasting hourly away, till already there was the look of the wraith about him. The wounds were bad enough, for he had sustained injuries that to any other might easily have proven mortal, and without Vandrel's skill at healing, most certainly would have done. It was the poison of the hyppohornbora that she could not combat, poison that withered flesh and ate at the will till the victim, should he live so long, begged for the mercy of death. For there was no known cure, save only for an infusion of blood into a vein of the victim—blood that came from one who was of the children of Shin, the Moon Goddess.

"You might as well look to Shin herself to come

215

down and cure him," Vandrel had declared in despair, "as to expect to come across one of the Shintari. So far as I know, no one's ever even caught a glimpse of that legendary tribe of hunters—except, of course, for Aurora and Frayne—and lived to tell of it. No, I'm afraid it'll take a miracle to pull him out of the coil he's got himself in this time."

Crane, gazing upon the hunter's ravaged frame, silently cursed the enchantress for not being there. If anyone could have found one of the silver-haired children of Shin, she could. Blast! What sort of mess had she fashioned for herself this time? he fretted, chastising himself for not having brought her with him to Vandrel's cottage when he'd had the chance.

"I'm going to find her, Elwindolf," he vowed, grasping the frail hand lying lifelessly on top of the counterpane. "I'll bring Aurora back. Then we'll see about this business of an antidote."

But he had not found her, nor anyone who might have seen a raven-haired girl borne upon the back of a fire-breathing dragon. Indeed, there had been not a living soul left in all that lava-strewn rubble that once had been the fabulous city of Tor.

Nor had there been much of anything else, reflected the young shape-changer, coming to rest in the topmost branches of a tree. He was exceedingly weary and depressed, nor had he had a morsel to eat for over a day and a night, which did not improve one whit his dour outlook on life. If only he could get out of this blasted shape and just think himself back to Vandrel and Janine! But for the time being he seemed stuck with the feathered façade of a bird, though he could not for the life of him figure out just how he had happened to fall into it, for he had thought that with the creatures from the Flux on the loose it would be far less risky to travel down the Glendaron as far as Tor in fish-form. Still, no sooner had he waded waist-deep into water cold enough to freeze the bristles off a boar and willed himself to become a fine specimen of a rainbow trout, than what must he do but turn into a blasted falcon! It was a wonder he had not drowned, and even though he had managed to extricate himself from the river, it had taken him at least ten miles or more to stop shivering from the chill he had suffered as a result of his dunking.

"Well, what now, birdbrain?" he asked himself and tried to ignore the rumbling in his belly. If only he had a little something to tide him over till he made it back to Vandrel's hidden glen. He could always think a little better on a full stomach than an empty one, and he had yet to come up with an argument convincing enough to persuade Vandrel to let him try Lil's spell of summoning to bring Aurora to them. Drat it all, they couldn't let Elwindolf slip away without giving it everything they had. And besides, none of them would rest easy till they knew the enchantress hadn't perished in the devastation of Skorl.

It was then he spotted far below him a hare behaving in a most peculiar manner. Indeed, it appeared to be crippled, for as soon as it made any attempt to leap from the small clearing at the base of the tree, it flopped and floundered in a pitiful manner. His curiosity aroused, Crane brashly determined on a closer look. The notion of hare roasted on a spit over an open fire, after all, was not all that unappealing, if that is, he could manage to get the spell right that would change him back into himself again. Flinging caution to the winds, the shape-changer launched himself into the air, then, folding his wings, plummeted straight for the hapless creature.

Perhaps, being a man in the shape of a falcon, he should have recognized a trap when he saw one, but he was Crane, who ever leaped before he looked, and, besides, he was tired and nearly ravenous with hunger. Too late, he saw the cord that bound the rabbit's hind legs together. Before he could reverse his headlong flight into folly, a net shot out at him from the cover of a thicket and he was fairly caught.

Instantly a tall, slender form emerged from the concealing brush to come toward him. In seconds the net was secured, Crane helpless within it. Apprehending the futility of beating his wings against the mesh, the shape-changer ceased to struggle.

"So, little cousin of Gesh, you are wise as well as handsome," observed his captor in obvious satisfaction. "It is well, for you will learn quickly to obey your new master."

With something of awe and a great deal of surprise, Crane blinked up into the exquisitely beautiful countenance of a silver-haired girl with translucent ivory skin and eyes of a light, piercing blue flecked with dazzling emerald green. She was tall, easily topping six feet, guessed the stupefied young mage, and her slender limbs were well defined with muscle. She was scantily clad, in a leather breechclout and a soft buckskin vest lined with silver fox fur and laced across the front with rawhide thongs. Her long legs were wrapped in leggings to the knee and her feet were graced with supple sandals. With a long-bladed knife slung in a sheath from a leathern girdle about her narrow waist and leather bands about the slim wrists, she looked, every inch of her, a huntress.

Crane, stunned by the sight of the magnificent creature, failed to notice when he began suddenly to change. One moment he was a proud peregrine and the next a tall, skinny youth trussed, knees to the chin, within the incommodious confines of a net designed for a chicken hawk.

"For pity's sake, get me out of this!" he wailed, too tightly bound even to save himself from toppling ignominiously on his face.

For a seeming eternity he was treated to a pregnant silence broken only by the ineffectual threshing of the hare attempting to escape its tether. He had begun to wonder if his captor had simply vanished into the woods, when a low, throaty laugh broke across the uneasy stillness. Working his head to one side, he managed to catch a glimpse of sandaled feet planted shoulder-width apart a scant foot from his nose. Then, seeing the razor-sharp blade of a knife coming at him with terrifying deliberation, he flinched and squeezed shut his eyes.

"The gods preserve me!" he gasped and nearly swooned as he felt the swift slash of the knife at his back. Then all at once he was free.

"Who and what are you, little man, that you may take on the form of a falcon?" queried the girl, watching the flailing mage struggling to disentangle himself from the ruined net.

219

"Little man?" thought the shape-changer, red-faced from more than his exertions. By the gods, he would wager he topped her generous height by at least an inch or more. Then Crane glanced up into the marvelous eyes and was stricken by a haunting shadow of sadness in their depths not quite banished by the lingering smile upon her lips, and unaccountably his momentary pique was utterly banished.

"Er—Crane. My name is Crane," he stammered, realizing of a sudden that she was waiting for an answer.

"Crane? But that is the name of a bird far different from the cousin of Gesh. Yet it suits you somehow," she added, observing the long, lanky frame unfolding from its undignified sprawl upon the ground. "Tell me how it is that you have come to Freyga in the guise of a messenger of Shin, the Moon Goddess?"

The mage, busy dusting himself off, jerked suddenly upright.

"D-did you say 'Freyga'?" he demanded, feeling the hairs at the nape of his neck stand up. Immediately he could have bit his tongue as he beheld the girl retreat behind a cold, forbidding mask.

"You have heard that name before," she declared flatly, her hand straying toward the knife at her belt. "Tell me how that may be, when the law of Shin forbids any outworlder to behold the camp of the children and live."

Nervously the youth shifted his weight from one foot to the other. Egads, she was everything that Aurora had said she was, and more, he decided, quite certain that his life hung by a thread unless he did some fast talking or whisked himself away. Yet it took only a fleeting recollection of Elwindolf, lingering at the edge of death, to dissuade the shape-changer from the latter alternative, except as the very last resort. The hunter had fought overwhelming odds with a fierce courage such as few men possess, saving the shape-changer's life half a dozen times at the risk of his own. He, Crane, Krim's bumbling grandson, could surely stand up to one woman alone, even if she was Freyga, the Warrior-Priestess of the children of Shin!

"Actually I am not unfamiliar with the story of Freyga, who chose exile rather than to see Shamar, the Winter-King, wed to Aurora, Elf-Daughter and Enchantress of the Glade," admitted the youth judiciously, his gaze studiously avoiding the slim hand that closed convulsively on the knife handle, half-drawing the blade from its sheath. "In a sense I was there at the time, though I missed seeing the unfolding of the tale. I was a hunk of cheese tucked away in one of Frayne's packs, though they never guessed it. Later I became a mouse, then a blue chalcedony—the god's stone that brings the bearer good fortune—and finally a vulture. I have the power of a shape-changer, you see, the legacy bequeathed me by my mother Shellandra, the Sea-Nymph, whom my father Tarn, Son of Krim, ensnared with a will-web because he was captivated by her singing, as is anyone who hears the song of a sea-nymph. But that's another story. Of course, if you're interested in hearing it . . . ?"

But it was soon made readily apparent that the

warrior-priestess of Shin had not the least desire to hear Crane's family history.

"Cease your babbling, fool, lest you would have me cut out your tongue," she commanded in no uncertain terms. "I would hear only the account of the Enchantress Who Has No Name. She, who challenged the judgment of Gesh and then sent him away. The outworlder, who came bearing the Undeciphered Symbols of Power and riding upon the back of the White Elk of good omen. Tell me what you know of that one, Crane, Son of Tarn, and let there be no more of your witless ramblings."

Crane, who naturally took exception to being referred to either as witless or as a fool, snapped abruptly to attention, his earnest young face rigid with dislike.

"Well, I like that," he declared in no little disgust. "You've about as much notion of friendly hospitality as a polecat on a rampage. Maybe I did drop in uninvited, but I fail to see how I was supposed to know the hare was not here for the taking. If you must know, I haven't had a bite to eat for so long that I was ready to devour the creature, hide, hair, and tail. But since then, I seem to have lost my appetite. So, if you don't mind, I'll just be on my way. This is one shape-changer who knows when he's not welcome."

Wheeling, Crane started to stalk away in a fine huff, when suddenly Freyga's command to halt cracked like the lash of a whip at his back. Instantly he froze, the nerves prickling along the vulnerable length of his spine. He jumped at the almost furtive touch of a hand upon his arm, and whipping his head around, gazed with a sense of startled wonder

222

into curiously defenseless eyes.

"Wait. Do not go, I-I beg you," said the imperious warrior-priestess hardly above a whisper. Then, letting her hand drop, she turned convulsively away. "It is true that I have not the gift for—for making strangers welcome in my camp. I am—I *was* Shintari, you see, and more. For I was the chosen priestess of Shin, the Guardian of Gesh, who was the emissary of the goddess. The children of Shin are a jealous race, who would have none share in their secrets, for they are Shin's secrets, the mysteries of a goddess." She drew a deep, shuddering breath. "It is—difficult to learn new ways, and yet I must try. Freyga is priestess of Shin no more, nor even Shintari. She must make her own life, her own place in this strange world of mortal men."

Freyga turned then to look again upon the youth.

"It would give me pleasure if you stayed to share my fire, to sup and perhaps to exchange tidings of the world."

She stood proud and tall, her back held straight as a spear, and, indeed, her voice had been gruff when she spoke. Still, Crane could not mistake the soft light of pleading in the remarkable eyes no matter how stubbornly she sought to conceal it.

"I would be honored to accept your very generous invitation," he said, steeling himself, "if I were not sorely pressed for time." Seeing the stubborn jaw go rigid, the shape-changer hurried to explain. "Freyga, someone's life hangs by a thread, and strangely enough only you can save him. No. Please don't turn away. I'm telling you the truth. Nearly a se'ennight past, a brave man did battle with a fearsome beast and

223

was wounded. Since then he has lain so close to death that if it were anyone else, I wouldn't have given a groat for his life. I wouldn't have, that is, until I found out who and what you are. You see, the only antidote for the poison in his veins is the blood of one of the children of Shin."

Freyga stiffened, her eyes flashing dangerously.

"You're lying," she stated flatly, "if you are speaking of the poison of the hyppohornbora. The wizards of Gnath banished them to the Flux long ages past."

"And now they have come back again. Or at least some of them have. You see, there was this sorceress who put together a magic potion, but it didn't do what she had planned for it to do. It created a rift between our world and the Flux of Timelessness, and before Aurora could seal it with the Circlet of Kerr, a score or more of the creatures of the Flux passed over."

"Aurora? She who was to wed the Winter King?" queried the priestess with rapierlike swiftness.

Crane gulped. Egads, they were back to that again.

"Yes, the very same. Only she didn't marry your precious king because she was in love with Frayne, and now Frayne's trapped in the Flux and the gods only know what's happened to the enchantress. So if you want to hightail it back to where you came from, there's nothing to stop you," he ended bitterly, and thrusting his hands deep into his coat pockets, gave the gimlet-eyed Freyga the cold shoulder.

Well, he had certainly muffed that one, he thought morosely, wondering how he was going to face Vandrel with the tale that, after stumbling across one of the elusive children of Shin, he had managed to return home without her. Blast! Who was he trying to fool? He couldn't just walk away. Not with Elwindolf's life on the line. He'd never be able to live with himself. No, he would just have to eat humble pie, then beg, bribe, or cajole the dratted female into going with him. And if that didn't work, he could always just . . .

"You will take me to this warrior who dies of the hyppohornbora's poison, that I may judge for myself the truth of your tale," spoke up the huntress, much to Crane's amazement. "But beware, shape-changer. I will know if you have laid a trap for me, and if it is not as you have said, you will pay dearly for your falsehood."

Crane, experiencing a sudden blaze of joy, had to restrain himself from letting out a whoop.

"It's no trap, Freyga," he said instead, grinning from ear to ear. "I swear it."

Crane sat on one of the benches in Vandrel's kitchen, his elbows propped on bony knees and his shoulders hunched in weariness. Egads, how much longer must he wait before someone thought to let him know what was going on in the attic room above him?

It seemed an eternity since Vandrel, in an absolute dither of resurging hope, had bustled Freyga upstairs, abandoning a disgruntled young shape-changer to a solitary vigil. At first he had hoped she might at least dispatch Janine from her post at the stricken man's bedside to keep him company, but he had been doomed to disappointment and thus, left to his own unrewarding thoughts, he had nearly worn a path in Vandrel's hand-woven rug and himself to the edge of utter physical exhaustion.

The youth's head came up with a jerk at the sudden creaking protest of the wooden stair. As if hauled up by a rope around his neck, Crane shot to his feet. Then he beheld Vandrel framed in the soft glow of candlelight, her face older than he remembered it, and suddenly he felt his stomach queasy with hunger and a nameless sort of dread.

"I've done all *I* can," she said in answer to his unasked question. "Now it's up to him." Setting the candle on the table, she sank heavily onto the bench across from Crane and shook her head in weary bafflement. "I'll never know what's kept him alive this long. It's like he wants to let go, but he can't. He seems to be waiting for something—for a sign, maybe." She heaved a long sigh, then added wearily, "Or for someone."

Thus it was that the man-wolf's friends despaired of his life, while somewhere far away the enchantress muttered disjointedly and writhed upon her bed of fronds, as, hollow-eyed and pale as wraiths, Garwin, Gleb, and Thegne the Elder appeared to her in the twisted coils of a nightmare.

"Go away. Leave me be," she mumbled, for they would seem to accuse her with their hollow eyes. Why? What had she done?

"What is your name, Anduan? What is your name?" echoed in her mind like a bitter accusation, then, as if in obedience to her command, they vanished. Yet what next appeared was more horrifying still.

"Oh, gods," Aurora groaned, seeing the creatures of darkness, aingealwyrms and iaronnycorns, cutting a wide swath of destruction through Endrith's Forest as they made their way from Grendylmere east toward Hawthorn Glade.

'Twas Gleb, gathering mushrooms by the light of the crescent moon, who heard them first, the crash of trees and roar of flame devouring a forest that had ever been protected by Endrith's magic. The little elf dressed in forest green, his peaked hat comically askew, and his plump cherubic cheeks above the soft brown beard puffing in and out as he whistled a lively tune, paused suddenly and straightened, his head cocked in an attitude of listening.

"The horn, Gleb!" mumbled the enchantress, her head turning feverishly from side to side. "Sound the warning!"

As if sensing his foster-daughter's alarm, Gleb lifted to his lips the curved horn slung on a cord across his chest and shoulder and blew three short blasts. Then he was running, his face turned back over his shoulder and his short chubby legs pumping for all they were worth.

"Gleb, look before you!" Aurora cried, but the swarm of mudgeons swooping from the treetops was upon the frightened elf before he ever saw them. Helpless in the three-toed grasp of four of the winged gremlin-kin, Gleb was borne, kicking and sputtering elfin curses, into the night, while behind him Hawthorn Glade erupted into flame.

In a cold sweat Aurora bolted upright.

"Kev," she groaned, weeping bitter tears. "Kev, why do you not come? I cannot stay here any longer. My father-elves have need of me."

227

"But I am here," observed a sleepy voice in some bewilderment. "In truth, I have never left you."

Aurora, scarce daring to believe her ears, swiped impatiently at her eyes with the back of her hand then stared in no little astonishment at the great, hulking beast curled up beside her, his ruby eyes glowing like embers in the darkness.

"Kev! But how can this be?" she gasped, for, indeed, it was he. "How can any of this be?" marveled the enchantress, as, feeling Andruvien throbbing against her wrist, she gazed down her length to discover herself fully clothed, her pack strapped firmly to her back and heavy with the weight of the cloak of power, and at her side Guthsweord, her mother's sword, and Glaiveling, the elfin blade.

"Was it then only a dream?" she murmured, but, nay, it was something more, she soon decided, for neither cut nor bruise nor even the faintest sign of any injury could she find on her shoulder or her hand or anywhere.

Truly it was a marvelous place, she thought, smiling to herself. But then 'twould have to be, for where else could Kev, the magician's dragon, have brought her but to Myrialoc, the country wrought of the stuff of magic.

Still smiling, she turned fondly to the dragon, yawning a great, dragonish yawn.

"Come, Kev, we've a long journey before us, and 'tis time we were on our way."

"A long journey?" echoed the dragon, snapping to eager attention. "Do you mean 'we' as in 'you and me'?"

"Aye," she said, laughter springing to her lips.

Then she gazed out into the starlit night, her eyes shimmering with a light all their own. "Aye, my friend," she murmured softly, "it shall be you and I, bound for the distant isles of Kylandros and, the gods willing, for Frayne!"

Thus was the mockery of Somn silenced, Aurora's wounded spirit healed and made whole, for she knew that the dream of her father-elves had been a true one sent by the god to summon her once more to the quest for her name, the name of an enchantress bound by destiny to Frayne. And, indeed, only in freeing him could she find herself.

And so it was that Kev, the dragon of Myrialoc, took the enchantress on his back and bore her from the mystic plane of Hylmut into the star-ridden sky. West they went, soaring on dragon wings over the great Plain of Shintari and the barren Land of Erg, till at last, coming to the Sea of Westerness, they left the land behind. Still they veered not from their course, but, following the path of the setting sun, headed ever west, hopefully to Kylandros and perchance the answer to a riddle.

And far behind them in a cozy little cottage tucked away in a hidden valley, Vandrel and a weary young shape-changer hearkened to a glad cry.

"Hakim Vandrel, Crane, hurry! The man of the forest comes back into himself. He is awake, Hakim. I beg you to come and see!"

Chapter 8

In the time of the Beginnings elves roamed the seas on sailing ships driven before Thymfolthrall, the wind-wraith that comes upon command. They were the Droons, the "seafarers," compelled by the vision of Oglach, the servant of Nem, who is the One, to depart from Blissia in search of Cridhelann, the Heartland, wherein they were to dwell as keepers of the Great Forest created by Nem. The record of their journey has been obscured in the mists of time, but 'tis certain many mortal years fraught with strange sights and harrowing adventures passed ere they came at last to a great body of land into which Oglach, proclaiming it to be the Cridhelann of his god-sent dream, would disembark. But not so Gallad, the Bold, and many others of the elfin tribe over whom the sea had cast the spell of wanderlust. Summoning the wind-wraith once more, they set sail to search out other lands, while the followers of Oglach pushed inland to the wooded hills and dales at the heart of the land. Gwyddllan, they named it, or

"Woodland" in the language of men, and, forsaking their previous nomadic existence, they became Hraldoon, "dwellers of the forest."

Many years passed in peace, and the Hraldoons became ever more at home in Cridhelann, till Blissia, Gallad, and their seafaring cousins were little more than memories preserved in elfin songs. Thus it was that not until the twilight of the Age of Throm when the dark forces loosed by Dred drove the Droonish ships ashore once again upon Cridhelann were the strange tales of the islands of Drui first related to the elves of Gwyddllan.

Far to the west they lie, obscured in cloud and surrounded by perilous shoals. Fraught with savage storms that leap out of a calm sea like fierce beasts of prey upon passing ships, they are steeped in mystery, for rare is the vessel or the crew hardy enough to brave the Maurstom, the dark maw of the Vorbyss through which one must pass to enter the Straits of Tantalleth and the enchanted sea of Drui. Yet one such vessel was the *Wind-Harp*, Gallad's ship, with Gallad's crew, who, following the haunting euphony of the Tantalleth, were swallowed up by the Maurstom. Cloaking his vessel in an elfin spell of concealment, the intrepid Droon slipped past the grasping arms of the Snaigh, the sea serpents that reach out of the black void to ensnare seacraft, and thus emerged beyond the pall of darkness in a wondrous mist-enshrouded sea sighing songs of enchantment meant to lure the unsuspecting on to the treacherous coral reefs of the Tantalleth. And before him, looming out of the mist like a brooding world veiled in secrecy, was the island Gallad named "Saur," the Lizard, for its pointed snout reaching out at one end into the still waters and the long, slender tail of jagged reef trailing into the sea at the other. 'Twas on this island that Gallad disembarked with a small party of elves and was never seen again.

It is told in the Song of Druce, the Droonish bard, that the Ban-sidhe swallowed up the *Wind Harp* and bore her far from her moorings so that when at last the shriek of the dread spirit carried in the swirl of cloud and storm departed, no sign was there of the Tantalleth or of the enchanted islands, but only the small fleet of Droonish ships, which had waited beyond the Maurstom for Gallad's return, and the great, swelling sea, boundless and empty all around them.

Gallad's fate was taken as a sign from Nem that no elf should again venture forth over the sea till the Ages of Magic should give way to Reason in the Realm, whereupon the magic folk shall return again to Blissia, the Land of Blessed Dreams. Then it is written in the Tome of Prophecy that men shall be scattered like seeds among the stars and with them they will carry the Light of Truth and the Darkness of Dread throughout all the worlds within the Nous, the Universal Mind of the Creator. And thus shall the struggle begin anew, this time to be waged without the power of magic or magic folk but among men who, with powers of their own making, rule the Universe as gods. Still, that is a story for another time, a time far removed from the flight of the enchantress and the dragon of Myrialoc in search of the isles of Kylandros.

With a start Aurora awakened from the light sleep

into which she had fallen just before daybreak of the third day. Though the sun was well above the shimmering horizon of foam-rippled sea, she shivered. How odd that it should be so cold skimming beneath the ceiling of white, vaporous clouds, she ruefully mused, blowing into her hands and chaffing them against the chill air. Had she previously given the matter any thought, she would have supposed that the airy heights, being so much nearer to the sun, must surely be blessed with uncommon warmth. Yet she had quickly learned that that was not the case at all, that, indeed, if anything, she was like to turn quite blue from the cold. For the first time she was glad to have the detested raiment of the man-beast to wear, and still it was not enough to keep her warm. In truth, had it not been for the marvleous cloak given her by Endrith upon her return from the quest for the unicorn horn, she doubted not that she would be in dire straits indeed.

In the forlorn hope of putting her misery from her mind for a time, the enchantress drew a handful of dried herbs and seeds from her pouch and ate her meager breakfast with less than relish. How much longer could they go on? she wondered bleakly. Already her small supply of food and water was perilously close to being depleted, and Kev had had neither sustenance nor sleep since they had departed on the ill-conceived trek. Though she was not well-versed in dragon-lore, it seemed highly improbable that even a dragon of Myrialoc could go on forever without food and rest. Still, thus far he had seemed virtually indefatigable, she thought, experiencing a surge of affection for the valiant beast. Then, feeling herself beginning to nod off again, the enchantress forced herself to sit straighter in the saddle Kev had rummaged from her grandfather's peculiar collection of odds and ends still cached here and there in the magic country of Myrialoc. Carved from the shell of a giant tortoise and luxuriously covered with soft fur, it had once belonged to Chandra, the daughter of the Dragon-King, Lothe of Garn.

For a time Aurora lost herself in a fanciful daydream of the beautiful young spell-singer as she fled the Island of the Dragon-Lords with Rab, the magician, who had tricked Lothe into giving him the princess's hand in marriage. Like as not they had bestrode this very saddle, mused the spell-singer's granddaughter, seeing Chandra perched on the back of a mighty dragon, her lover's arms wrapped securely about her. Inevitably such fancies caused a rending of her heart, as she pictured not Rab and his bride soaring on dragon's wings, but Frayne and Aurora.

Oh, gods, she must not think such things. She could not bear it. Reeling in the saddle from the unexpected thrust of her reawakened sense of loss, she squinted her eyes against the brilliance of the sun slanting through the wispy trails of cloud and strained to pick out some sign of the islands in the vast expanse of sparkling sea. But her vision was clouded by the sting of tears and by the ache of weariness that dulled her mind and dragged at her body.

"How much farther, Kev?" she demanded, sending her thoughts outward to the dragon. "Are you certain we are on the right course? I shouldn't like to think we are lost out here hundreds of leagues from anything."

"Well, I can't be absolutely sure, never having been there before," came the answering wisp of thought, "but I think we cannot be so very far from the magic isles. It's something I feel inside, you understand."

But she did not understand at all how Kev, who had never ventured from Myrialoc until she herself had called him to her atop Tor, could possibly be so sure just where the islands of Kylandros lay in the Sea of Westerness. Yet he had insisted from the first that he needed neither compass nor map to take them there. And, indeed, he had never wavered from his course. It was as if he had been there before, a long time past, and was now guided by a distant memory, she mused whimsically. Upon which it inexplicably came to her to wonder what had become of the dragon that had borne her grandparents back to Myrialoc. Doubtless Chandra had sent it home again, she decided, and taking out a small strip of prickly ash bark, began absently to chew it that the natural stimulant might help to keep her awake.

Nevertheless, it was not long before the enchant-ress fell once more into a light doze, her cheek nestled in the crook of her arm propped against the *braich*, the sturdy brace rising in a loop at the front of the saddle that served as a handhold for the rider. Thus she did not see far below her the swirling pall of darkness seem to leap from the shimmering sea or the dark shape belching fire rise out of the fuliginous cloud on powerful wings. Larger and larger it loomed, a great beast glinting emerald and gold in the sunlight and ascending on a deliberate course for Kev and the enchantress, but the dragon of Myrialoc, himself close to utter exhaustion, likewise failed to apprehend their danger, as muttering beneath his breath, he concentrated on maintaining the rhythmic beat of leaden wings.

"Oh, aye, trust old Kev to find a speck in the ocean. Old Kev, who's naught but an empty-headed dunderhead. Why, oh, why did I not just stay in Myrialoc where I belong? Then would my master's heir yet be safe and myself not ready to drop into the blasted sea."

'Twas then he caught a glimpse of something hurtling at him from below. Hastily dropping his tail and braking himself with furled wings, Kev was only in the nick of time to avoid the rake of cruel talons as the great beast shot past, shrieking a blood-chilling cry of venomous dislike.

"Good gods, what was that?" gasped the enchantress, jarred to sudden wakefulness.

Kev, dipping and curling round to keep a startled eye on the creature vanishing into the clouds above them, could not fail to notice the distinct similarity between himself and their bellicose assailant.

"By the One, I believe it must have been a dragon," he observed, scarce able to contain his astonishment at having nearly collided with a real, live specimen of *Draca* countless leagues from anywhere. But then Aurora was shouting something at him with uncommon agitation and it was only by dint of immense concentration that he finally understood that they were in immediate peril. Indeed, the strange beast was even then swooping down at them with terrifying speed, the wicked, taloned feet extended with what would seem something less than a gesture of friendly welcome.

"Yipes!" shrieked Kev, and veering precipitously to one side, escaped by a hair's breadth being clutched in dragon claws. Without waiting to see what the ill-tempered creature intended doing next, Kev made a mad dash for the safety of the clouds.

"He's coming after us!" yelled the enchantress. "Kev! Hurry! Egads, he's on your tail!"

However, the unfortunate dragon, his great strength having been already taxed by three days of nonstop flight, was quite obviously at the disadvantage in what showed every manifestation of being a grossly uneven race. Puffing smoke instead of flame, Kev strained heavenward, while his adversary inevitably gained, till Aurora, staring back in dread fascination, saw clearly the fierce red glitter of dragon eyes closing fast upon them.

"Oh, Kev, it's no use," she cried. "We must turn about and fight."

"Aye, *waerloga*, turn and fight, if you dare," rang the dragon's challenge as orange flame seared the air behind them.

"'*Waerloga*'?" echoed the enchantress, startled, for in the Old Tongue, a *waerloga* was a traitor. But that was absurd. Whom could Kev, a creation of her grandfather's experiments in animated ceramic sculpture, possibly have betrayed? Instantly she was overwhelmed by a notion so boggling in its utter plausibility that she could not imagine how she had failed to consider it before. Kev must be her grandmother's very own dragon, whom Rab, the Crystal-Master, had transformed into glass, even as he had similarly transmuted Myrialoc into crystal long ages past. No wonder Kev had been so certain he knew the way to the magic isles. The Kingdom of the Dragon-Lords must surely be one of them!

No sooner had the thought come to mind than Kev groaned and perceptibly faltered in his flight.

"Egads, it's all coming back to me," he shuddered and nearly unseated Aurora as he dropped suddenly into a hair-raising dive.

"KEV!" shrieked the enchantress, clutching desperately to the *braich*. "Kev, for the gods' sake, come about!"

It appeared, however, that Kev either did not hear her or that he was powerless to do anything about their perilous descent toward the roiling black cloud growing more ominously distinct with every passing second. Indeed, it seemed they must surely plunge into its forbidding midst and from thence into whatever lay beneath, when, just as precipitously as Kev had begun to plummet, he bottomed out to skim gracefully scant feet above the steamy mass.

Aurora, only barely managing to swallow the bile that had risen to her throat, heard the dragon muttering distractedly as he began to circle in a wide arc.

"It's here somewhere. I know it is. If only everything weren't so blasted hazy."

"Why not ask me, Kevyn-rhi of Garn?" insinuated a chilling voice from behind them.

Kev whipped around to hover in dragon fashion, with head up and tail trailing down, and thus came face to face with their assailant, whom he had quite forgotten in the turmoil of recalling a past he had not dreamed he had.

"Dalchor!" he rasped with such uncharacteristic animosity that Aurora was taken totally by surprise. Yet no less unsettling was the single name that he had uttered. Dalchor! The dragon who had ravaged the countryside in the War of the Mages and who had carried Krim to the summit of Estrelland in the aborted attempt to steal the Vendrenin. What was *he* doing so far north of Careg-sunth, the black marble cliffs that formed the southern boundaries of the Known Lands?

"Even so," acknowledged the villain of a hundred tales, inclining his horned head with an arrogance that grated on the nerves.

"There may be a great deal that escaped me as I lay dreaming in Rab's Crystal Kingdom," observed the wholly astonishing dragon of Myrialoc with unearthly calm. "Yet I seem to recollect quite clearly that you and all your ilk have ever been denied the corridors of Drui. By what right do you claim knowledge of the Dracadorus?"

"But the secret of the Dragon Door fell to me long ages past," Dalchor replied. "Now *I* rule the corridors above the Sea of Drui, I, Dalchor of Careg-sunth, once shunned by the proud race of dragon-kings and by your kind, their puling dragon-thralls. I am Rhi, and you are Waerloga, the traitor to your tribe."

The unlovely lips curled in an obviously satisfied smirk to reveal twin rows of snaggle teeth. Green and gold, with a wing-span of ninety feet or more, he was easily of a size with Kev, who measured some eight rods from nose-tip to tail-end. Yet Dalchor was all malevolent fire and ice encased in steely armor, and Aurora shivered at the thought of the bone-weary Kev in combat with the legendary dragon-rogue of Caregsunth. But not so Kev, who seemed determined to wave the red flag before his age-old enemy.

"If in obeying the wishes of the Princess Chandra to bear her from Garn I may be judged *waerloga*, then so be it," Kev answered with quiet dignity. "I am not ashamed. It was ordained by the gods that Chandra should wed Rab of Zelig and thus take up the strands of a greater destiny than could be hers as dragon-queen of Garn. Mayhap I have been gone too long, but I am returned now, and so I say to you: Begone, Dalchor, lest you incite the wrath of Kevyn-rhi."

Aurora, listening to the transformed dragon of Myrialoc, could scarce believe her ears. Was this the same Kev who had cowered before Frayne's sword lest he be shattered into a multitude of proliferating glass frangibles? Was this the childlike creature who, ignorant of the fact that dragons could fly, had had to wait for a young shape-changer to instruct him in dragon-flight? Nay. Kev, her dear, childlike dragon, was no more. Dalchor, and perchance proximity to Garn, which, she doubted not, lay somewhere beneath the pall of cloud, had awakened him to his true being kept dormant through the years within Rab's sustaining web of magic. He was Kev no longer, but Kevyn-rhi, chief of the dragon-lords of Garn.

"Fool!" thundered Dalchor, no longer smiling. "Can you truly believe you are a match for me? I have seen you fly. Think you I cannot see how soft you are grown? Bah! You could not offer fair challenge to a dragon *flegge* ready for its first flight."

"Then so shall it be," uttered Kev, undaunted, though he knew himself to be less indeed than the Kevyn-rhi of old. "I ask only that I be granted time to set the heir of Garn safely down. This battle is none of hers."

A protest sprang to Aurora's lips, but it was Dalchor who voiced it.

"It is the pride of the race of kings that the princes of Garn bestride their champions into battle. So shall it be with this one, misbegotten though she be," decreed the usurper of Rhi, laughing hideously. Then, without warning, he attacked, lunging at Kev's exposed throat with deadly fangs.

Yet it is not given to a dragon-lord of Garn to be Rhi, lest he be gifted with both cunning and valor in battle. Kevyn-rhi had been no less than those who came before him. On the alert for treachery, the dragon of Myrialoc twisted sharply to the side, and striking with the swiftness of the adder, sank his teeth in Dalchor's neck behind the head. Shrieking in pain and rage, the emerald dragon writhed and twisted, slashing at Kev's underbelly with vicious claws, till Aurora, clinging desperately to saddle and *braich*, feared Kev must surely be disemboweled. Then the dragons had broken loose, Dalchor soaring on powerful wings into the sky with Kev fast behind.

It was as if the Usurper had kindled some ancient flame long dormant within the dragon of Myrialoc, as Kevyn-rhi swooped and soared in perfect synchronization with Dalchor, his weariness forgotten. And, indeed, it was the fighing spirit of a dragon-lord reawakened, the raging fire that burns within the

242

heart of Dracadern to slay the enemy or be slain. 'Twas this that had made them legendary as fearless and savage fighters. Nor was that all that inspired Kev's fierce pursuit of Dalchor, for along with all the other memories that had inundated his mind at the sight of the emerald dragon was the resurgence of an age-old hatred of Dracarog, the Rogue Dragons of the South, who had rebelled against the rule of Gathrhi in the old days to plunder the far lands in the name of Dred, and who had thus incited against dragons the enmity of all men. All men, that is, save for the Dragon-Kings of Garn.

Thus it was that Kev flew as one possessed, duplicating Dalchor in speed and endurance and in ferocity of attack. Time and again they careered apart to come together again, breathing flame and slashing at each other with rending claws and fangs, till Dalchor's overweening arrogance suffered an irreparable blight. Then did he know the icy clamp of fear within his entrails, for he saw at last that he was no match against Kevyn-rhi's insatiable fury. Without warning, he disengaged and streaked away, reaching for the clouds into which he might vanish, to fight another day. Yet, though terror lent strength to his wings, still was he unable to shake off his old enemy. Indeed, the dragon of Myrialoc was steadily gaining as Dalchor fled ever higher.

So swiftly did they rise that tears stung Aurora's eyes and the darkness of Somn threatened to flood her mind. Near to swooning, she felt Andruvien throb against her wrist, awakening her to crystal power pulsating through her veins. Instantly her vision cleared to reveal Dalchor beneath them as Kev shot

243

suddenly up at a nearly vertical slant. Then, with wings folded, he dropped his head to swoop with terrifying speed at the fleeing dragon. Aurora saw Dalchor veer sharply to the side, felt the powerful thrust of Kev's wings flaring out to catch the wind as he swerved in a tight arc with the other dragon. Then Kev was on him, the wicked talons biting deep, piercing the steely scales covering the dragon's back.

With a bloodcurdling shriek, the stricken Dalchor fell, carrying Kev and Aurora with him in a dizzying spiral of death.

"Kev, let him go!" shouted the enchantress, knowing full well that Dalchor would thus live to fight again. Yet to do otherwise was to die with him, which seemed pointless in the extreme.

It seemed an eternity had passed, though it could not have been more than a minute or two, and still the dragon of Myrialoc held grimly to the death hold, when finally Kev's head dropped with dreadful deliberation. Aurora heard the sickening crunch of bone. Dalchor gave a convulsive shudder and went suddenly limp, his spine neatly severed at the base of the serpentine neck. Then he was falling away, growing smaller and smaller, till, little more than an insignificant speck against the blue expanse of ocean, he plunged beneath the waves.

Aurora, hunched over the *braich* and shivering helplessly, stared dully at the mysterious pall enveloping the enchanted islands as Kev drifted slowly earthward. Silently she cursed, discovering her face wet with tears that would not stop. Egads, she was not a child to break down in the wake of danger, she chided herself, knowing in her heart that she wept for Kev, who had fought so magnificently. Instinctively she realized that things would never again be the same between them, for he had come once more into his own. Indeed, that other Kev, whom she had awakened along with Myrialoc from the magician's spell, had never been aught but a dream. When Rab had spun the dream-web about the marvelous creature, had he known that one day his heir would have need of the dauntless dragon to carry her to the land of her mother's fathers? Somehow she sensed that he had, and that in his wisdom he had granted Kevyn-rhi a merciful oblivion during the long years of waiting. Inevitably, it would have required time for the dragon to recover from centuries of sleep as measured in mortal years. Perhaps Rab had even intended that Kev should be as innocent as a child, in order to give Aurora and the dragon-lord of Garn time to form the sort of link that normally only a hatchling developed for a human. Whatever his reasons, she knew that she would always feel a special bonding with the dragon of Myrialoc, no matter how great the time and distance that might separate them, and for that she would be eternally grateful to her grandfather, the Master Magician of Sib.

The enchantress was not given further time to ponder her grandfather's motives, however, as Kev's thoughts impinged suddenly upon her own.

"We are come to the Dracardorus, Princess, which is known only to the dragon-lords of Garn. Or at least that was the case before Dalchor penetrated its secrets," he added rather apologetically, so that he sounded endearingly like the Kev of old.

"'Princess,' Kev?" she queried, smiling a trifle crookedly, for it had never occurred to her before that as Chandra's granddaughter, she was indeed a true princess of Garn. Somehow she was not easy with the notion. "I have been called many things, but never 'Princess.' Indeed, Aurora is sweeter to my ears by far and shall suit me well enough till I find my true name."

"Well, maybe," replied the dragon doubtfully, "but like as not the old King, be he still alive, will view things differently. You cannot avoid the fact that on Garn you are the Princess Aurora."

Princess Aurora, however, was paying no heed to what might very well have been a warning, as she soon made quite apparent.

"Sh-h, Kev! Listen. What is that marvelous sound—like a song of wind—or—waves washing against sand or of moonbeams dancing over still waters. Like a dream of quiet depths made wondrous with worlds of mystery, beckoning, beckoning. Oh, Kev, my heart is filled with an aching, a yearning for such loveliness as I have never seen before. Take me there at once, I beg you!"

"You mustn't heed the enchantments of the Tantelleth. They are sung by nixies and *meremagdens*. And sometimes even merrows, though *they* mostly do not venture far from Cymlic-niud, the Isle of Fair Desires, which lies much farther west and vanishes at the approach of outworlders—unless, of course, the seafarer happens to be cloaked in a spell of concealment. They are a shy and gentle folk, who love music above all things. But the nixies and *meremagdens* are mischievous and like nothing better than to beguile mariners, even going so far as to lure them onto the coral reefs of the Tantalleth if they can. So let there be no more talk of aches and yearnings," he added with a harshness that was so unlike him that it quite took Aurora by surprise. "Entering the mists of Drui even through the Dracadorus is hazardous enough without letting oneself fall to the allurement of the spell-singers and such."

Then, before the enchantress could puzzle out the vague feeling of unease Kev's tone had aroused in her, the dragon had slipped into the murky cloud with only a last-minute warning to hold tight no matter what happened.

It quickly proved that heeding Kev's final words of caution was not so easily done as might have been supposed, for no sooner had the thick curtain of fog closed about them than Aurora felt herself drifting into a pleasant quiescence, attended by a delicious torpor that was not quite sleep but yet not wakefulness either. Mesmerized by the beguiling song of the mermaids and nixies, the enchantress beheld tendrils of fog weaving dream-visions all around her, teasing and tormenting her with images of people and places she had known and loved—Garwin and Gleb seated beneath the Hawthorn Tree sent smoke rings wafting on a gentle breeze, while Minta and Valesia, nestled in the boughs of Truewood, Father-Oak, smiled and beckoned to her to join them. She saw Agrypha, Sky-Dancer, drifting on invisible pillars of air, and Tasha, Elk-Lord, limned against a pale morning sky as he stood atop a treeless ridge. Then it seemed that she wended a narrow path through a thicket of grasping willow, till finally she came to the

247

edge of a shimmering lake, and there, emerging like a god from the waters, was Frayne, his skin golden in the waning sunlight and sparkling with waterbeads.

"Oh, gods," she groaned, seeing him in all his manly beauty as she had that first day upon the shores of Grendylmere a lifetime ago. This time, too, she felt all the wonder of his glorious manhood, the powerful arms and shoulders, the muscled chest adorned with a golden mat of hair tapering to a V over the firm, flat belly. Then, she had gazed into silver-grey eyes as piercing as a falcon's and been spellbound, so that she hardly knew she had left her hiding place among the willows to go to him. Yet how much greater was her longing now!

She felt her hands loosening their grip upon the *braich*, knew herself to be leaning ever more perilously in the saddle and could not stop herself. There was Frayne, his arms outstretched to her, and she was so weary of the battle. Vaguely she heard the echo of Kev's thoughts, warning her to hold tight, telling her to heed not the enchantments of the nixies. But she was slipping from her precarious perch on the dragon, her fingers powerless to hold on.

"Frayne," she murmured deliriously. "Frayne . . ."

The image of Frayne shattered with the thrum of harp strings quivering golden in the air, and suddenly the enchantment was broken. Aurora, freed from the dream-web, clutched at the *braich* and quickly righted herself. Egads, what had happened to her? Had she truly been about to fling herself from Kev's back to certain death? Shuddering, she strained to hear the pure tones of the harp, like sweet sorrow

248

or magic wafting through the mists, but there was only the rush of wind in her ears and the heavy beat of her own heart gradually slowing to a normal pace. Had she merely dreamt it, after all?

Then Kev was through the pall and sailing on outspread wings toward a misty isle, rugged with sheer cliffs of weathered rock reaching down into an emerald sea.

"Saur," breathed the enchantress, recognizing from the Song of Drui the pointed snout and fluted tail of the island upon which Gallad had been stranded long ages past. "But is it Garn, too, the Kingdom of the Dragon-Lords?" she called out to Kev.

The dragon of Myrialoc answered not. Indeed, he seemed singularly preoccupied as he made for the bulge of the "Lizard's" back. And suddenly it came to the enchantress that the beat of the dragon's wings was ominously erratic. In truth he was wavering from his course, his great strength ebbing with each passing second. Then did Aurora's heart ache for Kev, who clearly was striving with every fiber of his being to reach the safety of the island. But he was flagging, falling below the steep ridge of barren rock, and at last she knew he would never make it to the top.

"Merciful gods, grant him aid," she pleaded, feeling the shudder that coursed through the length of the faltering dragon. "By the One, Kevyn-rhi must not be allowed to perish!"

It seemed the melliflous notes of the harpist's playing reached out to them in answer to her prayer and like sunlight breaking through cloud infused their hearts with new hope. Aurora saw Kev's head come up, felt him gather himself for the final effort. Then, miraculously, they were climbing. The weathered cliffs that had reared up before them like inescapable fate were falling away beneath them, and suddenly they were over.

Aurora glimpsed a rugged land of steep, wooded slopes and green valleys before Kev dropped into a broad basin, which looked rather as if it had been scooped out of the encroaching forest of old oak trees and pine. The earth seemed to rush up at her as the dragon came in recklessly, too spent to brake their swift passage. Then they were down, the very earth seeming to shudder with the impact, and Aurora was flung from the saddle into a mercifully thick growth of bracken.

Dazed and more than a little shaken by her fall, the enchantress struggled to rise, only to sink down again with a groan. For a long moment she lay, panting for breath and fighting to hold off the threatening curtain of darkness. Then she heard it again—the harpist weaving magic with his harp—and summoning the last of her rapidly fading strength, the enchantress raised her head.

Perhaps it would have been better to succumb to the swoon so close upon her than to behold the noble dragon, battered and broken, blood oozing from countless wounds—mute evidence of the fierce battle he had fought with the Usurper of Careg-sunth. What a fool she was not to have realized before that even as Kev struggled so valiantly to bring the heir of Garn safely to the land of her ancestors, the lifeblood had been steadily flowing from him. Bitterly she recalled his words to Dalchor. Aye. Kevyn-rhi was returned to the land of the dragon-lords, but at what a terrible cost!

"Oh, gods, Kev!" she moaned, catching sight of the red gleam of a slitted eye slowly closing. Carried by her terrible grief, she began to drag herself through the brake toward the dragon of Myrialoc, till at last she flung her arm across his neck and wept bitter tears.

"What have I done to you?" she choked, burying her face against the scaly neck. "You mustn't die, Kev. I could not bear it if you died."

The hand coming to grip her shoulder was infinitely gentle.

"Softly, child, you must not grieve," soothed a marvelous voice, deep and richly vibrant. "Kevyn-rhi has come home. He shall sleep peacefully now."

The enchantress looked up into eyes that were remarkably clear and cool yet seemingly possessed of an inner fire carefully veiled and unreadable. They were like distant stars shining on a still night or like sunlight glancing through crystalline water, she thought whimsically even as she slipped soundlessly into a deep well of darkness.

Aurora awakened slowly to an awareness of stiff muscles and an indecently soft bed draped in thick furs. Reluctant to open her eyes just yet, she nestled more deeply into the snug warmth and mentally chided herself for being so shamefully lazy. Vaguely she knew that she had been ill, indeed, had lain for a considerable time in the grips of some sort of a fever, for she seemed to recall crying out in delirium as she

251

struggled to surface from the icy currents sweeping through her body. These had given way to terrible dreams in which she fought savage dragons and suffered the torment of searing dragon-fire. Through it all there had been strong, but gentle, hands bathing her face and neck with cool, damp cloths, and sometimes, in the midst of her most tormenting dreams, there had been the sound of harping to draw her out of the labyrinth of horror wherein she wandered, so that she would lie for a time in blessed slumber. Yet other than a certain weakness of limb and numerous small aches and pains, she felt marvelously rested and well again. So much so, in fact, that at last she began to grow weary of her bed.

Rolling over on her back, the enchantress yawned and stretched luxuriously. Whereupon, she sensed immediately a quiet movement near the bed and opened her eyes to a tall form made hazy by a nimbus of dazzling light issuing from a window behind it.

"So you have decided to come awake at last," observed a singularly familiar voice, which served suddenly to bring everything she had mercifully forgotten during her illness crashing once more in on her.

"Kev!" she cried, bolting upright with such violence that the room tilted and threatened to recede into darkness.

"You might learn to curb such impulsiveness, Your Highness," mildly observed her companion, compelling her gently back against the pillows again. "It would save you a great deal of discomfort, I should think."

"What care I for comfort, when my friend has

suffered the final agony and solely because of me?" rejoined the enchantress, embracing the stranger with tragic eyes in which yet glittered a spark of resentment at what she perceived as unpardonable levity on his part. But immediately he gave her cause to revise her hasty judgment.

"Forgive me, child. I should have known you would be like your maternal grandmother," he said with simple sincerity, and an oddly whimsical smile hovered briefly about remarkably handsome lips. "In her youth she, too, was all fire and passion for those she loved. Come, it is time to end your grieving."

And so saying, he gathered her up in his arms, bedclothes and all, and despite her startled protest bore her across the room, which, aside from being rather chill and damp, was made cozy by brightly woven tapestries on the stone walls and luxurious fur rugs strewn about the floor. Then settling her in a cushioned seat within a bay window that overlooked green lawns hedged by thick forest and, in the distance, a stark ridge of weathered granite shimmering hazily in the sunlight, he stepped back to gaze down at her flushed face with a most peculiar gleam in eyes that were every bit as remarkable as she remembered them to be.

Suddenly, seeing him clearly for the first time with the sun falling upon his face and form, the enchantress felt her senses reel. He was attired plainly, with neither jewels nor other finery, in a day robe belted at the waist, and he was tall and graceful, with wide shoulders tapering to a narrow midriff. There was strength in the still face, which looked young, yet, framed in silver hair plaited at the sides and left to flow freely down the back, somehow gave the impression of an ageless wisdom, or was it patience, or even sorrow? She could not tell, but of one thing she was certain. She had seen that face before.

"Who are you?" she demanded in a strained voice hardly above a whisper.

"No one of importance, Highness," he answered, smiling a little. "Merely the king's bard."

"Y-you were acquainted with my grandmother, Chandra, Lothe's daughter?" she queried, turning her face away lest he see the sudden eagerness in her eyes. Indeed her heart was pounding so, she thought she could not bear it, and her head felt feathery light. Yet her mind was crystal-clear, her thoughts coming with rapierlike quickness.

Could he truly not know her? Garwin had said she was amazingly like the warrior-woman who had suckled her in the Glade. Even Kev had had to be persuaded that she was not that other raven-haired girl who had left her home and never returned— Almira, Chandra's daughter, who had sculpted out of granite a likeness of Amaur and Gawr to stand watch at the sealed gates of Seraisharaqa. The one figure had been furtive, his face hidden within the shadows of a black, hooded cloak symbolizing the darkness of Dred, but the other, the Fire-God, who was known as Harmon to the peoples of the eastern lands, had stood out boldly, the strong chin and stern-lipped visage turned to the rising sun.

It had seemed to Aurora as she stared up into the stone god's face that the sculpture was inspired by the enduring memory of one who had been greatly beloved, for there had been sensitivity and compassion in the sculptor's rendering of the patron-god of warriors that she had thought strange. And, too, though he had worn a shield on one arm and a great sword at his side, in his other hand he had carried a harp. And how should he not, she mused, glancing up at the king's harpist out of the corner of her eye, when Almira, in rendering her creation of Harmon, had given him the likeness of a living, mortal bard?

"Aye, I knew the princess, years ago in Myrialoc." He had spoken quietly, his marvelous eyes distant with the memory, and there was a smile in his voice. Yet Aurora hardly noticed as her head shot up, her glance flying to his face.

"You were in Myrialoc?" she exclaimed incredulously. "But when? How could you, when Rab transmuted the magic plane of Hylmut and all within to crystal at the end of the First Uprising in order to preserve Myrialoc from Dred's forces? Are you a magician to have lived so long?"

"No, not a magician," he said easily, laughing a little at her obvious disbelief. "I was a soldier."

"A soldier?" she echoed faintly, feeling even more confused. Yet it was true that Kev had said he was a commander of Harmon's combined forces, but that had been in the Second Uprising, and Almira had fought at his side. Surely she could not be mistaken in thinking he was Alain, the Bard of Naefredeyan, and her father!

"Yes, a soldier, but I did not bring you to the window to pass the time in talk. Look there, Highness, above the fringe of the escarpment. They have eaten, and so they come now to sun themselves

255

on the crags overlooking the sea."

Her attention fairly caught by something in his voice, Aurora turned to look where the bard pointed with a graceful hand. It was then she realized they were in a castle of sorts perched along the stony ridge of the Lizard's back, and the park below them was the basin in which Kev had come finally to rest. Feeling again the sharp edge of grief, she uttered a strangled gasp and started to turn away.

"No, look, Aurora," commanded the bard and, gripping her firmly by the shoulders, forced her around.

Then she saw them, the dragon-lords of Garn, gliding in, singly and in twos and threes, eventually to settle atop the sun-drenched cliffs. By the One, it was a glorious sight, with the sun glinting off emerald, red, and amber scales, and the great beasts flirting with the wind in a sublimely beautiful dance of dragonflight. And last, limping in alone, one larger than the others, the scales so dark as to appear jet, lest one should catch a close enough look to see the greenish sheen like a fine patina—he was the only true Dracadern among them. Then suddenly Aurora became aware of a swift, sharp pang in her breast, for perched easily on the dragon's back, red-gold hair flying wildly, was a slender youth, who seemed somehow an inseparable part of it all—the scent of sea and wind, the sun glinting against the barren thrust of weathered rock, and the great beasts swooping from a boundless sky.

"'Tis Kev, isn't it," murmured the enchantress, glancing up at the bard then back again at the magnificent dragon settling a little apart from the others. "And who is that who bestrides him as if he were born to it?" she added carefully.

"That, Highness, is Ellard, the Dragon-Prince. Your distant cousin. Had you not returned, it is he who would one day sit upon the throne."

"I see," she murmured, wondering how the young prince had received the news that a previously unknown granddaughter of the Princess Chandra had materialized suddenly to supplant him. And not only had she sprung out of nowhere, but she had done so astride Kevyn-rhi, the chief of all the dragon-lords! Surely he must despise her, she thought with a sinking heart. But then she forgot her cousin as it came to her to rejoice at the marvel of Kev's survival.

"B-but I don't understand. I-I thought he was . . ."

She could not finish it, for suddenly there was a huge lump in her throat, and it was left to the bard to extricate her from her embarrassment.

"In the norm it's hard at best to kill a dragon," he said, striding forward to gaze out the window at the marvelous creatures lying like great torpid lizards among the crags. "And Kevyn-rhi had the advantage of being among a people who have at their command centuries of knowledge concerning dragons. Ellard himself tended Kevyn-rhi, and every true dragon-prince has a special gift for healing the creatures of wind and flame," said the bard quietly, turning toward the enchantress with what she considered an all-too-meaningful glance. Was she, then, no true princess of Garn? she wondered, for so far as she knew she had no such special talent.

"Add to this the fact that dragons were among the first of the One's creations," the bard continued then, "and as a result are naturally long-lived, possessing something of the rejuvenating potency of the earth itself, and you have Kevyn-rhi, almost indestructible and thus the most ancient of his kind. You see, he is the last of the Dracaderns, the Black Dragons of the Beginnings."

"The last? But what happened to the others?" queried the enchantress, saddened that Kev should still find himself one of a kind even as a real, living dragon.

"Most were lost in the upheaval created when Dred released the dark forces of earth—the drakes in battle with the wyverns and manticores and the females to the devastation of massive earthquakes and tidal waves. For it was the time of *brod*, when the females retreat to the lairs to lay the eggs, so that they were caught beneath the earth with little chance of escape."

"All the females perished?" Aurora asked, horrified.

"All," pronounced the bard, and Aurora shivered at his look. "Though it was believed that a few might have managed to transmaterialize into the Flux, that hope has long since been laid to rest by Harmon, who went in search of them."

"The Flux?" uttered the enchantress, startled. "But why should they have gone there, and how?"

"But how not," shrugged the bard. "A Dracadern can travel freely to and from the Flux, for it, like the gods, is a creature of infinitude, created to span all time, all possibilities, save one: the bounds of its own mortality."

Aurora's incredulous glance flew to the bard's

granite face.

"What are you saying?" she demanded, her heart of a sudden heavy with a strange feeling of dread. "That the gods, like dragons, can die? That they, too, are mortal?"

"The gods are mortal only in the sense that they can die—either by choice or by a power greater than their own. Dragons, however, have not that choice. Thus it was that all but a handful of the Black Dragons were destroyed and all the eggs, save for one that the Princess Chandra herself recovered and preserved with a song of enchantment. Unfortunately, it was lost shortly after Chandra fled the island—stolen, some say, by Rab, to punish the king for having refused to honor his promise of Chandra's hand in marriage. But I place little credence in such a tale. Such an act would have been beneath the Master Magician of Sib, who, I suspect, chose to flee with Kevyn-rhi for the very purpose of removing the last surviving Dracadern from almost certain death in Dred's wars."

"But that must be it," said the enchantress, "for why else should he have sealed Kev in a dream-web, thus not only halting the natural process of aging but in a sense granting Kev a sort of rebirth by transmuting him into glass? How wise he was to have foreseen so much! Indeed, he must have known that I would one day come in search of a perfect crystal rose, though had it not been for Frayne, I might still be only a nameless foundling in Endrith's Forest, spinning fantasies about who I am. And Kev and Myrialoc would still be crystallized essences awaiting someone to come along to release them.

259

And instead—well, instead, I have a borrowed name and am upon an unfinished quest for my true one. No longer am I Anduan or Tree-Child, but the enchantress, the guardian of Andruvien. Further, I have discovered myself to be the granddaughter of a great magician and a princess of Garn, for I am the daughter of Chandra's daughter, who was wed long ago to a bard of Naefredeyan. But who are you, king's musician, that you know so much about dragons and gods and so many other things?"

"Don't play the innocent, wench. You must know he is Alain, the Bard of Naefredeyan. And I am Lothe, the Dragon-King who, long ago, was fool enough to admit a magician into my court!"

In startled awe, Aurora turned to gaze upon the fierce old man studying her from beneath white, bristling brows. He stood just within the doorway, his spare frame weathered and bowed with the weight of countless years, propped heavily upon a long staff carved all over with runes.

"My lord," murmured the bard quietly, going to the old king's side to offer the sustaining aid of his arm. "You honor us with your presence. Perhaps you would care to sit a spell while you become better acquainted with the Princess Aurora, your great-granddaughter?"

"*My* great-granddaughter, Bard?" parried the dragon-king, pinning shrewd eyes on the other man. "And am I alone to acknowledge the upstart? Oh, I do not deny she has the look of the magician," he conceded, stumping deeper into the room to sweep Aurora with a distempered glance. "Indeed, who *could* say she has not his heathenish hair, black as

Dred's night, or his unnatural eyes. But I see nothing of my daughter in her. Nor little of you, Bard. Who, then, shall say for certain that she comes of my seed, or yours?"

"*I* shall not say it! Nor should I wish kinship with anyone so mean and disagreeable as you, my lord, or so loath as the Bard of Naefredeyan," declared Aurora, who had come swiftly to her feet to stand, white-faced and swaying slightly, her glorious eyes flashing hurt and angry sparks, but her head yet held high. How dare they discuss her as if she were not there! And, worse than that, to make it obvious neither wished to acknowledge her as his kin. Who were they to find her lacking? "In truth I should rather remain nameless than claim either of you."

Aurora blushed, angry at herself, as her voice broke slightly at the end. Yet instantly she drew herself to her full height to face them proudly. She was Aurora, the enchantress, a name of which one could be proud, for had not Frayne given it to her out of a love that had awakened her to the god's power? She had no need to beg. Quickly she got hold of herself.

"Forgive me, my lords, if my demeanor has been less than seemly," she said with a quiet dignity that would have surprised Crane no end, but did justice to the endless lessons in etiquette to which Vandrel had subjected her in the hopes of molding her into a lady. "I am in your debt for your generous hospitality and now would take my leave of you. The Kingdom of Garn was never my intended destination, and I have pressing business elsewhere. I ask only one favor more, that you give me leave to speak one last time with Kevyn-rhi."

261

"What, and give you opportunity to bewitch him with your magic as the trickster did before you?" demanded the irascible old liege, slamming the heel of his staff hard against the floor. "The magician stole my daughter and the most prized of my dragons. Nay, it shall not be said that Lothe was made twice the fool by one of Rab's cursed seed. You will see or speak with Kevyn-rhi only at peril of your life, wench. Upon my word I swear it."

"The dragon-king of Garn does not need me to make him foolish," the enchantress retorted, all aflame again at his unreasoning distrust. "He does that all by himself. I will bid Kev farewell, my lord. And there is nothing that you or anyone can do to stop me."

"You dare speak so to me?" demanded the king, white-lipped and indignant. "Is there not one drop of Chandra's blood in you that you see fit to treat her father with such insolence?"

"'Twas you who said I had not, my lord," she answered bitterly. "As for my insolence, I have only answered kind with kind."

At once Aurora regretted her heedless words, spoken out of anger, as she beheld the old man grow ashen of face, and clutching at his chest, seem suddenly to sag. Instantly she was at his side, grasping a spindling arm about her neck as she supported his frail weight with her youthful strength.

"Softly, my lord," murmured the bard, who, no less quick to come to the king's aid, helped ease him into a chair.

Aurora, looking up, locked glances with the bard and for a long moment was held mesmerized by something in his eyes—a look not unlike those Garwin had been used to give her when, as a child, she had been in one of her obstreperous starts. Then the spell was broken as Lothe feebly waved them both away.

"Take your hands off me. I'm no infant to be coddled."

"Nay, sire, you are a man old enough to know better than to work himself into an unseemly fit," the bard observed calmly, waving a vial of smelling salts beneath the king's nose, but it was at the bristling young enchantress that his meaningful gaze was directed. "Now see if you can behave yourself."

"One day you will go too far, Alain of Naeffredeyan," choked the dragon-king, eyeing the sternly handsome countenance with a baleful eye. "Meantime, you will see this ill-mannered female from beneath my roof without delay, and off the Isle of Garn. And make sure she takes nothing with her that is not hers. Do I make myself clear?"

"Oh, you make yourself quite clear," the enchantress interjected dangerously, though she strove to keep a tight rein on her uncertain temper. Egads, but he was a despicable old man upon whom she would gladly turn her back. Still, she had no wish to cause him to fall victim to an apoplexy, she firmly told herself. Indeed, she had not needed the bard's pointed look to tell her she had behaved quite badly. She knew it all too well. That she had acted thus more out of hurt at the man who had refused to admit he was her father than out of anger at the king who had openly rejected her, she refused to acknowledge. She knew only a need to remove herself as far away from

263

them both as was humanly possible, and with as great a dispatch as was seemly.

"You needn't bother to see me out, Alain of Naefredeyan," she thus added stiffly, staring at a spot somewhere beyond the man's shoulder. "I am no thief, nor is there anything in all of Garn that I either need or desire."

"Is there not indeed," Lothe rejoined with a slyness Aurora immediately distrusted. "But then I doubt not that you are a resourceful lass who can as easily conjure a ship out of seaweed or a dragon out of vapor as you can breathe. Or perhaps you had forgot Garn is an island?"

Egads, in the heat of the moment she had indeed forgotten it, she realized with a sinking heart, and saw as well that the king was enjoying her discomfort. He thought to see her humbled before him, as he had often dreamed, she doubted not, of humbling the magician who had tricked him into giving up his daughter's hand in marriage. But she would not be brought to beg, she vowed. If need be, she would swim to Kylandros ere she asked Lothe of Garn for so much as a by-your-leave. But then immediately she thought of Frayne and knew full well that she had no choice but to swallow her pride. No matter what the price, she must let nothing keep her from Kylandros.

With as much dignity as she could muster, the enchantress, who had sworn never to bow to any man, bent her knee in supplication to the dragon-king of Garn.

"I humbly beg your pardon, my lord. I was wrong to speak with less than respect before one who is both my elder and my host," she said with lowered eyes,

264

and surprisingly discovered that she meant every word. "In addition, I fear Garwin was quite right when he warned long ago that I should come to regret my hasty temper. In my pride I have been quite foolish, for I must implore not only your forgiveness, but a boon as well—the loan of some form of conveyance in which to make my way from Garn."

She had spoken with the simple eloquence of truth and a noble heart, and though for a moment Lothe's fierce old eyes appeared briefly to waver as he gazed upon her bent head, he soon made it apparent that he was not so easily to be won, for, after all, had not Chandra, his lovely little princess, meant the world to him, and was not this hoydenish, outspoken female the very likeness of the man who had stolen her?

"How you choose to make your way is none of my concern," he uttered gruffly, flicking an ancient hand at her as though to dismiss both her plea and her presence. "Go, go, you weary me. See her gone, musician, then return at once to soothe my shattered nerves with your harping."

And, in truth, the old reprobate did appear as worn as he had claimed, thought the enchantress with an unexpected stab of pity, as she took in the rather abject figure slumped heavily in the chair, his bearded chin sunk to his chest in what one might have suspected to be an attitude of despondency, did one not know better, that is. One hand, seemingly of its own accord, reached tentatively toward the king, only to be snatched quickly back again. And though Lothe did not see it, one other, keener pair of eyes was not so unfortunately remiss.

"It grieves me, sire, that I cannot in this instance heed your desire to hear me play," said the bard, watching the slender girl turn determinedly away to begin gathering up her few belongings.

"'Cannot heed' say you?" the king demanded imperiously, coming instantly upright in the chair. "You have, I trust, some acceptable explanation for refusing your king?"

"Indeed, sire. I shall not be here. For since you have denied her passage in a king's ship, it naturally falls upon me to convey my daughter wheresoever she would go. If, that is," he added, his gaze never straying from the youthful face that had turned to regard him with such agonizing uncertainty, "she will deign to allow me, her rightful father, that singularly precious honor."

Chapter 9

Sighing contentedly, Aurora curled her toes into the fur rug and watched the sparks fly as the flames licked at the rain-dampened billet of wood she had just thrown on the fire. They were in the great hall of the keep—she, the dragon-king, and the Bard of Naefredeyan, who had persuaded her to stay the length of a fortnight on Garn—and, outside, the night was cold and blustery with the storm that had been gathering all day, finally breaking into a hard-driven shower as dusk set in. In a way she was glad the rain and wind had come to delay her departure yet another day, for she was loath to bid farewell to Kevyn-rhi, who, despite the reawakening of his memory, was yet somehow just as gentle and endearing as the Kev of old, or to Ellard, the free-spirited prince, who had befriended her and tried to teach her the rare art of dragon-mastery, and—aye— she was reticent even to leave crotchety King Lothe, her stiff-necked great-grandfather.

She owed that unexpected development to Alain of

Naefredeyan, who had manipulated both his king and his fiercely independent daughter with a subtlety that would have done credit to the most talented diplomatist. Aurora glanced from beneath thick lashes at the bard, who sat across from her quietly strumming the strings of an exquisite *crwth*, the favored harp of the ancient tribe of Volcae, renowned as lyricists of great power. She could hardly believe yet that this strange man who was her father had brought the old king so easily to relent toward her, his legitimate heir. But that was exactly what Alain had done, and when later she had asked him about it, he had merely smiled enigmatically, saying that it was no great matter to persuade the old king to what in his heart he had wanted all along, be he ever too stubborn to admit it even to himself. And 'twas true that even though Lothe persisted in his gruff manner toward her, she had come to suspect in the past few days that he disliked her far less than he let on. Indeed, she almost believed that he enjoyed having her near, for she had heard the halls resound more than a few times with his bearish growl, demanding to know where the impertinent young upstart who claimed to be a dragon-prince of Garn had got off to.

As for herself, she could not deny a growing fondness for the fierce old drake. He reminded her a great deal, somehow, of Garwin, who, as Gleb had been used to say, might seem on the outside as "prickly as a hedgehog," but was as "soft as plum pudding" on the inside. In truth she wished time did not press on her so just when she had found him, for she would have liked to be able to come to know him better ere she had perforce to lose him again. And, indeed, the matter of her departure for Kylandros, which had been rescheduled for dawn of the next day, had become a bone of contention between them.

So greatly had she withdrawn into her thoughts that when the king abruptly demanded that she tell him more of what she had been about while growing up nameless in far, heathenish places, Aurora had to gather her wits about her ere answering.

"I was not unhappy as Anduan living among the elves in Hawthorn Glade," she said dreamily after a time, propping her chin upon knees folded to her chest to gaze deeply into the fire leaping in the great stone fireplace. "Indeed, I had everything I could want. Garwin and Gleb instructed me in the Beginnings and saw that I learned what every young elf should know about the Cycles of Being and the Hraldoonish secret rites and mysteries. And the Eleven Hundred Curses of the Droonish Cant, as well," she added, with an impish giggle, "with which Gleb once gave sow's teats and a mare's arse to the Black King of Kern in return for kidnapping him. Even dearest Garwin was taken quite by surprise to learn our timid little Gleb had been so resourceful in bringing about his escape. Though of course Crane was helpful, too, for 'twas he who in mouse-form gnawed through the ropes that bound Gleb."

"You mentioned this Garwin earlier," Lothe interrupted in his usual crusty manner but with what might have been the faintest hint of jealousy. Indeed he had not once taken his eyes off the lovely creature who sat curled like a contented kitten on the fur rug at his feet in the Hall of the Dragon-Kings as she described with innocent candor her childhood in

Endrith's Forest. "Who is he, and this Gleb of whom you speak so fondly?"

"They are my father-elves," she said simply, smiling a trifle wistfully as it came to her to wonder if she would ever again see the dear folk of tree and glen, "and Minta and Valesia are my dryad mother-pair, who took me into their keeping when I became too large for the elves to look after. I learned how to steal unseen from tree branch to tree branch dryad fashion and to sing the songs of the father-oak, which are of ageless things, like wind and sun and rain, and the strength of the earth itself. I ran with Tasha, Elk-Lord, and hunted with the wolves. I saw through the eyes of Agrypha, the Falcon, how the world appears from the sky. The birds and animals, even the trees, were extensions of myself, so that I seemed almost to *be* the forest."

Suddenly the smile left her lips, and a shadow flitted across her face.

"Then Frayne came one day to Grendylmere and taught me that the world is much more than Endrith's Forest, and nothing has since been the same. When first he held me in his arms and taught me the wonder of love between woman and man, I felt the god's power move within me. 'Twas then I began to understand that the dreams of my childhood had been god-sent visions of a power that was to be mine—the power of the god whose vassal I am. And I knew that I was no longer a child in search of a name, but the enchantress on a quest for her true destiny."

The raven head lifted then so that the bard, his face obscured in the shadows cast by the fire, saw the huge eyes flash golden and the small chin jut with a hint of the same stubborn determination he had witnessed

270

that first day as the young enchantress had confronted the dragon-king with both courage and audacity. And there had been something else as well—a depth of compassion and understanding that, breaking through the ice of her proud disdain, had taken him off guard. Though she immediately had sought to cover it up again, he had yet seen it, the sudden translucent softening of those glorious eyes, into which to look was to know both a fierce joy and a rending pain. Nor had he failed to note the tentative gesture of her trembling hand toward Lothe's shrunken figure slumped into the melancholia of a childless old age. By the One, she was a marvel, this lovely creature of earth and flame, whose spirit seemed to quicken all that came within her sphere. Indeed, her laughter had been like elixir to the weary king, who, ere she had come to dispel the haunting shades of his lonely existence, had taken to his bed in anticipation of death's final embrace.

Watching the king's spindly fingers tighten on the carved armrests of the chair till the knuckles shone white, the bard frowned thoughtfully. Lothe would be more than reluctant to set free this rare fledgling of the dragon-kings, and yet he must be brought to reason. So much depended on it.

"I know he is the Thromholan, sire," Aurora was saying, beseeching the king with her eyes, so that neither Lothe nor the enchantress was aware of the slim youth who entered the hall to stand watching them from the shadows.

"Then would you have us believe you know not what has been written of him?" Lothe demanded incredulously.

"I know the prophecies," she answered steadily,

"yet *still* would I free him."

"Then you are either mad or a traitor!" thundered the king, flaying her with a look that both entreated and damned her.

"Nay!" she cried passionately, "I am neither."

"No, you are even worse," said Lothe bitterly. "You are a woman blind with love."

"Yes, I love him! I say it freely, for what shame be there in love? What harm, Ealdathir?"

She saw him wince at her use of the old title for a loved and respected partriarch, an "elder-father," and came to her knees, one hand going out to Lothe in supplication.

"Please, try to understand," she said softly, though her eyes were eloquent with unshed tears. "Frayne and I are inextricably bound—his spirit and mine, our destinies one to the other. That is why I must make with all speed to Kylandros. I cannot explain how I know it to be so, but you must believe me."

For a long moment the old man stared into the lovely, upturned face as if mesmerized by something he alone could see. Then suddenly his lips thinned to a hard line, and he seemed compelled to jerk his eyes away.

"And what of Garn?" he demanded coldly, staring beyond her with such fixity of expression that she knew he was thinking not of her, but of another young girl who had left him and her legacy of a kingdom to pursue a destiny of love.

A smile trembled to her lips.

"Garn was never mine," she murmured with an aching tenderness for the fierce old monarch, "nor ever shall be. Garn is Ellard's destiny, not mine. Oh, don't you see, Grandfather? 'Tis Ellard who has the healing gift of the true dragon-king, not I."

"Yet it is you with whom Kevyn-rhi formed the bond of *gemynd-plegan*," Lothe answered ringingly, "even as he did with Chandra before you. So say not to me you are no true prince of the dragon."

The bard's head turned fleetingly toward the soft scrape of feet and the faint creak of a closing door. Then thoughtfully he looked back again at the enchantress and the king, whose face appeared suddenly carved of stone.

Aurora, reeling at the sudden lance of bittersweet pain, felt as if she had been struck a knife-thrust to the breast. Oh, gods, he could have made no greater declaration of his love, and what must she do but fling it back in his face in the one way that would damn her in his eyes forever. Nearly blinded by the tears streaming unheeded down her cheeks, she stared up into the proud visage of the king and thought that she could not bear to hurt him. Where was the power of the god now? she thought bitterly. Of what use the crystal sword or the symbols woven into the fabric of the Crimson Cloak? In matters of the heart she was no enchantress, but only Anduan, Elf-Foundling and Tree-Child.

Then it came to her that Lothe offered her far more than a kingdom and a throne, or even the wonder of his love. He had said she was a true prince of the dragon, and in those few words had given her roots and ties of blood and home and family. She need go no farther in search of a name. She was Dracareg, of the ancient lineage of the dragon-kings! Was that not enough?

Was this, then, what Rab had foreseen when he bound Kev in the will-web, knowing that when the dragon was made flesh again, he would bond with the one who awakened him—Rab's heir and Lothe's, the hereditary queen of Garn? It might have been done in pledge to his beloved Chandra, who had forsaken her heritage for a greater love. Or even in revenge against the king who long before had forced the magician to flee the island of the dragons with his bride. But, nay. The man who had wrought the magic of Myrialoc preserved so lovingly in crystal could not possess a heart that yearned for vengeance. Why then had he made certain that Almira's daughter should one day be granted the heritage denied the lovely Chandra? And why not his own daughter Almira instead of his granddaughter? Gods, it made no sense, yet it was not chance that had brought her here. Of that she was certain.

The ripple of harp strings reawakened her to another facet of the puzzle—Alain of Naefredeyan. What irony that she should have found her father only to discover that he loomed an even greater riddle in the flesh than he had as a fleshless name. For in truth, he had told her less than nothing of himself or Almira, always smiling that elusive smile whenever she pressed him, and murmuring some evasive something, such as advising her to be patient, for all in time would be made clear to her, or telling her to trust in him for the present, for she was not ready yet to have all the answers to her myriad questions. Then would he gently turn her to other matters, usually leading her with his inescapable subtleness into talking at great length about herself, Frayne, Van-

274

drel, and Leilah—indeed, he had demonstrated a most particular interest in the sorceress of Tor and in Almira, too, going so far as to ask Aurora to repeat the elves's tale of the slaying of the warrior-woman and her companions in the Glade several times ere he seemed satisfied she had told him everything she knew. Finally he had questioned her about the Crimson Cloak, asking her to bring it forth to show it to him. Then, as she had slipped it over her shoulders at his request, she had for the first time beheld a brief fissure in his cool reserve, the banked fire she had sensed smoldering behind the crystalline opacity of his eyes leaping forth in brilliant flame, quickly to be doused again. But'twas Andruvien that had sparked the incident that was to trouble her the most.

At dusk of that first waking day in Kylandros, as she had sat with Alain beneath the laburnums blazing yellow in the fading sunlight, he had first asked her about the bracelet clasped about her slim wrist. Thinking to let him examine the crystal, which lay dormant at her command, she slipped it from her arm and held it out to him.

"'Tis the Andruvien," she remembered saying, "the sliver of Vendrenin that Harmon left beneath the Black Mountain after his final battle there with Dred." Then suddenly she had been struck with the notion that perhaps this was why the god had led her at last to her father—that he, being of greater experience and knowledge than herself, might be the one for whom the thing of power was intended. For had she not taken it from the Crystal Room solely to safeguard it till she could determine where best it might be kept hidden from Dred? Might not her

275

stewardship now be at an end and herself freed at last from the dreadful burden?

"Please, take it if you will," she had pleaded most earnestly, "for I have ever been tormented by the fear that I am unfit to be its keeper. Doubtless it is a task more suited to a soldier able to defend it from those who covet it for themselves or Dred than for one untutored in the ways of the world."

But rather than accept it from her, the bard had flung himself hastily away to stand with his back to her, his hands knotted into fists at his sides and the broad shoulders hunched as though he suffered the throes of some deep and painful emotion. Hastily slipping the bracelet back onto her wrist, she had waited, feeling helpless and miserable with the belief that she had somehow offended him. It was thus with a feeling of awe that she watched him turn back again and saw not loathing on his lean countenance but a wondrous, warm affection and an odd sort of humility.

"Forgive me, child," he murmured, the old glimmer of a smile less guarded than she had yet to see it, but the strange eyes as unreadable as ever. "I was unprepared for such evidence of trust and of your innocent faith in me. I have seen Harmon wield the Vendrenin, have even felt a yearning to possess such a marvel of pure power for myself. But, nay, Andruvien is not for me. I fear you shall have to keep the crystal safe yet a while longer, and I doubt not that you shall be equal to the task."

He had turned to other concerns immediately, and never again had she dared to broach the subject, though she had not ceased to wonder about it. She, who had never desired it for herself, indeed, had ever feared its terrible power, could not truly understand what might drive a man to want it so dreadfully that he dare not even touch or look at it, for so it had seemed to be with Alain of Naefredeyan.

Suddenly, then, as she gazed up into the dragon-king's eyes and saw in them both his guarded vulnerability and his yearning to hear her say she would remain with him, Aurora cursed the fates that had brought her here apparently for no greater purpose than to test her. It was unjust and cruel that Lothe should be made to suffer for it. Yet the thing must be done, for she saw clearly that more than just her love for Frayne must in the end drive her from her great-grandfather and from Garn. Indeed, she would never know any peace till she had found the means to divest herself of the burden of Andruvien.

Steeling herself to withstand the terrible contempt of the old monarch whom, unbeknownst to herself, she had come to love from the first moment of their meeting, the enchantress rose to her feet to meet Lothe's look square on.

"Aye, Kev and I are mind-bound," she said, seeing Lothe draw suddenly in upon himself, as if he read her answer in her eyes, she thought. "Rab intended that we should be, in order that one day the last of the proud breed of Dracadern should be returned to his own land. Thus did he hope in some small measure to make up to you the loss of your beloved Chandra."

She saw his hand come up as though to stop her ere she had finished, but sternly she ignored it and the mute pleading in his frail frame held taut as a bowstring.

277

"God grant that you find it in your heart to forgive me, sire, for I intend to release Kevyn-rhi from the pledge of memory."

"You cannot!" he rasped, swaying to his feet. "The pledge is binding: Dragon-king to Dragon-rhi, till a new king shall need be.' Thereby is the king designated from generation to generation, through the bonding of the rhi with the one who would succeed to the throne."

"Aye, but I would not be a king, or a queen, of Garn," she answered, though it hurt her. "As a true prince of Garn, I may relinquish the pledge to another if I so choose, and if Kev, too, is willing. My lord, the matter has already been settled between us. Kevyn-rhi has agreed to accept Ellard."

Lothe winced as if stung by a whiplash and clenched tight his eyes.

"Grandfather? Sire?" uttered Aurora in a low, anxious voice as she took an uncertain step forward. But the king stopped her with a savage gesture.

"Go. Get you from my presence, servant of the viper!" he commanded harshly and refused to look upon the girl's wretched countenance turned up to his. "Henceforward you are nothing to me."

Helplessly Aurora sent a pleading glance at the bard, who had risen quietly.

Shaking his head ever so slightly, Alain said softly, "Go, child. I will join you when I can."

Briefly Aurora's shoulders sagged, her head bowed with the terrible burden of grief. But then she straightened, and dashing a sleeve across her eyes, nodded her head in convulsive acquiescence. Blindly she lunged for the door and flung it open almost savagely, only to halt suddenly, her knuckles white where she gripped the door's smooth edge. Slowly, as if compelled, she looked back again, her heart in her eyes.

"Farewell, Ealdathir," she murmured, her voice a bare whisper in the great hall yet deceptively cheerful with the crackle of the fire. "The One be with you." Then she turned and was gone.

For a long moment fraught with a shrieking sort of silence, both men stood immovable, till finally the bard, seeming to shake himself from a brief reverie, walked deliberately across the chamber to shut the gaping door against the shadows of the vestibule beyond. Then turning, he gazed piteously upon the dragon-king of Garn still standing rigid as the granite from which the stone keep was carved.

"That was ill-done, my lord," he said, coming back again to meet Lothe's savage glance, which was yet full of anguish.

"I will have none of your impertinence, Bard," growled the king and sank heavily into the chair. "The wench is gone and good riddance."

"And are you the better for having sent her on her way unblessed? Perhaps to eternal imprisonment or even death? Just so did you send your only daughter fleeing in the night from you. Chandra you never saw again, or her daughter, who bore that rare and lovely creature you have just wounded to the heart."

"Enough!" thundered the king, shaking with wrath and something even deeper and harder to bear. " 'Twas not I who robbed the kingdom of its queen, but the magician, rot him."

The bard came closer, his robed figure looming over the king like a fateful apparition.

"We have known each other far too long for untruths, my king," he said quietly, but something in his voice brought Lothe's head sharply up. Then did a shudder seem to shake the king as he gazed into eyes gleaming palely in the gloom, and his hands like withered claws closed hard about the armrests.

"You dare to accuse the king of lying!" he rasped.

"I accuse you of having twisted the truth to still the whisperings of your conscience, lord," replied the bard implacably. "Let us refresh your memory. Is it not the truth that Dred placed a curse of silence upon the dragon-lords, who were set to be the vanguard of Harmon's offensive that they might serve as the Eilderood's eyes and ears? And is it not also true that someone offered his daughter's hand in marriage to anyone who might lift the curse?"

"Yes, yes, it's true, but . . ."

"And was not that someone you, sire, for were you not wroth to learn that Harmon, in consequence of the curse, meant to change his plans, removing Garn from the vanguard and relegating the dragon-kings to a lesser task, indeed, a lesser glory."

"He would grant Britshelm and Gunther *my* rightful place in history, *my* immortality!" uttered the king with bitter loathing, his eyes distant with the hated memory. "Gunther, who held his forces home till the winds began to turn in Harmon's favor. It would not be Lothe who led the offensive to turn the tides of war. No, for Garn was to be sent to guard the flank while the womanish king of the south took all the glory."

"But you had fought too long in the thick of battle to take defeat lying down, had you not, my lord," continued the bard. "And so you sent for the Master Magician of Sib, offering him the Princess Chandra to wed if he could right the wrong."

"Yes, yes, I sent for him," admitted the king, waving his hand impatiently. "And since lived to rue the day. He came in a magic boat wrought from crystal. Which," he added, his eyes sliding sideways from the bard's, "fell to Dred, I heard, when the dark prince tried to take Myrialoc. 'Twas all he got, for, as ever, the cursed magician was too clever for him. I give my former son-in-law that much, at least. He was slippery as a snake and no coward. Else he'd never have braved the Land of Somn the way he did and lived to bring home the staff he called 'Mum.'"

"No finer man ever lived than Rab of Zelig. Nor none braver," the bard unequivocally agreed.

The king snorted.

"He was a clever thief is all. He stole the staff from Dred and my daughter from me. I'll not thank him for the latter."

"And how did you demonstrate your gratitude for the former, sire, except to deny him your part of the bargain? Indeed, no sooner had he used the staff to remove the curse of silence, than you denounced him as a charlatan."

"And so he was," Lothe declared, bringing the flat of his hand down hard against the armrest. "Dred let it be known that he himself had removed the curse to punish the magician's temerity, as Harmon could bear witness. The warrior-god was here when the

281

Black King sailed into the harbor beneath a flag of truce. Hedron, the emissary of Somn, declared the staff was nothing but a forgery. And it was, for when Rab tried to disprove Hedron's claim, it would neither give speech nor take it away."

"But how not," the bard remarked drily, "when you yourself had substituted the counterfeit for the real Staff of Mum, my lord? Tell me, was not Hedron satisfied with Dred's staff, which you had promised him for his little part in the drama, but you must give him Rab's crystal boat, as well?"

"That's a lie! I . . ."

"Do not perjure yourself further, king," the bard warned chillingly.

"Aye, my lord," rang out a youthful voice from out of the shadows, "let there be no more lies."

Lothe's sharply indrawn breath sounded harshly in the sudden silence. His eyes cavernous in a face gone grey, he watched the enchantress, her raven hair and her clothes wet from the storm and clinging to her, stride across the chamber toward him, and a step behind her, a slender youth with disbelieving eyes.

The bard, suddenly grim, moved quickly to intercept them, one hand closing with gentle firmness about the girl's arm.

"You were instructed to wait for me to join you," he said, his quiet voice edged with steel.

Aurora, tearing her eyes from the shrunken figure of the king, glanced accusingly at her father.

"You had no right to keep me ignorant. I am no child to be sent from the room when men talk." Then she blanched, her teeth catching at her lower lip as the bard's hand tightened painfully.

"I had every right, impertinent little fool," he murmured dangerously. "What you overheard was never meant for your ears. Or for *his*, the dragon-prince of Garn, lest Lothe himself decided to reveal it. Now take Ellard and get you hence, till such time as I send for you. Perhaps I can still mend whatever damage you have wrought here this night."

Aurora's eyes flashed golden sparks of anger and resentment, as she bowed up, ready to defy him. But then she seemed to read something in the bard's look to give her pause for reflection. Her gaze wavered, then gradually she relaxed, the tautness easing from her frozen countenance so that she appeared suddenly very young and vulnerable.

"I-I never meant to eavesdrop," she said distractedly. "When I was ordered from the king's presence, I wanted nothing except to escape for a time, to feel the rain upon my face and let the fury of the storm cool my own, inner tempest. Ellard was waiting for me. He had been in the hall and heard everything. Everything, that is, save for my intention to relinquish Kev's pledge in Ellard's favor." Fleetingly she glanced over her shoulder at the youth standing slightly apart from them. He was slender and well knit, and though he had the proud bearing of a prince, there was neither vanity nor arrogance in the fine-molded face, but intelligence tempered with sensitivity. Like Aurora, he was soaked to the skin, his red-gold hair plastered to his head and hanging in sodden strands about his shoulders. He had seen sixteen passings of the seasons, but there was a quiet strength about him that made him seem somehow older.

"He wanted to be the first to swear loyalty to me," Aurora murmured and smiled a little as she recalled how Ellard had appeared suddenly out of the storm-ridden night and gone to his knees before her.

"I have been reared to believe I would one day be king," he had said, gazing earnestly up at her, "yet you have done what I could never do. You have given life back to the old king, and you have returned Kevyn-rhi to Garn. Gladly would I serve you all the days of my life, if you will but have me, my liege."

"Get up out of the mud this instant, Ellard," she had replied, laughing to keep from bawling again, for she had been embarrassed and deeply touched by his noble gesture. "I am not your liege and never shall be. You were born to be king, and I—I have yet to know what I am meant to be or do."

He had come slowly to his feet, his eyes on her face searching for an answer to the riddle that was the enchantress.

"You are leaving Garn," he said, his voice filled with wondering disbelief. "Why, Aurora? Not because of me? I admit I was hurt and angry when I heard Lothe delcare you his rightful heir. But that was only at first. I stole from the hall seeking to assuage the bitterness in my heart and found myself near the lair of the Dragon-rhi. He spoke to me from the mouth of the cave, calling me Gimako Ellard. And when I asked him why he had used the title of 'Companion,' he told me it was your will that he and I be one in *gemynd-plegan*, the pledge of memory, for it was I who had healed him. Then did I understand for the first time what it was to be a true prince of the dragon. The king was right, Aurora. It is not healing hands, but generosity and wisdom of the heart that make a king."

"It is not generosity to give what was never meant to be mine," replied the enchantress, "nor wisdom to follow a trail when it is the only trail I have before me. So let us speak no more of such things. Tell me instead the way back to the keep ere I contract a fatal inflammation of the lungs," she laughed.

And so they had come back to the hall, thinking to find the fire deserted and Alain and the king turned in for the night. But instead they had overheard the bard accuse Lothe of bribing the Black King with the Staff of Mum. Shocked at what she had heard and loath to believe the dragon-king capable of so dreadful a deceit, Aurora yet could not dismiss the damning evidence that pointed to his guilt. For it was true that Hedron had possessed the Staff of Mum; indeed, he had sought to use it against her in the Treasure Room of the Kings. As for the crystal boat, she had no knowledge of it or its whereabouts. Yet in her heart she had not doubted that Lothe could tell them what had become of it if he wished.

Consequently, she had demanded the truth, and still desired it, though she had looked into the bard's eyes and experienced something she had never felt before. Indeed, she had not the words to describe it, for it had been more than a will that would not be gainsaid, or eyes that shamed one and yet at the same time demanded one's unquestioning trust. Had she but known it, it was the look a father gives a daughter who has erred unwittingly, but in the erring, done a possibly irreparable harm.

"Very well, I will go, Alain," she said, angry at

herself for giving in to him and troubled because she had never before bowed so tamely to anyone's will, not even Frayne's, when she believed herself in the right. "But know this. I will not rest till I have uncovered the answer to this riddle for myself."

The bard, inclining his head with proper gravity, yet failed to keep the brief, wry glint of amusement from his eyes.

"I stand forewarned. Now, go. I have kept the king waiting far too long."

"No, let them stay."

It was Lothe who had spoken, the voice of an old man who was both resigned and unutterably weary.

"Come, sit by me. It is time the truth was told."

Aurora and Ellard exchanged an uncertain glance, but then the bard of Naefredeyan had nudged them gently forward. Slowly they advanced toward the king and obediently seated themselves on the fur rug at his feet, one on either side of him.

Still, for a time, it seemed that Lothe had forgotten them, as he stared long into the fire, his eyes blurred with private thoughts. And when at last he did break the lengthy silence, it was not of Rab that he spoke, nor of his own part in discrediting the magician, but of things far removed from them.

"Our people were once a seafaring tribe who preyed upon ships and distant ports for their livelihood," he said, apparently irrelevantly. "We were wild and savage fighters, and every man's hand was against us. Till it came about that we could land nowhere except that we must in the end fight our way out again. Still, man since the beginning of time has been a creature of the land. Eventually he must ever yearn for a home port, a place to moor his ship that he may rest for a time beside a hearthfire and tell bold tales of his adventures, and it was no less so for us. Many passings of the seasons we roamed the seas, taking what we would and fleeing the reprisals of our fellow man, till at last it seemed that the gods, too, had turned against us.

"The merchants who depended on the sea-lanes between the Lands of Dagian, the Rising Sun, and of Aefnian, the Setting Sun, amassed a great fleet to free the seas of pirates. We were set upon and in the fighting lost many ships before at last Garn, the foremost warlord among us, entreated the intervention of Heaf, the god of the sea, imploring that he grant us passage to a safe harbor where none might ever find us. Then did he give sacrifice, blood for blood and kind for kind, the greatest of all offerings, for ere he could stop him, Arvyn, his youngest son, whom he loved well, gave himself into the depths that his people might live.

"No sooner was the thing done, than Heaf sent forth a dread storm such as no man before had ever seen. It was the Maurstom, which is the guardian of the Islands of Drui, and it swallowed up the ships of the sea-raiders and brought them to the Enchanted Isles in the emerald sea. But the gods have ever loved to make fools of mortals, and though Heaf delivered our people unto a safe haven where none might ever find them, he dashed our ships against the reefs of Tantalleth and laughed to see us foundering within sight but not reach of land. When all seemed lost indeed, Garn cursed Heaf and vowed that if Scio, the god of the sky, who has ever viewed with jealousy mankind's many offerings to Heaf, would send them aid, none of their kith and kin would ever more go forth upon ships across the sea, nor give sacrifice again to the god of the watery depths lest they bring down a dreadful curse upon them. Then did his ship, too, break upon the reefs, and Garn was swept into the sea.

"It seemed all would perish, down to the last man, woman, and child, when suddenly there appeared a wondrous sight—dragons, two score or more, swooping out of the clouds. They plucked us from the sea, as many as they could carry, and bore us to safety on this island. Again and again they went back for more, till all those who could be saved had been brought to the island of the dragon-lords.

"We called our new land Garn that we might never forget the vow he made that none of our race should sail in ships or honor by word or deed the god who betrayed us. Indeed, we are bound by it, lest in disobeying, we bring the wrath of Scio down upon us."

"But Rab came in his magic vessel to rid Garn of Dred's curse of silence," Aurora interjected, her eyes filled with sudden understanding. "And you had given your word that Chandra should wed him."

"Aye, in my jealousy for Gunther and my lust for an immortality preserved in songs of glory, I promised my daughter to an outworlder, who would return from whence he came."

"And so you thought to discredit him in Chandra's eyes," Aurora said, "and in Harmon's, that you would not be bound to uphold the bargain. And when Chandra yet would go with Rab, out of love and perhaps a sense of destiny, you bade Hedron take the crystal boat and leave."

"I never believed she would choose to take Kevyn-rhi from Garn. Nor would she have done, had it not been for the magician's conniving tongue."

"But, Grandfather, Rab must have understood that she could not break the vow. Surely there could have been no objection to making their journey upon a dragon."

"*I* objected to it!" answered Lothe, piercing her with tormented eyes. "She was bound to Kevyn-rhi, the last of the Dracaderns—dragons created at the Beginnings from three of the four elements—earth, air, and fire. Kevyn-rhi is the heart and soul of Garn. 'Tis he who holds the sea at bay, and Heaf, who would destroy us if he could. All these years I have known that the Rhi of Garn yet lived only because Garn yet stood. And now you, like my daughter before you, would tempt the fates yet again. You, no less than any of us, are bound by Garn's oath to Scio. You cannot leave here except on dragon's wings, and only Kevyn-rhi can bear you."

"But neither can I stay!" cried the enchantress, realizing then why it had been so easy for Alain to persuade the king to accept her presence there. He had never intended that she should leave, and if she would not stay to *rule* the Kingdom of the Dragons, then she would remain instead its prisoner!

Aurora wandered distractedly through the forest of old elm and oak, her brow furrowed with worry. Everything about her shone fresh and sparkly in the early morning sun breaking through the thinning clouds, and the bracken was sweet with the lingering scent of rain, but she did not notice. Nor did she hear the raucous cry of the chough from the cliffs overhead or the chiffchaff calling repeatedly to its mate, or even the chuckle of water tumbling over the rocky bed of a small bourne nearby. She had come into the woods to think what she must do, but thus far she had managed to do little more than further convince herself of the hopelessness of her situation and to get herself good and lost in the bargain.

The latter little disturbed her, however, as she felt reasonably certain she had only to head east toward the cliffs, which she doubted not formed the barren ridge of the lizard-shaped island, and eventually she would come to the corrie scooped out of the granite escarpment honeycombed with dragon lairs. Still, she was not anxious to return to Maendin, the stone fortress of the dragon-kings perched atop the crags. Within the grey, ancient walls, she was ever reminded that she was a prisoner with no prospect of escape, while here she could at least pretend that she was free and at home once more in Endrith's Forest, with the elfin glade hidden amid the trees only a stone's throw away. Indeed, she could almost imagine, as she swung easily into the boughs of a great oak and climbed above the leafy ceiling of the forest, that she heard Gleb humming the haunting melody of the Song of Blissia of the Sidhe as he had used to do when he gathered mushrooms after an evening shower, for the scent of rain ever bestirred an elf's heart with yearning for the Fair Land. But then the humming broke into song, and suddenly she realized she had not imagined it at all. Her curiosity piqued, Aurora followed the lilting refrain through the treetops till she came to a small clearing, the bourne burbling cheerfully away into the deeper wood, and an elf gathering mushrooms. Hardly able to believe either her eyes or her ears, she settled noiselessly in the low branches of an elm and waited for the elf to finish singing.

> "A fair land, a far land,
> A jewel in the sea,
> A dreamland, an island—
> Fair Blissia of the Sidhe—
> Lies west of east and north of south
> 'Twixt the realms of day and night
> Beyond the gaping Dragon's Mouth
> Amidst the spell of gloaming light.
> 'Tis an isle of ancient mystery—
> Fair Blissia of the Sidhe.

> "Rising 'neath a cloud of mist,
> The island in the sea,
> By enchanted waters kissed—
> Fair Blissia of the Sidhe.
> The sound of gleeful laughter drifts
> Upon the gentle breeze.
> The enraptured song of faerie lifts
> In gay frivolities.
> 'Tis an isle of magic revelry—
> Fair Blissia of the Sidhe."

The elf's voice drifted into a soft hum as he came to the end of the refrain and paused to rummage through a knapsack that lay at his feet. Out came a cloth-bound jug from which he took a generous swig, then, swiping a sleeve backhanded across his mouth, he drew forth a long-stemmed pipe and a pouch. A smile trembled on Aurora's lips when after a moment or two the familiar aroma of elfin weed wafted sweetly on the breeze.

" 'Tis a fine day for the gathering of mushrooms," she called out in the Hraldoonish dialect of the Old Tongue. "Mayhap you'd not mind a little company whilst you go about it? I've a sharp eye for morels and a nose for finding truffles—Nay, wait! Don't go," she cried, as the elf, recovering sufficiently from his first startlement, spun and made for the cover of the thick furze and bracken growing beyond the stream. She dropped lightly from the tree. "I am *eadwinaldas*, elf-friend," she added as the little man hesitated, his bearded face turned back over his shoulder. "I mean you no harm."

He was rather taller than the elves of Hawthorn Glade, she thought, taking in the trim figure clad in forest green, his peaked hat slightly askew atop silver hair floating in wisps about his head. Skeptical eyes the color of the emerald sea swept the enchantress an appraising glance from her raven head to her bare toes.

"Ye've th' manner and raiment of a tree-nymph, but not the face and form," he observed, cocking a doubtful eye at the thigh-length dryad gown into which she had changed upon entering the familiar aegis of the forest. "By what right does ye lay claim to *eadwinaldas*? No Droon of Saur ever give it ye."

292

"Nay, 'twas Thegne of Cridhelann," she answered carefully, suspecting the elf would be totally unfamiliar with either Endrith's Forest or the Hraldoons of Hawthorn Glade. "I was called Anduan by the elves and Tree-Child by the dryads. Both had a hand in rearing me. But in sooth I am Aurora, the great-granddaughter of Lothe, the Dragon-king."

"Are ye now," said the elf, eyeing her askance. "An' belike ye might call me Oglath, the Dreamer, were I t'swallow such a taradiddle as that."

"Nay, never Oglath, who found the heartland far to the east of Drui and never more set out upon the sea. Rather say you are kith to one of Gallad's crew, then might I believe you."

"Pshaw! And what could ye know of Gallad, wench?" he hedged, though clearly he was caught. "Not even the old king himself has heard the likes of that tale."

"Nay, 'twas Druce of the *Wind-Harp* who carried the Song of Gallad back to Cridhelann. And Oglath himself, who declared it part of the Droonish Cants and Mysteries. But if that is not enough to convince you that I am a friend," she added, growing suddenly sober, "then I must needs evoke that which none of elf kindred may deny:

Thréllen du kréllen shan thróndel Hraldóon.
Ahndu loríndu hae glénden naght Dróon.

"In truth be ye *eadwinaldas*," murmured the elf all agape, for she had recited the first of the elfin chants

293

of summoning and aid, which all elfkind are sworn to heed. "And 'tis Pic, son of Pipkin, who stands here before ye."

"Actually, I doubt that anyone can help me," Aurora sighed as she finished telling Pic the details of her plight. "If I sail in a vessel over the sea, I shall bring the wrath of Scio down on Garn. And I can't ask Kev to take me, for I cannot be sure that I shall be able to return him to his rightful time and place once we have entered the Flux. If Kev is lost, then so will Garn be lost, and thére you have it, Pic. I am in an impossible situation. I cannot stay here and leave Frayne trapped in the Flux of Timelessness, but nor can I leave. By the One, I know not what to do."

Suddenly an image of the king's bard obtruded on her thoughts, the lean face and still eyes, which had seemed worried somehow, despite his calm assurance that all would be well.

"We will find a way," he had said for her ears only, and his look had compelled her trust. Indeed, she had felt infused by the certain something about him that she had never been able to define—not strength exactly, though she sensed that in him, too, a latent power like the banked fire smoldering behind his eyes. Nor was it the unmovable calm that exuded from him, the unrufflability of one who was never surprised at anything—or disappointed either. Sometimes he made her feel that he had lived forever, seen all that there was to see and done all that there was to do, and, indeed, he must have lived many ages to have known Rab in Myrialoc. If he were a magician, he would possibly be in his ninth or tenth magical age of power, or if he were a dragon-king, preserved by the power of dragon-craft, he would doubtless be older even than Lothe. Yet he claimed he was no magician, nor was he bent and withered with more mortal years than were given to a dozen men to bear. He was Alain, the king's bard, and he was an enigma, for she sensed that he was much more than just a mere harpist, but as to what he was, she had no clue.

"Hm-m, 'tis a heavy coil ye've wrought fer yerself," agreed the elf, nodding his head sympathetically.

They were seated on a low rock near the bourne, and the morning was already well advanced when Aurora finished her tale. Absently she wriggled her toes in the cold water trailing over her bare feet. Despite her doldrums, the pleasant little glade had imperceptibly begun to work its spell on her, awakening her by slow degrees to the inevitable feeling of hope engendered by sunlight, flower-perfumed air, birdsong, and a gentle breeze rustling through leafy, green trees. The elf drew thoughtfully on his pipe, his face hazy behind a cloud of smoke, as he mulled over the ins and outs of the situation.

"I've never been off th' island, meself," Pic said, tapping the pipe lightly against the rock to knock the dregs from the bowl. "The truth be told I've never had a wish to go a-rovin'. Y'see, I like things the way they be, so it just don't make sense to old Pic why a body'd go alookin' fer adventure, though there's been some what has done it. 'Tis said that Gallad himself made it to the farthest island, which is surrounded by will-webs woven by the merrows, them that men call 'sea-nymphs.' And there he stayed, caught in a wish-net cast by the loveliest of all the merrow-maids." A whimsical smile touched his lips. "Belike he's not suffered over much, if th' tale be true."

"If only we had a ship that could float on air," the enchantress murmured, paying scant attention to the elf's apparent ramblings as she watched puffs of white cloud drift lazily to the west. "A soap bubble, perchance, with sails made of cloud," she giggled, and tossing a stick into the brook, watched it shoot downstream till it floated out of sight.

"Aye," speculated the elf dourly, unamused by her foolishness, "or a bubble hitched to a basket, belike. But 'twere better did ye have a wish-net like that what caught Gallad, methinks."

"Oh, aye, a net that catches whatever one wishes would be a good thing to have indeed," agreed Aurora blithely. "Only, if by chance one did come my way," she added wryly, "I don't really see how it would help with the hobble I've got myself in this time. It wouldn't bring me Frayne, after all, for even a wish-net is hardly powerful enough to reach beyond the barriers between this world and the Flux of Timelessness. So what could I possibly wish for that would take me to Kylandros, other than a dragon or a boat?"

"But that's simple," Pic answered, eyeing Aurora as if he suspected her of being just a trifle slow-witted. "Ye'd wish for the merrow-maid what had woven the net. Or did ye not know that sea-nymphs not only sing enchantments and possess the power of shape-changing, but they can . . ."

"Send things from one place to another at a

thought or even forward and backward in time!" exclaimed Aurora, wondering that she had not thought of it immediately. "Good gods, I *should* know it. Crane has gotten me out of more tight spots than bear looking back on and with those very same talents. His mother was the sea-nymph, Shellandra."

She had spoken with a great deal of excitement, but suddenly the light faded from her face as it occurred to her that a wish-net could hardly be easy to come by, especially since the island of the merrow-maids was even farther away than Kylandros.

"I don't suppose you happen to have such a marvel just lying around, have you?" she queried with a short little laugh that sounded rather hollow even in her ears.

"Well, if I didn't, I'd be a fool fer bringin' it up, wouldn't I," retorted the elf and, digging into his knapsack, drew forth a shimmery mesh wrought of moonbeams intertwined with mists of mother-of-pearl. "Ah, here it be," he said, shaking it out so that it flowed from his fingers like fine-spun gossamer on the breeze.

"Oh, but it is beautiful," breathed the enchantress, reaching out a tentative hand to touch the wisp of gauze. "How in the world did you come by it?"

"I found it caught in the branches of an elm this very morning. Belike the merrow-maiden lost it in the storm and 'twas carried there by the winds. Lest there were a god's hand in it," he added with an odd glint in his eye.

"Indeed, you must be blessed of the gods to be granted so wondrous a treasure," agreed the enchantress in all innocence. "And what shall you wish for,

Pic? For a ship to bear you to the Land of Blissia? Or perchance to Cridhelann that you might be with the Droons who settled there? Or," she added, thinking fondly of Gleb, her father-elf, "a bushel of blueberry tarts swimming in golden butter?"

"Pshaw! And did ye not invoke the chant of summoning and aid what no elf can refuse?" he demanded, as if that were sufficient answer to her foolish question. "Here, take it. 'Tis all the aid I can give ye. Now be on yer way that I may get about me own business."

The enchantress drew back, her eyes shimmering at so generous an offer.

"Nay, I could not take it," she said, slowly shaking her head. "'Twas meant for you. You must keep it and wish for something marvelous."

"Did ye not hear me say I were happy wi' things just the way they be?" Pic retorted, thrusting the wish-net at her. "I've no need for the thing. Why, belike it'll turn out t'be more trouble in the end than what 'tis worth. That's the way wi' wishes. Now, take it, I say, ere I toss it to th' winds jest to be rid of it."

"Well, then, I suppose I must accept it," she murmured, her smile tremulous as she gathered up the gossamer mesh and tucked it carefully into her own pack, which contained the Crimson Cloak and her elfin clothes. Then wishing she had something to give the elf in return, she stilled as her fingers touched metal. Slowly she drew forth Glaiveling, the elfin blade given her by Garwin and Gleb when first she set out on the quest for the horn of a unicorn. Holding it up so that it caught the sun, she turned solemnly to her Droonish benefactor.

"I own nothing of any value, save for this," she said, extending the knife, haft first, toward the elf. "'Tis Glaiveling, 'Little Sword,' and it bears the elfin runes of protection. I beg you will accept it in remembrance of our chance meeting, for an exchange of gifts between friends is a blessing to the heart."

For a moment it seemed he would refuse her offering, and Aurora was aggrieved that he had found the gift and her wanting. But then suddenly he seemed to shake himself, and clearing his throat noisily, took Glaiveling from her hand.

"Ahem! 'Tis a noble blade," he said gruffly, touching a finger experimentally to the point. "Fine craftsmanship. A gift worthy of both giver and receiver."

Awarding him a dazzling glimpse of golden eyes, Aurora rose to her feet.

"The One be with you, Pic, son of Pipkin," she murmured, bending down to salute his whiskered cheek with a kiss. Then with a last fleeting glance, Aurora turned to leave him gazing whimsically after her till she had slipped from view into the deeper shadows of the forest.

Thus the enchantress did not see the little elf suddenly begin to grow and alter form, till it was not Pic, son of Pipkin, staring at the place where she had vanished, but Alain, the Bard of Naefredeyan.

"Godspeed, Daughter of Earth and Fire," he murmured softly, then, smiling oddly, he strode swiftly along a different path into the woods.

Chapter 10

"Elves?" Lothe echoed, his bristly brows drawing sharply together. "There are no elves on Garn."

"Oh, but there are indeed, Grandfather," Aurora earnestly assured him, "for I have seen and spoken with one. He is a descendant of those who came to Garn long ages ago led by Gallad the Bold. His name is Pic, son of Pipkin."

"I'm afraid that's not possible, wench. Gallad's party were granted leave to construct their own vessel from the oakwood of Garn. None chose to remain behind when the fool Gallad set sail for the islands further west. Naught's been seen nor heard of them since. There's little doubt they shipwrecked, lured to the rocks by the mere-magdens or ensnared by the Snaigh in the Narrows. You must have been dreaming."

"Nay, 'twas no dream," declared the enchantress, slinging her pack from her shoulders to the stone floor before the king in his great hall.

She had only just returned from relating her

301

marvelous adventure in the forest to Ellard and Kev, and her eyes glistened with a strange mingling of excitement and the sorrow that had been engendered by her final leavetaking of her friends.

"Now I can make my way to Kylandros without endangering you or Garn," she had said to them as she proudly displayed the wish-net Pic had given her.

"A wish-net!" Ellard had exclaimed in awe. "I've never seen one before, though it is said that Chandra learned the art of weaving them from the merrow-queen. I've often wondered at it, for Lothe denies the tale, which claims that with her net Chandra wished for any surviving eggs of the Dracadern."

"Oh, but it's true enough," spoke up Kev, his dragonish face wearing that odd expression that came over it when he was remembering something from his forgotten past. "The merrow-queen did come one day to the shores of Garn, summoned by one of the Princess Chandra's spell-songs. I was there and saw it all—the lovely queen, the weaving of the net, and the egg, plain as day and black as night, popping out of nowhere into the meshes. Chandra begged Harmon, the Warrior-God, to keep it safe from harm the very night we fled from Garn for Myrialoc on the plane of Hylmut. I don't know what became of it after that."

"The legend says Rab stole it," Ellard blurted, then flushed, his glance sliding guiltily away from the enchantress.

"The legend is wrong," she stated flatly, and began folding the net back into the pack with fingers that trembled slightly. Egads, did everyone on Garn believe Rab to be a thief and a scoundrel? she wondered heatedly, then forgot her pique at sight of Ellard's downcast face.

"Never mind all that nonsense about Rab—and that is all it is, as I shall one day prove to everyone," she said bracingly. "There must be no ill will among us now that we must part, perchance never again to meet."

Made uncomfortable by the knowledge that the dread moment of final departure was upon them, they watched her silently till she had the pack firmly in place on her back again and had turned to embrace them with a misty, rather twisted smile.

"I-I have to go now," she managed around a sudden lump in her throat and laid her cheek tenderly against the dragon's scaly neck. "I shall miss you ever so much, dearest Kev. Promise you won't forget me."

"I would be more like to follow after you, even into the Flux, rather than to forget you," declared the dragon with the new assertiveness of Kevyn-rhi of Garn.

"You will do no such thing," she instantly admonished, alarmed, for there had been a distinct gleam in the fierce, dragonish eyes that she had little trusted as she pulled away to face them both squarely. "Ellard, swear you will not let him do anything so foolhardy," she added, fixing the youth with a look that made him squirm. "Swear it, Ellard, on the word of a true prince of the dragon, for you must know that your place, and Kev's, is here with Lothe and the dragon-lords, that you may be prepared when the Realm has need of you. That time is not far off, my friends. I feel it in my heart."

She had spoken quietly, but her voice had seemed to ring with utter conviction. Indeed, she could have found no surer way to remind them of their sworn duty to Garn and the race of Dragon-kings. Reluctantly they had promised to abandon their scheme to follow her into the Flux of Timelessness, and she had left them, her heart full with the knowledge that, concerned for her safety, they would have dared so much for her. She had thanked the One, as well, that she had discovered their plan in time to avert it. Then she had dismissed them resolutely from her mind, having reminded herself that in moments she would be standing on the island of Kylandros and that much nearer to being reunited with Frayne.

Thus it was that she had gone in search of Lothe and her father with an unencumbered heart. Indeed, she had been buoyed by the wondrous stroke of luck she had had in finding Pic and the wish-net of the unknown merrow-maiden. Surely the god was with her, and, once on Kylandros, somehow she would discover out of all the infinitude of possibilities the one avenue in the Flux that would lead her to her love. She could not doubt it now, nor allow anyone to shake her in her resolve to make with all haste to the island, no matter what awaited her. And, indeed, Frayne filled her heart and mind to the exclusion of all else as she removed the gossamer net and held it up for the king and Alain to see.

"Behold, Grandfather, the wish-net of a merrow-maiden," she said triumphantly. "The elf gave it to me."

The old king's bristly brows swept darkly together

as he beheld the fragile thing of indescribable beauty. Then suddenly his glance darted fiercely to the Bard of Naefredeyan standing quietly in his usual place at his side. It seemed that Lothe would speak, but something in the bard's still face silenced him. His lips firming to a grim line, the king turned back to the enchantress, who was watching the two men curiously.

"Is something wrong?" she asked, her glance flicking from one to the other. "Surely you see now that the god's hand is upon me and that it is meant for me to journey to Kylandros."

"I see only a foolish, headstrong woman determined to fling her life away for one who will in the end bring her nothing but grief and bitter desolation," grumbled the old man and gazed stonily into the distance, unable to meet the girl's suddenly stricken glance. Thus he was not aware when she drew uncertainly to his side, until he felt strong, young fingers close gently about his withered hand. Starting, he looked up to find the enchantress kneeling before him, her lovely face turned compassionately up to his.

"It grieves me that our time has been short, sire," she said in a low voice vibrant with sweet tenderness. "But I belong to the god, and I must do as my heart tells me. Bid me godspeed with your blessing, *Ealdathir,* I beg you."

For a long time he said nothing as he stared into the mesmerizing eyes and beheld them shimmering with the power of the god. Then did he see not only that she spoke the simple truth, but that in spite of all his hopes, she had defeated him. She was Aurora, and she could not be caged, any more than one could cage the light of the sun as it banishes the darkness at dawn. An unfamiliar stinging behind his eyelids, Lothe laid a hand that trembled upon the raven head.

"I had thought to keep you by me till the One called me from this life. Nor do I gladly relinquish the rightful heir of the dragon-kings to this god of yours." His glance went to the bard and curiously lingered for an instant before turning back again to Aurora. "May he guard you well, Daughter of Chandra's daughter, as you go forth with the blessings of your king."

Aurora, her soul singing with gladness, pressed her lips to the old king's hand, then, rising, she turned to gaze upon the Bard of Naefredeyan.

"Shall you, too, bid me godspeed and grant me your blessing, Alain?" she queried, her heart in her eyes as she waited for his answer, for she did not see how she could bear to lose him ere she had been given even the chance to know him.

"My blessing I give freely, Enchantress," he said, smiling enigmatically, "but not godspeed yet a while, if you will have me."

Then was Aurora's heart full indeed, for he would come with her, the king's bard, who was her father.

"Aye, I would have you," she answered, laughter spilling joyously from her lips. "And may you never live to regret it, for I must warn you that I shall not promise always to be an obedient daughter. Indeed, Frayne says I am headstrong and appallingly prone to plunge heedlessly into danger. You may find it in your heart to wish me to the farthest ends of the earth ere we are through."

"I promise I am not so fainthearted," he smiled. "Now, if you are ready, let us summon the merrowmaid that we may put this wish-net to the test."

The enchantress moved with alacrity to do as she was bidden. Grasping the wish-net firmly in one hand, she recited the words of summoning:

> "From the land or from the sea,
> Wheresoever thou might be,
> With a wish I summon thee,
> Maker of the net, to me."

Often in the past Aurora had tried to envision from Crane's description of the beautiful Shellandra a likely image of a sea-nymph. She had imagined long, flowing tresses and eyes the color of seaweed, a lissome form either with the graceful tail of a fish or perhaps with long, tapering legs, as she had appeared to Crane in dreams. But nothing had prepared her to discover captured in the fragile meshes of the net a hornless cow of diminutive proportions, indeed, no larger than a small hound.

Her heart sinking, Aurora stared dumbfounded into bovine eyes, which, surprisingly enough, though shy, were yet unmistakably intelligent.

"Egads, there must be some mistake," she muttered, rapidly reviewing the words of the spell for any possible error. Yet she had said them just as she remembered them from Vandrel's *Catalogue of Magic Spells and Summonings.* "By the One, the fault must lie, then, with the net," she decided out loud, bending to make a closer examination of the meshes for any possible rents or tears.

"I do beg your pardon if my wish-net has been in some way unsatisfactory," said the cow apologetically. "It has never failed to do my bidding, till yestereve when I bade it fetch to me the harpist who played so sweetly from the cliffs that I was drawn despite my better judgment to the shores of Garn from far out to sea."

"*You* made the net?" Aurora uttered in startled accents and stepped back to better view this oddity, when suddenly she became aware of the bard's deep chuckle ringing pleasantly in the hall.

"But of course she made it," he said, his voice yet vibrant with amusement. "Do you not know a merrow-maid when you see one?" he teased, then, observing the enchantress's blank look, he took pity on her, explaining that whereas merrows may take on any manner of shape or form while in the sea, when on land they appear most often as hornless cattle. "It is one of their peculiarities. And now perhaps you might relieve our timid guest of any fears she may have that we mean her harm. It is time, Aurora, that you made known to her your request."

"Huh? Oh, aye," Aurora stammered, startled out of her brief reverie, for she had been thinking the sea-nymphs most peculiar indeed to choose a cow's shape in which to venture forth from the water. Then seeing that the creature was in truth trembling in trepidation, Aurora made haste to make her wishes known.

"But no one could possibly wish to be sent to Kylandros," shuddered the merrow-maid. "Those who go there are never seen again. Please, I beg you to reconsider. I should feel very sad at having condemned anyone to the Flux, even if they asked me to do it."

"Nevertheless, I most earnestly do desire it," Aurora assured her unhesitatingly. "Further, I freely absolve you of all blame, no matter what the outcome. Indeed, I shall be eternally grateful to you, for, you see, the one I love more than life itself is trapped within the Flux of Timelessness, and only I can save him. Please, say you will do it, and I shall return to you your wish-net before I go."

Aurora, having made her plea with all the eloquence at her command, could yet see the odd creature hesitate. Then she heard the soft ruffle of harp strings, and suddenly the room was filled with sweet music. Time itself seemed to stop as the harpist wove spellbinding tapestries of melodies, till the final note, seeming to hang in the air, died slowly away and released her from the harpist's enchantment.

Dazed, Aurora blinked, and like waking from a dream to unfamiliar surroundings, she found herself in the shadowy depths of a forest enshrouded in fog. With a sense of unreality she stared at the now-empty wish-net still clasped tightly in her hand and at her pack lying just as she had left it at her feet. Her stomach tightened to a hard knot as she realized she must be on Kylandros and that apparently she had been transported there alone.

"Alain!" she cried, straining to pierce the trailing clouds of vapor for some sign of the bard. "Alain!" She felt Andruvien throb against her wrist, then uttered a strangled scream as a hand came out of nowhere and clasped her by the shoulder.

"Softly, child, I am here."

"Oh, gods, I thought you hadn't come!" she gasped, turning instinctively into the warm comfort of his chest. She felt him stiffen, then slowly, as if unsure of themselves, his arms lifted and enclosed her in a firm embrace.

The chill clouds of formless time swirling past the two forms huddled near a fluttering campfire distorted and obscured the hulks of trees looming out of the gloom like grotesque shadow-phantoms. Aurora, her knees clasped to her chest, stared fixedly into the flames and marveled that the Bard of Naefredeyan could appear so maddeningly calm. He sat across from her, his head bowed over the harp and his fingers brushing the harp strings seemingly aimlessly, as he waited tranquilly—for what?

It had been at his insistence that they settle here before they had even made an attempt to explore the island for some clue as to Frayne's whereabouts, saying there was little point in spending effort on a fruitless venture.

"Kylandros is but a portal into the endless flow of timeless possibilities," he had told her, his hands firm on her shoulders as he compelled her to listen to him. "Trust me, Aurora. When the time comes for us to go, I will know it."

"Go where, Alain? How will you know it?" she had insisted, in a fever of impatience to be about the task of finding Frayne, though it was true that she knew not how to go about it. But then, how did the bard know so much? She shivered, watching the slender fingers at the harp in helpless fascination. Who was he, this harpist with magic at his fingertips—a king's musician, a soldier, Almira's consort—what *else* was he?

"Tell me about Almira," she said before she thought, for it was a subject she had learned to avoid since her first eager queries had been turned resolutely aside. Thinking that perhaps her uncanny resemblance to her mother, coupled with the unexpected appearance of a daughter he had never known, had reopened old wounds too painful for him to discuss yet awhile, she had discreetly thought to spare him. Besides, their acquaintanceship had been too new, and she had been too unsure of him or herself to put it to the test with persistent questions, no matter how strongly she felt the need to know about her mother and father and why Alain had not been with the warrior-woman in Endrith's Forest. Yet there is something about a campfire that breeds confidences between people, even strangers, and suddenly she wanted more than anything to have this man who was her father trust her with the truth. "Please, Alain, what was she like?"

For the briefest moment his hands stilled on the harp, then once again they played over the strings, working a delicate web of melody, which seemed to touch a chord of memory within her. But she was only half-listening as she struggled with a sharp stab of disappointment, for it seemed he would not answer her. Aurora released a pent-up breath, unaware that her hands clasped about her knees tightened till the knuckles shone white against the skin. Then the bard's marvelous voice sounded quietly against the background of music and the wind groaning in the trees.

"Almira was the most remarkable woman I ever knew," he murmured, lifting his head so that Aurora could see his eyes glimmering uncannily in the firelight. "Till I met her daughter," he added with a smile that brought a blush to Aurora's cheeks. "We were amassing troops along the fringes of the desert bordering the Plain of Shintari when she rode into camp one evening, a slip of a girl with golden eyes and hair the color of raven's wings. She was Almira, Rab's daughter, and she had come to fight the enemies of the One—on her own, if need be."

His smile was wryly reminiscent.

"I knew her father well, of course, and would have sent her home where she belonged, only I could see her mind was set. When she was hurt or angry, or obstinately determined on a thing, her eyes would go all glittery—the way yours did when you decided you wanted none of Lothe or the Bard of Naefredeyan, who had treated you so shabbily." Aurora grinned appreciatively, just as he had meant for her to do. "Then, too, her chin would go up, which was ever an unmistakable sign that she had dug her heels in. But she had a sure instinct for reading people's minds, a trait that proved invaluable on more than one occasion and that very likely brought about her own end, even as it preserved the life of our only daughter."

Aurora jumped as his fingers ran harshly across the harp strings.

"If only I had listened to her!"

There was a bitterness in these last words that tore

312

at Aurora's heart. In wonder she beheld his eyes glint metallic fire, and then he was playing softly again, the same melody as before; indeed, she suddenly realized he had been playing the same haunting tune with minor variations for the past hour or more.

"You know already that Leilah had her killed, and why," he murmured, his voice distant, almost dreamy, so that Aurora stared at him, unable to believe he could speak with such unearthly calm when seconds before he had seemed literally to burn within. "What you do not know is that I sent Almira from me, believing she had plotted against me, against Harmon, against the One. They were Leilah's lies, and somehow I could not see past her lovely face to the wickedness within. I even believed the scheming sorceress when she said the child was the prince of Garn's, not mine; and, indeed, the infant Leilah brought to me, saying she was Almira's, bore more resemblance to Almira's cousin than it did to me. Still, when I learned that Almira and Garn had perished in Endrith's Forest, I kept the infant by me, telling myself I did it out of duty. She was, after all, of Rab's seed and the descendant of kings. And if I came soon to love that poor, gentle creature, it was because she seemed some fragile flower too delicate for life. Yet, as I watched her, dying a little more day after day, and knew that because of her mortal condition I could do nothing to save her, I suddenly realized I grieved not only for her brief life, but for Almira, who had taught me what it was to be a mere mortal—powerless before what seemed the laughter of the gods, prey to heartache, loneliness, fleeting heights of rapture and joy, despairing depths of grief, sorrow, hatred, anger, and yes, the bittersweet agony of love."

"You loved her, even when you thought she had betrayed you," Aurora said softly, remembering her own confused anger and pain at what had seemed Frayne's betrayal, and through it all, her inability to drive him from her heart.

"Yes," he answered, his expression unfathomable. "Even as you love Sulwyn Idris."

"Sulwyn Idris?" she repeated blankly. "But that is the Old Tongue for the 'Sun-Prince.' I don't understand."

"That is his name, even as it once was Dred's—before the Rebellion. 'Frayne' was convenient so long as he wished to remain unknown, but that time is past. He is the Thromholan, half-mortal, half-god. He can evade that truth no longer, for Dred will soon have in his possession Efluvien and Vendrenin. The tides of war are upon us. Behold."

Aurora gasped as the fog seemed suddenly to swirl and coalesce into solid shapes, so that where before there had been ancient trees draped with moss, she now beheld a sea of crystals sparkling brilliantly in the light of a setting sun, and standing far out from the shore, a crystal tower rising in solitary splendor toward a sky streaked with crimson clouds.

"Estrelland!" she breathed. "The tower of Efluvien."

"Aye. And there against the skyline, Dred's creatures from the Flux."

Oh, gods, it was true. Great winged shadows swooped about the tower, while others scaled the crystal heights like huge black spiders. Aurora cried

314

out as she saw crystal shatter and an ominous web of cracks spreading downward from the apex of the tower. Then suddenly the clouds closed in again, and the enchantress found herself once more on Kylandros before the dying fire, and calmly seated across from her was the bard still strumming quietly on his harp. For the space of several heartbeats she was not sure which was the reality—the island obscured in cloud or the faded vision of Estrelland besieged by the creatures who served Dred. Then she remembered she was on Kylandros drifting through the Flux. Perhaps she had been made to see what was only a possibility. Afraid to know the truth and yet compelled to ask, she turned huge, haunted eyes to the Bard of Naefredeyan.

"Was it a true vision or only a possibility?" she whispered huskily. "Is Estrelland even now falling to the forces of Throm?"

"It is a possibility became an actuality," replied the bard with steely calm.

Aurora shivered and glanced away from the strong, chiseled features. Gods ,with his hair flowing silvery on the wind and his eyes fey with some distant vision, he had seemed suddenly eldritch, something other than flesh and blood. How could he be so cold about the destruction of Estelland and the loss of Vendrenin to the Lord of Somn? she wondered, repelled.

"But why doesn't Efluvien do something?" she cried in frustration. "Surely the creatures could not stand against the Vendrenin."

"Efluvien is the Peace-Keeper, the Guardian of the Vendrenin, nothing more. Only Harmon ever dared wield the thing wrought of purest power."

315

"Then where is Harmon? Why does he not come forward to put a stop to things ere it is too late? Does he not know we have need of him?" she demanded, trying desperately to understand why the world seemed to be crashing in all around her.

"He knows," replied the bard strangely, "and doubtless he will come when the need is the greatest. But not to wield the Vendrenin. That is for some other."

"Then who? Where is this other?" she asked, but then she knew without his answer. With a sort of awe she recited the Prophecy of the Chosen One:

> "In the time of the Third Upheaval Dred shall walk the land. And the harmony of the Realm shall be disrupted, for in his hand he shall wield the Vendrenin. And Harmon, the warrior-god, shall seek the mage-child born of mystic light, whose soul commands the music of the spheres. And from Dred shall the Chosen One wrest the instrument of power and for seven times seventy ages vanquish Dred to darkness."

"It is that one, is it not?" she queried steadily. "The one chosen to be the savior of the people is come to retrieve the Vendrenin. But then that is the one to whom Andruvien must belong. Alain, you must tell me how I may find the mage-child. Please, who is this new god of the Eilderood?"

"Not a god," smiled the bard, "but a mortal child. And only Harmon could tell you who, for it is *his* quest to find the Chosen One."

"Is that what he is about, then, while Estelland crumbles and the Vendrenin is lost to Dred?" she demanded, unable to keep the bitterness from her voice, for, indeed, she could not understand how it was that Immortals—the Eilderood—could seem as helpless as those who were so much less than they. "And will he find what he seeks?"

"I doubt not that he waits only for the child to find it out. Then, and only then, will Harmon make his presence known. But that is not why we are come to Kylandros, is it?" he reminded her, and laying aside the harp, rose to gaze upon her with a warmth that softened his stern features so that he no longer seemed an unearthly being, but only the king's bard—Alain, her father. Smiling into her eyes, he extended a lean hand toward her. "We have our own quest, have we not?"

She did not answer at once, as it came to her to wonder how he could know so much about the Flux, the gods, and so many other things she somehow sensed about him. He had, of course, fought with Harmon as one of his commanders, and he had known Rab and Chandra. And, too, he had won Almira's love, so perhaps it was not so strange after all that he should be someone quite exceptional.

"Aye, we have," she said at last, and taking his hand, let him pull her to her feet. "Just tell me how we are to go about it."

He laughed at her wry expression, his deep chuckle seeming to roll over and through her, so that she found herself grinning back at him, her heart lighter than it had been since they had come to the dismal island of grey, insubstantial fog. But then suddenly

317

he sobered, and instinctively she steeled herself, expecting some dire warning of peril. She was thus taken aback to hear him begin what smacked very much of a fatherly lecture on the larger questions of life as viewed from the perspective of one of far greater experience and maturity. It was the sort of thing Garwin had been wont to do whenever it appeared she was about to launch herself heedlessly into some sort of bumblebroth, and always just when time seemed most pressing and she chafed to be about the business of living her life that she might draw her own conclusions about it. With the result that not only had she found it trying to attend to him, but she had been hard put as well to make any sense of his gnomes of wisdom.

"Every life," Alain began, "is made up of variations on a single tune—the music of existence, like the cycles of being, repeated endlessly. If I had not, for example, listened to Leilah's lies, Almira would not have been forced to flee my protection to save her daughter's life. You would not have grown up nameless among elves and dryads, and your life would have been far different from what it has been. But you would have been different, too, for it is possible you would never have met the knight of Tor, or having met, not loved him as you do now. Then might your destinies have been separate strands, the songs of your lives sung quite differently. You see, the possibilities are endless, and yet still, the underlying theme remains unchanged, for it is based on the cycles of being."

"But what has that to do with the Flux?" she interrupted, unable to contain her impatience.

Everything he had said so far seemed painfully obvious, and, besides, this hardly seemed the time for philosophic conjectures on the nature of the universe. She would be about the task of finding Frayne!

"The Flux," he persisted, ignoring her importunate tone of voice, "is nothing more than all the possible variations on that single theme. And so it is with you and Frayne, your lives, each a melody with its own variations, until they become joined, one to the other, to create a harmonic entity—one song out of all the possibilities."

Suddenly Aurora's interest quickened as she began to grasp glimmerings of the purpose of his discourse. Indeed, it struck her that earlier he had not been harping idly, for while the music flowing endlessly from his fingertips had varied from rhapsodic flights to lyrical sublimity, it had always returned to the same haunting melody that yet echoed through her mind like a half-awakened memory.

"'Twas my song you were harping all this time," she said, "the strands of my existence, which are joined with Frayne's and thus form the continuum through all the flux of possibilities to wherever Frayne is trapped. I see it now. But how shall we trace the melody? By what means see where the strands lead?"

"I have prepared the way," answered the bard, and suddenly she could see he had withdrawn from her again. "Now the harp shall be your guide."

"My guide? But you are coming with me? Alain, I am not ready yet to lose you," she pleaded, turning the full force of her eyes upon him. But already he seemed to be fading, his tall form growing blurred as he appeared to recede beyond a thickening curtain of fog.

"This is your journey into the Flux," she heard him say, and his voice was hollow and insubstantial, as if it came from somewhere far away. "Whatever awaits you along the way is for you alone, Enchantress. But you have not lost me, nor shall I ever be far from you. Fear not, I'll be waiting for you beyond the realm of possibility wheresoever you emerge."

The fog closed in around her then, and she was alone save for the harp lying on the ground beside the dying embers of the fire. Slowly she crossed to it, and kneeling, picked it up as if it were some fragile thing that might crumble at her touch. Oh, gods, it was yet warm, she groaned, clasping it to her as though to cling somehow to her father's lingering presence. Weeping softly, she rose to her feet again to stare blankly at the grey shroud of vapor into which the bard had vanished.

"But I-I know not how to play it, nor how to find my way out again," she shouted. "Alain! By the One, Alain, you *cannot* leave me here like this!"

Within the grey cocoon of fog, the enchantress ran her fingers again and again across the harp strings, listening for some familiar note, some clue as to the beginning of the harpist's oft-repeated melody. Doggedly she kept at the task, till the skin of her fingertips was rubbed raw and she thought she could not bear to try again. Then wearily she laid her cheek against the harp-frame and wept with bitter frustration.

"Oh, gods, am I thus meant to linger for all eternity in this dismal place, alone and bereft of any living thing? Shall I dream of Garwin and Gleb and the Hawthorn Glade till even they are naught but faded memories?"

Never had she felt so alone, she who had thought always to be one with the earth and one with Frayne. Cruelly she had been cut adrift, and only the harp could lead her back again—the harp, which she could not play.

"By the One, I shall go mad," she cried, then shivered as a chill gust of wind hurtled past her.

Well, at least she need not suffer the cold, she thought rebelliously, and rummaged through her pack for the cloak given her by Endrith. Then did she know true despair, as she discovered the pack empty save for the wish-net, the Circlet of Kerr, and Almira's Cloak of Power. With hands that trembled from the cold and from an utter sense of hurt bewilderment, she pulled the crimson cloak from the pack and draped it around her.

Why should the bard have taken the other cloak, the one wrought of Endrith's magic to ward off the cold of deepest winter? And, indeed, it must have been he, for she was sure it had been there when she pulled the wish-net from the pack in the Hall of the Dragon-Kings. What else had he taken? she wondered suddenly and hastily felt for the bracelet about her wrist and Guthsweord in the scabbard at her belt. Both were there. Egads, it made no sense. Why the cloak and nothing else?

But the answer was obvious. He had known she would be forced to seek warmth from the chill damp and had thus made sure she would have to wear the Cloak of Power. Why?

"Because it is inextricably entwined with the song of my destiny!" she whispered, her heart beginning to pound excitedly. "And because woven into its fabric are the symbols of the Song of Power." Summoning the light of Andruvien, the enchantress gazed with dawning understanding upon the symbols wrought in gold, which glittered in the subdued fire of the crystal like a message of hope. No wonder the melody had been familiar, she thought. It was the Song of Power Alain had played over and over. Then suddenly much was made plain to her.

She thought back to the first time the song had come to her. Gleb's spirit had wandered in the dark land of Somn as Hedron, the Black King, searched the farthest recesses of his mind for the identity of the young enchantress whom Frayne had taken as his lover. Thinking Gleb gone forever from her, she had been overcome with grief, when suddenly the song, whose words and melody she had never heard before welled up within her and burst forth to still the forest. The song had broken the power of the wraith and freed Gleb's spirit from the Land of Somn. After that the song had come to her in times of great trial—in Sheelar's sylvan glen when she had charmed the Serpent-Lord and escaped his treacherous coils, in the Crystal Room when she had mastered Andruvien, in Endrith's Forest when she had called upon the song to quell the blood-lust of the wolves as they circled for the kill, and again in Seraisharaqa when she had raised Al-tabl-ur-ras, the Drum of the Heavens. And then suddenly she knew that it had not come from outside her but from somewhere deep within, for had not Alain said that it was her song of

322

being, the melody which was uniquely Aurora, the enchantress with strange and wondrous powers?

Therein lay the riddle to her true name, and to resolve it and find Frayne, she must somehow learn to play it on her father's harp, the Harp of Naefredeyan. But how? The answer must lie in the cloak, she thought, else Alain would not have gone to so much trouble to render it significant by its singular presence. Perhaps it was enough just to have it on, she thought, remembering how, as she had raised the Drum of the Heavens, the cloak had intensified the empyrean power commanded by the song and thus by the symbols woven into the crimson fabric. Then she had believed the cloak served to channel the power through the one who wore it, and it had come to her that the undeciphered symbols on the cloak, the song of power, the harp that was part of the sculpture of Harmon, even the crystal power of Andruvien and thus the Vendrenin, too, were all connected, all parts of a riddle she must somehow resolve. Now she knew as well that the riddle was herself.

Each time in the past the song had come to her unbidden as within her she felt the first stirrings of the god. The One grant that it would this time, too, she prayed and lifted the harp onto her lap once more.

Her fingers trembled as she began to play haltingly, listening and waiting for something to happen—waiting for the hand of the god to touch her and listening for the song to awaken within her. But she felt nothing. Nothing but bitter emptiness.

"Oh, gods, Frayne, where are you?" she cried,

weaving with weariness and despair. "Without you I am powerless, and even the god does not hearken to my need." Then, as if summoned by her words, a vision of the godlike face supplanted the threatening darkness within her mind. She saw him—Frayne— and felt his strength melding with hers. He was one with her, his power calling forth hers, and suddenly music welled up within her and burst forth in song, even as her fingers found the hidden chords upon the harp strings.

Endlessly the music flowed, carrying the enchantress on a dream-trek through the unknown or half-forgotten landscapes of her life. She was Almira and Alain joined in the sweet tides of love's passion, and she was the seed and the egg made one. She was warm, moist dark, a dream of contentment growing without knowing toward a wondrous, terrifying light and the comfort of her mother's love. She was a babe suckling at Almira's breast and a melody of power summoning the miracle of a unicorn into her presence—Endrith, bowing before her as her mother wept.

"You behold before you the daughter of earth and fire," she heard her mother say. "In due course all that I have seen reflected on the still waters of Sheelar's mystic pond shall come to pass. Already the god turns from me, for Alain is soul-weary from battle and filled with the darkness of destiny. He listens to Leilah and believes her lies. My death even now stalks my trail, old friend. I rely on you to watch over the child till the power is awakened within her. Then shall you sing to her the Song of the Unicorn that she may know the way to the truth of her destiny."

"It shall be as you say," replied the unicorn, his purple eyes filled with sorrow. "The One grant her strength and goodness of heart, for the Path of Rebirth is meant to try the soul."

Then Endrith vanished and in his stead was a young prince with red-gold hair.

"Nay, Cousin," cried her mother, "I will not have your death on my hands. Leilah's black knights shall be granted the victory over Rab's younger daughter and any foolish enough to side with her. It is the will of the gods, who believe I have betrayed them."

"Then so be it, Almira," said the prince, his voice like steel. "My place is with you and the infant of destiny. If it is into the arms of death you must ride, then you shall not ride alone. By the gods, I swear it."

It seemed then that she viewed a kaleidoscope of events: a terrifying ride beneath thick, leafy boughs; Almira, singing the song of power as Aurora nursed at her breast; battle cries, death, and elves appearing out of nowhere to bear an infant into the deeper solitude of a woody bower. She was a child again among elves and dryads—Anduan, Elf-Foundling, and Tree-Child. She beheld Breatha, She-Bear, slay the panther that had slain her cub and Arkon, Rogue-Wolf, driven from the pack, and still did the song go on, till she was a girl in her eighteenth summer setting off through the woods in search of the dreaded man-beast. And at last there was Frayne in all the glory of manhood, and she was Anduan no longer, but Aurora awakening to an enchantress's power.

Aurora opened her eyes to a field of starflowers and

fairy-wand and thought she must be dreaming, for before her was a cozy thatched cottage nestled among tamarack trees at the edge of the meadow, and sunning lazily in the knee-high grass mottled with flowers was a graceful young Dracadern. Nor was that all, for she soon became acutely aware that her head rested most satisfactorily in the cradle of a broad shoulder, and that lean, powerful arms held her tenderly against a hard chest. Aurora's heart gave a leap as her eyes lifted to behold a firm jaw and finely molded lips, at the corner of which was a small scar that gave the mouth a slightly cynical cast.

"Oh, gods, Frayne!" she choked, hugging him convulsively about the neck. "Thank the One I have found you at last."

She felt his arms tighten about her, and then his lips had found hers, and the world seemed suddenly to tilt and whirl away, leaving only the wonder of Frayne's mouth hungrily devouring her.

"Aurora, you little fool," he groaned as he kissed her feverishly—her eyes, her cheeks, the delicious vulnerability of her neck, and then her mouth again, long and tenderly.

"Frayne, Frayne," she cried weakly. She was weeping softly, the tears streaming unheeded down her cheeks, when at last he pulled away to gaze long into her eyes, his own burning with a silvery fire.

"You shouldn't have come," he began, but she stopped him with a hand placed gently to his lips.

"Don't," she whispered, smiling at him through her tears. "I am Aurora, and you are Frayne. Can you truly think I could do otherwise?"

A shutter seemed to close over his face as he

released her legs, and letting her slide slowly down his length, set her on the ground.

"I had hoped you would," he said with an odd sort of bitterness that wounded her. "I prayed that you would forget me. But you are here now, and I must live with the knowledge that you are now a prisoner here with me. Damn it, Aurora! I am the Thromholan, and you—" she trembled as his hand came up, seemingly of its own accord, to cradle the side of her face with infinite tenderness, "—you are something rare and precious, like the Dracaderns Kev and Lynwen, who are the only ones of their kind. I had believed that so long as I must remain in the Flux, you at least would be spared."

"Spared without you?" she demanded huskily. "Can you not see that that would be to live a half-life? Always empty, incomplete and forever yearning—is that what you wanted for me? For yourself?"

She felt a shudder shake the lean frame.

"No," he groaned, the single utterance seemingly torn from his very depths as he crushed her to him. — "Oh, gods, Aurora, you defeat me at every turn. When I am apart from you, I see my way clearly, and I know it is wrong for me to love you, *wrong* to let *you* love Dred's cursed bastard. But when you are near, you fill my senses with sweet madness, and I know only that I want you, need you desperately. I cannot stop myself from loving you any more than I can stop myself from breathing."

She felt the leap of his desire and knew the sweet ecstasy of the god's fire ignite within her.

"Then do not try to thwart what is the god's will," she whispered throatily, and reaching up with both hands to pull his head down to her, she kissed him with all the desperate yearning of her woman's heart.

Never had their need been greater. Indeed, she thought she must be consumed by the uncontrolled fury of their love as hurriedly he undressed her and then himself, then lay with her on the crimson cloak spread amid the starflowers and fairy-wand. His breath harsh in his throat, he found her lips and kissed her deeply. Indeed, he seemed to draw upon her very soul as she answered him passion for passion with an urgency not one whit less than his own. Then his hand trailing liquid flames along her thigh found the wellspring of her desire. She shuddered, sigh after sigh escaping from her lips. And at last he mounted and drove deep into her so that she cried out with the rapture of their joining.

Flame for flame, they burned as one, their joined powers cresting in a glorious blaze of incandescent fire that rendered Aurora weak and trembling, but feeling gloriously alive. She was filled with a sweet, aching tenderness for the man cradled in her arms, his head resting delectably against the soft mound of her breast. Trailing her hand over the powerful muscles of his back and shoulders, she rejoiced in the mystic rite of love between woman and man that could exceed the barriers of time and space, transmuting flesh into fire and thus melding separate bodies into a single entity of spiritual transcendence.

As if he had read her thoughts, Frayne stirred, turning his face to nibble tantalizingly at the pink thrust of her nipple. Aurora's eyelids drifted over her eyes at the answering pulsation of desire rippling deliciously upward through her belly. A sigh shuddered through her, as, his strong hands infinitely loving, he roused her once more, this time with slow deliberation.

Their first joining had been the violent conflagration of the god's purging flame, but in its wake they found a passion that, while gentler, was no less strong, for it was the ineffable harmony of love's blissful song. She was the harp and he the harpist, whose exquisite touch elicited the sublime music of her innermost self. With a moan she opened to him, moving with him to the age-old rhythm of love.

In a delirious rhapsody of mounting ecstasy, she gazed deeply into falcon eyes gleaming silvery with love and knew such heart-rending rapture as she had never imagined possible before. Oh, gods, she thought she must die of it, this terrible, sweet passion of the soul. Tenderly she caressed him, her eyes feverish, as her fingers trailed a path through the hair on his chest. He was so beautiful. Save for the marks of old wounds upon the lean torso, his skin, rendered tawny by exposure to the sun, was smooth, the muscles rippling beneath it well formed and powerful. Through half-lidded eyes, she beheld the strong column of his neck, the muscles standing out like cords as he carried them both toward the apex of culminating desire. Then she was lost to the crescendoing rhythm of his driving passion and her own swelling need, till at last he drew back and thrust powerfully, and she nearly swooned with the explosive burst, which set off wave after wave of pleasure rippling through her, like harp strings vibrating to an exquisite song of celestial sublimity.

Then at last she slept, blissfully snug within the circle of her lover's arms.

Aurora awakened slowly to the ominous rumble of a building storm and to Frayne's gaze, silvery upon her.

"I had almost forgotten how beautiful you are," he said as he read the unspoken question in her eyes. "In sleep, how like a child." His handsome lips twisted in a half-rueful smile. "And within, such passion as must inspire the gods to sweet ecstasy. Long ago, it seems, I sensed you reaching out to me as I struggled to decipher those blasted signposts. Indeed, your thoughts seemed to pierce my mind, and suddenly I knew what I must do. The road brought me here, to Ariana and the agony of not knowing what had happened to you. Then, today, as the sun rose, I awakened to the sound of harping and the feeling that you were in some kind of trouble. I sent my thoughts outward, and for one blissful, heart-rending moment, it seemed that somewhere we touched. Was I dreaming, Aurora? How did you find your way to my prison?"

Smiling, she raised her hand to run her fingers through his hair shining golden in a shaft of sunlight streaming through a hole in the clouds.

"My father's harp brought me," she said lightly; then, grimacing comically, she added, "And 'twas no dream, I assure you. I might still be wearing my fingers to the bone trying to pick out the right notes, had I not called out to you in utter frustration and felt you meld with me. After that, the harp seemed to play itself, though my fingers yet moved over the strings. I saw my life pass before me like the landmarks along a winding road. And when at last our songs were joined, as they were when you made love to me beside the still waters of Grendylmere, I seemed suddenly to fall into a deep sleep from which you awakened me. I was in your arms, and I thought I must be dreaming. And if you do not kiss me soon, I shall still think you naught but a dream."

"I, on the other hand, could wish it to be," he retorted, pulling away from her.

Drawing her bottom lip between her teeth to keep from crying out at him in angry frustration, Aurora watched her maddening love rise with sinuous grace and begin to shrug on his scattered clothing. Drat the man! Why must he erect all the old barriers now, when she sensed that he needed her? Indeed, she could see the muscles bunched like steel bands across his neck and shoulders. Blast! Why could he not see that she was no child, but the enchantress whom he himself had awakened and named? He need only trust her, and together they could surmount whatever difficulty he envisioned before them.

Then he turned to impale her with light, piercing eyes, and instantly she knew that he had heard the whisper of her thoughts.

"Since I have been here, I have sensed other things as well," he said icily, and it struck her that he had yet to assume the old, impenetrable mask of the knight of Tor. Indeed, there was a new hardness about him, like tempered steel, which she had often sensed before but seldom seen revealed, and she could not help but

331

wonder at it. "I can feel my father awakening from his brooding sleep. Dred, rising from the plasmic stuff of Somn, taking on the solidity of shape and form, as he stretches stiff limbs and probes the farthest reaches for whatever it was that roused him. My mind is haunted with an image of darkness, like a shadow spreading across the land. In my sleep I have been visited with images of Hawthorn Glade, charred and blackened, the great tree beneath which your gentle Gleb lay wracked with pain naught but a ruined hulk. I have heard the weeping of dryads who mourn the slow passing of their father-oak and felt their own spirits withering and dying within them. I have felt the shape-changer's bewilderment and beheld the man-wolf and the Shintari huntress stalking beasts whose names are evil whispers spoken in dread. Would you know more?" he queried brutally. "Shall I tell you that I have seen Endrith embark upon a long, tortuous journey, the same treacherous path that ended for another, hopefully less fortunate unicorn in the bowels of the Black Mountain in the Confounded Lands?"

"Nay!" she cried piercingly, her hands tearing at her hair as with lowered head she writhed in pain. "Oh, gods, I pray you. Let not all that is good and wondrous pass from the earth. Spare Endrith, I beg you."

For a long moment the man stood staring at the girl, his lean countenance seemingly hewn from granite, save for the eyes, glowing like white-hot embers in the cold rigidity of his face. Then he glanced up at the approach of a slender woman whose gentle aspect wore a look that both pitied and reproached him. The muscle leaped along his jawline, and abruptly he turned and stalked wordlessly across the lea, finally to vanish into a thick spinney of encroaching tamaracks.

The woman watched him go, a haunting sadness hovering about her, then, kneeling to cover Aurora's nakedness in the soft folds of the crimson cloak, she gathered the weeping girl in a soothing embrace.

"There, there, child," she murmured, gently stroking the ebony curls. "You mustn't mind him, for he can't change what he is. He'll always do the noble thing, no matter what the cost to himself. And if you love him as I think you do, then you must know that he's hurting far more right now than you are."

Aurora, her mind reeling from shock, clung senselessly to the woman's sustaining strength and struggled to come to grips with her own terrible grief. Endrith dying! And Minta and Valesia, too, her dryad mother-pair, whose life forces were one with the stricken father-oak. Oh, gods, she could not bear it! But then gradually her weeping subsided, her grief giving way before the swelling tides of an icy rage.

Only then did she become aware of the woman, and pulling abruptly away, looked up into the still-lovely countenance of Ariana, the Holy Maiden of Sedgewick.

It seemed that with that single glance into eyes as soft as a hind's yet translucent with a shimmering inner strength, Aurora's tumult was stilled, her anger quenched in the cool depths of the Valdoran's boundless compassion.

"Ariana," she uttered hoarsely and blushed as

helplessly she hiccupped. "Oh, dear, what must you think of me?"

"I think that you have been ill rewarded for the courage of your heart, my child. And further, that you will feel much better once you have bathed your face and put something warm in your belly," pronounced the woman who had willingly given herself as sacrifice that Dred's evil might be laid to rest for a time. "When you have washed and dressed, come inside, my dear. I cannot promise a lavish meal, but what we have I offer in the hopes that you shall forgive the poor hospitality thus far afforded you."

Aurora, her eyes darkening nearly to amber, looked quickly away from the woman's all-too-discerning gaze.

"I-I cannot promise to accept your offer in the same spirit in which it is given," she managed after a moment. "But in no way do I hold you accountable. *You* have been everything that is kind."

"I see," murmured Ariana, studying the frozen young countenance. For a while she was silent as she seemed to consider her next words. But then she spoke with an infinite gentleness that somehow shamed the enchantress into looking up again. "I have never loved as you love my son," she said, "so I cannot know what you are suffering. But I do know that he would die before he harmed you. The thing is, do you love my son enough to make him want to live for you? No, do not try to answer me. That is for you and you alone to decide. I shall go now. Come whenever you are ready. Only promise you won't tarry too long. There's a storm brewing, and it would not do anyone any good for you to be caught out in it.

A cold, after all, is a miserable thing, even for someone with a great deal to think over.''

Smiling then, Ariana turned and strolled easily toward a cottage, pausing only long enough to bat playfully at the young dragon nipping at the hem of her plain robe of unadorned homespun. With a vague sense of unreality, Aurora watched her vanish into the shadowed interior of the house.

For a long while the enchantress sat unmoving, prey to a whole gamut of disturbing thoughts, not the least of which concerned the Valdoren's unsettling suggestion that Frayne meant to die rather than harm her. In a way it explained much about her love's mysterious behavior, for he had from the first warned her to have nothing to do with one such as he. But she had thought he had acted thus merely to keep from her the dark secret of his birth, and once that was out and still the worst had not turned her from him, she had believed that surely there was no more need for him to hold her at arm's length. Yet still he persisted in his determination to drive her away, for she could think of no other reason that he should wound her with such deliberate cruelty, unless, of course, he was truly as black as he wished her to think. But, nay. She could not be so mistaken in him or in her own heart, which would not let him kill her love for him. If he was evil, then so must she be, for they were immutably made one.

Then why did he fear himself so greatly that if he could not destroy her love then willingly would he destroy himself? That the riddle was in some way bound up with the prophecies of the Thromholan was obvious. He was Dred's son, who, it was foretold in the Tome of Prophecy, would one day lead the Thromgilad to victory, and yet that in itself did not seem sufficient reason for him to fear for *her* life in particular. She was naught but the daughter of a warrior-woman and a king's musician. What was there in that to dread? Lest he believed they might one day stand as enemies over drawn swords, Andruvien against Thrimheld, she mused with a sinking heart. And, indeed, she was committed to uphold the Realm and would gladly give her life in the name of the One. But then so was Frayne, who was a sworn knight of Tor. Egads, she could not envision the circumstances that could cause him to turn from his blood oath to the One. He was Frayne, the hero of a hundred tales of valor. Naught could ever change him.

Oh, gods, if she could only make him see that once and for all! And indeed she must if what his mother had hinted was anywhere close to the truth. It would be just like him to fling himself into the heart of danger in the mistaken belief that in so doing he might avert any chance of bringing her harm, she thought with a sinking heart. Nor did she see that she could in any way stop him, for he was, as Gleb had been wont to say, as stubborn as a bear after honey when he took a sudden notion. But then so was she, she mused with a wry grin. And what if he was half-mortal, half-god? Was she not a descendant of magicians and kings? And of what else? whispered a small voice in the back of her head as a fleeting image of silvery hair and strange opaque crystalline eyes came briefly before her.

Well, no matter, she shrugged and bent resolutely

to gather up her discarded clothes. It was enough that she was Aurora, the enchantress with the power of Andruvien and the wiles of a woman irretrievably in love. She would be more than his match when the time came, she told herself and made her way with a firm step to a small spring gurgling out of the earth near the Valdoran's cottage. She would wash and render herself more presentable to break bread with her hostess. Then, she vowed with a dangerous glint in her eye, she would be ready for anything her obstinate lord might have in store for her!

Chapter 11

Frayne stood at the edge of a precipice, his face set in hard lines as he stared out over an infinitude of formless dark. He had wandered seemingly for hours, oblivious of the sheets of lightning scintillating in the heavens and the downpour only just receding to a slow, steady drizzle. Wet and disheveled, his hair clinging to his forehead and his clothes plastered to limbs heavy with weariness, he had still gone on, driven by the torment of his soul and by the haunting image of a slender, raven-haired girl with eyes the color of gold, till at last he had found himself here, at the Abyss of Possibilities.

When first he had heard the distant sound of harping, he had thought it naught but an echo of memory come to torture him. He had tried to put it from him, but it had persisted, changing from the smooth flow of a master's touch upon the strings to the halting uncertainty of an untutored searching. Then suddenly, inexplicably, he had known it was she—Aurora, reaching out to him, Aurora in need—

and he had responded without thought or hesitation, his soul's yearning greater than the cold, hard logic of reality. Whereupon the answering swell of melody had seemed to pierce his heart with a fierce, aching joy.

Could nothing daunt her, this exquisite creature whose essence was all sweet innocence and fiery passion? he marveled as he felt her drawing nearer and nearer, the song of her being, the music of an ineffable power, crescendoing till it seemed to vibrate within his very soul. She had come, against all odds had found him amid the infinitude of possibilities, and the knowledge had both humbled him and filled him with bittersweet torment. For he could not tell her that deep within he had welcomed the solitude of a prison, which, though it might be naught but the eternity of emptiness and despair without her, yet had still seemed to insure that so long as he remained within the Flux he should never be a threat to her. Indeed, not even to destroy her love for him could he bring himself to confess that he was no prisoner at all, that, in truth he could find his way through the drift of insubstantiality with as great an ease as he made his way in the dark. Therein lay the greatest irony of all, because he could only travel in such a manner alone. Thus she had, in a sense, made what was previously only a self-induced exile a prison in reality, for though he would never leave without her, he saw no way to take her with him. And yet he must return her somehow to complete her quest for her identity, else Dred's victory would be as complete as if he had the Thromholan fighting at his side.

Egads, what a fool he had been to believe he might

thwart destiny. Indeed, he should have known he had never had a choice from the day he had come across the slithery-tongued Sheelar lying in wait for him on the outskirts of the Tamarack Grove, he thought, seeing again in his mind's eye the monstrous green serpent coiled on a moonlit rock at the edge of a sylvan pool.

Three days after his return to Tor with the enchantress his prisoner, he had gone to the forest in search of Crane and the missing slave girl. For it had ever been the sorceress's practice to closet herself in the Chamber of Visions for a lengthy meditation after she received each new ingredient for the potion, and thus the knight, knowing his mistress would be occupied for several days, had been free to steal from the stone fortress and make with all haste for the abandoned camp in the Tamarack Grove. Unfortunately, he had arrived only to discover that a storm had obliterated any lingering sign that either Janine or the young shape-changer might have left behind, and though he had remained as long as he dared, doggedly combing the brakes till he was quite certain further search was pointless, he had found nothing but a trail left by a band of mounted horsemen less than half an hour before him. One of the several outlaw bands that sheltered in the forest, he had judged and dismissed them from his mind. It was on the third day, as Ciaron doused the light of Eo, that he turned wearily for home, only to discover himself suddenly hemmed in on three sides by a seemingly impenetrable growth of rosehedge and bramblebush. A grim smile had come to his lips, for he had known instantly that he was caught in a will-web of considerable magnitude.

Still, he had not been overly concerned, for he was not unversed in the art of such enchantments, and even a web as intricately wrought as this was easily unraveled by one who knew how to see through the illusion to the reality. His curiosity, however, had been piqued, as the web-weaver had no doubt intended that it should be, with the result that Frayne had decided to follow the tangled trail wheresoever it might lead.

That it had eventually brought him to Sheelar's sylvan glen had not surprised him overmuch. Whom else, after all, *should* he have found in the midst of a rowan wood overgrown with virgin's bower and teeming with mushrooms, toadstools, elfin cap and enchanter's nightshade *but* the mightiest of the Seventy-seven Serpent-Lords of Somn? What *had* caught him totally off guard was the serpent's purpose in luring him into its lair.

"Ah, the mortal s-son of S-Somn has-s found his-s way at las-st to Sh-Sheelar's s-sylvan paradis-se," hissed the snake, lazily lifting its wedge-shaped head to regard the knight out of soulless eyes of glittering emerald.

"Even so, Serpent," the knight drawled sardonically, but his nerves had tingled with a premonition of danger not yet apprehended. "I was curious to know why the mighty Sheelar should go to the trouble of issuing an invitation, and so I came. But know this: my time is short and I'm in no mood for lengthy discourse. So if you will come simply to the point, I should be best pleased."

"S-so impetuous-s, thes-se has-sty mortals-s,"

sighed the serpent-lord, languorously unraveling its coiled sinuosity. "In s-seven times-s s-seventy ages one attains-s a certain temperance, the wisdom of patience, as it were, mos-st regrettably denied mankind's ephemeral offs-spring. Now let's-s s-see. What was-s it you wished of Sh-Sheelar, S-son of S-Somn?"

"Your purpose in bringing me here," supplied the knight with an amused quirk of an eyebrow.

"Ah, yes-s. S-so it was. S-Strange that I sh-should have los-st my train of thought."

"No doubt," Frayne retorted drily. "However, I suggest that unless you keep your distance, 'twill not be the thought, but your head that's lost." And, indeed, the slippery snake had crept by slow degrees to within a few feet of the mounted knight.

"Pssst!" spat the serpent, recoiling precipitously from the threat of Thrimheld flashing silvery in the moonlight, and, oozing back upon itself, coil after slithery coil, the creature sullenly retreated.

"Sh-Sheathe your s-sword, knight," he sibilated from the safety of his rock. The reptilian tongue licked the air as he eyed the knight with cold disdain. "I am Sh-Sheelar, mighties-st of the S-Seventy-s-seven. What poss-ssible interes-st could *I* have in harming S-Sulwyn Idris-s?"

The knight, coolly obliging, returned the weapon to the scabbard, then dropped lightly to the ground.

"Oh, come now, Sheelar," he retorted amiably, flicking the dust from his travel-stained cloak, "we both know one who would be greatly interested. Tell me, how does my dearest father? Still up to his usual skullduggery?"

343

"The prince does not confide in serpents, even the mightiest of them, my lord," interjected a new voice, seemingly out of nowhere. "*I* asked Sheelar to bring you here." Then, as if having shed a concealing cloak, a slender girl appeared, her gaze fond as she reached out to stroke the serpent's wedge-shaped head.

"Thank you, old friend," Frayne heard her murmur. "I am forever in your debt. I ask you now to leave us, for it is best that you know nothing of what transpires between this one and myself."

"If it is-s your wish-sh, I sh-shall go," susurrated the serpent-lord with what seemed an affection most peculiar for a snake. "Yet s-still will I s-say that you was-ste your time and ris-sk far too much on this-s feckless-s s-scheme. This-s one's-s heart is-s clos-sed to you. He will not be brought to reas-son."

"Nevertheless, I must try," she whispered hauntingly as Sheelar, the Serpent-Lord, vanished into the night. The illusion of the sylvan pond set amid a rowan wood disappeared with him, leaving in its stead naught but an oak and maple forest bathed in moonlight and a small spring bubbling out of the earth where the sylvan pool had been. At last she turned to Frayne. "If it please my lord, I would most earnestly speak with you."

The knight's eyes flashed cold steel as he looked upon the girl simply gowned in pale orchid, her fair hair, straight and parted in the middle, falling in a shimmering mass down her back to below her waist. She was of dainty proportions, the wrists finely boned, as was the face turned beseechingly toward him. Everything about her bespoke a lovely, untu-

344

tored innocence that must surely disarm the most cynical of hearts. Yet Frayne wore the grim aspect of one confronting his most deadly enemy.

"Then speak, damsel, if you would," he said dangerously, "but of your depth of earnestness, let me be the judge."

"You do not trust me," she cried, clasping her hands before her in an attitude of maidenly distress. "Oh, I feared as much. It's because of Sheelar, isn't it? But though he may be of Somn, I assure you he is no servant to the Dark Prince."

"Is he not? But then to believe that, I must accept your word on it—the word of a Thromgilad," uttered the knight chillingly. "Tell me, damsel, which of my father's cursed race are you?"

The girl straightened and met him glance for glance, her head lifted in proud defiance. She played her role well, he thought cynically as he beheld her lips trembling as if with hurt and anger. Almost one could believe he had offended her.

"It is your race, too, Sulwyn Idris," she reminded him in a voice that both accused and entreated him. "You are one of us."

"Yes," he answered, his voice bitter. "I am the bastard son of Dred, who raped a Valdoran virgin to beget me." The muscle leaped along the line of his jaw. "But I am no Thromgilad. My sword is pledged to the One and my soul to no one. You have no claim on me, Immortal; nor does the Dark Prince, who has tried other schemes less subtle than this to be rid of me."

The girl came toward him, her face white with a passion Frayne had not thought possible in an

345

immortal Thromgilad.

"Is that what you think?" she cried, her eyes like black burning holes of disbelief. "That I have been sent by Dred to slay you?"

"And have you not?" he drawled, his lip curling in a cold, mirthless smile.

"No! I came unbeknownst to anyone and must return before I am missed. Indeed, if Dred knew . . ." Suddenly she shuddered and turned away to stand stiffly with her back to Frayne.

A frown darkened the knight's brow. There had been a ring of sincerity in her impassioned denial, and the fear that had distorted her face as she spoke Dred's name had not seemed feigned. And yet she was Thromgilad, a race noted for treachery and deceit. Deliberately he hardened his heart against what logic told him was naught but artful illusion. Yet something deeper than cold, hard reason prompted him against his better judgment to pursue the matter further.

"You dissemble well, damsel. Indeed, I have seldom been so well entertained. Perhaps you would humor me further by revealing how you managed to slip through the barriers between this world and Somn. I find I am vastly intrigued by so singular a feat."

The girl uttered a short laugh and turned back again to face him.

"Oh, indeed. I should not wish to disappoint you," she said, flaying him with her eyes. "Someone from this side spoke the words that may either bind and conceal or unbind and reveal, depending on the speaker's need. I felt a ripple in the fabric of existence, and it chanced that I was near when suddenly a portal opened." She shrugged, her lips curved in a brittle smile. "I slipped through before it could close again. It seemed at the time an answer to a prayer," she added bitterly.

Frayne arched a disbelieving eyebrow. To whom did a god pray? he wondered ironically. But immediately another, more disturbing riddle took its place. If one were to assume it was the truth that had been told, then one must only speculate as to who had evoked the spell. At that point he was assailed with a sudden startling premonition.

Without warning his hands shot out to grasp the girl's arms in a punishing grip. Uttering a small gasp, her form seemed momentarily to waver, and for an instant he glimpsed his death in eyes that blazed with a hardly restrained power. Then she had herself in control again, and her face solidified once more into the mask of a fearful maiden.

Frayne drew in a sharp breath, his own glance piercing.

"If there is such a spell," he said in a voice edged with steel, "then tell it to me. Now!"

She hesitated for only the barest instant before answering him with what seemed a convincing candor.

"I heard the words only once, and then but indistinctly. Still, I will repeat them as they came to me:

> I invoke the spell which hides and binds,
> Conceals, reveals, and sometimes finds,
> The stricture which releases souls,

The yawning rift which yet mends holes,
That which is both in and out
And whispers, groans, but cannot shout.
'Tis an end and a beginning,
A farewell and a welcoming,
A haven of a kind,
Or a prison of the mind,
For indeed the name
Remains the same—
A spell that ye revoke
With that which ye invoke."

Abruptly the knight released her, a gleam of grim humor leaping to his eyes.

"Crane!" he said. "I might have known. No wonder Vandrel forbade its use," he mused aloud, recalling how troubled Aurora had been to discover the young shape-changer, in order to protect Janine from Baldrac and the others, had evoked Lil's forbidden spell, thus creating an impenetrable barrier about their cozy little bower nestled beneath the Shrine of the Holy Maiden. Then he was recalled once more to the business at hand as he saw the girl looking at him strangely.

"You believe me now," she said, but her smile was yet uncertain.

"Perhaps," he hedged. "Who are you, and if it is true that Dred knows nothing of your presence here, then why have you come?"

"To find you," she said, moving suddenly toward him. "To persuade you to . . ."

The whang of a bowstring and the muffled thud of an arrow striking flesh cut short whatever she had been about to say. Frayne cursed softly as the girl staggered and fell against him, her eyes fixed in startled bewilderment on his. Then suddenly her eyelids drifted closed and she went limp in his arms as the night rang with the harsh cries of men and horses coming at them from out of the depths of the forest. Hastily the knight laid the lifeless form in the shelter of a fallen log, then, leaping astride Boltar, the warrior-steed of the breed of Zendar, he turned to meet his assailants.

There were six outlaws, uncouth louts roughly garbed but well-armed, their faces brutal with greed as they rode at the knight mounted on the great black charger, a jeweled sword flashing silvery in his hand. In their brutish hearts they gloated, beholding what seemed a rare prize for the taking, for while he was one, they were many. Still, it was Frayne they faced, and before they had struck a single blow, two had fallen to Thrimheld, Swift-Blade, and another to Boltar's powerful, slashing hooves. The other three had broken and fled, leaving the fearsome knight the field.

Sheathing his sword, Frayne dismounted and went swiftly to the place where he had left the wounded girl. She was gone, and the grass still flattened where she had lain was the only sign that she had ever been there. A mirthless smile played briefly about his lips. For a moment, as he had looked into her stricken eyes and felt the slight form crumple in his arms, he had forgotten she was an Immortal. Indeed, he had been pierced by a sudden, sharp regret, which now became relief that she had fled ere he had proved a greater fool.

Suddenly, his limbs leaden with weariness, Frayne flung off his cloak and made his way to the spring. Shrugging out of his shirt of silver mail and the woollen undertunic, he splashed cold water over his face and chest, then settled back on his heels as he thought of Aurora waiting in dread for him to come to her in her cell in the sorceress's fortress. A swift thrust of pain bowed his shoulders at the memory of that first night of her captivity when he had taken her against her will. Gods, he would never forget her look of loathing as he had left her, his lust satisfied, but his heart bitter with self-contempt. He had not gone near her since, except to take her some gowns and other articles of clothing, which he had hoped would make her imprisonment somewhat less onerous. A wry smile twisted his lips at the recollection of the way she had flung them in his face, declaring she would die ere she wore a one of them. Nor would she, if he knew his proud enchantress.

With a groan he rose blindly to his feet. Curse the gods for this torment of his soul! Was it not enough to be a bastard son of Throm without this added burden of forbidden love? he anguished. Then suddenly the scent of orchids was thick in the air, nearly suffocating in its cloying sweetness, and he felt a slow heat pervade his veins. Turning, he saw her standing in the moonlight—the goddess who had stolen through the portal—her body pale beneath a gossamer gown of translucent silver. Smiling, she moved toward him with slow, sinuous grace, the nipples of her breasts peaked against the thin transparency of her gown. Holding him with eyes that transfixed and rendered him powerless, she ran her hands sensuously over his bare chest.

"Yes, you are worthy to be the prince of Throm," she whispered, her voice sultry as she pressed moist lips to the muscle that leaped across his chest at her touch. "Come, my lord, that I may teach you what it is to be a god," she murmured, and sinking to her knees, drew him down to her on a soft bed of grass.

Frayne groaned at the memory of the goddess's liquid caress, which had roused him to a feverish pitch of desire. His groin afire with an aching need, he had been lost to everything but the sensuous witchery of supple limbs and silken skin, of lips that drained his soul and drove him to a mindless frenzy.

"My prince, my prince," whispered the seductress, and clinging to him with her legs, she compelled him to her with hands cupped about the muscular firmness of his buttocks. "I shall make you forget the raven-haired tormentress. You shall become one with Sehwan and one with Throm. You shall be as a god, then none shall stand against us. Not Dred himself."

Then had his blood run suddenly cold, dousing the devouring flames of his lust. He drew sharply back and thrust himself away from her, his breath coming in hard, swift gusts as he struggled in the agonizing throes of unsated need. At last, as his pain receded to a dull ache, he shook his head to clear it of the smell of orchids still cloying about him. Hers was the spell of the seductress who enthralls the will and subverts it to her own desires, he thought, drawing in a long, shuddering breath, and suddenly he felt the sweat break out in cold beads on his forehead as he realized how close he had come to succumbing to it.

"My lord, what is it?" She had risen to her knees, one hand reaching out to him, her face, the mask of the innocent, eloquently pleading.

"Enough," he rasped, lifting his head to impale her with his falcon eyes. "The game is finished. Return to Dred and tell him I am not so easily purchased."

"No, you are wrong," she cried passionately, leaning toward him so that her silken hair flowed off her shoulders to veil the rounded loveliness of her breasts. "I was not sent by Dred. Please, you must listen to me!"

"I have listened," he said, his smile coldly mocking. "You are Sehwan, and you came to woo the Thromholan to your cause."

"Not to *my* cause. I am not alone in desiring that Sulwyn Idris should see where in truth must lie his destiny." She drew back, the seductive loveliness of her face altering to a strange sort of wistfulness. "Once we were a proud race, a race of gods created by the One to grace the fair land of Blidseafeld. Like the Eilderood, who took our place, we, too, were creatures of light—fair of face and form, our hearts rejoicing in the beauty of creation that surrounded us. Indeed, I had almost forgotten the serenity of moonlight playing through the trees and the intoxicating joy of sunlight sparkling on wind-ruffled water."

Suddenly her expression hardened as she lifted brittle eyes to look once more upon the uncompromising planes of the man's visage.

"We were gods," she said bitterly, "with wondrous powers at our command, and yet we were children,

352

too, for we were as innocent as Blidseafeld itself, knowing nothing of the dark things, the dread things, which lie concealed beyond the fringes of the light. Dred betrayed our trust. And for many ages we have wandered in the twisted maze of his ambition, lost to the light, lost to hope, lost to the beneficence of the One. Yet in the midst of despair, a dream was granted us—a vision of a promise made even before Dred delved the depths of darkness to release the evil upon the land. For in the Book of Throm in the Tome of Prophecy it is written:

> From dreadful Night and purest Light
> Is born a noble Prince of might.
> Fair of face, of godly grace,
> The scion of a fallen race,
> With him lies the destiny
> To lead the Throm to victory—
> The mortal son of Somn—
> The mighty Thromholan.

"You are that promise, Sulwyn Idris," she said passionately. "For you are the Thromholan. Return with me to the lightless depths of Somn, my prince, not as Dred's thrall but as the rightful heir of Throm. I swear to you that your father's race will rally to your flag in the Third Uprising. With you to lead us, we shall turn on Dred and fight in the name of the One that we may at last atone for our transgressions against Him who made us. And you *will* need us, knight of the One, as will Harmon and all his immortal Eilderood, for Dred and his army of trolls, goblins, dragon-rogues, monsters from the Flux, and misguided mortals with their false dreams of power will have the Vendrenin on their side!"

"And if I am fool enough to succumb after all to your cunning, Sehwan of Throm," he had answered coldly, "shall not the army of Somn have the Thromholan as well—the mortal son of Throm to whom the victory has been already decreed? And when the deed is done, and you and your race hold the world in thrall, what then? Shall I be made the king of all the races, perhaps with you as my queen? Or shall there be some other to supplant me in your favor, to rule in my stead? No, Goddess of Passion. I am not such a fool. Death would be better than damnation in Somn."

"But I agree," she uttered fervently. "Such a victory would be no victory at all for us. Can you not see that the triumph promised us is the triumph of the One? We yearn not for the subjugation of the light, but for our own sublimation into its blessed realm. We ask only for the chance to prove ourselves, but without you, our own 'Prince of Light,' to lead us, we are powerless against Dred's greater might. Come with me, Sulwyn Idris, I beg you!"

She had been very persuasive, but he had not gone, for he had thought still to thwart the threads of his own destiny. Nor could he have gone then, even if he had trusted Sehwan's eloquence, for Frayne, the knight of Tor, had had unfinished business with the sorceress, who yet held Aurora and Ariana hostage. Thus had he returned to Tor and the wonder of Aurora's love, which not even the revelation of his dark secret or the hoax he had perpetrated against her had been able to destroy. He had lain with her, knowing in his heart as he did so that he betrayed her innocence and her sweet love, for he had come to her straight from the arms of the seductress.

It was that, as well as the sudden certainty that not even in the Flux could he escape the kismet of Dred's son, that had driven him in anguish from the enchantress that morning as she had gazed upon him with eyes of love, the very image of a wood nymph with flowers and blades of grass entangled in her raven tresses. Her thoughts as ever had been open to him, so that he had been pierced to the heart by her youthful naiveté. And all at once, thinking to destroy her illusions, he had with an inhuman brutality imparted to her the visions of possibilities that had been revealed to him here at the edge of the precipice.

Suddenly he raised his arms toward the lightless void, which was his to sculpt into likenessses of possibilities that had become, or might yet become, actualities. For he was the Thromholan, whose natural element was darkness, but whose heart and mind had been molded by the Valdoran into a receptacle for the Light of the One.

From out of the dark came a vision of Aurora and himself sailing in a crystal boat through a sea of rainbow-ridden mist that flowed from a fountain at the center of the sea. The heart of the fountain was a great cloud-draped peak, and at its base gleamed the bleached bones of countless unicorns, the skeletons draped in a multitude of tiny fragile blooms the color of moonbeams.

"Tears of Eldwenwood," breathed an awed voice at the knight's back, and he did not have to look to know it was Aurora. "And there, Frayne, do you see him? 'Tis Endrith scaling the peak! Oh, brave-hearted unicorn, fear not. Soon your pain shall be ended, for you tread the path to rebirth and oneness with the One.''

Then the vision faded, and all was darkness and an eternal sort of silence, save for the muffled sound of weeping. Slowly Frayne turned and gathered the enchantress in the circle of his arms.

"It was the Unicorns' Burial Ground, wasn't it,'' she sniffed, laying her cheek gratefully against the knight's hard chest. "And the river of mist flowing from the peak must be the Veil of Tears.'' Tilting back her head, she tried to pierce the darkness to see his face. "From the very first we were meant to finish the quest begun so long ago. The quest for the horn of the unicorn was only the beginning. The end lies somewhere beyond the Veil of Tears, I know it. For I heard Almira, my mother, tell Endrith to watch over me till the power awakened within me. Then he was to sing to me the Song of the Unicorn that I might know the way to the truth of my destiny.'' Suddenly she smiled and hugged him close to her as she laid her cheek once more over his heart.

"I'm glad that you shall be going there with me after all,'' she murmured dreamily, "for I confess I am weary of having to track you down whenever you take a notion you're not meant for me, as you did this very day. I had a fiendish time following your trail here in the rain. But surely you must see now that your destiny and mine are but a single strand.''

She felt him stiffen and experienced an odd sort of pang somewhere beneath her breast. Yet he said nothing, but only continued to stroke her hair in long, even strokes.

"But Alain himself told me that Dracaderns can move freely through the Flux!" Aurora insisted stubbornly as she faced a skeptical Frayne and the Valdoran, who thus far had offered no comment on the enchantress's suggestion that Lynwen fly them to Garn.

"And perhaps they can—fully grown dragons who have been guided through the Flux before," Frayne answered wearily, for they had been mulling over the possibilities for better than an hour without coming up with a really workable plan. "Lynwen is a *flegge*, who has only just begun to fly. Furthermore, having been hatched here, she has never been outside the Flux, let alone to Garn. There is no telling where she might end up, even if she did not founder and become lost in the drift itself."

"Well, even a slim chance is better than none at all," retorted the enchantress with a flash of golden eyes. "How did the missing egg of Garn find its way here anyhow?"

"Efluvien brought it to me for safekeeping," Ariana offered quietly.

Aurora stared in dumbfounded amazement at the Valdoran sitting serenely knitting by the fire in her cozy one-room cottage. How lovely she was! Indeed, in the soft glow of the firelight, with her flaxen hair pulled back from the marble purity of her brow and her still-smooth cheeks slightly flushed from the heat of the blaze, her gentle beauty seemed untouched by time. She was a marvel of compassion and understanding, and already Aurora loved her, but she had a way of springing things on one that took one totally by surprise.

"Efluvien?" Aurora queried with a frown. "But how did he get it?"

"I believe Harmon had left it with him in the hopes that Thaelous, the peace-keeper's silver-winged swan, might be able to hatch it with her own imminent brood," replied the Valdoran, laying her knitting aside and rising to stir the fire. "When that failed, apparently Efluvien decided that the special ambience of the Flux might be needed, so he brought it here to me."

"Efluvien came here? You saw him, *spoke* with him?" the enchantress demanded incredulously.

"But of course, my dear," she said, a gleam of amusement in her eyes, "It would have been extremely rude *not* to have spoken to him after he was kind enough to come all this way just to visit me, and to bring my Lynwen. Even as an egg, she served to make the burden of timelessness less tedious, for it was something of a challenge to keep the egg at an even temperature. And since her hatching, she has proved a blessing indeed, for it has been very like having a child around. Doubtless that was part of the reason Efluvien brought her to me, for he seemed most solicitous of my comfort at his parting."

"You mean he just left you here, imprisoned in timelessness? Why did he not take you with him?" demanded the enchantress, incensed at such callousness.

Smiling at Aurora's youthful indignation, Ariana resumed her seat and calmly took up her knitting

358

once more.

"Because it was impossible that he should. He is, after all, a god," she said matter-of-factly, "and thus bound not to interfere with the destinies of mortals. Just think how greatly so simple an act would have affected events. Why Frayne would never have gone in search of the unicorn horn for the sorceress's potion, and thus he very likely would not have met you. You would have been delayed in discovering your latent powers and might even conceivably have never gone in search of your true name. There's no telling how the fabric of history might have been altered."

"Which brings us back to the problem at hand," Frayne observed acerbically.

Ariana gazed thoughtfully at the tall figure of her son silhouetted against the open doorway. His back to the room, he stood staring out into the night, and from the unnatural rigidity of his stance, she judged his destiny lay heavily upon him. Had she been wrong to conceal the truth from him when he was a boy yearning toward manhood? she wondered, not for the first time. She had thought only to give him time to grow in strength and understanding before he must take up the burden. And in spite of everything, she could not truly regret having given him those peaceful years of his boyhood spent roving the forests of the Valleys of Mists in the Mountains of Thunder. But time had betrayed her, and before she had ever found the right time to tell him about himself, fate had taken her from him so that it was Leilah who had revealed to him the secret of his birth. Leilah, who had hated her and who had no doubt relished the task of robbing her son of both his illusions and his innocence! And yet the fault had lain not with the sorceress, who was only another of Dred's poor, tormented victims, but with herself, for not having provided him with the armor of truth.

This had been the true punishment through all the seeming eternity of her imprisonment, and it was her punishment still, for even knowing how greatly he must have been hurt, how disillusioned he must have been, she had not been prepared to see her son so bitter, the youthful contours of his face honed to a lean hardness, the fine, sensitive mouth stern-lipped and cynical, and his eyes, oh, gods, his eyes, which had once shimmered with ready laughter, and now wore the hooded look of the falcon. How great had been her anguish for that lost youth when first she had seen him emerge out of the grey mists of timelessness. Wounded and weary in both body and soul, he had yet worn the aspect of a god. By the One, she had not known him!

Indeed, there was little in this gimlet-eyed warrior to remind her of the youth who had left her a lifetime ago to make his oath of fealty before the Menhir of Tor. The boy scintillating with restless energy and a hunger for adventure was now a man, soft-spoken and remote, a man in whom one sensed danger and a sternly controlled power, and something else, something that had troubled her more than all the other changes she had seen or sensed in him. Still, it was not until she had come upon him standing like something hewn out of granite before the girl weeping brokenly at his feet that finally she had understood what disturbed her. One look in his eyes and she had seen that he was a man fleeing more than his destiny. And suddenly it had come to her that this lovely raven-haired child who shimmered with a golden fire had been sent by the One to save her son from a greater danger than any he had ever faced before. In truth, she had come to save Frayne from himself.

"The child may be right about Lynwen," Ariana mused aloud. "The dragon is young, but she might do to carry you and Aurora safely out."

"No, Mother," Frayne said without turning. "We go together—*all* of us—or not at all."

"He's right, Ariana—for *once*," murmured Aurora, and dropping to her knees beside the older woman, gazed earnestly up into her face. "We could not leave you here alone. You have given up enough, that others might enjoy a measure of peace. Besides, there must be some other way out of the fix we're in. We have only to discover it."

What a lovely child she was, marveled the Valdoran, pulling the girl's head down to her lap and affectionately running a hand over the raven curls. No wonder Frayne was in such a turmoil. He had never had a chance. Even a single glance from those glorious eyes must have been enough to wreck the bastions of his fiercely guarded heart. And then to feel himself not only unworthy of such a boundless devotion as hers, but, even worse, to believe he was his beloved's instrument of death! It did not bear thinking on. If only he could see beyond his dark side to the infinitely greater good, she thought despairingly. The One would not have granted Dred's son something so precious as the love of this child born of light had he not meant it as a sign of His favor. Sulwyn Idris was *not* destined for evil. She would stake her life on it.

"If only we had the amulet!" muttered Frayne, ramming the side of his fist without warning against the door jamb. "Curse the sorceress's rotten heart. I should have wrung her neck when I had the chance."

"The amulet?" queried Aurora. Her head came up with a jerk at this sudden, unwonted outburst, and the enchantress observed her beloved's lithe form moving restlessly about the room with a good deal of interest and a glimmer of wry amusement. "Can you mean the Circlet of Kerr?"

"Yes, the circlet," he said, searing her with a glance. "With it, we might at least have found our way to wherever Hedron secreted the other. They are bound, one to open the portal in the Flux, the other to seal it."

"Then I don't see how the amulet could help us," Aurora rejoined with a frown. "The one I won from Hedron closed the portal. Would we not require the other one to open it again?"

"Kylandros is our portal. What we need is a lodestone to guide us through the drift to our own time. And since the circlets are either end of a single continuum, it stands to reason that one would eventually lead us to the other. It would, of course, have been a perilous undertaking, since only the one in possession of the amulet would be able to see where it led. That would mean that anyone who became separated from the bearer of the circlet would be lost forever in the drift where none could ever find him—or her," he added with a grim smile. "It little

362

signifies, however, since we have not the circlet. It were better to turn our thoughts to some other possibility, if there is one. Perhaps in time you might even learn to play your song of destiny backwards and thus lead us out hindmost first. It is, after all, as promising as anything else we've come up with thus far."

"Oh, dear. I cannot think it at all likely that I should ever manage anything quite so extraordinary as that would be," mused the enchantress soulfully, but with a decided gleam of mischief in her eye, which was not lost upon the woman watching her with amusement. Now what was the child up to? she wondered, thinking that if ever these two survived Dred's war and all the other obstacles before them, Frayne would yet have his hands full with his unpredictable enchantress.

"Indeed," said the one destined to cut up the knight's peaceful prospects, "I should much prefer to let the circlet lead us out, no matter how perilous it might be, to an eternity of uninspired plucking at the strings. And since I just happen to have brought the king's amulet with me, the real question is: Do we try it now or in the morning?"

It was soon decided, *after* Frayne had roundly berated his troublesome love for not having informed him sooner of the silver circlet nestled snugly in her pack, that they would rest and then put Frayne's theory to the test with the first light of dawn. It was thus not until Aurora and the knight made ready to seek their bed laid out in the shelter of the woods that Ariana thought to bring up the question of what should be done with Lynwen.

"She is quite attached to me, you know," she said with a troubled frown, "and I should not like to leave her here by herself. For despite her size, she is really little more than an overgrown infant."

"I am sorry, Mother," Frayne answered gravely. "I know how fond you are of her, but it simply cannot be helped. Lynwen will have to remain here till someone can return for her."

"I'll send Kev and Ellard for her just as soon as possible, I promise," Aurora added fervently, clasping the older woman's hand in pledge to her.

"Yes, I know you will, my dear," Ariana nodded, smiling and patting the hand that held hers so earnestly. "Think no more about it tonight. You both need your rest for the morrow. I'll just go out and try to explain things to Lynwen. She's really very intelligent and doubtless will do quite well on her own. Goodnight, children, and the One be with you always as is my love." Then turning, she left them to stare after her, Aurora with tears in her eyes and Frayne with a pensive frown in his.

"Do you think she *will* be all right?" queried the enchantress as Frayne led her at last beneath the Tamaracks to the small brook beside which they had earlier set up a makeshift camp.

"Perhaps," he said, drawing her down beside him on the blankets spread over freshly picked fronds. "At any rate we have little choice in the matter. It will be difficult enough for the three of us to remain together in the drift without having the impossible impediment of an infant dragon to contend with as well."

"I suppose you're right," agreed Aurora, but she felt no easier about abandoning the last living female

Dracadern to shift for herself. After all, there was no knowing when she might be able to send word to Ellard and Kev about Lynwen's existence, nor was she at all certain that once informed, they would be able to find the young *flegge* on their own. Drat! What a damnable coil.

Thus it was that she lay for a long time staring up at the treetops swaying with a gentle breeze before at last utter exhaustion eased her into a troubled sleep.

The enchantress groaned as an ungentle hand shook her urgently by the shoulder. Cautiously she uncovered her eyes only to close them again against the brilliance of the sun rising above the treetops.

"Aurora, wake up. Quickly! We may already be too late. Something's happened to Ariana."

"Wha-at?" Aurora mumbled, raising herself on one elbow the better to see the knight, half-dressed in breeches and boots and hastily shrugging on his shirt.

"Ariana and the dragon," he said grimly. "I've just come from the cottage, and there's no sign of either one of them. It looks as if she may have tried to ride Lynwen through the Flux. You'd better hurry and get dressed while I take another look around."

Fully awake at last, Aurora sat bolt upright.

"Oh, gods, if she has done anything so foolish, what can we do to help her? How, indeed, can we even know if she has made it somewhere to the other side? Or somewhen," she added, shuddering at the thought of the gentle Valdoran trapped in some distant time.

"We can do nothing to help her," returned the knight, his eyes like slate, "but we can try to find her in the Abyss of Possibilities. Make haste now, if you would go there with me."

"Aye, I'm coming," she shouted after him as he strode swiftly away. Moments later, fully dressed, her pack slung hastily over her shoulder, she was fleeing lightly through the Tamaracks toward the Valdoran's cottage, a prayer winging silently to the One that all might be well with Ariana and Lynwen. Her heart sank when she found Frayne, grim-lipped and silent, waiting for her at the door to the cottage. Without a word, he struck out through the forest toward the rocky bluff and the black void that marked the boundary of their own span of possibility.

The morning was clear and crisp and they made good time, so that the sun had not yet reached its zenith before they came to the precipice overlooking the abyss. In awe Aurora watched as Frayne once more wove the fabric of darkness into images. This time she saw Ariana's cottage as it had been the night before and herself and Frayne wending their way across the meadow to vanish into the trees. She beheld the Valdoran seated on a rock before the dragon, its head lowered to nuzzle playfully at the woman as she appeared to speak at great length to it.

Time seemed to speed by as the stars overhead scudded across the sky toward dawn, and still Ariana remained with the dragon, but silent now, her words having long since run out. Suddenly the enchantress stiffened as she spied a dark form slink around the corner of the cottage, then pause to peer through the window. After a moment the intruder straightened and turned so that for an instant Aurora glimpsed a countenance possessed of a hard, glittery beauty that made her blood run suddenly cold.

"Leilah!" she gasped, glancing up at Frayne's still profile.

"Quite so," remarked the knight, and Aurora shuddered at the chill edge of steel in his voice.

Wordlessly, Aurora turned back to the silent drama unfolding before them and saw the sorceress steal across the open ground to come up behind the Valdoran. The dragon, perhaps sensing something evil in the intruder, lurched up to its full height. A tongue of flame spouting from its mouth shot over Ariana's head to singe the sorceress. Leilah, scream-ing invectives, drew back as the Valdoran came to her feet and wheeled to confront her old enemy. Words were exchanged, then Ariana spoke soothingly to the dragon, till Lynwen, still shuddering, lowered her head and crouched down behind the Valdoran for all the world like a frightened puppy. In helpless rage Aurora beheld the sorceress, the soulless perfection of her beauty distorted by cunning, appear to threaten the other woman—with what vile lies, she wondered, clenching her fist. She saw Ariana glance briefly toward the woods into which Frayne and Aurora had disappeared some hours earlier. Then, seeming to draw a deep breath, she called the dragon to her.

"Nay, Ariana," Aurora muttered, feeling helpless as she watched the woman climb to the dragon's back followed by the sorceress. Lynwen, turning her had to gaze quizzically at the two women, flinched as Leilah rapped her sharply on the nose, and for the first time Aurora beheld something like anger flash

367

across the gentle features of the Valdoran. Then the dragon, spreading its wings, lifted into the night sky and simply vanished.

As the abyss of darkness swallowed the vision of the cottage, Aurora drew herself up to her full height.

"A curse on my mother's sister!" she cried, shaking with grief and rage. "How I wish I had her here before me that I might put an end to her evil once and for all!"

No sooner had the words left her mouth, than suddenly it came to her that such a wish might not be beyond the range of possibility. Her eyes flashing golden sparks, she turned eagerly to Frayne.

"Is it possible they are still within the drift?" she demanded, reaching out to grasp him by the arms in her excitement. She felt his muscles tense beneath her hands, and his eyes, like blades of ice, seem to pierce her.

"Let it go, Aurora," he said, his voice wintry. "Wherever they are, they are beyond our reach."

"Mayhap beyond *our* reach," she rejoined, abruptly releasing him to drop to one knee beside her pack lying where earlier she had carelessly tossed it. Without further preamble she dumped its contents out on the ground, and with hands that shook gathered up a thing of shimmering gossamer. "But perchance *not* beyond the reach of a wish-net spun by a merrow-maid," she finished, rising once more to her feet to embrace Frayne with a dazzling smile. "What think you?"

An answering gleam flickered silvery in the falcon eyes.

"Time here has no real meaning," he answered

368

consideringly. "What seems like hours may be only seconds, or seconds hours, depending on the way one chooses to perceive them, for they are only possibilities, and here anything is possible. It's worth a try, at least. Only, perhaps, my ever amazing love," he added, the look in his eyes suffusing her with a warm glow of happiness, "it were better to wish for the sorceress alone. If they are so far away that the spell works imperfectly or fails altogether, only Leilah can be affected. But if you direct the wish at Lynwen and Ariana under the same conditions, you might conceivably do no more than alter the course of the dragon's flight, thus placing them in danger. At any rate, it would seem far better in this case to wish for too little than for too much."

"Then so be it," said the enchantress, and holding firmly to the net, spoke the words of summoning.

For a long moment nothing happened, and Aurora was gripped with a dreadful feeling of despair at the thought that the sorceress had escaped the Flux with the Valdoran as hostage. Oh, gods, they would have it all to go through again! she inwardly groaned, wondering what despicable punishment Leilah would exact against her rebellious knight.

Then suddenly the net bulged and was nearly dragged from Aurora's hand as the sorceress appeared within its meshes, a translucent, insubstantial apparition with eyes like glittery black holes that glared at Aurora with a malevolence terrible to behold.

"You!" she uttered with the virulence of a striking adder and flung herself at Aurora through the net,

369

her hands reaching for the enchantress's throat. Then Frayne had grasped her wrists in a grip of steel and forced her to her knees before him.

"Where did you tell my mother to direct the dragon, Sorceress?" he said with an icy fury.

Leilah, her form within the net yet wavering between solidity and shimmering incorporeality, threw back her head and laughed.

"I thought it time your precious mother was reunited with your loving father. You may seek the Valdoran in Somn, Prince," she sneered, "and what a reunion that must be. Indeed, had it not been for my sister's interfering brat, I would not have missed it for the world."

"She's lying," declared the enchantress flatly. "She dare not go to Dred, for he must know that she betrayed him. Nay, she would try to reach Garn in the hopes of exchanging the last female Dracadern for a safe asylum. Doubtless she planned to lose Ariana somewhere in the enchanted mists surrounding the island, that there would be no one to denounce her for the conniving wretch that she is."

"But then she would have had to know that the bard was elsewhere," mused the knight with a sudden glint in his eye. "You heard his harping just as I did, did you not? It was that which led you here to Ariana."

"Yes, curse you," Leilah hissed, then, straining toward the enchantress, she spat maliciously. "Would that I had flung you from the walls of Skorl when I had the chance. By the gods, I pray that you and your bastard lover suffer the eternal torment of Dred's reeking pit for what you've done to me."

"For what *we've* done to *you?*" Aurora gasped.

"Oh, *such* innocence. Such righteous indignation. And yet it was you who wrecked everything with your vicious lie. The crystal of Andruvien indeed. How the two of you must have laughed behind my back. But the last laugh would have been mine had you not dragged me back with this blasted net. Indeed, I was savoring the moment when I should have flung the cursed Valdoran to her death. To hear her beg for mercy as I forced her from the dragon's back," she gloated, her lips parted in a distorted grin of perverted pleasure.

Then suddenly the imperfectly transmaterialized figure began to flicker and grow more and more translucent.

"Oh, gods, Frayne!" Aurora cried in horror. "The net is not powerful enough to hold her. She's slipping back again!"

"Stand back!" ordered the knight, as his hands, clenched grimly about the sorceress's wrists, passed through the insubstantial transparency of flesh and bone to come up empty. "It's no use. Nothing can hold her now."

"*No!*" shrieked Leilah, clawing hideously at the mesh. "No-o-o, don't let go of me, I beg you-u-u!"

Instinctively the enchantress leaped forward to grab at the net in a last, desperate attempt to stave off the tragedy. But though she clung doggedly to the gossamer strands, the sorceress simply vanished, her final cry of despair lingering like the thin wail of a dying wind.

The enchantress fell back as the delicate web fluttered emptily in her hands. Retching violently, she recoiled from the ghastly memory of horror-stricken eyes, which had gazed with utter certainty upon a doom too dreadful to contemplate. Flinging the limp net from her as if it were some noxious thing, she sank to her knees.

"Oh, gods, I cannot bear it," she gasped. "Why was she so twisted and full of hate that she should bring such a gruesome end upon herself? Why are there so many like her—poor, tortured souls deaf to the harmony of living at one with others, indeed, at one with the earth and all the creatures thereon? And Dred would plunge the land into chaos and darkness, if he could, so that *none* should ever again know peace of harmony or joy. Why? Why does he hate the light of the One?"

The knight stood over her, his face granite-hard as he gazed upon her wounded innocence.

"He doesn't hate the light," he answered, dragging his eyes away from her. "He is envious of it."

"Envious?"

"Indeed, how not?" he drawled, his smile coolly cynical. "He was Sulwyn Idris, the brightest of all the One's creations. Yet, fair as he was, he was still only a lesser glory than the One. Thus it is hardly surprising, is it, that, unable to exceed the light of the One, he chose instead to exceed all others in the darkness of his soul?"

The enchantress shivered. Ye gods, she had never thought to feel pity in her heart for Dred, and yet surprisingly she did. For how sad it was that the brightest of all creations should have been so blinded by the light as to be rendered impervious to the light itself. Yet was it not so with Krim as well? Krim, the Mage-Lord, who had coveted the scintillating fire of

Vendrenin that he might become as a god—immortal and possessed of a godly puissance. And as a result had he not become pure flame, for was that not the only sort of immortality that could be granted by a thing of unadulterated power? Indeed, of the man there was nothing left but his memories and hate and the devious workings of his own tortured mind. And now that same lust for a power that even Harmon, the greatest Eilderood, had learned to fear had condemned Leilah to an eternity within the insubstantiality that existed between possibility and reality.

What was this terrible hunger that could drive gods and mortals mad? Aurora wondered with a strange feeling of foreboding. But then Frayne reached down to pull her to her feet, and the thought was lost as she faced the more immediate uncertainty of their own passage through the drift. Indeed her tongue clove to the roof of her mouth as she beheld Frayne with the talisman of the Black Kings in his hand and realized that he wished for her to take it from him.

"But I don't know how to make it work." she said, drawing back.

"You have only to look through the center and direct your thoughts outward toward the circlet's twin," he answered, taking her hand and curling her fingers firmly about the thing of tarnished silver. "The amulet will do the rest."

Aurora stared at Frayne and felt insanely like giggling. Ye gods, he made it sound so absurdly simple. And yet if it were, why did the hairs at the nape of her neck prickle with the feeling that something was amiss? And why had her ever-elusive love assumed that old, detestable mask of boredom he knew so well how to wield? By the One, he meant to send her on alone! She knew it as well as she knew that blasted veiled look that concealed his thoughts so perfectly. Curse the man! Was it indeed so dreadful a fate to love and be loved by her? she fumed, thinking of all she had suffered just to come to him. Was *he* the fool or *she?*

In her sudden, hurt anger, she was almost tempted to leave him there. Why should she, after all, have to beg him to save himself? From the very first it had always been she who must toss pride aside and plead, cajole, or connive to be allowed just to stay with him a little while longer. Well, almost always, she amended, inexplicably recalling how he had tricked her into going on with him after the horn of the unicorn instead of remaining in the camp of the Shintari to wed Shamar, the Winter-King. Naturally, one thing leading to another, it was inevitable that she should next be reminded of the night they had spent on the moonlit plain half a day's journey from the runed portal leading into the Confounded Lands. It was then that, pretending to be a simple shepherd and she a shepherdess, he had loaned her his heart till the sun should rise again. How sweetly had he made love to her, wooing her with tender words such as he had never used before. Oh, gods, who was she fooling? She would rather die than go on without him!

Thus it was that the knight was treated to a glance from huge, limpid eyes, which had the power to bewitch.

"You're sure that's all there is to it?" she queried, smiling with an innocence that set him on his guard.

Suddenly his glance narrowed. Now what was she up to, this young fledgling enchantress whose power over him had been enough to break the spell of Sehwan, the Thromgilad Goddess of Passion? he wondered darkly.

"Can you doubt my word?" he murmured, arching a quelling eyebrow.

"Oh, I have never doubted your *word*," she replied, and kneeling, began folding her scattered belongings once more into her pack. "Indeed, I am quite sure you have never lied to me," she added thoughtfully as, slinging the pack over her shoulder and rising with the wish-net in her hands, she looked him guilelessly straight in the eye. "'Tis what you do *not* say that I have learned to distrust."

How he next found himself bound by the fragile strands of shimmering gossamer, Frayne was never afterwards quite sure. Yet, indeed, that was the case, and whether it was the woven moonbeams intertwined with mists of mother-of-pearl that held him powerless or the spellbinding beauty of eyes glimmering with an indestructible love, he was never certain either. The fact of the matter remained that he was fairly caught.

Torn between anger and reluctant amusement, he stared into the bewitching countenance and demanded that she release him.

"This is hardly the time for childish pranks, witch," he said at his sternest, yet the slight twitch at the corner of his mouth would seem to betray him.

"'Tis neither childish nor a prank," she retorted,

her laughter ringing golden in the stillness. Then suddenly the imps vanished from her eyes to be replaced by a compelling look that seemed to probe his very soul. "You never meant to leave here with me, did you," she said flatly, and inwardly he marveled at her. She was like quicksilver, forever changing, forever unpredictable.

"No," he answered, meeting her look for look.

She winced a little at so blatant an admission, her glorious eyes darkening to amber, and he steeled himself for the inevitable.

"Why? I know you love me. My heart could not be so misled. I know who and what you are, and it makes no difference. I cannot help loving you. If it is the prophecy of the Thromholan that stands between us, then I say 'tis you who are being childish. For though I am pledged to the One, no less are you. You *are no danger* to me—indeed, why should you be, even if you are Dred's son?—except that you would wound me to the death by leaving me. So tell me what it is you dread so greatly that you would remain a prisoner of the Flux."

"Don't be a fool, Aurora," he said, his lip curling in self-mockery. "If you know so much, then surely you must have guessed I am no prisoner here, nor ever was. I have traveled through the dimensions of timelessness countless times before."

"But—I don't understand," she faltered and shook her head at him in disbelief. "Nay, it makes no sense. Everything you have done, everything *we* have done, would be meaningless. What need had you for the potion—or the circlet—or any of it, if 'tis true you could come and go at will? Why did you not return to the Mountains of Thunder with Ariana long ages ago?"

"Because only one of an immortal race can mold the Flux to his will. And because, while I might enter by way of Kylandros, the only certain way out for the Thromholan is to go through the Land of Somn," he answered bitterly. "Perhaps you can understand why I should be reluctant to take undue advantage of such a route. Hitherto, I ran little risk. Dred, after all, has been immersed in a brooding sleep, stirring only rarely as he waited for the time when events should be set into motion for his final awakening. That time began when I lay with a raven-haired wood sprite in Endrith's Forest and awakened her to the powers of an enchantress. It is that power I fear, and the name that is your destiny. And I fear it still, enough to set you free to pursue it, even as you must set me free."

"Nay!" she breathed, her eyes huge in her face. "If what you say is true, there can be only one reason why you would choose now to risk the peril of Somn. You mean to confront him, to face Dred alone. Why?" she cried, flinging her arms around him as if by that she might keep him forever with her. "What can you hope to accomplish against an immortal prince? Can you not see that you would be throwing your life away for nothing?"

A rending pain distorted the stern features. Clenching his eyes shut, Frayne pressed his lips convulsively against her hair.

"Not for nothing," he murmured so low that she barely heard. Then he had straightened, and his face wore the derisive mask of the knight of Tor. "I am, after all, the Thromholan," he said, and whether he mocked her or himself, she could not tell. "Doubtless it is time I put my destiny to the touch."

Drat the man's obstinacy! Aurora fumed, more frightened than she had ever been before. If indeed he must one day stand before Dred, it was not yet, for she had seen the vision and they had yet to cross the sea of mist together to the Unicorns' Burial Ground and the mystical Veil of Tears. In her heart she knew it had been a true vision. Now she had only to make him see it, too.

Turning the full force of her eyes upon him, she compelled him to listen to her.

"Once long ago you said you believed we were meant to go together in search of the unicorn horn. But you were wrong. 'Twas not the horn, but the Unicorn Burial Ground we were meant to find, and that quest is yet to be completed. If you would have me set you free, then you must swear first to finish what we began. My love, I beg you. Let us seek the end of Endrith's Song together, for in my heart I know 'twas written by the gods."

Without waiting for Frayne to answer, she threw herself against him, and clinging tightly to him, raised the amulet.

"Let that which closes seek that which opens," she whispered, sending her thoughts outward through the center of the ring. As the precipice overlooking the Abyss of Possibilities vanished within a grey shroud of uncertainty, she felt his arms close instinctively around her and smiled at his muttered curse.

"If you break the bonds that bind us as one," she shouted back at him, "I swear I shall toss the amulet

378

away. For to lose you is to lose myself, and I dread that far more than eternity in the drift."

His answer was lost in the formless wail of a wind that deadened her senses and filled her mind with an awareness of total desolation. Within the Flux anything was possible, but in the drift nothing was certain, so that she came soon to doubt even in her own existence. Yet doggedly she clung to Frayne, the one reality amid all the uncertainty, and to the circlet, which was their only hope, till even they assumed the mere qualities of dreams half-forgotten. Then in dawning terror she realized that she could no longer feel the circlet in her hand or the muscular reality of Frayne's arms clasped around her, and suddenly she knew the most appalling uncertainty of all. She could not feel herself!

Then truly did Aurora apprehend the horror she had seen in Leilah's eyes as the sorceress had slipped toward insubstantiality within the drift. Oh, gods, she could not bear it! To be consciousness without physical being was to be a mind trapped within a vacuum without light or dark or sound or silence or sensation of any kind. It was to be constantly aware of nothing, which was infinitely worse than being nothing, for it was to be utterly alone.

In that first instant of dreadful comprehension, she thought she must go mad. Or perhaps she was already mad, and none of this was real. Could one dream of nothing? she wondered. Indeed, how could one know the reality from the dream within the context of nothingness? One couldn't, she decided, but could one know anything at all? Then it came to her—the one certainty in all the infinitude of uncertainty. One could know one's self. She was Aurora, a song of scintillating power, and she was one with Frayne. She had no need to feel his arms around her. She could meld her mind with his!

Still she hesitated, for had he not forbidden her ever to invade the private realm of his own thoughts? Aye, he had, and she had thus far kept her word, save for one brief glimpse as he had come to her in the pool on the edge of Endrith's Forest. He had frightened her, for he had clothed himself in an illusion of Dred, and she had not known him. Nor had she understood then that he had sought thus to reveal to her the dark secret that had ever been an invisible barrier between them. Summoning the strength of Andruvien, she had seen behind the mask to the glory of his love and the torment of his soul. And now she would look again, for to do otherwise was to go mad with this terrible sense of aloneness.

"Frayne," she whispered in her own mind, sending the thought outward into the vacuum of uncertainty. "Frayne, my love."

She thought she heard the echo of her name reverberating through the universe of her own consciousness, and then sensed a pulsating energy radiating outward, seeking something, seeking her. Instinctively she reached toward it with the full force of her need. And suddenly she had found him, a probing thrust of bitter anguish. Without thought she opened to it, without fear embraced the throbbing entity that was Frayne's powerful essence, and with a sense of mounting ecstasy she knew the wonder of becoming one with him—one thought, one mind, a single awareness of two separate worlds of memory. For a single instant she glimpsed the forbidden corridors of awareness that were Sulwyn Idris, and then suddenly they were closed to her and she was sent careering back into the void of uncertainty.

Briefly she knew the horror of consciousness without identity, of awareness without memory, and then as from a great distance she thought she heard the sound of harping.

"The harp," she groaned, a single strand of memory awakening to fill her with a terrible, rending pain. For it was the memory of her father's harp left forgotten within the Flux of Timelessness and thus irretrievably lost to her. "Alain," she murmured. "Father." Then utter darkness enveloped her mind.

Chapter 12

Janine, daughter of the desert tribes, wandered aimlessly through the elderberry wood, her thoughts far from the snowy clusters of blossoms perfuming the air or the fading light of day slanting through the trees. Every now and then she would stop abruptly, her head cocked ever so slightly to one side, as if listening for a footstep or for a voice to call out her name. Then after a moment or two, when it was clear that she had heard only the soft scutter of a rabbit in the brakes or the cry of a dove calling from a tree overhead, the brief light would die out of her eyes and she would continue her solitary vigil in Vandrel's hidden glen.

Why was it that she must ever be judged too young or too weak or too lacking in *almah-ur-gabat*, the knowledge of the forest? she fretted, yanking a brilliant red and yellow bloom from a trailing vine and absently plucking the petals out one by one to let them flutter to the ground as she walked. *Marhakim!* She had seen nearly sixteen passings of the seasons.

Among her people she would be a woman nearly past the age of marrying, but here, in the land of *kafir,* the infidel, she was a child made to suffer *kalmak,* the curse of always remaining behind.

Seven times the sun had risen and even now for the seventh time was setting, and still the man-wolf and the Shintari huntress had not returned from their journey to the north to warn the forest elves of the danger loosed upon the land by the sorceress's potion. And now the young *mogush,* filled with *al-fatwa-atha,* the feeling of impending doom, had determined to go in search of them, and nothing, not even her tears, could persuade him to take her with him. Thus in the grips of *ghadib,* the anger which makes fools of men and women, she had run from him into the woods, hoping that he would follow after her. Yet still he had not come.

Oh, he was of the most stubborn, was her Sayyid Crane! she fumed, brushing impatiently at her eyes with the back of her hand. In truth, he was little different from the men of her tribe, who believed a woman was meant to submit to their rule or suffer *al-darb,* the beating with the stick. But she would show him that she was no longer *salama,* resigned to humility and obedience, for had she not beheld the priestess of Shin and Aurora, the Daughter of Zarcun-nar, which are the Golden Flames, and had not her eyes been opened to the truth? Women need not be less than men. For she had seen the women of the *kafir* claim the right of *jarid,* the lance, and go into battle even as the men. Why, then, should not she? For had she not faced the perils of *fesh-fesh,* the shifting sands, and had she not proven she could find her way in the desert as well as any man? She was no *haramie* girl in need of protection, and so she would tell her pigheaded young *mogush*, she fiercely vowed, then shuddered as she realized the sun had set, transforming the woods into an eerie twilit world of shadowy recesses and unfamiliar noises.

"*Marhakim!* What have I done?" she cried softly, for no longer did she stand amid the blooming elderberries of Vandrel's hidden glen, but in the midst of a forbidding forest of towering trees and dense thickets rife with unknown perils. Struggling against the first suffocating wash of terror, she whirled about, searching frantically for the way she had come, but in the deepening shadows of dusk, with not even the sun or stars to guide her, she could distinguish neither direction nor recognizable landmark. Slowly she sank to her knees, the knuckle of one fist between her teeth to stifle a rising scream. She had suffered *al-fatwa*, the judgment of the gods for her pride, and she was lost and alone in the land of *ghuwallin*, the wood demons.

Night closed irrevocably over the forest as Janine huddled in fear beneath the swaying phantom of a tall tamarack and fought against *shah mat*, the panic that robs one of reason. Her fear was of the mind only, she told herself. Already Crane and Vandrel must be looking for her. She had only to wait. Soon they would find her. But then the howl of a stalking wolf sent her scrambling to her feet, and all at once she was running heedlessly, her breath coming n painful gasps as she plunged deeper into the tangled forest. Oblivious to the hidden snags and the low-hanging branches like grasping hands that tore at

385

her dress and cut her tender flesh, she fled the remembered terror of Phelan, the wolf mad with the blood lust, who had tracked her down and led the pack in for the kill. She ran until she thought her heart would burst and still she could hear, in close pursuit it seemed, the cry of the wolf who scents the prey. Then suddenly the forest was alight with flame leaping out of darkness, and all about were the harsh cries of men. Stumbling to a halt, Janine flung herself instinctively behind a dense thicket of dwarf oak and clenched a hand over her mouth to still the ragged sobs that shuddered through her.

Again the night blazed with a leaping tongue of flame, and Janine flinched as a savage curse rang out scant feet from her hiding place.

"Fools. Craven sons of the jackal. It is but a half-grown lizard. Any churl with a club could kill it."

"No! Leave her alone," cried a woman's voice. "She will not harm you, I promise."

Startled at the rather odd exchange, one of which, the man's, had been couched in accents strongly reminiscent of the Wendaren tongue, Janine found the courage to work her way up to her knees. Parting the branches, she peered cautiously out, only to find her view blocked by the cloaked figure of a tall, powerful man standing with his back to her. Stifling a gasp, she drew back. Then somewhere before her the forest seemed to erupt into flame and the sounds of trees crashing and men screaming. Curiosity getting the better of caution, Janine began to edge around to one side, trying to see past the cloaked figure into a clearing surrounded by burning trees. A strangled cry rose to her throat as she glimpsed a

386

monstrous, fire-breathing dragon threshing about in a tangle of rope fetters, and before it, a slender woman, her hair streaming wildly about her. With hands folded at her waist, but her head high, she waited as a dozen or more armed men stole furtively toward her. Then a hand closed roughly over Janine's mouth and dragged her back into the dense shadows of a tangled windfall.

Struggling frenziedly, she landed a punishing kick against a hard shin and heard a man's low grunt before her assailant's fierce whisper effectively immobilized her.

"Janine, for gods' sake, it's me!"

"Sayyid Crane!" she sobbed and threw herself into his arms. But then instantly she had pulled away again. "The woman! They will kill her," she cried, her eyes huge in the white blur of her face as she tugged frantically at the shape-changer's arm. "Quickly, we must go to her aid."

She had half-turned as if to launch the proposed attack single-handedly when the youth clasped her by the wrist and hauled her back again.

"Janine, wait, you little spitfire," he uttered between clenched teeth. "You'll ruin everything."

"But it is the woman of the shrine," she insisted, desperate to make him understand. "I could never forget the face of our protectress. Please, you will change into the lion or the tiger, or—or into the winds of *simoom*. Then, when you sweep down on the *ghuwallin* and bewilder them with the fury of *al ghawl*, which is the attack of great suddenness, I will steal the woman away."

Crane, apparently dazzled at the prospect, regarded

the girl with a peculiarly frozen look.

"Of all the hen-witted schemes," he unwisely blurted when he had got his wits back again, "that takes the cake. You, my girl, will wait here till this business is over. Then, when we are all safely back at Vandrel's, we will discuss this damned annoying habit of yours of running away at the slightest provocation. Now, have I made myself clear?"

Janine, understandably incensed at the youth's less than sympathetic response, drew sharply back to flay him with a withering glance.

"But of course, Amiru'l-umara, oh, great prince of princes," she said, making a fine show of touching her hand to her forehead in the gesture of humility. "I am as ever your obedient slave."

"Yes, well, that's more like it," rejoined the shape-changer, eyeing his anything but meek-looking odalisque with a deal of suspicion. "Stay here, mind you, till I can come back for you. You'll only muddle things up and likely get yourself or someone else hurt if you try to follow me. This is no business for a kid, especially a female."

"Then perhaps, Sayyid Crane," Janine murmured sweetly as he turned to go, "it were better if you, too, remained here. For surely a fool is of less use even than a child or a woman."

The young shape-changer came up with a jerk, his back peculiarly rigid. Then, without turning, he growled, "Stay *here*," and lunged off into the darkness.

Janine muttered something less than complimentary in her native tongue and whirled sharply about, her arms crossed over a heaving bosom. For all of ten seconds she remained thus, obedient to her lord's command. And then suddenly her chin came up, a dangerous glint sparked in her eye, and without further ado she turned and stole swiftly after him.

The forest seemed suddenly aswarm with darting shadows as the girl fled the safety of the thicket. Once she imagined she saw the lithe hunter, Elwindolf, wielding Valarc, the long-bow made of Glinden wood. Then the long, grey shape of a wolf bounded past her, and, stifling a scream, she lost sight of the tall man dressed in buckskin. There were strange, miniature warriors, as well. No taller than her knee, they swarmed past her, their voices raised in battle cries couched in the tongue she had only heard one other speak—Aurora, the golden-eyed enchantress, who had seemingly dropped off the edge of the earth.

Breathing a sigh of relief that at least the cloaked warrior who had ordered the death of the dragon was nowhere in sight, Janine darted from cover to cover. Her heart was hammering as she peered ahead through a thickening pall of acrid fumes for the shape-changer. *Marhakim!* It was as if he had simply vanished, poof, into the air, she thought with a sinking feeling in the pit of her stomach. Then she saw him, a tall, gangling figure bent nearly double, skirting a thicket engulfed in flames. Flinging caution to the wind in the fear that she might lose him, Janine shouted, "Sayyid, wait!"

She saw Crane straighten, and glancing over his shoulder, wave his arms frantically at her. Then she was racing boldly for the open, only to blunder full tilt into a gorbellied brute who loomed suddenly out of the smoke directly in front of her.

389

In the grips of *shah mat*, the panic that robs one of reason, the girl screamed and rammed her elbow hard into the soft paunch. With a startled "oomph!" the villain sagged, clutching at his midriff. Then, before her deflated would-be assailant had time to regain his composure, Janine feld in terror straight into the arms of the highly distraught shape-changer.

"Damn it, Janine, of all the *obstinate, hare-brained, perverse* females in the world, you are undoubtedly the worst. If I had any sense, I'd have hogtied you and sent you to Vandrel's before I trusted a *woman* to do what she was told to do." He shook her furiously by the arms as he sought release from the unbearable pressure in his chest. Then, seeing the brute barreling at them like an enraged bull, he cut short his lecture on the vagaries of the female character, and hauling her, unresisting, out of the way, stuck out a gangly leg to send the fellow crashing headlong into the trunk of a tree.

"Blast! What am I to do with you?" Crane continued then, as though he had not been so rudely interrupted. "Can't you see that there's a war going on? Someone has drawn together all the outlaw bands in Endrith's Forest and maybe a few more from outside besides. They've raided all the settlements between the Mountains of Thunder and here on their way to join Dred's forces gathering in the Confounded Lands. The word's out that Estrelland has fallen to the creatures from the Flux, and the Vendrenin is on its way to the Black Mountain. Do you understand what I'm saying? Dred has broken out of Somn, and he's only waiting in Helynderne for the crystal to arrive. When it does, nothing will stop

390

him from making his move against Harmon and the Eilderood!"

Janine, who had hardly had time yet to recover either from her near mishap with the brute or her subsequent astonishment at having finally been acknowledged a woman by her blustering lord, now struggled to grasp the meaning of this latest unsettling news.

"This army of outlaws," she uttered faintly, "why have they come? Surely there is nothing here for them."

"Oh, yes there is. There's the Valdoran's shrine," he answered grimly. "Thegne of Hawthorn Glade figured they would come here to destroy the Crystal Tear, but no one guessed that when they did, Ariana herself would drop into their laps like an overripe plum. Which brings us back to our present difficulty. Elwindolf and Freyga, along with an assortment of wolves, elves, and whomever else they could find to help, are doing their best to throw this bunch into a stage of confusion. It's up to me to get through to the lady. So what do I do about you? I can't send you to Vandrel. She's out somewhere *looking* for you."

"There is no more time, Sayyid," Janine quickly interjected, judiciously ignoring the harassed shape-changer's rather pointed look. "You have no choice but to take me with you."

In truth, Janine did not know how they managed to break through the barrier of flames into the heart of the fighting. One moment she was standing looking up into Crane's freckled face, and the next she was dodging a soot-blackened warrior who lunged at them, swinging an axe. It was only after Crane disabled the rogue with a well-placed kick to the groin that she realized the shape-changer must simply have thought them there.

The clearing was in a turmoil, with perhaps a score of outlaws in full rout caught between the blazing forest and the dragon, spouting flames in a fear-maddened frenzy at anything that moved. A tangle of frayed and badly charred ropes littered the ground about the dragon, evidence that the outlaws had tried to capture the beast alive. Still, it had obviously broken loose from its fetters and appeared to be unhurt despite the numerous spears, axes, and other miscellaneous weapons lying about. Thus it occurred to Janine to wonder why the creature did not simply fly away, when she caught sight of a woman's inert form lying between the dragon's front feet.

"The Lady of the Shrine!" she breathed, her throat suddenly tight as she realized the dragon refused to leave the stricken woman. Then Crane had caught up her hand and was pulling her in the direction of the shrine's carven statuary.

"Quick," he said, propelling her toward the figure of the Valdoran surrounded by animals, "under here." Then, after nearly thrusting her into the narrow space beneath the carved representation of a hind, he paused for the barest instant to look her straight in the eyes. "There isn't time to weave a spell of hiding and binding, as I did before." He grinned a trifle crookedly, recalling their single night spent together beneath the safe haven of the shrine. Then the smile faded to be replaced by a compelling gravity that made Janine's heart beat ever so much faster. "I couldn't stand it if anything happened to you, Janine," he murmured, his voice unwontedly husky. "Promise me you won't do anything foolish?"

"I-I promise, my lord," she answered simply, scarce knowing what was happening to her as suddenly he bent and brushed his lips fleetingly against hers. Then he had gone, and she was left feeling weak and trembly. *"Marhakim!"* she whispered, touching her fingers to her lips. "So this is what it is to be a woman."

Crane, emerging once more from the shadowed haven of the shrine onto the scene of utter chaos, tried resolutely to force his thoughts from the lingering image of violet-blue eyes and rosebud lips. Drat! Why did the troublesome brat have to be so blasted stubborn? he fretted, uneasy at having to leave Janine unprotected. For he was well aware that if anything happened to the little Wendaren, his life would no longer be worth living.

Still, he had done all he could for Janine, and now there was nothing for it but to trust that the One, who looked after innocents and fools, would keep this maddeningly headstrong, but infinitely precious, young girl safe until he could come back for her. Meantime, he reflected dourly, he must somehow reach the Valdoran and contrive to get her to safety, which, from the looks of the dragon, was going to be no easy matter. Then with a pang the young mage thought suddenly of Aurora. Drat! Where in Throm *was* the blasted female? Egads, but he'd give his eyeteeth to have her materialize suddenly before him. Then, by god, he'd give her a piece of his mind. How dared she leave them in the lurch just when all of Somn was about to break loose! If the raven-haired enchantress *were* only here, he thought, shuddering at the sight of an outlaw who, trying frantically to dodge the red-hot spew of dragon's fire, was singed ignominiously on the behind. At least she could have tried reasoning with the creature. But since it seemed unlikely in the extreme that the enchantress was anywhere within the vicinity, there was nothing for it but that *he* think of something, and fast. For there was no telling how long Elwindolf's small band could hold off the bulk of the outlaws still beyond the circle of flames.

After reluctantly discarding the notion of trying to reach the unconscious Valdoran by burrowing underground in the form of a mole, Crane was suddenly and inexplicably visited with a fleeting memory of the maddeningly intractable cud-chewing dromedary, whimsically misnomered "Mouse," or Mush in Wendaren, who had been tamed into submission upon being confronted by Crane in the form of a bull camel. It had been love at first sight for the unfortunate female, who thenceforth had displayed a docility of temperament astounding in one of her recalcitrant breed. And suddenly the germ of an idea began to take root in Crane's fertile brain. Why not? he thought. It had worked, after all, with the camel.

"Just because one dromedary with the intelligence of a gnat had the poor taste to fall for a mage in

394

camel's clothing does not mean that the last living female of Dracadern lineage would be equally absurd," observed a dry voice behind him. "Indeed, she would be more like to fry you for supper, my lad."

"Van!" exclaimed the shape-changer, his face lighting up at the sight of the elderly scholar. "How in Somn did you get here?"

"Never mind, boy. I have my ways, and you can be sure nothing could keep me from so marvelous a sight as *that*," she said, indicating the dragon just then putting a hastily abandoned catapult to the torch. "But to business now. It's time we put an end to the poor little darling's distress. First, I think we must provide an exit for these scoundrels, and for that, my lad, we shall require a little old-fashioned conjuring:

> Out of air, from here to there,
> An element of cloud prepare:
> A twist of mist, a dash of splash.
> Begin with a thunder clash!"

No sooner had the words left her mouth than a bolt of lightning slithered out of the night followed by a shattering clap of thunder. And then it began to rain in torrents.

Without waiting to see the ragtag band of outlaws scramble for the safety of the smoldering forest, Vandrel picked up her voluminous skirts and bundled through the downpour toward the dragon, who even then had lowered its head to nuzzle the inert form at its feet with every appearance of bewildered grief. Crane, who understandably pictured the monstrous creature more in the light of a virago of destruction than a "poor little darling," followed his former mentor with rather less enthusiasm. He was fully prepared to behold the creature erupt into an outraged frenzy at their foolhardy approach. Nor was he to be disappointed. At first sight of the scholar and her reluctant companion, the dragon uttered a blood-chilling screech and reared up to some thirty feet in height from the top of its head to the hideously clawed hind feet.

Thus it was that, his gaze fixed on the dragon in every expectation of being momentarily reduced to charred rubble, Crane failed to see a tall, caped figure steal into the Valdoran's Shrine. Indeed, the shape-changer had frozen instantly into a complete state of immovability. Not so Vandrel, who dropping her skirt hems and planting her fists firmly on plump hips, proceeded to deliver the creature a scolding as if it were naught but a small, rather grubby, misbehaved child.

"Shame, shame on you, my little pet. Don't you know friends when you see them? Come down now and tell us your name. I'm called Vandrel, and this is Crane. We've come to help your lady."

To Crane's astonishment, the dragon cocked its head to one side and blinked a single ruby-red eye at the two in timorous uncertainty. Then slowly the wedge-shaped head lowered.

"That's a good girl," crooned the elderly scholar, chuckling as the creature shyly nudged her with its horned snout. "Now, tell old Vandrel your name while I have a look at this poor lass."

"Lynwen," mumbled the dragon, never taking her

eyes off Vandrel as the scholar knelt in the mud beside the unconscious woman. "Lynwen, the Fair. You won't hurt her, will you?"

"No, no. Of course we won't, but you must let us move her to a dry place so that we can tend to her properly."

"Mathair's going to die. I know she is," blurted the infantile dracadern, her head beginning to weave on the serpentine neck in renewed agitation, "and it's all my fault. Mathair told me there was nothing to fear, but they threw ropes at me and shouted and I-I just couldn't help it. I was so frightened. Oh, I *wish* we could go home. I don't like it here."

"Now, Lynwen," said the scholar in her firmest, no-nonsense voice, "you shall not let yourself go into a pet. Mathair is not going to die. You must trust me. Now you will please stand back and let Crane carry Ariana to a safer place. Well, what are you waiting for, boy?" she demanded then, frowning impatiently at the thunderstricken youth.

Crane shot a horrified glance at the Valdoran lying at the oversized taloned feet of destruction and shuddered. Egads, Vandrel could not truly be serious, he thought, but one look at the scholar's expression of blatant expectancy was enough to convince him otherwise. Resigning himself to the inevitable, the shape-changer eased forward through the nearly ankle-deep mud, and kneeling gingerly, slid his hands beneath the woman's shoulders and knees. So far, so good, he thought, running his tongue over dry lips. But then as he struggled to hoist the limp form up in his arms and simultaneously to heave himself to feet none too firmly planted in the slippery mud, the Valdoran stirred and uttered a soft groan. The sudden reek of dragon-breath full in his face brought the shape-changer up short in a most damned awkward position. Without moving a muscle, Crane slowly lifted his eyes from the ground to look squarely into a frigid, rufescent glare.

"Vandre-el," he caroled between teeth clenched in a grin.

"Oh, for pity's sake. Enough of this foolishness, both of you. Crane, get Ariana to the shrine, and you, Lynwen, cease to tease the poor lad."

Thus it was that the Valdoran was returned at last to the shrine erected in her honor by Lathrop of Sedgewick long ages past.

Crane, entering with his precious burden, felt an instant frisson of danger. Indeed, the statuary was hardly in the same shape that he had left it. The figure of the Valdoran and most of the carven representations of animals had been ruthlessly hacked by an axe or a stout blade so as to be rendered virtually unrecognizable. For the space of two heartbeats, the shape-changer stood in stunned horror. Then dropping heavily to one knee, the Valdoran still clasped hard in his arms, he uttered a terrible cry of despair.

"JANINE! Oh, gods, Janine, what have I done?"

Vandrel, coming softly down the steps from the loft in which she had left Ariana peacefully sleeping, paused at the sudden loud outburst from the room below.

"I don't *care* about Dred's blasted war! I've been to

the Land of the Mages *and* to Britshelm and Fengard. The armies of the south should be halfway to the Plain of Shin by now. Someone else can summon the desert tribes. I *know* the bastard has taken Janine to Helynderne beneath the Black Mountain. And that's where I'm headed just as soon as Elwindolf gets back."

"Now, lad, we all know how ye feel, but that's the talk of a hotheaded fool. What good can ye be t' th' lass if'n ye be likewise a prisoner? Or, dead, which be more likely."

Crane ceased his fitful perambulations about Vandrel's cluttered kitchen and glared at the old elf who had spoken kindly.

"No, Garwin," he said, his boyish face hard in the subdued light of the fire burning in the open grate of the fireplace, "not a prisoner. Maybe you've forgotten that I'm not likely to be easily captured. And I mean to do my level best to see that no one kills me, either. But either way, I'm going. It's my fault Janine's in the fix she's in, and I'd just as soon be dead as do nothing to get her out of it."

The elf's sigh was clearly audible to Vandrel, listening at the head of the stairs. The gleam of a smile hovered briefly in the bespectacled eyes. The lad had spoken like a man. Indeed, he was a long sight removed from the bumbling young mage who had been ever uncertain of his powers and uncertain of himself. The enchantress had played a large part in the molding of this steadier, more mature Crane, but it had taken Janine to add the finishing touches.

A sudden loud rap, followed by a howling flurry of wind as the door was thrust open then quickly closed again, heralded a new arrival in Vandrel's already crowded kitchen.

"Elwindolf," murmured a low voice thrillingly, and a tall, graceful form detached itself from the shadows to cross quickly to the hunter wearily divesting himself of a fur mantle streaming water.

An unwonted warmth relieved the pale glitter of the man's grey eyes as Freyga took the cloak and hung it on a wooden peg near the fire, then, pouring a generous measure of freshly brewed tea laced with Vandrel's potent elderberry wine, handed him the cup.

"Come sit by the fire," she said, "and tell us what you have learned."

"Was there any sign of the girl?" Garwin asked, making room for the man on a low wooden bench.

"Aye, we found her trail—Stahn, the Hlafard of Bredan, and I," Elwindolf said and drank gratefully of the steaming brew.

"And?" Crane prodded from across the room, his long frame taut as he waited for the taciturn hunter to tell his tale.

The man raised expressionless eyes to the youth's face in which the freckles standing out against the pallid skin seemed somehow incongruous with the stubborn set of his jaw.

"We followed the spoor to the abandoned town of Sedgewick and there caught sight of the girl with another." The hunter's lean features hardened. "She was the captive of the Black Knight, who came forth out of the Flux, him whom I had thought slain in the sorceress's chamber the night the enchantress was taken from us."

"Xerxes!" Crane uttered in a low voice, his brown eyes glinting.

"Aye, the very same," murmured the hunter.

For a long moment the youth stood with fists clenched tightly at his sides, his throat working as he fought some inner battle. Then suddenly he turned eyes that accused upon the hunter.

"But if you saw them, why did you let them get away? What happened to Janine? Why is she not with you?"

Elwindolf peered into the cup in his hands, his stern features unreadable in the shadows cast by the firelight.

"We stood atop the ridge overlooking the town. It was Stahn who first sensed the coming of the evil ones from out of the black of night. The aingeal-wyrms, breathing fire, descended on silent wings into the wold. 'Twas then we saw the flare of the signal fire and the Black Knight with the girl in bonds at his feet. The creatures took them up and bore them into the west ere we could reach the fell. The girl Janine hath gone beyond our reach, Mage-Lord, borne unto Dred's Confounded Lands."

"No. Not beyond *my* reach," Crane said in a steely voice. "You forget I have been to Helynderne before."

"Aye, lad," spoke up Garwin, his hazel eyes worried, "but then ye had the enchantress wi' ye, an' Dred yet slept in Somn."

"And now Dred is on the loose and the gods only know where Aurora is or even if she's alive," Crane retorted bitterly, flinging himself away from the elf's discerning gaze. Standing with his back to the room, he stared blindly out at the storm raging beyond the single curtained window. "And if she is alive, how can we know she gives a tinker's damn about what's going on? She left *us* to deal with the creatures of the Flux, while she went on some wild goose chase to save her Thromholan lover. Frayne is all she cares about."

The room went deathly still. Then Elwindolf deliberately looked up from his silent contemplation of the cup between his hands.

"We don't know that, boy," he said ever so quietly, and suddenly Crane shivered. But still he would not be silenced. He spun about to face them, a wild look in his eyes that yet radiated a sort of hurt bewilderment.

"Don't we?" he demanded, daring them to deny it. "Is there anything she wouldn't do for the bloody knight of Tor? Anything she wouldn't do to be with him? She is obsessed with him, bewitched. By the gods, she would sell her soul for him—if she hasn't already."

"Enough!" It was the elf, the wizened countenance markedly devoid of its earlier sympathy. "Ye'll say no more against th' lass. Innocent be her heart of what ye wouldst imply, as innocent as is that of the lady what lies ill in the loft above us. She be Anduan, Elf-Foundling and Tree-Child. I know her as I know meself. She could not betray the Realm."

Then Freyga spoke, her eyes troubled as she gazed at the silent hunter.

"I do *not* know her as do the rest of you. But I have wondered. If she is the Symbol-Bearer, the one chosen to be the savior of the people, then why has she not shown herself? Indeed, where *is* the Nameless One, if she yet lives?"

"Oh, she's alive," Vandrel answered, cheerfully descending at last to join her troubled houseguests. "Alive and nearer to the Prince of Somn than even she realizes."

The old scholar waited patiently for the inevitable uproar to calm before finally she raised her hands for order.

"I'll thank all of you to be quiet," she admonished, the gleam in her eyes robbing the words of their sting. "There's a patient upstairs who needs her rest. After all, the Valdoran's come a long way from the Flux to what could hardly be construed a hospitable welcome. I'll not have her disturbed so long as she resides beneath my roof."

"But Aurora," Crane broke in impatiently. "Tell us what you know of her."

"Aye, where is th' lass?" chimed in Garwin, glaring balefully at the youth. "There be some what doesn't trust her."

"She's with my son—or at least she was," answered the Valdoran from the head of the stairs. "And by now they are most likely in the Confounded Lands, the gods help them."

For a moment the company fell into an uneasy stillness as the slender figure, draped in a white robe, her flaxen hair falling freely down her back and her eyes translucent with an enduring sorrow, came slowly down the stairs.

"My dear," Vandrel exclaimed disapprovingly as she bustled forward to take charge of her patient, "whatever are you about? You know you shouldn't be out of your bed just yet."

"You mustn't worry about me, dearest friend. I shall be fine," murmured the Valdoran. Still she did not resist when Vandrel insisted she be seated in a padded rocking chair placed solicitously near the fire. "Now," she said, smiling as the scholar straightened from tucking a goose-down comforter snugly about her, "you must not keep these good people waiting any longer. Tell them about Aurora."

"Yes, I suppose that is the first order of business, since there has been some question raised as to the girl's loyalty," began the scholar, glancing significantly at the stone-faced young mage. "Far from selling her soul to Somn, however, you will doubtless be pleased to hear that, on the contrary, our young enchantress has had the temerity to challenge Dred in the sorceress's fortress and did in the process destroy the Seeing Eye. Along with Skorl, incidentally. Now the Black Prince is as blind as everyone else, which cannot have made him easy. Doubtless he's wondering like the rest of us where Aurora is, and little does he guess that she is outside his very door. Indeed, at the feet of the Black King himself, unless I miss my guess. For the circlet of Hythe was used always to reside atop the likeness Dred had raised for Hedron on the shores of the Blessed Sea," she finished, fairly beaming upon her rapt audience.

"Like as not ye've reason t' seem pleased as a bear wi' honey at th' news," grumbled the elf, when he had had time properly to digest the scholar's somewhat disjointed revelations. "There be some, however, what can't make nary a smidgeon o' sense out o' all yer yammer, woman, an' would be best

404

pleased were ye t' begin at th' beginnin'."

Thus it was that Vandrel had, perforce, to relate the events that had kept the enchantress from them since the fall of Skorl, even as Ariana had earlier reported them to her. She spoke at great length, leaving nothing out of the telling, and when at last she had finished, she was met with a grim silence broken only by the fire crackling cheerfully in the fireplace.

"Well, have *you* nothing to say at least?" she queried of Crane, who stared stonily at the scuffed toes of his boots.

"I say that what you've told us changes nothing," answered the shape-changer, flushing as he looked up to meet the scholar's keen-eyed glance. "If the enchantress is about to enter the Black Mountain, that's all the more reason why I should be there. Janine won't stand a chance otherwise. There's nothing anyone can say to change my mind. I'm going, and that's that."

"But of course you're going. And so are Elwindolf and Garwin, unless I miss my guess."

"And I," spoke up the Shintari priestess. A faintly ironic smile touched her lips as the man-wolf's pale glance rose sharply to hers.

"The mage hath given his reasons for daring the black depths of Helynderne, and Garwin would go for the sake of the elf-foundling, Aurora," he said evenly, his lean face questioning. "But Elwindolf goes to repay a debt owed Brenna of the golden eyes, for it was she who freed him from the curse of *faege*. Yet the huntress of Shin lays claim neither to friendship with the enchantress or the child nor to a

405

debt owed. There can be no reason for her to risk her life needlessly."

"Not for the child would I go, nor for the enchantress, though perhaps my debt to her is as great as yours, Hunter," she answered steadily. "Yet would I claim the right of one whose blood flows in the veins of another to go wherever he would go. I will not be denied, Elwindolf. I will not be left behind."

"Oh, that's just great," Crane blurted, glancing irately from one to the other of his determined companions. "Next I suppose Vandrel will want to go, and why not the Valdoran and her insufferable fire-spewing dragon as well?"

"Whatever are you talking about?" queried the scholar, eyeing the red-faced young mage in mild surprise. "I cannot, of course, speak for Ariana, but I for one have no intentions of doing anything so foolish. As a matter of fact, it has recently occurred to me that, as I'm not getting any younger, it is time I pulled up stakes and renewed some old acquaintances. I've decided to take Lynwen home to Garn where she belongs. And, of course, while I'm at it, I suppose I might as well elicit the aid of a certain stubborn old drake for his great-granddaughter. It's high time Lothe stopped feeling sorry for himself and thought of someone else for a change."

"But then that is the perfect solution to my own dilemma!" Ariana exclaimed softly. "I have been wracking my brain trying to think what I should do with Lynwen. For you see, far from wishing to inflict myself on you, young man," she said, smiling gently at the discomfited Crane, "or anyone else for that matter, I had hoped to do what I could to right some of the things that are wrong here in Endrith's Forest. Unfortunately, I have since discovered that a half-grown dragon would make that impossible. But now that I am free of that worry, I shall hope to discover someplace where I am truly needed."

"If ye mean that, me lady," Garwin interjected in his gruff manner, "then mayhap ye'll hasten to th' aid o' th' dryads. They be dyin', the father-oaks what spawned 'em witherin' away from blight what no elf or dryad can name."

"Maybe no elf can give it a name, but I can," Freyga said abruptly, her marvelous eyes glittering strangely. "It's the poison spread by the creatures released from the Flux. The poison that nearly did in Elwindolf and has done for Endrith. No, it's true. The unicorns are gone. Driven into hiding or, like Endrith, taken in despair so that they follow the path of the dying unicorn to the ancient burial ground. The father-oaks die because the magic is gone from the forest, and till Dred is banished once more, there's nothing anyone can do to stop it."

"I might have known," uttered the shape-changer in a voice of self-loathing. "Oh, gods, why did I listen to Aurora? We could have stopped Leilah before she completed the potion. It's my fault Endrith is gone. And Frayne's, curse him."

"Crane . . . !" Vandrel began harshly, but the Valdoran silenced her with a look.

"No, the boy has a right to speak. But know this: no one has cursed my son so mercilessly as has he himself since first he learned the bitter truth of his birth. He is the Thromholan, but he is my son, and

Aurora's beloved. What he did he did for me. Whatever he does now will depend on the gods and the enchantress."

The gathering about Vandrel's kitchen table for the last time was anything but merry. Ariana had been finally induced to return to her bed. Gently wishing Elwindolf and Fregya godspeed, and after promising Garwin she would do all in her power for the dryads of Grendylmere, she had next drawn the reluctant young mage aside for a brief, soft-spoken exchange, after which she had left him staring after her, his boyish face hard and yet strangely vulnerable. Thus Crane brooded at the window, and Garwin sat by the fire predicting they should, like poor Gleb, who had been carried off by mudgeons, all come to a bad end. The scholar herself had soon given over trying to dispel the pervading gloom as she busied herself preparing a savory vegetable stew, fresh apple turnovers, and, last, a goodly supply of pasties stuffed with potatoes, onions, and turnips, which she insisted the others must take along with them despite Garwin's assurance that starvation would be the least of the perils they faced in the great mines inhabited by blood-drinking Valkar, distempered gnomes, and flesh-eating giants, not to mention whatever loathsome creatures Dred might since have dragged up from the vile depths.

During all of this, Elwindolf occupied his old place at the far end of the table. His broad shoulders propped against the wall at his back, he drew thoughtfully on his pipe and watched Freyga move quietly about the room as she helped Vandrel in the preparations of the evening meal.

The Shintari priestess loomed as something of a marvel to the woodsman, whose unfettered existence had hitherto precluded many meaningful contacts with members of the gentler sex. Yet, weak and dazed, his spirit still drifting in a nebulous dream of half-reality, he had awakened from his long sojourn at the outer fringes of death to the silver-haired Freyga, and somehow he had known nothing would ever again be the same.

The wounds to his body had healed quickly, thanks to Vandrel's magic and the blood of the Shintari, which now flowed in his veins. It had taken longer for his mind, which had delved deeply into the darkness of death's subtle spell, for he had been *faege*, bound to the cursed spirit of the slain Phelan. Still, the oath, which had linked him in spirit to the enchantress as well, had proven the stronger. Brenna of the golden eyes had freed him of the curse of the father-wolf, but it had been Freyga's strength in the end that had banished the lingering shadows. Indeed, it was ironic that just as he should have found a reason for wanting to live, he was confronted with the prospect of almost certain death, a prospect that she willingly would face with him, he marveled.

The thought both uplifted and appalled him, for while he had long since discovered that the warrior-priestess could track a quarry and wield a sword, spear or bow with the best of men and that she displayed a cool head and a dauntless courage possessed by few of either sex, still it distressed him to think that so wondrous a creature should die because of him. Yet neither could he deny her, for he was the man-wolf reared in the ways of the Bredan, and ever had the she-wolves hunted equally with the pack. Nay, he could stop her from going only if he himself refused to go, he realized, suddenly conscious for the first time in his life of weariness and a deep reluctance to place himself in danger. Nor did he delude himself that his malaise could be attributed to his recent bout with death. Nay, it was the woman and the feelings that she aroused in him that unmanned him. Indeed, had circumstances been different, he, Elwindolf, would have taken Freyga to mate.

Thus it was the Elwindolf, who had been Ealan, the Lone-Wolf, shunning fellowship with either man or beast, was brought to an awareness of love's first torment. Nor had his preoccupation with the silver-haired Shintari gone unnoticed. Vandrel, observing her inscrutable foster-son in a brown study, was hard put not to break into glee. Indeed, unless she missed her guess, the formidable man-wolf had at last met his match. As for Freyga, she was more difficult to decipher, for she was by nature stubbornly proud and displayed a cool reserve that the scholar had never been able to penetrate. Still, it promised well for Elwindolf's suit that the girl had boldly declared her intent to go with him. No, she had little enough to worry about so far as Elwindolf and Freyga were concerned. The man-wolf had never more to be Ealan, the Loner. Indeed, it was Crane who troubled her now.

It was not that she did not understand the boy's hurt perplexity over the enchantress's prolonged absence at a time when the very air seemed rife with the fulfilling of prophecy. Nor did she condemn him for his seeming lack of faith in Aurora. Deep down he did not believe his harsh accusations. In this, his heart warred with his brain, and both were heavily taxed with anxiety over Janine's well-being and a sense of guilt that he had not somehow prevented the child's abduction. He blamed himself for all the misfortunes that had befallen with the fateful completion of the sorceress's potion. Poor lad. As if he could have done anything to stem the tides of destiny! No, she did not blame him for anything he had said or done. Crane's love for the golden-eyed Aurora was not one whit less than it had ever been, despite his growing tenderness for Janine. In truth they were separate and distinct emotions. Aurora he would ever worship from afar as some sort of unattainable ideal, but to Janine he would give his heart. It was in this that his dilemma lay, for the lad had yet to make the distinction in his own mind.

Somehow his feelings for Aurora had become all jumbled up with his guilt at having failed Janine. Indeed, she suspected that Crane felt the enchantress had betrayed him by her very absence, for was not she, who had mastered Andruvien and wielded the heart of crystal fire, capable of anything? And therefore was it not probable that she could have prevented Janine's misfortune had she not instead been off in pursuit of her Thromholan lover, the very man who had caused the rift to be formed through which Janine's abductor had escaped into the Realm? Oh, what a tangle of cause and effect it was! No wonder Crane was all mixed up inside. And only Janine's safe return could unravel it all for him. By the One, she prayed it would all come about for them, and *before* the young shape-changer did something totally brash and irrevocable!

The domed roof and marble arches of the Vardos gleamed palely in the moonlight as Crane and his three companions materialized on the lava-strewn slopes of the Black Mountain. Crane shivered at the utter stillness, realizing suddenly that the incessant winds that had swooped over the barren plains of igneous rock on his last visit here were uncannily still. A muttered curse from the elf brought him around sharply, his nerves tingling.

"By th' One, 'tis th' whole world comin' t'gether. An' the gods help us when they meet!" exclaimed Garwin, staring in awe beyond the black expanse of the Confounded Lands to the distant Plains of Shintari, mottled by bivouac fires. "There t' th' south must lie the armies of Fengard and Britshelm. An' to th' south and east, the elves under Thegne's command. An' near them, the mage-clans. Th' rest be Dred's, the gods rot 'em."

"The vanguard should reach the Lava Plain by noonday tomorrow," Crane conjectured gloomily. "Before sunset they'll be here."

"Nay, they'll not come to Dred's mountain to fight," Elwindolf murmured, his eyes gleaming palely in the moonlight. "They'll meet out there, beyond the Runed Portal."

Instantly Crane knew the hunter was right, for no battle could be waged on the wasteland of lava rock, which was treacherous with jagged edges and invisible pitfalls covered over with thin crusts that gave way beneath a man's weight. Dred would send his forces into the loosely organized armies of the One before they had even the chance to come together to form a solid front let alone devise a plan of attack. Suddenly he felt the sweat trickle down his ribs beneath his shirt despite the chill night air. The allies of the One hadn't a chance. From the size of the bivouacked armies, he judged they were outnumbered three to one, and Dred would have the Vendrenin as well. And as if that were not enough to daunt the staunchest heart, there had as yet been no sign that Harmon and the Eilderood were even aware that the Realm of the One teetered on the edge of destruction. Where in blazes *was* the warrior-god? fretted the shape-changer, on the edge of despair. For that matter, where were the enchantress and the cursed Thromholan upon whom the outcome of the coming upheaval had ever seemed somehow to devolve?

Then Garwin's demand to know if the shape-changer meant to stand there till the end of doom jerked Crane back to the present.

"I don't know the way inside from here," he confessed, flushing slightly at the elf's answering snort of disbelief. "I thought it would be better to try to get some idea of what we were up against before we popped in on Dred unannounced. For all I knew the place might be swarming with Thromgilad and who knows what else."

"So what do we do now?" Freyga said, seeming to drag her eyes away from the plain named for her people, the Children of Shin, who had roamed its vastness for centuries. "We still know nothing of what awaits us below."

"No, but we do know the bulk of Dred's army is out there. So there's a chance at least of materializing unseen in the western adit. I wouldn't recommend the Helynderne itself, since Aurora pretty well made a mess of it the last time we were here. At least part of it caved in when she removed the Andruvien from the Crystal Room. And the only other place I've seen is the Chamber of Lords, which is most likely where we'll find Dred and the Lords of Throm."

"Then so be it," remarked Garwin fatalistically. "Just make sure 'tis the corridor ye think us to. I've little wish to end up a permanent fixture in one of Dred's bloomin' walls."

"Not 'us,' Garwin, but 'me' alone," Crane said, shifting uneasily from one foot to the other. Now they had come to the touchy part of the scheme he had worked out earlier in Vandrel's kitchen after it had become apparent that he would not be allowed to venture forth to the Confounded Lands alone.

From his past experiences with the confusing network of tunnels that honeycombed the mountain's interior, he had known that to try to search every twist and turn would be fruitless in the extreme; indeed, a lifetime might not be sufficient for such a hopeless task. Which had meant that actually there was only a single avenue open to them, and it offered only a slim chance of success, for to pull it off, one of them must try to slip into the Chamber of Lords unseen in the hopes of learning something that would lead them to the kidnapped girl. Well aware that because of his peculiar talents, he alone of the four was suited to the task, he had wracked his brain for a place to seclude the others till he could return to them. Then it had come to him that the only realistic plan would be to leave them somewhere on the surface of the mountain, and since the Vardos was the only place he could visualize with any certainty, he had determined to bring them here. But now he had somehow to convince them that he must go alone the rest of the way.

"Now, hold on just a minute . . ." sputtered the old elf, but Crane, in no mood for a lengthy debate, cut in.

"No, by the gods, I won't. Can't you see that till we know where they're holding Janine, it's pointless for all of us to go blundering around down there? In fact, there was never any reason for anyone else to come here at all. Once I've found her, I'll simply think us both out again. The rest of you would only be in the way."

"Ye've got it all worked out have ye?" demanded Garwin, drawing up indignantly. "An' what if something goes agley whilst ye be playin' th' hero? What o' th' lass then, an' yerself? Might be ye'd be wishful o' a friend or two *then*, me lad."

"In that case not even a friend or two will be enough to help us," Crane said evenly, "and only one has paid the forfeit."

"Bah! An' I'd come t' think ye'd got o'er yer Tomfool notions that ye must prove yerself aught but Krim's bumblin' grandson. More th' fool be I fer it."

Blast! thought the shape-changer, scarcely able to

contain his impatience with this needless delay. *Why* had Vandrel to meddle with what should have been his concern and his alone? She was not usually so thick-skulled. Drawing breath to deliver a stinging retort, Crane was rendered suddenly speechless by the man-wolf's intervention.

"Nay, Garwin," he murmured in that way he had of cutting to the heart of things, "the boy be right. He alone can go unseen amidst the enemy." Then he looked at Crane, and the shape-changer felt a sudden lump hard in his throat. "We will wait here till the passing of Shin into the west, Mage-Lord. Yet know that be ye not then returned unto this place, we will follow after you."

Thus it was that scant moments later Crane found himself alone at the mouth of a long, dimly lit tunnel that would take him straight to the mammoth vaulted hall known as the Chamber of the Lords. And suddenly he was overwhelmed by a floodtide of bittersweet memories. For it was there that Frayne and Aurora had found the horn of the unicorn and there, too, that the knight of Tor had single-handedly battled the giant Grimshank, while Crane dragged the fiercely resistant Aurora from the hall to the safety of the intersecting tunnels, one of which formed the adit he now traversed. Blast! he thought, remembering how he had no sooner gotten Aurora out of the Chamber of Lords than she had spotted Fangol, the haggish wife of Kral, the gnome-chieftan, stealing into the other, lightless corridor, the enchantress's stolen blade, Glaiveling, clutched in her gnarled hand. A reluctant smile tugged at the corner of Crane's mouth. Egads, he had been mad enough to throttle the ever-impetuous Aurora when suddenly she pulled free and vanished heedlessly after the dratted gnome. And then to discover they had gotten themselves trapped in the Crystal Room, which Endrith's Song had warned must be avoided at all costs! It had been enough to curl one's hair, he thought, but then immediately the half-formed grin faded before the succeeding rush of memories— Dred's secret door slithering shut behind him as he darted into the darkness after the enchantress, Fangol cursing Aurora for spilling her pouch of gold coins—the gnome's blood money for having betrayed them to the giants—and finally the sliver of Vendrenin scintillating awesome flames of crystal fire from the hand of a slender, raven-haired girl, for such had been the forging of Andruvien, the Blade of Light, which was the sword of the enchantress.

Angrily Crane shook off the paralyzing spell wrought by his painful reminiscences and struck out grimly down the corridor. Of what use was remembering? Everything had changed since they had discovered the truth of Frayne's identity. Curse the knight for his cold-blooded deceit! And curse Aurora for refusing to see him for what he was—Dred's heinous spawn, the Thromholan who would stop at nothing to achieve his own nefarious ends.

Damn! What was the power Frayne had to mesmerize and enthrall so that, even knowing who and what he was, one still longed to believe he was the paragon he seemed, the hero of a hundred tales of dauntless courage and bold deeds? Why was it that he could with a word or a glance make one feel ten feet tall, a man who could do anything, face any peril, real or imagined, a man who was worth Frayne's regard? Blast! he cursed silently, writhing at the memory of Ariana's soft plea to wait before judging her son too harshly. Egads, he had not needed *her* to tell him that ofttimes appearances were deceiving, that, indeed, the knight might not be all that he had been represented to be. He had found it out the hard way. Once he would have given anything to be just like him, *done* anything to earn the faintest glimmer of approval from the impenetrable knight, but no more. Once and for all he had seen him for what he was—the Thromholan, who ruthlessly manipulated others for his own inscrutable purposes. Janine, himself, Aurora, yes, even the enchantress—Frayne had used them all, but he would never again use Krim's slow-witted grandson, vowed the shape-changer, and resolutely quashed the dull ache that persisted somewhere near his breast.

Having come to the junction of the adit with the blind corridor that led to what had been the Crystal Room, Crane halted and peered stealthily around the corner. The luminescent stuff that seemed a part of the very stone rendered the tunnel an eerie place of glaucous, unmoving shadows.

Cripes! It was like seeing down a giant's gullet into the putrid entrails. He shuddered, wondering if the ghoulish notion were an ill portent of his own imminent and odiously distasteful demise. Then a furtive step at his back sounded a warning in his brain. Crane spun about, and suddenly the tunnel roof seemed to cave in on him. With a groan he sank to his knees and tumbled forward, his cheek coming down hard against the cold stone floor. Egads, he had botched it, went fleetingly through his mind, followed by the bitter certainty that he must somehow get away. Struggling against the cold waves of darkness washing over him, the shape-changer tried desperately to think himself back to Elwindolf and the others, but it was useless. His brain, bursting with lights and reeling before a blinding pain, he could neither form an image of the Vardos nor recall the words of transmutation. By the One, he had been fairly caught.

A footstep sounded near and the brief sounds of a scuffle. Then through the glaze of pain he saw a boot halt within inches of his face. Summoning the last of his fading strength, he forced up his head to see who had struck him from behind. A face swam into focus, the features lean and hard, and the eyes, the eyes of a falcon—steely grey with dark rims about the irises.

"Frayne!" he rasped, a bitter travesty of a laugh shuddering through him. "Gods, I might have known it would be you." Then his strength gave way and Crane slid into oblivion.

Chapter 13

Aurora awakened to the susurrus of sand brushed by a cold breeze and to a white vastness shimmering in the pale light of a full moon. Licking parched lips, she raised herself on one elbow and stared out over an empty arenaceous waste seemingly bereft of any other living thing. Vaguely she wondered how she came to be in the Land of Erg and in befuddlement looked about for Frayne, Janine, and the young shape-changer, all of whom had been with her on the perilous quest for Saraisharaqa. But, nay, she thought, shaking her head to clear it of the confusing tangle of memories, we found Rab's palace and the Kingdom of Crystals and left the desert. And then suddenly everything came flooding back to her.

Oh, gods! she groaned inwardly, clenching shut her eyes. She had pierced the veiled depths of the Thromholan and for an instant had seen the image of betrayal. Frayne in the arms of a goddess. Frayne entwined with a seductress of Throm! She could not be mistaken, for in that brief glimpse she had beheld the glimmerous aura of power exuding from the lissome form, had smelled the intoxicating fragrance of orchids and known it for what it was—the scent of an ancient magic, the potion of desire. And Frayne had succumbed to it! When? she wondered bitterly. Before or after he had sworn his undying love for the "enchantress of his heart"?

Suddenly she thought she would be ill as she recalled their last moments at the Abyss of Possibilities when she had pleaded with him to escape with her. What a fool she had been to think he had meant to send her to safety while he pursued some mad but valiant scheme to thwart Dred. Egads, in truth, he had only wanted her out of the way that he might follow his Thromgilad lover to the Land of Somn! Indeed, in light of what she now knew it was hardly marvelous that Frayne should have been less than gratified to discover himself pursued even into the Flux by his erstwhile and unrelenting love, she thought, mortified beyond bearing. And that had not been enough, but she must forcibly abduct him as well!

Merciful gods, how could she have been so blind! And worse, what was she to do now, how face him with what she knew? In the grips of pain and disillusionment, she was certain of one thing only: somehow she must keep her discovery from him, for he had not only betrayed her, but the One, as well. Indeed, he was the Thromholan, and he had sold himself to Somn. Henceforth he would be a danger to the very survival of the Realm.

Then in truth did she suffer a mortal thrust, for suddenly it seemed clear what she must do. She must see that he never fulfilled the prophecy of the Thromholan. Indeed, she herself must destroy him!

Still, could he not be forgiven, even yet redeemed? whispered a small, insidious voice within. For had he not been the innocent prey of a vile plot, the blameless victim of a potent spell? Once more she conjured up the image of her beloved held thrall to the passion of a goddess, and suddenly the voice of reason was silenced before a tide of hurt and bitter anger. Aye, she could have absolved him of all blame for falling to the wiles of the seductress, but in seeking to keep it from her, he had failed in trust, failed in love. In truth, he had deceived her, and that she could *not* forgive.

Curse Frayne! And curse Dred for having spawned him. Gladly would she kill the false knight, and then herself! But not yet, she told herself. Oh, gods, not yet. For should she not first seek to learn more of the traitor's plans, and Dred's? And was there not yet the unfinished business of the Unicorns' Burial Ground—the vision of a quest to be completed and made reality? Nay, it would not do to be too hasty. She would be cunning and bide her time. If only she had not this dreadful ache where once her heart had been! she thought and silently cursed herself. For even though her heart had been wounded unto the death, to her shame her love yet lived.

She must not think of that, not now when she felt weak and ill. First she would turn her thoughts to the problem of where she was.

"But if this is not the land of Erg, where am I?" she muttered out loud, then froze, her heart thudding heavily as she glimpsed in the distance a solitary peak looming like a shadow of doom amid the glimmerous wastes. "Oh, gods," she groaned, "the Black Mountain."

"Aye," a voice murmured reflectively behind her. "I'm sorry that it should be so, for I would have spared you so grim a reality upon your return if I could. And yet I'm afraid it could not be helped. It seems that so little *can* in this game we play with destiny."

"Alain?" cried the enchantress, her heart leaping at the welcome sight of the bard standing at the foot of an immense monument wrought of jet-black stone.

"Even as you see," he answered, smiling a little at her look of startled wonder. Then she came to her feet to face him soberly, her huge eyes troubled as she seemed to gather her thoughts.

"You are alone?" she said at last, her brow furrowing as she grappled with the riddle of Frayne's absence. "Has there been no one else here with you?"

"No, no one," he answered, watching her with a singular intensity.

"But Frayne was with me. Our minds were—were one u-until—"

She stumbled to a halt, unable to say aloud what she had seen. A small silence stretched between them, then the bard spoke quietly.

"When the Thromholan separated from you in the drift, he came not to the Plain of Hedron, but to Dred's stronghold. Sulwyn Idris no longer flees his own destiny, enchantress. He is in Helynderne, beneath the Black Mountain."

"Oh, gods," Aurora choked, one hand rising to

cover her mouth as she wheeled away from the bard to stand with her back to him, her shoulders hunched as though she had sustained a physical blow. A shudder seemed to shake her slim body, then suddenly she drew in a long, tremulous breath and slowly straightened. Still with her back to him, the Enchantress spoke in a low voice, carefully devoid of all emotion.

"I have followed the strands of my life to Grendylmere and beyond. I have beheld my mother with Endrith and the prince of Garn and seen her fall to Xerxes in the Hawthorn Glade. And I have seen the visions of destruction wrought by Dred's creatures, the creatures I helped the Thromholan release from Timelessness into the Realm."

She stopped and turned deliberately, her face white and oddly frozen as she looked once more upon her father.

"The One be merciful," she said, "for I have lain with the knight of Tor and professed my love, but he has proven false. False to me and false to his oath of knighthood. Yet no less so am I, who dared to believe I was the vassal of a god."

"And are you not?" murmured the bard, a strange expression in his eyes.

"Are you my father?" she countered in a wintry voice.

"I have told you that I am."

"Then surely you must know who and what I am; and, indeed, 'tis more than I know either of myself or you. Who are you, Alain of Naefredeyan? Why do you deliberately cloak yourself in secrecy—and me? Cannot a father name his daughter?"

425

"Sometimes a father must allow his daughter to name herself," replied the bard enigmatically. "Tell me what has brought you to the point that you question the knight and all you once held true about yourself?"

For a moment a spark of anger broke through the controlled frigidity of her reserve. Almost she was herself again—the enchantress, all fire and passion. Then she smiled, and the spark gave way to the hard glitter of an ice crystal.

"I have seen behind the mask of the knight of Tor and beheld the dark secrets of the Thromholan. He is indeed one with Throm. One with Dred. He has taken a Thromgilad goddess as his lover."

"In truth?" queried the bard with an unwonted gleam of interest. "You surprise me. I believed somehow that the knight would prove stronger than even Sehwan's potent charms. But what would you? It is said a man is no stronger than the flesh. Doubtless you are right to revile him for the infirmity of his resolve."

"Nay, not for his resolve, or the lack of it. In time I might have come to forgive him that. But for his deceit, which is a breach both in trust and faith." Suddenly she swung away from him as if she could no longer bear to have him look at her. "In truth," she said, "I am more despicable than the Thromholan, who at least never pretended he would not in the end destroy my faith in him. In that, he never lied, but I have committed the supreme folly of lying to myself. I came to pride myself on being Aurora, the enchantress, who had faced Gesh and challenged Dred. And now I must pay the penalty for my

426

arrogance. I am no one, nothing. The visions I thought sent me by the god were as false as the name *he* gave me."

"I am to understand, then, that the knight lied to you, denied the truth when you confronted him with what you had discovered?" interpolated the bard with maddening rationality.

"Nay, how could he?" Aurora rejoined impatiently. "'Twas something I glimpsed as our minds melded in the drift. There was not time to question or contrive a defense. He broke away from me as soon as he became aware of what I had seen, and I was left in darkness. The next I knew, I awakened here."

"Then you did *not* confront him, and the knight neither affirmed nor denied what you think you saw," Alain reflected reasonably, then spread wide his hands. "In which case, I fear I do not fully understand you. Wherein lies the falsehood?"

Slowly the enchantress turned and looked at him as if she thought him either deliberately obtuse or peculiarly lackwitted.

"In keeping it from me," she declared, making it clear by her tone of voice that she was needlessly stating the obvious. "In swearing his heart belonged to me. In succumbing to the wiles of the enemy. He made *love* to her. Is that not falsehood enough?"

"Oh, well, if you saw him—his memory of himself—coupling with the goddess—you are, of course, positive she was a goddess—I suppose I see your point," mused the bard, tugging thoughtfully at his beard.

Of a sudden Aurora blinked and looked away.

"Nay," she said, her voice troubled, "I-I did *not* see

427

him actually—I mean, I *saw* him with her, and they w-were—but he shut me out ere I glimpsed the whole of it." The walls of her reserve crumbling at last before the bard's persistent logic, the enchantress turned on her tormentor with eyes that blazed hurt and helpless fury. *"Damn!* what is it that you want from me?" she cried in bafflement. *"Why* would you defend him?"

Then at last did Alain of Naefredeyan relent and draw near her. Gently he clasped her arms in strong, slender hands.

"No," he murmured, his gaze unflinching on hers. "I should never defend him. You are my daughter. If you say the knight has been false, then indeed he must be punished for what he has done. Tell me what you would have me do. Invoke the fury of the gods against him? Confront him with his infamy, then cut him down with the sword of vengeance? Strip him of his spurs and spurn him before his peers? Tell me, enchantress, and I swear it shall be done."

For a long moment Aurora stared into the boundless depths of eyes that seemed somehow able to soothe the very anguish of her heart, and suddenly it was as if a dark cloud had been lifted from her mind so that she could think again.

"You think I have misjudged him," she marveled. "You believe him innocent of perfidy. Why? He is the Thromholan, and he has gone at last to join his father. Does that not in itself convict him? Please, I beg you. Help me to see it as you do. Is he Sulwyn Idris, a traitor whom I must try somehow to destroy? Or is he the knight of Tor pledged to the One? Is he

428

truly Frayne, the man I love?"

"In truth, I know not what he is—No. Turn not away, but bear with me yet a moment longer," he said as her face hardened with bitter disappointment and she tried to pull free. Something in his voice made her go still. Then in wonder she felt his hand run lightly over her hair. Her heart pounding, she glanced up into his face, and suddenly her breath caught in her throat at what she saw there.

"I have lived a very long time," he murmured, his gaze distant as if those ages of his life were at that moment passing before his eyes. Then suddenly his vision focused with wondrous clarity on the troubled face turned up to his. "Long ago I learned that it is dangerous to read too much into prophecy. Indeed, it is better to leave such things to the infallibility of time. For that reason I would withhold judgment on Dred's son till time and events prove what prophecy can only imply. But more than that, I have come to trust in you. If you would know whether the knight is true or not, you must simply look into your heart, Aurora. As with Almira, therein lies your greatest strength, the true power of the enchantress whom Frayne awakened to her being."

"I-I'm not sure I understand," Aurora said, her brow furrowing in a puzzled frown.

"You will when the time comes," he answered, his smile tinged somehow with sadness. Then suddenly she shivered as the breeze quickened to a chill wind and the bard pulled away from her to stare with eldritch eyes at the mountain brooding in the distance. "And that time is nigh upon us," he said, seeming to withdraw once more into the impenetrable shroud of mystery that kept her ever at a distance.

"What is it? What's happening?" she cried, reaching out for the robed figure, which had begun to blur in her sight, seeming to thin and grow rarefied, till he appeared naught but an insubstantial vision woven from moonbeams, save for eyes that scintillated crystal fire.

"Who *are* you?" she uttered in a voice hardly above a whisper and drew back, her heart pounding within her breast.

"The dragons of war swarm to the Plain of Shintari," came like a whisper to her mind, "and I sense my old enemy waiting for me. In his hand he holds the instrument of destiny, which once was mine and shall be yours. Yet be not afraid. In your name resides a power that shall remold the face of the earth."

The terrifying orbs softened then to a warm, mesmerizing glow, and suddenly Aurora felt her fear give way to wonder.

"The time is come when I must leave you to find your own way, enchantress. Destiny presses hard upon me and I know not if it shall be given to us to speak like this again. Yet would I leave you with the certainty that I am well pleased with the Daughter of Earth and Flame, whom in all the ages of waiting I had never thought should be mine own child. Long ago I turned from the One in bitterness and despair, but in you I have beheld again the light of hope. And more—a rare and lovely woman with a heart of innocence who might teach a god the lessons of humility and enduring love. Those shall be the lights that sustain me in the darkness that lies ahead. Let them be your own guides as you seek the light at the end of your quest for truth.''

"Wait!" cried the enchantress. "Please, take me with you. Let me stand at your side in whatever peril you go to meet. Alain!"

But already the bard had vanished. As from a distance she heard her father's parting words.

"We shall meet anon. Till then, I leave the elfin blade in your keeping. Guard it well, Almira's daughter, for it and you are precious to me."

Then did she know he was truly gone as she stared in dazed bewilderment at the shiny thing lying at her feet upon the sand. Sinking heavily to her knees, she picked up the knife.

"Glaiveling," she muttered, shaking her head. "But how did he . . . ?" But then her eyes flashed with sudden comprehension. 'Twas not an elf she had seen and spoken with on Garn, but Alain, her father. Why? What game did he play? With a groan she clutched the blade to her breast and flung up her head to stare blindly out into the darkness of night before the dawn.

"In the name of the One, *who are* you?" she shouted, but her only answer was the empty silence.

Gods, was the whole world gone topsy-turvy? she wondered, filled with bitter frustration, for nothing was as she had dreamed it would be when first she set out upon the quest for her identity. Then she had been buoyant with the dawning wonder of a love she had never imagined possible and with a power that had both elated and awed, but had never filled her

431

with such dreadful foreboding as weighed upon her now. For Alain had said Frayne was with the Prince of Throm at Helynderne beneath the Black Mountain, and doubtless that was where he, too, had gone. After all, Alain had been one of Harmon's commanders, and thus it would be absurd to suppose that the "old enemy" who was "waiting for" him could be anyone but Dred himself. But where did that leave her, the enchantress, who was Andruvien and the bearer of the undeciphered symbols?

Wearily the enchantress dragged herself to her feet. What dreadful irony, she thought, staring vaguely at the monument towering above her, that even as the forces of war were gathering in the Plain of Shintari, she should find herself here in the midst of nowhere, a hundred leagues from the events that would determine the future of the world. And yet Alain had said they would meet anon, she recalled bitterly. Where? Indeed, how? Was she to make her way on foot to the Black Mountain? Egads, it would take days even if she did not first expire from lack of food and water. Drat the bard and his damned propensity for the obscure! Egads, he had said something about completing her quest as well, and yet she hardly saw how she might travel to the Veil of Tears and still somehow be on hand to encounter him in Helynderne. Besides which, she did not know how to reach the elusive Unicorns' Burial Ground. Endrith's Song had led them as far as the Black Mountain and the Crystal Room. From there, they had been supposed to "Seek the shaft of silver light/Which points the way from endless night."

Of course, it was possible, she suddenly mused,

that the shaft of silver light had referred to the sunlight she and Crane had seen shining at the end of the tunnel as they emerged from the Chamber of the Lords. In which case, "endless night" would simply have referred to the maze of tunnels they had wandered through beneath the mountain. Aye, it made sense, but what had come after that? Furrowing her brow, the enchantress sought to recall the final stanzas of the song. There had been something about a plain and—

"Aye, that's it," she said out loud. "'The plain/ Bereft of tree, bereft of rain'! I remember now.

> "Seek the shaft of silver light
> Which points the way from endless night.
> Beyond, the way lies through the plain
> Bereft of tree, bereft of rain.
> Along the shores of shifting sand—
> A sealess sea, a landless land—
> Make way before the headless king.
> Pass through the center of the ring."

The first light of dawn streaked the sky beyond the Black Mountain as Aurora gazed out over the desert of sand with new eyes. But of course! It had to be, she thought. And if this were indeed the plain of Endrith's Song, then—

Slowly she backed away from the monument, her pulse quickening as she beheld in the growing light of morning the carved likeness of sandaled feet protruding from beneath the hem of a flowing robe. And were not those hands resting upon the armrests of a kingly throne? Aye, what a fool she had been not to have guessed it before! In truth the Circlet of Kerr had brought her to the Monument of the Black King, complete in every detail save for one—this king had lost his head!

It seemed all at once that the riddles of Endrith's verse resolved themselves one by one, as it came to her to realize that if this were indeed the Headless King, then the "ring" must of a certainty be the circlet that once had crowned the now missing head and surely the same as that which had drawn its counterpart here from the Flux. But where was it? she wondered and began to search the barren sand for the statue's severed head. Still, she found no sign of it, and it was not long before she was forced to give it up as lost, buried somewhere beneath the shifting surface.

"Blast!" she shouted, scooping up a handful of sand and flinging it to the wind. "What does it matter anyway? Of what point is a quest to find myself if Frayne is not to be there with me? What reason can there be for living if 'tis to be a life without meaning? A name shall not make me whole again. Indeed, I should rather die nameless in the battle against Dred than to know the anguish of eternal emptiness."

In her despair, she turned away from the detested mountain, which seemed to mock her, and stared blindly into the west. And there, as if in answer to a riddle, she beheld the sky filled magically with dragons! Oh, gods, they were the dragon-lords of Garn, and there, at the forefront, was Kev, with Ellard, the boy's red-gold hair streaming freely in the wind. Suddenly the slim shoulders straightened. Nay, she vowed, her eyes flashing golden as she looked across the shimmering expanse to the Black

434

Mountain. She would go not to the Veil of Tears, but to Helynderne and Frayne. For therein lay her true destiny—either to fight, perhaps to die, at the side of her beloved, or to slay the traitorous Thromholan and so be slain.

Swiftly the enchantress donned the Crimson Cloak, which had been Almira's legacy from Rab. Then, lifting her eyes to the magnificent sight of the dagons soaring in a clear sky, she sent her thoughts speeding out to them.

"To me, Kev! Swiftly. For on the wings of a dragon would I fly to meet the Bard of Naefredeyan, the Dark Prince, and Frayne!"

Thus it was that the enchantress of the Glade was taken up and borne east toward the Black Mountain, and behind her, unseen, the quickening wind laid bare the crowned head of a king and beside it, a great silver circlet standing like a portal, half-buried in the sand.

"We be as lost as three rats in a hole, I tell ye," rasped Garwin, the Wise, as he glowered in perplexity upon the fifteenth intersection of passages that they had come to within the past hour. "Th' fiend's tale be as treacherous as these twisted tunnels, methinks. Like as not he knew as little how t' find his way through th' maze as those what's never been here."

"The Valkar bears the fruits of whatever deceit he may have wrought," rejoined Elwindolf with unwonted levity. And, indeed, the hideous half-man, half-bat was not likely ever to forget his unfortunate run-in with Garwin and the elf's two companions.

The darkness of Ciaron, which precedes the dawn, had found them searching among the ruins of Shallandorwas for a passageway into the mines below when a winged shadow had fallen on the elf. Sputtering elfin curses, Garwin had gifted the Valkar with donkey's ears, pig's hind feet, and a rooster's crow before Freyga had come to his rescue, knocking the creature senseless with the butt end of her spear.

Elwindolf, arriving belatedly on the scene, had ordered the Valkar securely bound in the hopes that they might persuade the creature to reveal the hidden entrance. And, upon reviving, he had talked readily enough, thanks to Garwin, who, harboring an understandable antipathy to the notion of serving as the Valkar's appetizer, which, he had been informed as he lay pinned beneath the reeking fiend, was intended to precede the rather more bountiful main course of Elwindolf's human blood—the delectable Freyga presumably had been ear-marked for dessert—the elf proceeded to review for the Valkar's edification a catalogue of the Eleven Hundred Droonish Curses still available to him. In evident horror of having a polecat's bouquet, a lizard's tail, or the flea-bitten hide of a bear added to his already disharmonious accoutrements, the Valkar had told them what they demanded, asking in return only that they spare him from the wrath of the gnome-kin with the tongue of a vindictive wizard.

Thus it was that they had found themselves wandering the entrails of the Black Mountain with not a single notion as to where they were or whither they were going. Nor had they encountered a single living being, neither gnomes nor giants, since they had entered the secret passage beneath the Vardos.

"It looks t' be fair deserted," muttered the elf for the umpteenth time. "Like as not ifn there ever were gnomes, they were made t' feed the giants long ago."

"Sh-h-h!" Freyga hissed, throwing out an arm to halt her two companions. "There's something moving about ahead."

The three froze in taut attitudes of listening, but for a time they detected nothing that would indicate the proximity of another in the tunnel, whether man or beast. At length the elf drew breath to voice an acrid observation on the nervous disposition of females, when suddenly the faint, but unmistakable patter of scurrying footsteps sent Elwindolf gliding noiselessly down the passageway in swift pursuit of their elusive fellow. Freyga was quick to follow, leaving Garwin to hump along in their wake as best he could, with the result that the elf soon found himself exceedingly winded and very much alone in the confusing labyrinth of tunnels.

"Of all th' Tomfool notions ye've ever had, Garwin Dandershorn, trailin' along wi' a couple o' long-legged hail-ho and fare-thee-wells be th' worst," he panted as he came lumbering to a halt, and dragging a scarf from his pocket, proceeded to mop the sweat from his brow. "An' now ye've landed yerself in a fair kettle o' fish, what do ye think t' do about it?"

"Ye might start out by sharin' a bite o' th' savories what ye be packin' in yer kit," observed a hopeful voice at his back. "'Tis nigh t' swoonin' I be from smellin' 'tiddy oggies' an' apple popovers an' thinkin' all along 'twere naught but one o' me fancies o' good provender what only an elf would ken."

Garwin, twisting aroud to view in amazement a bedraggled little fellow with a scraggly brown beard and blue wistful eyes regarding him rather mistily, took all of five seconds to recognize in this underfed caricature his old friend and comrade.

"B' gosh an' b' gory," Garwin ejaculated in no little astonishment, "does me eyes deceive, or be ye truly Gleb Thistledor recently o' Hawthorn Glade come back in th' flesh?"

"Gleb in some'at less flesh than th' Gleb what ye knew, but, aye, Gleb nonetheless. An' right glad t' see ye, Garwin Dandershorn," rejoined the second of Aurora's father-pair with a lopsided grin.

It soon transpired that Gleb, following his capture by mudgeons, had been turned over to one Xerxes of Sarq for quesitoning concerning the whereabouts of a certain golden-eyed enchantress.

"But th' joke was on 'im," chuckled the elf around a generous mouthful of Vandrel's turnip pastries, "for no sooner had I convinced th' black-hearted fiend I knew nary a thing about where th' lass had got herself off to, than he hands me over t' th' gnomes t' help work th' mines. An' nary another thought has he gi'e me, I doubt not."

One bristly eyebrow plunged toward the bridge of Garwin's rather prominent nose.

"Ye relish slavin' in these cursed mines, does ye?" he queried sarcastically. "Well, ye was ever a trifle lackwitted, Gleb Thistledor, but I never thought t' see ye daft as well. An' all this time I was feelin' sorry

438

fer ye. Next ye'll be tellin' me ye be fit as a fiddle an' twicet as sassy."

"Oh, 'tis well enough I am, considerin' I've had t' live on what doesn't bear thinkin' on. On th' whole, our gnomish cousins ha'e done their best by me, though it took a goodly dose o' the Hraldoonish Chants o' summonin' an' aid t' persuade 'em."

Then did enlightenment strike the old elf, who, despite his appearance of distemper, had been observing his formerly rotund and jolly fellow with a growing lump in this throat.

"Ye invoked the chants, an' th' gnomes were forced t' lend ye their aid!" he exclaimed in helpless amazement at the slow-top Gleb's resourcefulness.

"Eh?" grunted Gleb, rummaging through the considerably depleted remains of Garwin's food sack. "Oh, aye. Them bein' descendants o' the elves what come to Blidseafeld in th' company o' Dorn, they had no choice," he muttered distractedly. Then, having discovered an unrecognizable lump of squashed tart and jelly roll mashed together at the very bottom, he heaved a relieved sigh and set himself to the happy task of making it disappear again. "They're not such a bad lot oncet ye come t' know 'em," he added reflectively, "though they'd not hesitate t' rob ye blind or sell ye to th' giants if they took a notion to."

"Oh, fine fellows they sound. Th' kind ye'd dare not turn yer back on. An' where be these paragons now, I ask ye?" Garwin demanded, turning to eye askance the hodgepodge of cubbyholes and empty warrens surrounding the two elves, the misshapen windows and doors staring vacantly back at them. They were in what Gleb had called the Glangornshaft, a replicate of the giants' labyrinth of tunnels, done in miniature to suit the minikin stature of the gnomes that inhabited them.

"Th' bairns and babes they've hidden away where none'll tell ye, fer they've learned a mistrust of Dred an' his foul creatures. More than a few gnomes, it seems, ha've mysteriously vanished since their master's return, ne'er t' be seen again. Th' word is that they be taken as fodder fer th' giants what've been sent t' fight in the plain to the east o' here. Kral an' a handful o' his band o' cutthroats be all that's left."

The clamor of voices issuing from beyond a bend in the narrow tunnel interrupted Gleb's account of the gnomes and brought Garwin leaping to his feet, one hand grabbing for the elfin blade at his belt.

"This had better not be a trap, Kral," carried clearly to the listening elves. "You shan't live long enough to regret it if it is."

"Oh, th' elf be 'ere right enuf, me lord," spoke up a wheedling voice. "Kral's as good as 'is word, as ye'll see soon enough. An' glad I am t' be able t' turn 'im o'er t' ye safe and sound's as when 'e come t' us, poor lad. Not that we begrudges 'im what little we has, but 'e be like t' eat us out o' 'ouse 'n 'ome."

A pointy eared fellow, as broad as he was tall, and with coarse, brutish features dominated by a great, hooked nose, rounded the corner then, to stop and stare in rude astonishment at not one, but *two* of his distant elfin cousins.

"Nay!" he thundered, the swarthy visage darkening to an indignant red. "I'll not stand t' be saddled wi' another o' Dred's unwanted ticket-o'-leavers what always be spoutin' thim blasted chants o'

440

summonin' an' sech. Hain't I always been a honest gnome what nivver thought t' rob none o' th' prince's gold what be cached in places only I knows? An' 'twas me gramfer's gramfer what led th' delvin' an' th' diggin' o' th' prince's own Helynderne an' nivver oncet has I let slip th' secret words that opens it. When ye goes, me lord, ye takes both thim wi' ye, or Kral, begads, 'll fergit his vow nivver to' slit th' throat o' one o' 'is own kindred. Th' chants be damned."

"That'll be enough, Kral," drawled the soft voice of "me lord," and the tunnel seemed suddenly filled with the cloaked figure of a man who was forced to stoop to keep from braining himself on the ceiling. Gleb swallowed drily at the forbidding sight of a body draped grotesquely over the newcomer's shoulder. "You'll do as you're told, and you'll do it without a whimper or a nay, understand? Now go and fetch the girl here to me at once, and make sure you find your way back. I shouldn't want to have to come looking for you."

"Now, now, no need t' git het up o'er nothin'," crooned the gnome, beginning to back hastily past the elves observing the little byplay with a great deal of astonished interest. "I'm goin', I'm goin'." Then apparently having judged himself at a judicious distance from the stranger, the gnome turned and plunged headlong out of sight down the far end of the tunnel.

"And now, my friends, if you would be so kind as to help me unload this rather unwieldy encumbrance, perhaps we can revive the young whelp."

It was then that Gleb stepped timidly forward, a

slow grin breaking beatifically across his once cherubic face.

"Me Lord Frayne, by all that's wonderful!" he murmured softly, the blue eyes round with amazement. "How come ye t' be in this nasty hole?"

"And where else should he be, halfwit?" interjected Garwin, shouldering the smaller elf to one side. "'Tis the Thromholan come t' join his father, he is. An' ifn he's hurt th' lad, he'll have me t' answer to."

"As you wish," the knight drawled cynically, and dropping to one knee, lowered the unconscious shape-changer to the floor. "However, I suggest that if you have any wish to escape the mountain alive, it were best to do exactly as I say. In a very short time all of Somn is going to break loose, and it won't be a very healthy place for you and your friends."

"At this moment, it is not all that healthy for you, knight of Tor," murmured a low, deadly voice, and suddenly Frayne stiffened as he felt the sharp point of a spear at his back. Careful to keep his hands in sight, the knight eased his head around to regard his assailant with a slow, ironic smile.

"I am fast becoming bored with your propensity for prodding me with spears, warrior-priestess. I see little has changed since the last time we met. You were overly hasty in your judgment of me then, too, were you not?"

"Silence!" Freyga hissed, a bright tinge of color washing her cheeks at the knight's cool effrontery. "You two, take his sword, then bind his hands. We shall decide what to do with him once we have found Elwindolf."

Reluctantly and with great effort, Gleb dragged

the great sword Thrimheld from the scabbard.

"Beggin' yer pardon, me lord," he mumbled, his expression troubled as he glanced helplessly from the man's sardonic visage to Garwin's grim one. "I-I don't rightly understand what this be all about. Belike Anduan won't be pleased t' hear we've treated her knight so shabbily, Garwin. Can't we just sit down and talk this over calm-like?"

"There be nothin' to talk o'er, halfwit," rasped Garwin, uneasy himself about the turn things had taken. Thromholan or not, he had once been fond of the manly knight. "He be Dred's mortal son, an' till we know for sure what he's about, 'twere best t' see he can do no one any harm. Now don't just stand there. Let me by."

Then suddenly Crane stirred, uttering a low groan, and simultaneously a girl's anxious cry rang out.

"Sayyid Crane! *Marhakim*, what has happened to you?"

A slender figure tried to shove past the Shintari warrior-priestess, and suddenly Frayne's hand shot out to grasp the spear in an iron grip. In an instant he had disarmed Freyga and held her prisoner in his arms.

"Kral, get in here where I can see you. And you, Gleb, may kindly return my sword to me," he said, his tone tinged with an odd sort of gentleness as he addressed the shrinking elf.

"Er-aye," Gleb stammered, then, brightening at something he saw in Frayne's hooded gaze, he squared his shoulders and mumbling, "Pardon. Pardon me," made his way past Garwin and the girl weeping softly over a bedazzled young mage who had yet to gather his wits about him, till at last he halted a trifle breathlessly before the knight.

"Here 'tis, an' right glad I am t' see it restored to where it had ought t' be," he said, grinning a trifle crookedly. But suddenly he was all seriousness again as he blinked timidly up at the tall, stern-faced man and appeared to gather his courage to continue. "I may be a slow-top, me lord," he blurted, then reddened at what sounded very like a snort from Garwin. "An' 'tis certain I could never match me old friend Garwin in a battle o' wits," he added, flashing a pointed look over his shoulder at his scowling friend, "but I know what I know. An' beggin' yer pardon, me lord, but it just ain't right t' let folks believe things what can't be true. *I* know ye bain't what Garwin an' this lady think ye be, fer I saw how ye looked at me lass. But folks wi' brains hev got t' be *told* sometimes, or maybe *shown* what their hearts had ought t' know wi'out words."

For a moment utter silence reigned. Then Gleb, blushing furiously at his own temerity, ducked his head in embarrassment at suddenly finding himself the center of attention.

"Well—er—that's all I've got t' say," he mumbled, beginning to hedge his way back to the welcome obscurity at the outer fringes of the crowded enclosure. "'Ceptin' only, I hope ye won't hold it agin anyone fer misjudgin' ye an' all. An' mayhap ye'll see yer way clear t' squarin' things fer us wi' our lass when next ye see her."

"No doubt you will be able to do that for yourself sooner than you imagine, my wise little friend," Frayne said quietly.

"If she's still alive," interjected the shape-changer, shoving himself up on one elbow. A darkening bruise seemed to throb at his temple as he shot an accusing glance at the knight. "And if *we* are, after you finish whatever it is you plan to do with us."

"You, I would gladly throttle for what you obviously intended doing had you not stupidly allowed one of Dred's lieutenants to sneak up on you," uttered the knight in a chilling voice. Then, releasing the Shintari priestess with such abruptness that he nearly flung her from him, he swept the gathering with a piercing glance. "And the rest of you—especially you, Garwin, who should have had better sense than to allow a starry-eyed youth to tackle Dred's domain alone—"

"The blame for that be mine," interrupted Elwindolf, emerging from the shadows at the far end of the tunnel.

"No, don't let Frayne do this," Crane said, brushing Janine's clinging hands away as he pushed himself up on trembling legs. "He's hand in glove with Dred. Have you already forgotten that he's behind everything that's happened? He created the rift that brought the creatures here. *And* Xerxes. Egads, it's Frayne's fault Janine was kidnapped, never mind the fact that Xerxes's army of outlaws drove away the unicorns and nearly devastated Endrith's Forest! But then he made sure Aurora would follow him into the Flux, too. And *now* where is she? We only have Ariana's word that they ever left the Flux together, and she can't know anything for certain because she was already in the drift with the sorceress. How do we know he didn't leave Aurora there? Don't you see? He's trying to twist things around. I never saw anyone else in that tunnel. It had to be him, the Thromholan, who snuck up on me and struck me from behind."

"No, Sayyid," cried the girl, rising to capture the mage's flailing arm with hands that clung, "you must not say such things of my Lord Frayne."

"I'm sorry, Janine. I know how you feel about him and that it's hard for you to hear that he's not what you believed he was. You're only a girl, after all, and too young to understand about men like him. But you mustn't feel too bad. He had Aurora and me fooled, too."

It soon became apparent that the youth's attempt to soothe what he had mistakenly assumed to be the girl's grief at discovering her beloved former master to be false had drastically miscarried. Janine, her eyes flashing sparks of feminine outrage, flung up her hands in withering disgust.

"Oh!" she cried, beginning to pace forward and backward the meager two steps open to her in their less-than-spacious surroundings. *"Innaho-al-wallad--ur-khar wa muwallad-ur-maskharat!"* she ranted in her native Wendaren.

"What's that she be sayin'?" queried Gleb of Garwin in awed amazement.

"Belike ye doesn't want t' know, me lad," replied the older, wiser elf with a solemn shake of the head.

"I will not listen to you make of yourself the witless fool," she ended scathingly. "For it was Sayyid Frayne who only a short time ago freed me from the son of a jackal. And now you may fall prostrate on your knees before me and plead for a thousand

446

pardons, and I will not hear you. Not ever again shall I suffer the insult of *sakhira,* which is to be ridiculed and treated as *al-zan-kalmak-al-zanana,* the woman confined to the place of the women."

"Aw, Janine," groaned the shape-changer, but he was not to be granted mercy either from his infuriated love or the man-wolf, who added the final nail to his coffin.

"The knight hath spoken truly, lad," he said quietly. "I followed one who had the look of an elf and the tongue of a she-devil—"

"Fangol, me bloody wife!" Kral broke in harshly. "I'll lay odds she were sneakin' to the prince hisself t' spill 'er guts about th' elf. An' whatever else she'd got an earful of."

"Aye, for the small one led me by a secret way to the door of the chamber from which came the sounds of voices. There did I lose her, only to find another. The signs lie not, Mage-Lord. 'Twas Xerxes himself who discovered you in the tunnel as he came to make his report to the prince, for 'twas his body I found there and concealed that none might know of our coming."

"I'm grateful to you for a job well done," drawled the knight, sheathing his sword at last. "But enough of idle talk. Whether you believe that I am the Thromholan, in league with my father, or the knight of Tor, who would give my life if need be to thwart him, matters not. Either way, there is nothing you can do against Dred here. It will be the gods and the forces of destiny that decide the outcome of things within Dred's confounded mountain. Rather should you seek immediately either to return to Endrith's

Forest or to join the combined armies of the One now converging on the Plain of Shintari. No mortal can withstand the devastation that shall soon be wrought here, so I suggest that with the shape-changer's aid, you get yourselves hence at once."

"And you, Sayyid Frayne?" whispered his former slave. "Shall you not come with us?"

Briefly the hint of a smile softened Frayne's stern features as he gazed into the girl's eyes, huge and filled with fear for him.

"I think not, Bgim Janine," he murmured, brushing her cheek with his thumb as a single teardrop rolled from the corner of her eye. "Aurora will be on her way here by now, carried on the merciless winds of destiny. I would be at Dred's side when the moment arrives."

"An' so would I be there t' give what small aid I can," Garwin declared stolidly.

"And I," said Elwindolf.

"I would see the tale to its end." It was Freyga, her gaze steady on the man-wolf.

Then Gleb coughed to clear his throat.

"She be Anduan, Elf-Foundling and Tree-Child," he said, an unwonted hint of stubbornness in the tilt of his bearded chin. "Ifn she walks into danger, then we've a right t' be there wi' her, beggin' your pardon, me lord," he ended, blushing rosily as he stepped back again.

Then it seemed they would all go, even Kral, who, carried along in the spirit of the venture and a dozen or so belts of *grarg*, the potent gnomish brew, declared he were of a mind for a good row and like as not he'd jest tag along for the fun of it.

448

The knight swept them with a piercing look, which yet held a hint of bafflement. The fools, he thought. What were their puny weapons against the might of gods—against Vendrenin?

"Enough. This is the talk of madmen and fools. Rather than aid the enchantress, you will only be throwing your lives away needlessly. How can it help Aurora to see her friends slain hideously before her eyes? As it is, she comes blindly to the prince's lair, unsure of who or what she is and little guessing what will ultimately be asked of her. Can you not understand that Dred will use you against her?"

"Maybe and maybe not," spoke up Crane for the first time as he strode forward to stand eye to eye with the knight of Tor, his grin rueful, but his gaze steady. "None of us knows what the gods have written for us. Maybe we won't make any difference at all in the short or the long run of things. Maybe we'll all die for nothing. But Aurora's the enchantress, and we've all had a part, no matter how small, in making her what she is. Maybe, just *maybe*, it's destiny that we be there at the finish. Anyway, it sorta looks like you're stuck with us, whether you like it or not."

With the final words, Crane stuck his hand out with a jerky motion and held it there. For a long, suspenseful moment it seemed that exasperation warred with some deeper emotion within the knight as the silvery eyes probed the stubborn set of the boy's jaw. Emitting a short, baffled breath, Frayne slowly shook his head.

"You don't make it easy to refuse, boy," he said grimly.

"I guess I was just meant to be a thorn in your

449

side," Crane answered wryly, "but maybe with the proper influence," he added, sending a meaningful glance at the girl watching them with tears in her eyes, "someday I'll learn not to be a jackass as well."

Then the man's lean hand went out to close with Crane's in a strong clasp.

"I'll hold you to that in the next few hours," he said, suddenly flinty-eyed again. "It may be that the enchantress will have other friends as well, but till the moment of reckoning, nothing is certain. Which means I'll be playing it close and deep. I will have to be the Thromholan in all that that name would seem to imply, and not even Aurora must guess it is all a ruse. Meanwhile, I shall trust all of you to remain sight unseen until and *if* your presence is needed. On that we must agree, or we are defeated before we even begin."

"Then it's agreed," Crane said, in answer for them all.

After that, it was decided that Elwindolf and Kral would lead the others to the Chamber of Lords by the secret passageway down which Fangol, Kral's haggish gnome-wife, earlier had fled. There they would wait and listen for the arrival of the enchantress. Then, still troubled at this unexpected complication in what was already a desperate and deadly game, Frayne took his leave of them.

Cloaking himself in darkness that none should discover his presence before he was ready to have it known, the knight of Tor made his way swiftly along a different set of passages till he came at last to the intersection of tunnels in which earlier he had encountered the young shape-changer in dire circumstances. Drawing near the high, vaulted entrance to the Chamber of the Lords, the knight suddenly froze, the nerves at the nape of his neck tingling with the sense that something was wrong. Then it came to him that the tunnel and the chamber beyond brooded in an unnatural stillness.

Abandoning all caution in the utter certainty of what he would find, Frayne entered boldly into the chamber in which he had long ago fought and defeated Grimshank, the Giant. The hollow echo of his footsteps faded into silence as he halted and gazed once more upon the great hall, empty, save for the grisly remains that littered the floor, stark reminders that the giants had dined here, often and well. Allowing only time enough for that single searching glance, Frayne pivoted on his heel and strode out into the vestibule again. There, before him, was the long, straight stretch of empty tunnel, the circle of light shining silvery at the end beckoning him to freedom. And to the right, the lightless corridor that led to Helynderne, the Dark Prince's forbidding inner sanctum. The portal, which opened and closed at Dred's command, was agape, as if in leering invitation for him to enter the chamber, which ages past had seen the Dark Prince vanquished by Harmon into the lightless depths of Somn, and had witnessed, as well, the forging of the crystal into Andruvien, the enchantress's sword.

A mirthless smile came briefly to his lips, then without further pause, he went in.

"I have come, Dred, even as you knew I would. Surely you have some welcome for your one and only son?" he called.

From out of the blackness of the chamber bubbled forth an amorphous blob of viscid stuff from which a head and limbs appeared to erupt, till at last a recognizably human form took shape before the waiting Thromholan. And yet still the knight, gazing upon his immortal father, sensed the infinitude of shapes within the faceless prince, the multitude of fantastical façades that were the god of nightmare visions. Which, he wondered, had Dred used when he descended out of darkness upon the Valdoran?

"Welcome you, Sulwyn Idris?" came the god's mocking voice, like the susurrus of a chill wind in the night. "And how not? Does not a father ever wish the attendance of his only heir? You, however, have seen fit not only to ignore my every overture of fatherly regard, but, indeed, to plot against me. You would incite the Lords of Throm to mutiny against their prince. *That* is the welcome you had planned for me. Tell me, my son, how I should address such a grievous wrong, one perpetrated by the Thromholan against the prince himself?"

"I doubt not, my lord, that you have long since determined my meet reward," Frayne drawled ironically, "which you shall in good time make known to me. I do find it rather curious, however, that the great halls of Throm should be so singularly thin of company. I had thought to find the illustrious prince surrounded by his subjects."

The Immortal's laughter crackled in the air.

"You surprise me. I had not thought to detect even so little of myself in my half-breed son. Yet surely such drollness of wit cannot have come from that

452

paragon of insipidity and virtue upon whom I so foolishly fathered you out of spite for the One. You cannot truly believe I would surround myself with mutineers and rebels? It would hardly be politic, after all. No, I fear I found it necessary to leave the Lords of Throm confined in Somn. A minor inconvenience really when one takes into account that I now possess Harmon's incomparable weapon."

"And Sehwan?" demanded Frayne chillingly. "What have you done with her?"

"Ah, yes. Poor, deluded Sehwan to think she could keep anything from me. I have yet to determine what punishment shall be hers. But doubtless, she pines for her newest lover, and who am I to deny my son a last moment of pleasure, after all?"

With a gesture of the hand, the Dark Prince caused Sehwan to materialize suddenly before them, her lissome body shimmering through pale orchid gossamer.

"Prince Idris!" she cried, her eyes flaming at the sight of the tall knight. "The Lords of Throm wait at the doors of Somn for you to lead them against Dred's hordes. But the prince has sealed Hauldrws, the Gate of the Sun, against us." Her glance flew with bitter loathing to Dred. *"You!"* she breathed. "You tricked us. Else even now the tides of battle should otherwise be turning against you."

"Oh, but it is a capital jest," agreed the prince of Throm, his laughter mocking. "The forces of the One founder for want of leadership, and the Second Generation of Immortals watch and wait and do nothing. For so long as no Thromgilad strikes down a mortal, the Eilderood are bound by oath to their

453

almighty lord not to interfere. I, the prince of Throm, shall be victorious without even having to call upon the power of the Vendrenin."

"But *we* are not bound by any oath!" the goddess uttered, turning passionately to the tall knight. "Prince Idris, you must release the Lords of Throm ere it is too late. We will fight in lieu of the Eilderood."

"And how do you propose that this mere mortal perform anything quite so impossible?" taunted the Dark Prince. "Shall he ask it as a boon of his loving father?"

"He is Sulwyn Idris," answered Sehwan, glittery with triumph. "The Sun-Prince need only command, and Hauldrws will open."

"Oh, but the half-breed prince is not such a fool. The moment of destiny approaches. Even now his beloved enchantress is drawn here to me. Innocent of who she is and of the power which is hers to command. One word from your precious Sulwyn Idris, and I will touch her with the icy flame of Vendrenin. Like Krim, she, too, shall burn with the immortal flames for all eternity, a living death of unremitting torment. Ask him if that is what he would wish for his exquisite Aurora, Sehwan. Ask him if he dares to defy his loving father."

"Prince Idris?" demanded the goddess, impaling the knight with burning eyes. *"Prince Idris, what will you do?"*

The knight's lip curled in ironic self-mockery.

"My father knows me all too well," he drawled, the falcon eyes unreadable save for the glitter of cold steel as he gazed upon the prince of Throm. "I will do nothing."

Then did Sehwan know bitter defeat as she read in the granite-hard face the man's unyielding resolve.

"Can the love of one mortal woman mean so much?" she said in a voice hardly above a whisper. "The fate of one against the destruction of thousands of mortals and the eternal damnation of a race of gods?"

She saw the muscle leap along the lean line of his jaw, but the knight answered not, as Dred's laughter shuddered through the chamber. Slowly she turned away, her head bowed in despair.

"How very wise of you," chuckled the victorious Immortal. "No doubt, as you languish for all eternity in Somn, you will find our enticing little concubine as delectable as ever. I trust you will savor her voluptuous charms, while you may. I myself look forward to the rather more intriguing delights of your very own enchantress. A fair exchange, would you not agree—my trollop for your sweet innocent?"

The knight's hand clenched into a hard fist. Yet by no other sign did he betray the savage leap of an icy rage within his breast.

"Perhaps, my lord prince," he drawled sardonically, "you will not find the enchantress so easily tamed. Aurora is hardly a Valdoran Virgin offered up as a sacrificial lamb."

"If she were, I should sooner toss her to the Dogs of Gor than try to bed her, even though in so doing, I would have to forego the gratification of striking my old enemy a mortal blow. As it is, I shall have both the pleasure of breaking the bitch to my will and savoring the vengeance that is rightfully mine."

"Have you in truth learned so little, Forberan?" inquired a newcomer to Dred's black hole, and suddenly the chamber was suffused with a dazzling golden light, save only for the inky nimbus that exuded from the god of Throm.

Frayne, turning, beheld a warrior of godly aspect. Great-thewed was he, and piercing of eye. His hair beneath a golden helm was silvery and plaited in the manner of the Volcae, the ancient breed of warriors who go forth unto battle with the song of Wealas on their lips. He wore the white kirtle and flowing cloak of a great lord, and at his side a silver sword. Golden were his breastplate and shield. And golden, too, the war bracelets about his powerful arms and wrists. Upon his helm he bore Aon, the symbol of the One.

"But what have we here?" queried the Black Prince jeeringly. "The One's lieutenant in full war regalia? As I live and breathe, I had it on good faith that the One had traded a warrior for a bard. You disappoint me, Sean-oech, for I had thought to have you play for our amusement."

"Had you now," the warrior rejoined easily, a glint of grim humor in his eye. "And now I suppose I've spoiled your homecoming. But, alas, what would you? I have not my harp here with me. Yet doubtless anon shall come another with a greater gift than mine, one who shall sing with an even greater power."

"You intrigue me. And has this paragon a name?"

"By the One," breathed a voice, in stunned enlightenment. "It is Alanna, and she is Harmon's mortal daughter!"

The blood leaping in his veins, Frayne wheeled to behold a slender figure standing at the threshold of Helynderne, her lovely eyes wide and staring at the silver-haired warrior-god—Harmon, who was the One's lieutenant and the Bard of Naefredeyan.

"Aurora!" he murmured, and then, flinging the startled Sehwan from him, he strode boldly to confront the Prince of Darkness.

"By the power of my name," he said ringingly, "I, Sulwyn Idris, command Hauldrws to be opened!"

"Fool!" thundered Dred, as with an upflung hand he sent the knight hurtling against the stone wall.

"No!" Aurora screamed, seeing her beloved stagger, then pitch headlong to the floor to groan and then lie still. She started toward him, but with a gesture Dred frozen her into immobility so that she was left staring out of the prison of her own body at her beloved lying lifelessly before her.

It was Sewhan who knelt beside the stricken knight, her flaxen hair streaming off her shoulders to hide her face as she felt for the pulse at Frayne's throat. Aurora caught her breath as she saw the slender body seem momentarily to sag. Then the goddess lifted her head to reveal eyes burning with a fierce triumph.

"He yet lives," she said, rising fearlessly to confront Dred. "And he has released the Thromgilad from their prison. No longer shall you rule the First Generation of Immortals. We are free!" she cried, and lifting her arms as though to embrace the world now open to her, Sehwan seemed to dissolve into the air.

Then did the enchantress taste bitter gall, as it came to her that in the end Frayne had managed to fool even Harmon, the greatest of the Eilderood, who had thought to reserve judgment on the Thromholan. How she had clung to the hope that events

457

would acquit the knight of all wrongdoing, but instead he stood revealed as a villain and a blackguard. For had he not risked death for his Thromgilad lover? Indeed, had he not just loosed the cursed breed of Throm upon the already beleaguered Realm? The One give her strength to sustain the anguish of so bitter a disillusion, she prayed. Grant her the means and the power to right the dreadful wrong.

Then in a daze Aurora heard Harmon speak, his words reverberating through the chamber like the voice of judgment. Compelled by something she sensed but could not define, she looked up to see the Eilderood gazing upon the fallen knight with a wondrous warmth.

"It is done," he proclaimed. "Dred's son hath drawn the wrath of Throm upon himself that the Eilderood need no longer be bound by the strictures of the One. A mortal lies stricken down by Dred's own hand. By the One, let the Eilderood attack!"

"Wait!" rasped Dred as it came to him how the Thromholan had tricked him. "Think what you do. Call them back, warrior-god—both Eilderood and Throm—or bring Dred's wrath down upon you and all the seven races. By my oath, I will scourge the land with the flames of Vendrenin till the earth is naught but a charred and lifeless hulk."

"Then so be it, Forberan. My part is nearly done." Dred's venomous hiss susurrated through the chamber.

"On your head be it, Eilderood," he uttered like a curse, and in horror Aurora saw him summon forth from darkness a magnificent, living crystal shimmering with iridescent fire. Oh, gods, she thought, staring in awe at the multifaceted sphere as large as a man's fist. It was the Vendrenin with a heart of pure power a thousand-thousand times greater than that of the Crystal of Kerr, and Dred was about to release it against the Realm of the One! Her glance flew to the warrior-god, Harmon, her father, standing calmly, watching, not Dred, but her. Why? What was he waiting for? Why did he not *do* something?

Then like a distant echo of a prophecy uttered long ago, his final words of parting came back to her.

"I sense my old enemy waiting for me. In his hands he holds the instrument of destiny, which once was mine and shall be yours. Yet be not afraid. In your name resides a power that shall remold the face of the earth."

And suddenly she knew with utter certainty that he would do nothing to stop Dred, for he was Harmon, and ages past he had renounced the thing wrought by a god for a god's vengeance. Nor dared he take it up again, though he might have done, because to do so would have made him like Dred, a god reveling in a power greater than any other god's. Nay. Harmon's part was truly done. Now it was for Alanna, the Chosen One, to wrest the power of Vendrenin from the immortal prince of Throm!

In dread fascination she watched the Immortal pass his hands over the crystal, and she winced as the liquid flames of Elfuvium flared with terrifying brilliance. Then her heart nearly failed her as she saw Frayne begin to stir and drag himself to his knees. Blood streamed crimson from a gash over his left eye where his head had struck the floor, and his mouth was set in a hard line, as if his every movement cost him pain. Then he was on his feet, his eyes glinting silver between slitted lids as deliberately he launched himself at the immortal prince.

"Frayne, *no!*" she cried as the Vendrenin shot molten flame at the knight.

As quick as thought Harmon stepped in front of Frayne to take the full blast of the crystal fire. It seemed the warrior-god embraced the deadly bolt, drawing it into himself till he was a flaming pillar of immortal fire. Then suddenly he was gone, vanished in a dazzling blaze of light to reveal Frayne lying ominously still upon the floor.

Never had the enchantress known such bitter grief and fury as took her then. Like a tidal wave of white-hot flame, it swept over and through her, feeding the blood lust of Andruvien, building with every pulse-beat, till she knew only the all-consuming passion for vengeance. With a thought she reached out to the Vendrenin, summoned the cold heart of crystal fire, willed the Vendrenin to yield to her.

As from a distance she saw Dred straighten and turn toward her, the nimbus of black cloud thinning to reveal the features of the god distorted in startled rage. Oh, gods, how like Frayne he was, she thought with a rending pain, but then she beheld the eyes as black as his soul and the godlike planes of his face contorted with malicious hate, and suddenly she saw no resemblance at all to her beloved knight. He was Dred, and already he was drawing the obscuring veil of darkness once more in place so that his face and form were naught but an insubstantial vision of constant flux and change.

"So my headstrong young beauty thinks to

challenge Dred's might once more," he chuckled, his voice the slithery caress of a serpent who seeks to mesmerize its hapless prey. "Such fire and passion! Such mortal impudence! You never cease to amuse me. In truth, I have long waited for the moment when I should at last possess you. And I promise it shall be soon. But first you must learn the lessons of obedience!"

Suddenly the enchantress reeled before a searing burst of pain like the thrust of a red-hot blade through her brain. A strangled scream welled up from her very depths, and clutching at her head, she fell to her knees. It seemed that a bottomless pit opened up beneath her as she pitched forward into darkness, the sound of Dred's laughter trailing after her, and for a time she knew nothing but writhing pain and a fierce yearning for death.

Then out of nowhere came the thin whisper like a fragile thread of hope.

"Hang on, Aurora. We're all here with you—Garwin and Janine, Elwindolf, Freyga, and I. Don't give in to Dred. Think of Vandrel's cottage or anywhere, and by the gods I'll get us there."

"Nay, Crane. Flee!" she cried, her heart pounding with fear for the courageous young shape-changer. Gods, where was he? Had Dred heard, or were his thoughts turned elsewhere—to the battle raging on the Plain of Shintari and his vow to immolate the Realm? She must know. She must banish the blinding pain from her mind and free herself of the pit.

Deliberately she fanned the flames of her hatred for the Dark Prince, summoning to her mind the image

461

of Frayne lying lifeless at her feet. Frayne, who had dared Dred's wrath that the Eilderood might be free to fight. Frayne, whose destiny had been to lead the Thromgilad to victory, not over the One, but over Dred. Frayne, her beloved.

All at once the pain ceased as the darkness was shattered by a dazzling burst of light—Andruvien aflame with crystal fire. Then did she see Dred bent over the Vendrenin and in a flash knew that he meant to shatter the heart of crystal and thus set loose the awesome flames of destruction. Her first thought was for Frayne, who might yet be alive, and for Crane and the others, who had dared the perils of the Black Mountain for her sake. Yet even as the fleeting realization came that they would be obliterated in the first throes of annihilation, she felt the crystal essence giving way, sensed the liquid flames of Efluvium breaking through the weakened bonds.

Realizing in that single instant that there was not time to grapple with Dred for control of the thing of power, the enchantress instinctively directed her thought inward to the essence of her strength.

She was Alanna, Harmon's mortal daughter and Almira's, and Rab and Chandra's granddaughter. She was the descendant of mage-lords and kings. In truth she was the crystal-master, with the power to mold crystal flame.

Then the crystal heart burst asunder, and white-hot flame erupted forth in an earth-shattering explosion of crystal fire. It seemed that the earth itself must be immolated as the mountain gave a great shudder and spewed forth its heaving entrails of molten rock, yet Alanna, the Chosen One of the gods, was before it, summoning the flames unto herself. She, who was the vassal of a god, became the conduit for the unbridled energy, drawing it into herself and sending it outward again at Dred, till the Immortal was encased in liquid flame, a solid core of blackest night within the dazzling brilliance. Then it, too, began to dissolve before the unremitting blast of pure energy, and the god stood revealed unto the light. Dred, who had been Sulwyn Idris, the Sun-Prince and the fairest of all the One's creations; Dred, the prince of Somn, who in turning from the light, had sought to render the darkness mightier than the One; Dred, shorn at last of the concealing cloak of darkness, made manifest as he truly was—a writhing, shapeless thing, a hideous corruption of spite and malice, a creature to be pitied.

In revulsion Aurora turned her eyes away, and suddenly she found that the fury and hatred that had sustained her were giving way to a growing weariness and an overriding need simply to be done with the thing. Banishing Dred once more to Limbo with a thought, she sealed the Gates of Somn with the crystal of Andruvien and bound him there with the power of her name. Then did she stand forth at the summit of the mountain and look out upon the devastation wrought by the Prince of Darkness, and all about her scintillated with crystal fire, her failing will all that kept the awesome power that had been Vendrenin from finishing what Dred had begun.

In despair did the enchantress behold the Plain of Shintari aflame, the armies fleeing in unordered panic as the fundament heaved and ruptured, sending forth slithering fissures of destruction. And

463

suddenly she knew that Dred had won, for she saw earth torn asunder and consumed with fire, and her heart lay stricken and buried with the mortal son of Throm beneath the rubble of Dred's Black Mountain. Only Frayne could awaken the god within her. Without him, she was less than half of nothing, for her spirit had been irrevocably bound with his, their lives, each a melody with its own variations, had been joined to create the harmonic unity that was the Song of Power.

"Oh, gods," she groaned. The struggle to maintain control over the unbridled flames of pure energy was draining her very soul! It was over, finished, the quest for her true name but a mockery. She was Alanna, but she was powerless. "Frayne," she whispered, feeling herself slipping into a deep well of darkness. "Frayne."

And suddenly she dreamed that he was with her, his strength melded to hers, his lips murmuring her name. Then the hand of the god was upon her, and the Song welled up within her. Intensified by the shimmering Cloak of Power, which bore the undeciphered symbols, the music vibrated through her, calling forth from another plane of existence the energy of godhead, the empyrean power that stems from the universal soul. And suddenly the earth stilled, as if to listen.

Then was she truly Alanna, weaving crystal fire into a harmonic symmetry of scintillating crystal, till at last she had restructured Vendrenin, and with it, restored balance and harmony to the stricken land. Finally, calling from out of the depths a love that was boundless, she healed the scars upon the land,

464

quelling the flames and sealing the fissures. Flowers sprang up and grass, as she wielded the thing of pure power as it had been meant to have done with it, for she was the crystal-master, and to her was given the power to see into the essence of the crystal heart of flame.

Then it was done, and she was falling, her legs giving way beneath her. Still caught up in the dream of power, she felt strong arms close about her and the wonder of lips pressed tenderly against her hair.

"Frayne," she sighed, giving in to the fantasy. Oh, gods, she was so very tired.

"I'm here," murmured his beloved voice. "We are all here—all those who have beheld the marvel of your love. Aurora!" Then he was shaking her, compelling her from the torpor stealing over her.

"Nay, 'tis illusion," she murmured, her brow furrowing as she struggled with this troublesome last riddle. "Frayne is dead. Everyone is—"

He silenced her with his lips pressed passionately against hers, and suddenly she knew it was no dream. In truth, he was alive and with her. Then, as he released her, the darkness receded and she saw them—Crane, the freckles dark splotches against the pallor of his face as he grinned crookedly down at her, and behind him, Janine, weeping softly. There was Garwin, too, gruffly clearing his throat and shoving a blushing, much depleted yet glad-eyed elf toward her.

"Gleb!" she cried softly. "And Elwindolf. A-and, why I remember you. You are Freyga. And by the One, 'tis Kral!"

And at last she gazed into falcon eyes lit with

silvery flame that shone for her alone.

"Frayne!" she whispered, feeling her strength ebbing as the godlike face blurred and appeared to recede behind a veil of cloud. "Frayne, my love."

Then all was lost to her as she slipped into a labyrinth of darkness.

Chapter 14

"Aurora!" Frayne said in alarm as he felt the enchantress go limp in his arms. His heart was hammering as he eased her to the ground and with fingers that shook felt for the pulsebeat at the base of the slender throat. For a long time he remained thus, unmoving, afraid to breathe lest he miss the telltale sign of lingering life. By all that was sacred, she could not be dead, he thought in near despair. Then he found it, the faint flutter beneath his fingertips, and, breathing a prayer to the One, he glanced up at the anxious faces hovering over him and the slight form lying white and motionless on the ground.

"There is life within her," he said soberly, "but like a candle that burns with a fragile flame."

"But what ails th' child?" demanded Gleb, dashing a sleeve across his eyes. "There be no wound upon her. Her bones be firm. Belike she be only tuckered out an' after a long rest, she'll be herself again."

"Nay. 'Twas the fire what she took unto herself,"

Garwin said, then shook his head in marvel at what he had seen his Anduan do that day. "We asked too much o' the wee lass. 'Tis like she's been all used up, methinks."

"What's the use of talking? We've got to *do* something!" It was Crane, his eyes dark with fear and a sense of helplessness. "Blast! If only we knew where Vandrel had got herself off to. She'd know what to do."

Elwindolf, thinking his own thoughts, said nothing as he gazed out over the Confounded Lands to the sun descending toward a cloudbank in the west. It was nigh on to dusk, and with the morrow would come the dawning of a new age. Yet what meaning could be drawn from all that had happened if she who had banished the darkness saw not the sunrise? Then, sensing with the instinct of the wolf the eyes of another on him, he turned to see Freyga watching him. In truth, it made little sense that the promise of happiness should lie before him, when she who had given so greatly of herself lay now with the shadow of death upon her brow.

"She were like th' unicorn what fell t' th' giants," observed Kral, bleary-eyed, but sober. "All shimmery wi' somethin' what ain't o' this world. I were all a quivery jest lookin' in them eyes what no mortal had ought t' 've hed."

"Hold your tongue, Kral, less'n ye've a wish t' answer t' me," Garwin growled. "I'll not hear a word agin' me lass."

"I nivver said nothin' agin her, ye ol' fool. 'Twere honestly spoken, it were."

"Quiet, both of you," Crane cut in. "Arguing

among ourselves won't help. And Aurora wouldn't like it."

Then without a word Frayne had bent to take the enchantress up in his arms, and immediately the shape-changer forgot the two belligerents.

"Hey, what're you doing? Where are you taking her?" he cried, reaching out to grasp the knight by the arm. Then he looked into the hooded eyes of the falcon and swallowed hard, his hand dropping unnoticed to his side. Slowly he backed a step.

Janine, looking on, thought that her beloved Sayyid Frayne only then truly saw the white-faced mogush, for suddenly he halted, the silvery sheen of his glance seeming to soften as he turned his head toward Crane.

"With your help, to the one place where she might have a chance," he answered quietly. "To the journey's end, which has ever lain before us."

Thus it was that Crane, linked to Frayne's inner vision, thought Aurora and the knight of Tor to the carven monument overlooking Hedron's vanished kingdom. There, Frayne carried his precious burden through the great silver circlet, which had served as the king's monumental crown and which now stood half-buried in the sand, like a portal looking out upon a horizon of iridescent mist. Gently he laid the enchantress's lifeless form upon the sand and knelt beside her.

"Rest," he murmured, gazing down at the still face. "Soon we will be together—you and I—for all eternity."

It seemed, then, that a faerie maiden with translucent wings of rainbow-riven cloud sailed toward them out of the sea of mist. Lovely was the brow graced with a garland of fragile blossoms, and graceful her form as she came to rest before them, her arms outstretched as if in welcome. Then Frayne saw that the maiden gazing upon them with shimmering eyes was wrought of purest crystal, and that her wings were the sails of a vessel come to bear them across the sealess sea. And suddenly he knew it was Rab's boat, which legend said had fallen to Dred when the god invaded Myrialoc long ages past, for none other could have woven from liquid crystal a craft of translucent iridescence.

Taking the enchantress up in his arms, Frayne bore her with infinite tenderness into the ethereally lovely craft which once had carried her grandfather to Garn and thus to Chandra, his beloved. Instantly the craft set sail, tracing a graceful arc through the mist all aglow with every color of the rainbow. Perhaps he only dreamed it, but it seemed ever afterwards to the knight that they drifted backward through time toward the Beginnings at the center of the universe. Then suddenly the mist parted before them, and he beheld a towering, cloud-draped peak, streaming iridescent rivers of vapor down its sides and outward into the sea.

The gloaming light of dusk fell over them as Rab's crystal boat came finally to rest in a small bay and Frayne gazed upon the sylvan glade rife with the Tears of Eldenwood that had appeared to him in the vision of possibilities. Gathering his beloved to him, he disembarked in a land teeming with wondrous things, which he had thought only the stuff of legends. Wisps of faerie-bright darted from flower to flower shedding spangled trails of glamor-dust in their wake, while the ephemeral Edanabrid flared forth on fiery wings to sing its single impassioned song ere vanishing in a blaze of glorious multicolored sparks. Strange and lovely woodland creatures with tapered horns glimmering silvery through the swirling vapors bounded from view into the shadowy depths of an ancient glinden wood. And, perhaps most wondrous of all, a timid Weffe-wiht, one of the creatures of cloud and vapor from which fantasies spring of lovely, ethereal things, spread opalescent butterfly wings and fluttered away to the top of a great, gnarled tree that bore on its weathered trunk the likeness of an old man's face, the seamed eyes closed as if in sleep.

Yet Frayne took only fleeting note, as he bore his beloved to the edge of a swirling pool of mist, and laying her amid the silver-petaled blooms shed by the Eldenwood, tenderly disrobed her. Then quickly discarding his own soiled clothing, he lifted the enchantress once more into his arms and carried her through the eddies of vapor to the shimmering Veil of Tears. For a long moment he gazed into the lovely face, remembering the enchanting woodsprite who had appeared to him on the shores of Grendylmere, remembering the child-woman who had awakened to a woman's passion and to destiny's quest for truth, and suddenly tears dampened the strong planes of his face, and the dark-rimmed eyes of the falcon lifted to the mystical gauze flowing from the fountainhead, which was the Mountain of Rebirth.

"Hear me, god of the Veil, and hearken to my words, I pray," he said ringingly. "I, Sulwyn Idris, who was the knight of Tor pledged to the One, stand before you, shorn of all pretense, divested of all worldly trappings, humbled in pride. I am come bearing the burden of grief. Yet for myself I ask nothing, for I have been too much in the world, seen too much of the darkness which abides in the hearts of men, and surely I must be judged unworthy. But the one I have brought with me is pure of heart and as innocent as the unicorn in whom is personified all that is marvelous and beautiful in the world. For her I ask that you heal her heart of its wounds and unburden her soul, whose only error was in giving too much of itself that others might live."

Having spoken his piece, Frayne gazed once more upon his beloved.

"May the gods have mercy," he groaned, and pressing his lips to hers, stepped beneath the Veil of Tears.

Aurora, adrift in a nebulous world of formless nightmares and elusive memories, awakened to the distant sound of harping and a waking dream of ethereal loveliness beyond her wildest fantasies. And to Frayne, who lay beside her amid a profusion of silver-petaled flowers, his eyes closed in sleep. In dawning wonder she gazed upon the beloved features, serene in the golden light of dawn. How young he looked! she marveled, tenderly tracing the smooth line of his jaw with her fingertips. It was as if all the burdens of his past, the hard years that had etched fine lines of cynicism about the eyes and mouth, had been lifted from him, leaving his godlike perfection unmarred, save only for the small scar at the corner of his lips and the marks of old wounds upon his magnificent body. How beautiful he was with his fair hair clustering in damp curls about his forehead and his skin, golden from the sun, glistening with beads of water as if he had only just finished bathing, and lying down in the sunlight to dry, had fallen asleep. Truly he was a god! And she naught but a lowly creature who was come to worship at his shrine. If only he were not sleeping so peacefully, she thought with a small moue of regret. How delectable to awaken him with a kiss. How sweet to tease and tantalize him, to arouse his manly passion, till at last he carried them both to the mystical heights of love's magical paradise. Still, he must be very weary to be so deeply lost in slumber. Indeed, he lay so still that had it not been for the rise and fall of his chest as he breathed and the steady beat of his heart beneath her cheek, she might have thought he slept the sleep of eternity.

Suddenly her stomach lurched and she sat bolt upright, her eyes wide and staring upon the vaporous flow streaming down the mountainside. Oh, gods, it was the Veil of Tears. She could not be mistaken, for it was just as she had seen it in the vision. Why had he brought her here? And when? she groaned, trying to remember. Then it all came back to her—Ellard and Kev, descending at her summons to the sandy wastes of Hedron's Plain and full of glad tidings. For Chandra had returned to Garn on the wings of a female Dracadern, and all the time she had been living secretly in Endrith's Forest, waiting for the day that Almira's daughter should come to her in search of her name. Then had Aurora understood the riddle of the sprightly scholar who had taken a fledgling enchantress under her wing till she should be strong enough to fly on her own, for Vandrel and Chandra were one and the same.

Marveling at the intricate warp and weft of the fabric of destiny, she had rejoiced that at long last Lothe had been reconciled with his only daughter. Then she had turned her thoughts to Frayne and the final riddle waiting for her beneath the Black Mountain. Never had she foreseen that the answer should meet her on the threshold! And yet now she could not understand how she had been so blind not to have known it nearly from the first meeting. Had not Almira made it plain enough in the sculpture she had wrought of her beloved before the gates of Seraisharaqa? Indeed, had the warrior-woman herself not named Aurora long before that in the vision beneath the walls of Krim's Keep? "Daughter of Earth and Flame," she had called her, but Aurora, in her innocence, had made nothing of it. Nor had she put together all the other pieces of the puzzle that had lain strewn along her path toward the final moment of truth. How stupid she had been indeed not to have guessed that the truth had resided all along in anything so simple as his name, for in the Old Tongue Alain meant "harmony" and Naefredeyan was simply "never-dying," the old term for an Immortal. Still, not until she had seen Alain of Naefreydeyan shorn of his disguise and standing in a glorious blaze of light had she guessed that he was a god; indeed, Harmon, the greatest of the Eilderood, and she, his daughter, half-mortal, half-god. Then had her own name come to her like the swift thrust of a knife and with it, the terrifying truth of her own destiny, for she was Alanna, the Chosen One, and to her was given the task of standing alone against Dred and the Vendrenin.

"Nay," she whispered, tears springing to her eyes as she looked once more upon the knight lying in slumber beside her, "not alone. For you were there with me—you a-and the others. Oh, gods, how could you have risked such peril for me?"

Indeed, she would never forget the desolation of her soul as she had seen him lying covered with blood and still as death in the depths of Helynderne. She saw it clearly now, what he had dared for her and for the Realm, dared for his own imprisoned race. In waiting to utter the words that would release the Thromgilad to do battle against Dred's horde, he had not only freed them and freed the Eilderood, as well, but he had bought her time to discover her identity and to realize the enormity of the task before her. He had drawn Dred's wrath upon himself deliberately, knowing that she would be roused to a fury of grief, which in turn would awaken Andruvien, knowing that only then would she find the courage to challenge Dred. Nor was that all, for she remembered how he had come to her, bolstering her strength with his, that the power of the god should at last come into her. What had followed was a blur to her, for she had been borne on the tides of an empyrean power that had scourged her soul and left her empty and wearied unto death. Indeed, she remembered nothing after that, save for Frayne's arms closing around her and a sea of anxious faces gazing at her out of a thickening haze before she plummeted into a bottomless black pit.

How near to death she must have been for him to have brought her here, she thought, and suddenly the final words of Endrith's Song reverberated through her mind like a phantom of memory come to taunt her.

Behold the solitude of sylvan glade.
Of rainbow mists be not afraid.
Bathe beneath the Veil of Tears.
Shed the burden of the years.
Sleep the sleep of eternity—
Or choose the Path of Purity.

Scale the cloud-draped brooding peak.
Of thy pain thou shalt not speak.
But place thy trust in what shall come—
The oneness of being with the One.
Be brave of heart! Be not forlorn!
For thou hath come to be reborn.

Then did she understand the sudden stab of fear she had suffered as she gazed upon her beloved composed in sleep, his hair yet damp and his skin shimmering with beads of water!

"Nay!" she cried, grasping him and trying with all her might to shake him from his unnatural slumber. "Our path lies not that way. Awaken! Oh, gods, I beg you. Open your eyes to me!"

Suddenly arms like steel bands clamped about her slender waist and crushed her breathlessly to a hard chest. She heard the whisper of her name, then hard, demanding lips closed ruthlessly over hers, and she knew nothing but the ecstasy of Frayne's kiss bearing her to the mystical heights of a god's passion.

The sun had risen high above the leafy boughs of the Glinden trees nodding sleepily in a light breeze when at last Aurora lay spent but happy in the snug cradle of her beloved's arms.

"Are we truly free?" she murmured, almost to herself, for she could not yet believe that she no longer need fear that she would awaken one day to find Frayne gone from her side.

"Not you, my love. Not so long as I live and breathe," he answered, pulling her most satisfyingly close.

"Then indeed it shall be for a very long time, for I intend to scale the peak, and you shall come with me if I have to drag you, for I have no wish to spend all eternity waiting for you to awaken to me. How dared you choose to 'sleep the sleep of eternity' when you must have known I would choose 'the Path of Purity'!"

A wondrous warmth stole through her veins at the sound of his vibrant laughter. How unlike the Frayne of old to be so carefree, his soul unburdened of all the dark secrets of the past.

"It was not the sleep of eternity, my absurd little gudgeon," he chuckled when at last his laughter had subsided, "but the sleep of utter exhaustion. Even a half-mortal, half-god is not impervious to being smashed against walls and to missing by a hair's breadth being incinerated by the Vendrenin's exceedingly potent flames. And in future I should prefer that you choose a rather less volatile manner of rousing me from my just repose. A simple kiss should do admirably."

"But surely you jest?" she queried, all innocence, as she raised herself on one elbow to regard him with eyes shimmering golden with laughter. "We are gods now, you and I, for we have bathed in the Veil of Tears and shed the burden of mortal years. What need shall we have henceforth of sleep? Indeed, it seems highly unlikely that we shall have even need of a bed. Oh, dear, eternity seems suddenly like a very long time. In truth, I cannot but wonder if we shall not become exceedingly bored ere 'tis through."

Then did a dangerous glint ignite in the sleepy grey eyes, as he pulled her irresistibly down to him.

"Perhaps you are right," he drawled, rendering her suddenly breathless with his look. "Yet I doubt not that *this* god fully intends not only to have a bed, but to spend a great deal of the first hundred ages or so in it." And with that pronouncement, he proceeded admirably to demonstrate in exactly what manner he ment to pass the long years of his immortality, so that it was some time later when at last Aurora, who was Alanna, the master of Vendrenin, drew a long, contented breath.

"In truth," she murmured, her lovely eyes dreamy, "you are in the right of it, for surely even gods must sleep sometime. How else could they find the strength to make love to their goddesses did they not?"

Then, her eyes closing, she snuggled closer to Frayne's lean length. The sound of harping came sweetly to her ears, for there was about it the magical touch of the master bard, and suddenly she knew that somewhere Harmon waited for her and for Sulwyn Idris, who was Dred's immortal son. Soon they must rise and begin the final journey to whatever lay before them in the new age of peace. Like as not the path of their joined destinies would take them one day into new peril, for after all, did not the Tome of Prophecy record that Dred would rise again in seven times seventy ages? But for now, the peak, which would lead them to rebirth with the One and to Galesiad, the City of Immortals in the Land of Silver Clouds, could wait just a little while longer.